Chekago

NATALYA LOWNDES

Chekago

It was in derisive homage to the CHEKA, the original Bolshevik secret police, and the reputation of pre-war Chicago, that Moscow, during the brief rule of Yuri Andropov (November 1982– February 1984), a former head of the KGB, became known in some circles as *Chekago*.

E. P. DUTTON NEW YORK

Published in the United States by E. P. Dutton, a division of NAL Penguin Inc.,
2 Park Avenue, New York, N.Y. 10016.

Originally published in Great Britain.

Library of Congress Cataloging-in-Publication Data

Lowndes, Natalya.
Chekago / Natalya Lowndes.—1st American ed.
p.   cm.
"It was in derisive homage to the CHEKA, the original Bolshevik
secret police, and the reputation of pre-war Chicago, that Moscow,
during the brief rule of Yuri Andropov (November 1982–February
1984), a former head of the KGB, became known in some circles as
Chekago."
ISBN 0-525-24686-X
I. Title.
PR6062.093C48   1988
823'.914—dc19   88-16951
                              CIP

10 9 8 7 6 5 4 3 2 1

First American Edition

НЕ УМЕРЛА ДЕВИЦА, НО СПИТ

CONTENTS

PRINCIPAL CHARACTERS

Outsiders
Aleksandr Mikhailovich Biryusov (Sasha), dustman
Olga Sergeyevna Melentyeva (Olya), translator and interpreter
Boris Sergeyevich Melentyev (Borya), Olga's brother, mathematics teacher
Galina Semyonovna (Galya), his wife
Lizaveta Ivanovna Kiprenskaya, old-age pensioner
Lyov Davidovich Kuznetsov (Lev), Jewish university teacher
Anna Georgyevna, his wife
Xenia, their daughter
Tatyana Borisovna Lestyeva (Tanya), journalist on women's periodical,
    Feministka
Marina Andreyevna Korolyova, her mother
Roberta Weston (Bobby), American postgraduate student from
    Pawtucket, Rhode Island, USA
Valentina Dmitryevna Afanasyeva (Valya), widow from Starochersskaya,
    near Rostov-on-Don, USSR
Leonid Vasilyevich Bikovsky (Len), Sasha's workmate
Ivan Aleksandrovich Baranov, *dvornik* (janitor)
Vera Grigoryevna, his wife

Insiders
Marya Fyodorovna Osipyenko, editorial assistant, then editor of
    Feministka, daughter of a deceased member of the Politburo
Pavel Aleksandrovich Bogatii (Bogat), plain-clothes officer
Yuri Petrovich (Legless), surname unknown, uniformed militiaman
Another plain-clothes officer, known only as Rocky
Matvey Yakovlyevich Shkiryatov, Director of a literary agency, Olga's
    boss
Philip Ivanovich Kirilyenko, former editor of *Feministka*

I

MOURNING

1

The entire city was watching the dead. At a distance the world, too, watched. Sasha Biryusov knew the dead better than the living. He was a connoisseur of funerals now, with Gran, Mum and the aunts all gone the same way, the same year. Death meant being on your own and the isolation was as final for him as it was for them. All he knew about life was that his own was endurable, unsatisfactory, and, sometimes, too long.

Today it was the Boss's turn: a gorgeous do with bands, flags and the chief members of the Family Firm up there, large as life, saluting the open coffin. You never saw them at full strength anywhere else but, after all, they had to show they stuck together right to the end.

Although nobody else had a funeral so big, Sasha had no desire to see this one. Len had spent the day holed up with his fat girl and Sasha would have stayed at home too but for the broken waste-disposal unit at the hotel Sevastopol which carried with it the promise of a bonus for a quick job; and when Tassya rang him from the first-floor desk she had hinted at an extra:

"There'll be a bottle in it for you. And I get off duty at four."

As he came up the service stairs wiping the grease off his hands on Intourist serviettes, he spotted her boyfriend, a brawny policeman in snow-boots. He was manoeuvring the portable round to get a better view. Tassya got up from behind her desk, sniffed, gave what she would have called a roguish smile and slipped her hand into Sasha's overall pocket, trying to untwist the cap of the bottle they had given him in the kitchen. With two men around she evidently thought it safe to be kittenish.

"What's the weather doing out there?" murmured Legless, disentangling the TV lead from his Sam Browne.

The girl made jokes about him — had given him the nickname because he never moved a muscle unless forced — but only when he was on duty, never to his face. He might not move but you couldn't push him. Sometimes he borrowed the portable, late at night when things were slack; he was hooked on anything screenable and funerals were just up his street.

"There's Zhenya!" called Legless, forgetting about the weather and pointing at a fur hat on the far left of a wavery line of soldiers. Sasha flopped on to a hard chair behind the policeman's right elbow. Usually he only watched television if Army Central were playing away but this was exceptional. The girl took a sip straight from the vodka bottle, screwed back the top and worried at an uncurling strand of her perm.

Sasha gazed at the screen over the top of Legless's flat skull with its Prussian stubble glinting yellowly, and tried to remember how long it was since Gran died. Already he was forgetting what she looked like, but her voice, the last thing that's supposed to go, had stayed with him, lodged between brain and ear and it came over now, drowning out the dirge of the brass band: *No style, they can't do things properly, not Ours.* Her invariable gripe about Soviet Power had been that *they* didn't do funerals properly, with the plumed horses, and for the first time in his life, Sasha thought the old girl might have had something.

Tassya's knee touched his. Casually, so as not to disturb Legless, he flattened his hand over her tights and started to move it up her thigh. On the screen the policeman caught the reflection of the bottle.

"Now then, what about my share?"

His long, uniformed arm came over the back of the chair to snatch Sasha's bottle but he didn't take his eyes from the set as the music rolled on and figures shuffled under the clouded sky.

"This is rubbish, this," he said after only one gulp. "This all they give you, you poor sod?"

Under the desk lay a leather attaché case and, at a grunt from Legless, the girl went down on her hands and knees to fish out another bottle. Sasha watched her hips strain under the pale-blue skirt.

"Go on, test it for me," said Legless benignly, still not turning round. "You're in luck, mate. Don't see booze like that where you come from, I bet? We could make a night of it."

He chuckled and Sasha imagined his grin: healthy teeth and sleek, clean-shaven chin. Jammy bastard, he thought.

"You're in the wrong line," shouted Legless. "Other people's leavings, isn't it? For you?"

The next morning he was on early shift, rolling in the ten-tonner up Gorky Street, past the window of the music shop where, the previous Thursday, he had first caught sight of the portrait, wreathed in laurel and plonked down anyhow beside the trumpets and banjoes. Crêpe unwound from the lamp posts and streamed in the wind. He swung the truck past the lights, into the square and pulled up by the church on the far side.

A week's refuse had accumulated in the old quarter. He hated the Arbat, especially in autumn, when its genteel stucco crumbled in the wet and the acrid mush of birch leaves was scenting the courtyards.

Swearing to a man, the early team was gradually working through the huge back areas of tenements. Torpid crows flapped off their perches along the garbage skips which lay beside the pavement, brimming over with cabbage leaves, newspapers and fish-tins.

No bottles. He always checked in case someone had tipped out an empty by mistake.

As he dug in a skip, the wind gusted overhead; he gave a shiver and looked for his tattoo. To cheer himself up, console himself with thoughts of women, the women he hardly ever got, he pushed back the sleeve of his overalls. MAMA tattooed in big letters over a blue apple tree extended from his upper arm to the point of his shoulder; when he tilted his forearm to the left, into the light, the foliage intermixed with the motto transforming the whole into the breasts and triangle of a headless girl. He'd had it done in the Army by a friend who'd learned the trick from a bloke in the punishment block at Yaroslavl Jail.

The mere sight of its tastelessness pacified him.

Most nights when he got back to his flat he rang up girls. A telephone was usually the nearest he ever got to taking them out or getting them up to his room. If that ever happened he changed the newspapers stuck over his curtainless windows. The same issue of *Trud* had been there for months – ever since he took Irina from the Gastronom cheese counter to a tea dance.

And it was two days off payday which meant unless he blew the five-rouble note he carried for emergencies, he would be sober until he collected his wages.

The other tenants complained about his uncouthness. This weekend he'd give them something really uncultured to shout about; this Friday he was going to live up to them, get *superbly intoxicated* as the woman translator in the front room who only brought home in a month what he drew in a fortnight, might have said in her fancy way.

Len was stretched out in the cab, dozing, the sunlight inflaming the huge birthmark shaped like a horse's head which nearly covered one side of his face. After half a litre it blazed out redder, a warning that he was touchy. Sasha considered: so far it had been a bleak morning; he'd had enough, he was going home. And he could go home too, because his street, Bakery Lane, was just around the corner.

But Len was worth a try before he skived off.

"Look, mate, I've got five roubles. How about it?"

"How about what?"

Sasha flicked one side of his throat with thumb and fourth finger. "Making a twosome."

Len didn't budge. "Bugger off. I'm tired. I'll have you on a charge. The whole lot of you."

Len had been teamleader for the Arbat ward until he was elbowed out by the Union man. The demotion had been political; nothing to do with him personally, or the work. But now he was going by the rule-book until he'd regained command of the team. In a few weeks they'd be splitting a bottle again. Meanwhile, looking Sasha up and down, he let fly with the ethics of Soviet labour.

"You're disgusting, you know that? Decadent."

Sasha was indifferent. If they got rid of him they'd have to give him another job. He'd sunk through several after leaving the Army, but compared with the Army anything was a soft option.

He hopped down from the mounting step and set off home, leaving Len to fuel himself on life's humiliations and his forty degrees proof. Lizaveta Ivanovna would talk to Sasha because she talked all the time anyway, with or without an audience. Not that Bakery Lane was a real home. Home had been Gran. On the corner he stopped, remembering her disconsolately snapping the outcanes off the rasp-berry bushes, her humped shoulders towards him, with the fields spanning out in front of her, green in the summer heat. A pity she hadn't liked him more.

Another hour and the beer-shop on Little Arbat would be open.

Over the way from Sasha's block stood the former townhouse of some eighteenth-century nobleman or other, now an Embassy of an obscure little country. Sasha's place had been converted into smaller and smaller rooms while the Embassy building, "restored by the State in 1947", as the plaque said, was untouched because it housed foreigners.

Not important ones, but no one important had lived down these streets for a hundred years. A policeman stood by the gate.

There was a crash from the front as the big door at the bottom of the main stairs swung to and Sasha, as if suddenly recalling something, loped briskly through the archway to the entrance of his block. Back towards him, shuffling down the road, was Melentyev, Boris Sergeyevich, the only person in the Arbat to wear a homburg and carry a walking-stick, brother of the translator in Sasha's own apartment, school-teacher and occasional drinking companion.

The Embassy policeman watched as Sasha shambled up, waving his arms. "Boris . . . Borya . . . My old mate . . ."

Boris walked on. At the end of the next street traffic roared along the wide boulevard past row on row of shops. Just before the subway entrance he stopped and turned. "Today you are the last person I want to see."

Sasha's expectant face with the mole under the lower lip and the yellow hair in a spiky fringe, went blank.

"A twosome. How about it? Go on, we're friends, aren't we? You, me and your sister."

Olga Sergeyevna, the one with the foreign boyfriend. When Sasha had opened the door to him once, he sidled past and made a sheepish "Thank you," in the flat tones of a Balt. Too much of a fancy dresser to come from round here.

"Cheer up, Borya, for Christ's sake, it might never happen."

He opened his fist slowly to reveal a five-rouble note. "Got a fiver or a tenner, then? Here's mine."

Boris paused on the steps. "It has already. Happened, I mean. And I'm late for the appointment."

He leaned against the subway wall and began to cough. Sasha put a finger in his cheek and made the noise of a popping cork.

"To hell with your appointment. Let's treat ourselves, let him wait, whoever he is."

"Can't wait. It's the hospital."

Boris took off his spectacles and watched as his companion spat on the pavement.

"Dr Foster went to Gloucester," said Sasha, reciting the only English he knew, learned from Irina's little cousin on the train to Ivantyevka where they went on a day trip. "So you've time off, enjoy it."

"A lot of that, too," said Boris vaguely. "They think I'm dying."

Sasha's high-pitched, quavering laugh which his girlfriends found sinister, resounded in the tunnel. "Listen, all of us, we're all on the way out. Got any ones or threes, then?"

Mechanically Boris took off his hat, felt in the band, then reached for a plastic wallet in his trouser pocket. "Five in here, five kopeks for my tube. That's the lot. What am I doing?"

"Anything at home? You know, I mean, empties?"

Boris polished his spectacles on the red scarf round his neck. "There's some been down behind the fridge for years. I asked her to take them back to stiffen us against that TV funeral yesterday, but she said she was saving them. 'For the next funeral,' I said."

He wheeled round and began walking slowly back the way they

had just come, muttering to himself. "Old champagne bottles from weddings and birthdays . . . pregnancies, even, I ask you!"

People were staring. It was becoming a speech.

"Women. They all say they're more sensible than men, but what does it come down to in the end, all that caring? Watching television every night with the only woman you've ever had and handing over our savings to a doctor who's used them to do up a *dacha* for his third wife."

"She's at home now?"

"Lord, no. She's at the Institute conjugating Norwegian verbs, inflicting herself . . ."

By now they had retraced their steps to Bakery Lane and Boris was fiddling in his pocket for the flat key. "To hell with it all," he broke out.

Sasha put his arm round Boris's shoulders and hugged, squeezing the thin bones. The coat was unlined and Boris as cold as paper. The big front door was jammed open with a wad of newspapers. Lizaveta Ivanovna must have been scrubbing the landing and stairs.

"Haywire, that woman," said Boris, stepping gingerly. "A public liability. You stay here. I don't want you inside the flat. You know what she's like."

Sasha remained by the lift shaft. Peering up, he saw Boris disappear through a door on the second landing.

"Make sure you come back," he called. His world was full of people who disappeared; people moving in and out of doors, behind the stage scenery of death or buying railway tickets to remote places. He had seen it all happen, and now only he seemed to be left, searching for new faces, new drinking partners and new girls.

Boris had wrapped several sheets of newspaper round the bottles and put six in his pockets, their necks sticking out at odd angles. The rest he gave to Sasha.

"Must be fifteen here."

"Lord knows when we drank them all," said Boris squinting at the labels. "Women are queer, the way they keep things."

Sasha had forgotten about his overalls. "Hang on a tick. Got to get out of these, Borya. They won't serve me in working clothes."

It was warmer on the street. Propping one shoulder in the coign of the doorway Boris rested in the weak sunshine, suddenly peaceable and indifferent. It had started to cloud over. Reaching down into one of the pockets of his raincoat he found an old packet of cigarettes which had lain there since the result of his first X-ray.

Having no matches he crossed the street to the policeman outside the Embassy.

"I'm not supposed to smoke," he started pointlessly as the policeman stared ahead. "Got a light?"

"I'm on duty."

"Want one?" said Boris, holding out the open packet.

Taking a match out of his sleeve the policeman struck it against a wrought-iron curlicue of the gate, lit his cigarette and passed the flame to Boris.

They smoked silently for a minute or two. Boris shivered as clouds moved across the sun.

"It's the middle of the morning and I'm going to have a drink, I've never done anything like that since New Year. That was when I talked all night about going to live in the country."

"Ah," sighed the policeman. "Another child of the steppes. Me, I'd breed horses."

At that moment Sasha emerged into the patchy sunshine, blinking and looking round.

"He'll fall over with those empties in a minute," observed the policeman professionally. He dropped his voice and pushed two one-rouble notes into Boris's hand. "Here's a couple. Want to cut me in?"

"Hey, Aleksandr Mikhailovich, mind yourself. Don't smash Galya's bottles!" shouted Boris scurrying back to his own side of the street.

"And don't forget me!" the policeman called after him. Sasha turned and gave a mock salute. It began to rain.

Eventually they halted by a knot of people clustering round the entrance of a double-fronted shop. Sasha was grabbed by a drunk who had crept up along the pavement.

"For the love of God, I'm twenty kopeks short."

Over the cropped white hair of the beggar's head, Sasha glimpsed a long line of shoppers, mostly men, snaking down to the cash desk. Tossing some coins into the outstretched cap, he twitched his arm away and pushed forward but the drunk held on, squinting.

"That's only ten. I need . . ."

Sasha barged him back through the heavy spring-loaded door and the drunk staggered over to a group of workmen, the strings of their hat flaps dangling, who were drinking beer straight from the bottle under a notice: "The Consumption of Alcohol on These Premises is Strictly Forbidden."

The air was heavy with the autumnal odour of damp felt, cucumbers and salt fish.

The interior was undivided, one side of the shop mirroring the other. Behind the long brown counters ran rows of boxes like horse-mangers, with jars stacked above them: on the right, brightly-wrapped sweets and biscuits under jars of coffee beans at twenty roubles a kilo; to the left, across the uneven floor awash with water from dripping coats and shoes, greenish Cuban lemons, waxed Egyptian oranges, onions and dried apricots were stacked in glass display cases, topped by white Bulgarian stewed apples.

The symmetry terminated with the lay-out. A child, her green shopping bag trailing in a puddle, was buying three packets of tea at the confectionery counter, while the beer queue swayed densely, threatening at any moment to spill over the notional line which intersected the ground space.

Sasha elbowed his way to the cash desk and then tagged on to the queue, clutching his sales ticket. He had acquired a pink string bag and the necks of Galya's souvenirs poked through the weave.

Unable to get a sight of the contents of the glass cases at the far end of the counter where goods and prices were displayed, he craned shortsightedly at the range of bottles on the wall-shelf behind the girl assistant, recognising them only by their colours. Stubby bottles of pale Kolos beer stood at the edge. Not the best at eleven per cent, but only forty-nine kopeks. Carefully he worked out the score: enough for ten.

A shriek came from the workmen's counter. A dumpy woman in a padded donkey jacket streaked with limewash had begun a slow twirl round Sasha's beggar, her hips jerking obscenely.

Well away, mused the dustman, glad he was a man. She hung round the taxi-rank in the square. He had seen her accost a negro in the snow at two o'clock in the morning.

The assistant who looked about eighteen, was serving the whole queue singlehanded. Or trying to. She slid deftly on her espadrilles from the counter to the high stacks of beer crates with a grace out of keeping with her surroundings. The fluorescent strip overhead tinted the folds of her white overall a dolly-bag blue. Sasha's eyes were on a level with her behind which jutted out every time she bent down to one of the crates on the floor which contained the Brezhnevas – half-litre bottles of spirit.

He couldn't see her legs. He imagined his palms grasping her waist, thumbs caressing the curve inward to her spine, with that bottom rolling languorously under him.

"You've got a nerve."

She had taken his cash check without a word while he began tumbling his bottles on to the counter. One rolled off to the side. Now she brushed a wisp of henna-ed hair back from her forehead, adjusted her cap and reached for the bottle.

He tried to sound engaging. "That's not all I've got, sweetheart."

A faint grin at the corners of her red mouth, she held up Galya's empty between finger and thumb. The champagne bottles had a picture of an eighteenth-century woman in rucked-up petticoats and an immense wig pressing a tulip glass to the lips of a man inert under a bush. The scene was enclosed under a scrolly gold label.

"Pom-Pa-Dour," she read off, making out the Roman script with difficulty. "These aren't ours."

Sasha had seven of them. Hungarian champagne which Galya must have mistaken for French because of the picture.

"They don't need to be yours. They're not mine either. They're just bottles. I mean, you do take bottles, don't you?"

In your bleeding bottle shop, he ran on, silently, the image of her soft body dissipating.

She banged the empty down into the middle of his collection and pushed the whole lot up the counter past the wide dish full of loose change. Dark hairs shone on the point of her wristbone.

"We're a specialist shop. We only take our own. Come on, get a move on, I haven't got all day."

A one-legged man next to him shoved the padded end of his crutch into the dustman's side.

"Just a minute, just a *fuck-ing* minute," shouted Sasha, trying to gather up the scattered empties with one arm and fend off the cripple with the other.

Murmurs came from the queue. "Get out of it," "Bloody fool, coming in here . . ."

Scrabbling about in the litter of empties he retrieved a lone Kolos. "What about these, then? You take these, I know you do. You've bloody sold me enough, I know that."

The girl looked from him to the bottle, her brown eyes glassy.

"Ly-udmila!"

The drunk with the convict haircut appeared again tugging at Sasha's side and babbling.

"Don't you know the rules, a clever man like you, don't you know what to do yet, can't you get it right, can't . . . ?"

"Get off, get out of it, you . . ."

"Lyudmila, Ly-udy, it's *him* again!" shouted the girl.

"You slut!" grunted Sasha.

The stunted figure of Lyudmila, the manageress, slopped towards him, pattens clicking on the flags, a chunk of bread in one hand and *Sovietskaya Rossiya* tucked under her arm.

Business ceased in the section as they waited for her to put on her spectacles. The bottle, still suspended by the girl, trembled above her head. She squinnied at the opaque bottom.

"Cockroaches!"

The drunk cackled triumphantly.

Sasha leaned over to get a better look. He knew from experience that cockroaches usually wiggled at customers from hiding-places in the metal lining of display cases, not from bottles.

"I can't see anything."

"No, you fool, *there*." Lyudmila pointed her sandwich at a sugary deposit of crystals ringing the inside of the glass. "That's where they breed."

A smear of butter adhered to the bottle, marking the place.

The crowd dissolved into a hubbub of factitious disgust. "How can people be so filthy? Revolting!"

"Look, darling, do us a favour, just this once. Next time I'll bottle-brush them with soda, but I'm a bit late, and . . ."

"Don't you darling me." The whites of her eyes gleamed yellow in the neon. "I know your sort. You're the bastard who punched my little Oleg last Saturday. Daring to show your ugly Ryazan mug in here again. I'll have you run in! Swine!" She inclined her face skywards like the Frog-princess chained to a rock, appealing to the line of men ranked against the counter.

"Citizens!"

That's torn it, thought Sasha.

"*Citizens*, what kind of a Soviet man is this?"

He was getting the wind up. Any moment a clean-limbed citizen was going to take a lunge at him. He gripped one of the Pompadours by the neck and cast a wild glance round the shop.

Two policemen strolled in. Both unaware of the row, they were pulling aside the heavy skirts of their greatcoats and reaching for the money in their trouser pockets. The taller one switched off his radio and whistled to the manageress from the far end of the long counter.

In a flash, Sasha had scooped up Galya's bottles, along with two empty Stolichnayas belonging to the cripple, and slung the pink bag over his shoulder.

Halfway to the exit, he collided with the dough-faced woman who had been doing the dance. He stuffed the cash-chit for two roubles fifty down the front of her bib and brace.

"Save you showing your knickers to black men. Have this one on me."

20

2

From their sodden, peeling bench Boris and Sasha gazed up at the statue, glistening wet and hard-toned under the trees, one foot protruding from the hem of a heavy cloak. They were in a small square completely enclosed by railings except for gaps where gates had once been. The garden, squeezed between two busy streets, was deserted.

"Died here, didn't he – Gogol?" said Boris, pointing across to the little house. It was obvious that Boris was a reading man.

Sasha shrugged. Tolstoy's spread at Yasnaya Polyana had convinced him that the way writers lived was more significant than how or where they died. Even Tolstoy's coachman had had his own room.

Besides, literary talk did not enhance your mood when you were drinking. Prose was less dire than poetry for fetching up your shortcomings and glum speculations on the hereafter, but that was all.

"You see, Borya," began Sasha. "You see . . ."

Boris took no notice. There had been some entry-way to a block of flats, he seemed to recall, with Art Nouveau tracery outlining the panes of the glass doors, their woodwork thickened by the application of years of heavy paint. Sasha had stubbed out his cigarette on a grey mailbox while Boris swopped all his empties for Moskovskoye with a woman street-dealer who had a poodle on a string. At Skatertniy he must have mislaid his stick. The taxi-driver, half-asleep after coming out of the canteen, seemed amazed that anyone should want Stolichnaya from him at that time of day. He took the bottle from under his dashboard and overcharged them.

Sasha had got up and was pacing round the pink string bag now bulging with loaves and the litre of Stolichnaya wrapped in the *Moscow Evening News*.

"You see, Borya, it's a dog's life, I'm telling you. I get nothing out of it."

The rain fell harder. Trees, buildings and statue seemed preternaturally clear in the downpour. In Sasha's bag the newsprint soaked up the rain blobs, and the rigid lines of mourners and catafalque in the funeral photographs softened in the wet.

"Do you think anyone gives a damn about you? Here? In this place?"

A window slammed shut. Boris shook his hat free of water and put it on again. He recalled a line of prose: "A monstrous and inconceivable Russia . . . Like a multitude of bugs swarming in clothes."

A fat man in a trench coat glanced at them as he took a short cut through the square on to the main road.

"They all think I'm a joke, too, my mates. They've made up a dirty song: 'Thirty-three and never been . . .' You know . . ."

"Oh, I see," chuckled Boris, relaxed by the vodka. "Private problems."

"'Ask Sasha,' they say. 'Go on, give him the late shift. He's free.' Free? I'm always free. Thirty-three and no one to come home to. Gran used to say I'd never get myself a decent girl but even you're married."

With an embarrassed snort he patted Boris's arm. "No offence meant but you know what I mean? All I want is a woman. I'm not too fussy, clean, a hard worker. Nice blouse with roses on it. Brooch at the throat. It's the homemakers that count." He drank deeply, rain trickling down his upturned face.

Boris crunched the gravel under his heel. "Try living with the same person for fifteen years," he said. "That's the real thing."

A light went up in a window of the distant flats and the clatter of plates came from a kitchen.

"Do you think an advert would work? You know, in the paper, the small ads, one of those agencies?"

Boris shifted on the damp seat. "Not everybody's born to get married. Look at that old woman in your flat, the widow. She's independent, isn't she, does what she likes, goes her own way?"

Lizaveta Ivanovna, he meant: Olga had once shown him her room, full of empty birdcages, boxes of unmatched china, mirrors and seatless chairs.

Sasha hooted. "Her? She's cracked."

"She has her freedom. Like my sister." Boris's face softened. "Olya . . . now there's an admirable woman. She enjoys her privacy."

"Well, it's different for women, isn't it?" said Sasha. "I mean, they don't have feelings, not like men." He remembered Irina's devastating unresponsiveness. "What's wrong with me, Borya?"

The older man stared back. "Wrong with you? How can anything be wrong with you?" He sat up. "In your state of health?"

Sasha proffered the bag. "You're so touchy, just like your sister."

"You don't know anything about her, either," said Boris. He fiddled with his hat once more, ignoring the bottle.

"I hear her crying at night."

"Crying?" Boris glared. "Nonsense. She never cries, she has better things to do. We grew up together. You've been listening at the wrong wall. Not that having to live with the likes of you wouldn't make the Mother of God weep."

"Well, you haven't seen her since that foreigner went home a few days ago," said Sasha. "She's not been the same."

"What foreigner?"

There was a silence.

"Come off it, Borya. You know who, he came in a taxi the first time and, Hello, I thought, some Embassy bloke's lost his way. Couldn't believe it when he rang our bell."

"So you watch her, do you? Spy on her?"

"You can't help noticing what goes on in a place like ours. And your sister isn't exactly careful. Got a thing about foreigners, hasn't she? I mean, this isn't the first."

Boris threw up his hands. "You're an imbecile. It's part of her job to go round with them. Officially."

"Official, is it?" said Sasha, leaning forward. "I don't care what she calls it, mate, but four o'clock in the morning, that's official, is it?"

The street lamps changed from red to yellow and lights twinkled through the trees.

"Big bloke he was. Sort of square in the shoulders. Tall. Dark, too, like a gypsy, except no gypsy ever wore *that* sort of suit."

"I don't believe you," said Boris slowly.

"Ask her yourself but all I know is that last week was one big scene: flowers, a tea-party, that sort of thing. – You know, before the Boss kicked the bucket and we didn't get down the Arbat because of the hoo-ha. I cleared out our bins this morning and you should have seen the tea-leaves: fat as mushrooms. Chinese they were. That's all she does lately. Cry and drink tea."

Boris massaged his stiff knees, then got up from the bench. "I've neglected her. I'm a selfish bastard." He walked away, almost out of sight, beyond the trees.

All that was visible now of the statue was a dark, smooth curve, silhouetted against the glow of the city. Sasha came stumbling across the grass, trying not to drop the yellow beer-carrier with its three empties and one full one.

"Hold on, I've got to get you home, Borya, you've overdone it."

Olga Sergeyevna would have a fit when she saw them dripping wet and stinking of the beer-shop. There'd be a row and he'd be blamed, he knew.

By the time they crossed the main road he was propping up Boris who was now more tired than drunk. Behind them lay the shops. Ahead was a tangle of small, narrow streets.

The bolt needed oil. Lizaveta Ivanovna had to tug hard and her apron rode up over her long black skirt and cardigan.

Sasha's voice came through the door: "Hurry up. My friend's sick."

"Friend?" murmured the old woman. "You have no friends."

Absently she smoothed down her apron, enjoying the feel of the knobbly silk flowers worked on the bib. She had embroidered that garland on the day of Stalin's requiem with the Patriarch's clear voice still singing in her ears: "Our Josip. Our Josip . . . Our Leonid." So many funerals. The apron was still too good to make into dusters.

Outside, Boris leaned his head against the landing wall. The lift was silent. They had walked up not wanting to be noticed, hearing only the click as the spring-loaded time-switch snapped off as usual, leaving them in complete darkness, one flight of steps short of their floor.

Olga was in her room, Lizaveta knew, but she wouldn't stir because the foreigner had gone. The Kuznetsovs never opened the door, but last week Olga Sergeyevna would have answered quickly enough if anyone rang from downstairs.

Lizaveta took her time with the bolt, muttering to herself. Suddenly the hinges squealed outwards and she stood revealed on the threshold, dust on her cardigan, trembling from her efforts. In the hallway Boris took off his hat. Lizaveta knew his wife, Galya, and she inched forward smiling but was suddenly aware of the reek of spirits emanating from the two men.

"It *is* you, Boris Sergeyevich, isn't it?" She peered myopically, shook her head and her gaze moved from the yellow plastic bag to Boris's dirty hands and sodden raincoat. "Your sister's in."

Boris turned abruptly to Sasha. "I've left my gloves on the bench and lost the two roubles. That policeman's. He'll know by now."

As they walked back along Bakery Lane they had seen the policemen make their routine shift-change at the Embassy gate but neither man was familiar to them.

Sasha chuckled at the old woman. "Come on, Gran. What about some *kasha*, eh? I've had nothing all day."

She tutted under her breath. "You've had too much of something else if you ask me." She frowned as the dustman tried to push past her into the kitchen, still wearing his cap. "Lord, bless us, far too much."

"Don't get on your high horse," he pleaded, half-seriously, stroking her sparse hair.

She wasn't listening. "I've served men all my life. But not men like you, if you don't mind my saying so," she said addressing Boris, who was in reality quite outside her experience of men: a gentleman she might have called him. "And I don't like to see you in the state you're in. Drink, drink, it's all right for *him*. But it can destroy a sensitive man." You couldn't blame Boris, thought the old woman. It must be Galina's fault. She'd never had any idea how to treat a man.

"Never belonged here, that woman," she said to Sasha who was familiar with her wool-gathering and rarely replied.

"Not her. My rule about men was: give them what they want, whenever they want, and never ask for a thank you. I've never been wrong about men." She looked up at the ceiling.

"She'll go on like that for ages," whispered Sasha. "I reckon those two roubles went in the shop, you know. Not that it matters. I get paid on Friday, he can wait till then."

A child's fur boot lay in the corner under the coat-rack. The Kuznetsovs had placed two pairs on a sheet of newspaper to stop muddy street water staining the lino, and they had fallen over in the scuffle at the door.

"Look at it, can't bloody move in this place. All women's, this clutter."

Sasha didn't count Lev Kuznetsov as a man, any more than the little nine-year-old Xenia Kuznetsova.

Lizaveta smiled at Boris. "You can always be sure of a welcome in this flat, my dear man."

"I've come to see my sister, actually."

Pointing to the first door on the left, Sasha winked. "Want me to give her a shout?"

"You'll do no such thing," said Lizaveta placing her hand round the polished brass knob, and easing the door open a crack. They could hear someone humming, moving round the room, picking things up and putting them down. The door was suddenly pulled wide open and Olga Sergeyevna appeared, her eyes large and questioning, her mouth set in an irritable line. Behind her the corners of the room were very dark in the muted glimmer of the table lamp.

"Olga Sergeyevna, my dear, you look *so* much better today," said Lizaveta leaning forward obsequiously.

"What do you mean, today? I was perfectly well yesterday, and the day before that. Why *do* you have to make these pointless remarks all the time?" Small, with a tight coil of grey hair set back from a straight, thick fringe, she gestured rapidly, elegantly punctuating the words with precise movements of her hands.

Behind the door was a kind of lobby where a refrigerator and wardrobe stood; Olga's skis lay up against one wall. An archway led into the main room.

Intimidated by her brisk articulation Sasha took off his cap and made a slight bow. Lizaveta was not so easily cowed.

"Your brother's come to see you. Isn't that nice?"

"Lizaveta Ivanovna, the day I no longer recognise my brother I'll send for you. Until then, *please* leave me alone."

The two men in the hall were embarrassed. In the silence they heard the lift hum, its doors clanging shut on the top floor.

"Borya, you're soaked," said Olga, taking her brother's arm and leading him inside.

Boris shut the door in Sasha's face. Lizaveta picked up the string bag and started off to the kitchen.

The corridor stretched round the corner in an L-shape, with rooms on the long side and the bathroom, lavatory and store-cupboard opposite. Doors ranged all down the passage: Olga's room beside Sasha's; Lizaveta's in the corner and the Kuznetsovs' next to the kitchen which was right at the end. The Kuznetsovs had two doors because their one big room had, at some time, been subdivided by a chipboard partition. A tiny alcove led off from the main room and that was where Xenia slept, in a curtained-off space the size of a cupboard. Lizaveta resented it. She resented all the Kuznetsovs because they had two rooms *and* the alcove; she resented Olga's little entrance-way where the silver samovar with the Romanov coat of arms stood on the refrigerator. But Sasha was exempt from all this, even though he had the biggest room, the one with two windows and a marble fireplace, a fine airy room which he filled with empty bottles, newspapers and remnants of food, exempt because it was there he had nursed his grandmother for seven and a half years. Lizaveta Ivanovna was sentimental.

When Xenia grew up the Kuznetsovs might lose a room. By then, Lizaveta reckoned, she would be eighty. Her own daughter, who lived on the other side of town, rarely called or telephoned. The Kuznetsovs gave her lonely life a focus; they were too well organised, they made little noise and no mess but it was impossible to tell what they did. Lizaveta could deduce all about Sasha and Olga simply from the clues they scattered in the course of everyday existence: Sasha's heaps of washing, Olga's dirty crockery; they were as informational as telegrams.

Sasha threw the carrier bag on to the table. "We had a good day, me and Borya. I've still got a beer," he said, examining the bottle.

Four small gas-stoves stood along one wall and Olga's was the cleanest. Over it, she had hung a tinplate clock. On the face two bears circled a woodcutter while a hunter took aim at them behind the cover of some trees.

Sasha twisted off the bottle cap with a coin. "Borya's well-read. He knows languages."

The old woman frowned. "Literature! Languages! You and Boris Sergeyevich? Impossible."

Through a long window, beyond the sink, vast forms of other buildings were darkly visible round the back courts.

Lizaveta could see Sasha's reflection in the glass. "Impossible," she repeated irritably, watching the window. "I saw you today when you came in and threw your overalls on the floor. You hadn't got Boris Sergeyevich with you then. And he wouldn't go round with you. Not him. He's a gentleman." For a second time she used the word, unaware of its modern derogatory implications.

Sasha ruffled his hair. "No, no, it's true. We were talking about writers and Russia and then he wanted to see his sister. He even told me how to get a girl. I had to help him across the main road in the end."

Lizaveta laughed. "That doesn't sound like Boris Melentyev, more like that idiot, Leonid Bikovsky, you go around with, the one you always drink with, that riff-raff."

Sasha, unmoved, swilled his beer round in the bottle. Soon he would be eating. Though Len was his mate, she had a point. He looked down at the table which Lizaveta scrubbed twice a week. There was no sound from Boris, Olga or the Kuznetsovs. "Too quiet, this place," he breathed. "Weird sometimes, don't you think?"

It was Lizaveta's turn not to answer. She put a bowl and spoon in front of him, and sat for a moment, gazing into his eyes. "What *will* become of you?" she said gently.

The lights flickered for a moment and a spatter of rain dashed at the window, rattling the panes.

"I'm going to get married, Granny."

She laughed a throaty, harsh laugh, and went back to the stove, smoothing down her apron and stroking its faded flowers. "It's only an old woman like me, my dear young man, who'll put up with your sort."

She watched composedly as he ate. Sasha concentrated on his own thoughts. Olga Sergeyevna or Boris might help him frame the right sort of advertisement. A postcard, perhaps, on the wall beside the beer-shop; or something in the newspaper. Boris said there were too many women in Russia; there were too many here, in this flat. There should be one for him, somewhere, he knew.

Olga switched on the centre light and helped Boris off with his coat.
The direct beam reduced the room to a white box with dark furniture
on two sides. At one end stood a high window, looking as if it ought
to have been another door opening out into a further, larger room.

Boris sat down on the most masculine of Olga's precious, pre-
Revolutionary furniture, a heavy chair with stout legs.

"Oh, what *do* you smell of?" Laughing, she fanned the air in front
of her, her full lips widely parted. He lit a cigarette.

"All right, all right, I know. One gesture of independence and I'm
unfit for the human race."

As he smoked she watched him intently from her favourite cane
chair, the back of her left wrist at her forehead as if to shield herself
from the light. The cigarette made him cough.

"I've been all over the place . . ."

Behind Olga was a narrow flowered divan, flanked on one side by
a chest and on the other by a cheval glass. A fine 1890s bureau, too
wide to fit along the wall without jutting out across part of the only
window, was at the far end of the room. The writing flap was dropped
down to reveal four ranks of tiny drawers with turned brass knobs
set amidst identical greenish, pale inlays of fruit and flower swags.
All round the edges of the drawers and the little cupboards were
slivers of white and green woods set into the darker grain of the
mahogany.

Twenty-two years ago she had moved in with Aunt Lily's bureau
and cupboards, the tea-service and the gold earrings their grandmother had bought on honeymoon in Darmstadt. Even then the room
was too small for the furniture and the balance of the plaster vine
clusters at each angle of the ceiling had been ruined by partitioning.

She had made the pink curtains almost immediately and they still
hung elaborately over the architraves of the window.

Over the divan a photograph of a moonlit sea hung beside a cheap
ikon from Novodyevichii Convent.

"Tell me about that Sasha you're so pally with, now. He keeps
giving me pictures. I never know what to say. Appalling things, but
I had to frame that one in the end. He would have been so offended
if I'd not. Is he really a brute?"

"Harmless, darling," said Boris. "He worries about you, says you
look miserable these days . . . that you had a new friend. Foreign."

The table was laid for one but there was a second chair. Olga went
over and rummaged in a wooden box containing her hair-brushes,
combs and small bottles. Brushing past her brother she gave off an
aroma of lavender, soap and dry tea.

"That's not concern, it's simple insolence. Sheer artful prurience.

Ugh!" She tapped her foot, enjoying the stress of the phrase. "There's something not quite nice about that man. Haven't you heard what he gets up to? Telephoning women at all hours, and such common ones, too. You should have seen . . ."

Boris yawned. The effect of the alcohol was wearing off and he had had enough of Sasha for one day.

"I shan't go into the kitchen tonight. Not while your precious Aleksandr and that old woman are tittle-tattling." With a small key Olga opened one of the cupboards of the bureau and took out a jar of preserved raspberries which she proceeded to spoon carefully into two minute porcelain bowls. As Boris took his place at the table he was surprised to see that the fine hair on her neck was still blonde.

A half-litre of vodka, smoked cheese, bread, and sliced, salted cucumbers quickly appeared on the table. Boris stared at the food, gripped his matchbox in his left palm and crushed his cigarette stub on the top.

Olga licked the raspberry spoon, her eyes bright. "At first I thought he must be a poet. Quite different from the others, with deliciously grave manners."

Ah, the well-tailored stranger. Boris waited resignedly for further confidences. This habit of unheralded, confessional speech was common to brother and sister.

She crossed the room with the kettle and a clean ashtray which she placed at his elbow.

"He wasn't reserved or snobbish, Borya. He sat in the kitchen for hours with Lizaveta, talking and talking. I don't think he understood much – you know how she speaks – but that was all very nice."

Brought up on schoolroom versions of the English character, she thought she could cover each of its manifestations by juggling with those three words. She piled Boris's plate with food and pushed the raspberries nearer his teacup.

"Could it ever have worked out for you, Olichka? Could you have had a future together?"

"Well, in the end it made me cry, if that's what you mean," she said brusquely, not wanting to be pressed but waiting for the right moment to reveal more. He sat there, feeling foolish as he had always done with her from boyhood, dropping crumbs on the pink cloth.

She soon brightened up again. "Eat up, darling. It's a change to have an intelligent person to talk to . . . So young, so distinguished. Too young, perhaps? Was that it? I'm older, of course, but . . ."

She was once more oblivious of him and everything around her. Boris worried about going back upstairs at midnight when Galya was

29

alert and motionless in the double bed, hardly breathing but conscious of his every move. If he died in bed, it certainly wouldn't be alone. He poured himself a big glass of spirits and sipped the hot tea which tasted smoky and unpleasantly of fish.

"He was shy, like you, but I knew at once he liked me. You see, he didn't *have* to like me. There was no necessity for it, you understand."

Boris took a large gulp of tea and burnt his mouth. It was too easy for foreigners. One minute, promises. Next minute, the airport. You couldn't blame them, though.

"I used to love to go walking at night. We'd wander about seeing nobody except drunks or crooks or policemen."

Boris shuddered. There was no point in saying anything to her. She wouldn't listen, she never had, not even as a child when he was several years older and as a boy ought to have had some authority. All he wished now was that she was less ingenuous and a bit more level-headed.

"Paradoxical, isn't it? I mean, starting to live at the end of your life," he said quietly. He was thinking about himself. How ill he was neither of them knew, and both usually managed to evade discussion of any subject which lay outside their particular expertise.

A thump came from behind the partition. Sasha was going through the evening paper looking for a wife and would soon be pounding up and down the bare floor of his room.

"Don't fuss," she said. "I know, we'll go to Tanya's. She and Marina generally have something nice to drink. I usually call round on Tuesdays, anyway."

As Olga was clearing away there came a knock on the door.

"That'll be your friend, I know it. Always about this time. Will you let him in?" she asked, her eyes wide and mocking as she wiped out the teapot.

"Oh Lord, I know he means well, but he's not really a friend."

"A hard-working, decent chap," said Olga, delighted to change moods by teasing her brother.

Boris was reluctant to move but the knocking grew louder. "How's Tanya?" he asked, walking to the door.

"What do you expect? Living with that potty husband? It's no joke. Still, she'll enjoy the company."

"You don't mean Sasha's coming too?"

She looked up and to his astonishment he realised she was serious. "Tanya wants me to meet a new friend of hers. *She'll* love him. But, Borya, Borya," she added swiftly, "promise me you'll go to the doctor's again, just once more, and get a second opinion. You could be wrong."

Sasha still had the carrier bag under one arm and an evening paper in his hand.

"I've got . . ." he began eagerly, evidently on the verge of a well-rehearsed preamble.

Irritated by his sister's strange determination, Boris cut him short. "You're going to a party."

"With you both?" said Sasha, more surprised than touched by the unexpected kindness. "Is Olga Sergeyevna coming too?"

Olga nodded from in front of the cheval glass where she was knotting a broad red scarf over her hair, neatly pinning two folds together at the side of her chin.

As if trying to make himself smaller the dustman squeezed his shoulders and upper arms tightly against his body and almost tiptoed up, stopping a little to the right, just behind her. She followed his reflection quizzically, tucking errant wisps of hair under her headscarf.

"Olga Sergeyevna, excuse me, but I've brought something for you."

It was a picture from an illustrated magazine. The middle fold buckled inwards and he looked down trying to smooth out the whole page with his big hands. "If you put something heavy on it . . . Or use your iron . . ."

"It's very kind of you, Aleksandr Mikhailovich," murmured Olga, indistinctly, intent on the fit of the scarf, the unclasped brooch gripped in her teeth, "but what on earth can I do with that? There's no space left on my wall for one thing."

"You could always shift some books." Sasha had never seen such a collection stacked on the walls of any flat. There was an awkward pause while they all contemplated his picture of a heavy glass bowl full of red and yellow tulips on a cottage window-sill. The light caught the sheen of the hot-pressed paper, making the flowers stand forward like cut-outs against the unnatural, intense white.

Boris pulled on his coat. "Shall I stick it up in the lavatory, Olya? That could do with a bit of . . ."

"No."

"Don't you like it?" asked Sasha, disappointed.

"Oh, really, just look at those colours."

Sasha turned the photograph round towards him, passed his tongue uncertainly over his lips and crumpled it up. "You're right. Tasteless." He looked brightly at Boris. "Off then, are we? Where's the party?"

"At Tatyana Lestyeva's, the journalist, my sister's friend," said Boris frowning. "And behave yourself, Aleksandr Mikhailovich. She's a cultivated woman."

The dustman nodded and sidled up holding out the newspaper.

"Look, there's a widow here. Thirty-eight with her own furniture."

"Are you ready?" shouted Olga from the lobby where she had been changing into outdoor shoes. The pessimistic Tanya would be waiting, expecting them not to turn up. "You know what a state she's always in, Borya."

She turned to Sasha, inspected him for a long moment and then burst out: "Whatever you do, don't ask about her husband."

"Why not?"

"Just don't, that's all."

The dustman was anxious to get out of the room before she had time to make him feel more uneasy. "I'll get the lift for you, Olga Sergeyevna, shall I?"

"What an idiot he is!" she laughed, straightening Boris's tie and mimicking Sasha's awkward manner.

"He likes women, Olichka, and he could be a friend to you."

Her eyes widened. "You must be out of your mind, my dear."

"Well, you could do with a friend. You can't be happy without different sorts of people around . . . The saint from the book, the well-mannered, the isolated, even the drunk. Isn't that true?"

In the hall Olga turned to look at him."Shut up. Just shutupshut-upshutup . . ."

3

Outside, it was cold. In the rising wind, the rain of the afternoon had given way to a fine, dry snow which frosted the bag of yellow apples by Tanya's front door. A friend must have brought them in from the *dacha* at Chernogolovka and gone before she had got round to answering the bell. They had to ring three times before she heard.

"Poor things! Why didn't you bang on the window like all the others? You'd let anyone walk over you if they wanted," said Tanya, a lanky, melancholic-looking woman, a good six inches taller than Sasha, giving Olga a hug in the doorway. The remark, Olga knew, was directed at her. They had been at school together and Tanya, however badly things had turned out for her afterwards, had never quite lost her playground bossiness with the younger woman. The texture of her pale-blue angora jumper (a birthday present from Olga) had degenerated over the months into grubby ringlets of fluff, and her maroon ski-pants looked a couple of sizes too small. Her white hair, usually massed on top of her head to give her figure a grandeur bizarrely out of keeping with her odd clothes, was now unpinned and streamed unkempt down her long back.

Sasha lagged behind, nervous of this towering woman, and thought of trying to make an impression by dead-lifting the fifty-kilogram bag from the pavement. But deprived of his audience, he decided against it and dragged the apples after him along the parquet and into the kitchen.

The room was cramped and overheated. Shelves ran from floor to ceiling, cluttered with a mass of household items, which, to judge by the dust covering jam-jars, meat tins and cheap Polish enamelled pots and pans, had not been touched for years. At the far end was a lavatory partially hidden by a curtain; someone had pushed in a bicycle beside the cistern and the back wheel bulged out under the material.

"Are you back at work yet?" asked Olga quietly.

"Blasted men and doctors," whispered Tanya. "They've ruined my life."

Sasha gave a low whistle when he saw her face. The bruises must have been about a week old and their colours reminded him of the flesh of the skinned rabbits gone off in the heat, the kind he'd never been able to stomach on the survival course in Kazakhstan. The green and blue and yellow had puffed up, making butterfly wings of the tissue round her eyes, and the bridge of her nose stood out bluish. Not a mark on her pale forehead, nothing on her cheeks, but her nose had been broken in two places and, by the look of it, not properly reset.

"It'll never be any better," said Tanya. She obviously meant with Andrey, her husband, whom Biryusov knew by reputation. As something of an expert, he could have told her she was wrong: he'd seen the same thing with his mother, and his mother had married again, and her nose had got to be fetching in a funny sort of way. Olga was already introducing him.

"Aleksandr Mikhailovich couldn't wait to meet you, Tanichka," she lied. "Next thing you know it'll be the policeman from over the road." Sasha mumbled his greetings and turned away quickly.

The table looked as if the contents of several shopping bags had been emptied all over it. There must have been two dozen scarlet and white packets of cigarettes – English or American, Sasha could not tell, but foreign, anyway – five bottles of vodka, at least two of which he had never seen the like of before, a neat heap of Russian chocolate bars, books, a map of Moscow, a photoguide to Zagorsk, postcards, a huge jar of freeze-dried coffee, and, everywhere, box upon box of matches sold in sets at tobacco kiosks all over Moscow and bearing pictures of Russian flowers, Russian birds, Russian dogs, Russian masterpieces of architecture and a whole collection of portraits of Yuri Gagarin. A pair of pigeons cooed eerily from the makeshift coop tucked between the table legs, and then there was a giggle from someone in the corner between the bicycle and blocked-up fireplace.

A girl, dressed completely in white, was seated by Tanya's old gas-stove. She had on the whitest blouse, the whitest skirt, and the whitest cardigan he had ever seen in his life; even her lips were paled by some faintly iridescent cosmetic. He found a chair, sat down and smiled broadly. Without a word he stared, marvelling at the gold rims of her spectacles, her rope of pearls, her long fingernails, her white-blonde hair. For variation of tonality it was like looking close up at a candle when the flame had burned down inside, deep into the wax; or at a glass of Czech lager when the bubbles were stilling in the foam. Dazzled he looked down at the cigarettes with their unfamiliar lettering and coats of arms. The girl quickly seized his hands, unclasped his fists and thrust a pack into each palm.

"Help yourself, courtesy of Amex, just take what you want."

The accent was almost faultless but her name sounded odd. Amex? Alex? Still, who cared about names when she looked like that?

The older women had pulled out stools from beneath the table and were sitting opposite, deep in talk of hospitals and the villainy of men.

"They set it crooked, I was sick after I saw myself in the mirror. They wanted me to prosecute Andrey."

Tanya's insistent chatter about wards, the rudeness of doctors, saline drips (she couldn't have had one of those, surely?) and whole families camped out in corridors, began to get on Biryusov's nerves. Besides, her voice was so high and loud that it would have been hard to break in with a query or even to make himself heard to the girl who was, by now, poring over the map, so he turned to Boris who was standing behind his sister listening to this dismal recital.

"Think I should open this?" he muttered, slowly revolving a bottle of Kubanskaya and wondering if he could start on it and whether or not it belonged to this Andrey who might or might not appear.

"Why not?"

Andrey was why not, but Sasha said nothing and untwisted the cap. The foreign cigarettes lay untouched at his elbow.

"Tanya, darling, don't worry, he must simply hate the sight of himself at this moment. Men. Why don't they hurt each other instead? And they're always the first to weep because of their delicate consciences. Don't you think so, Borya? Aren't I right?"

About to hand his glass for Sasha to fill, he timidly checked the movement. "Olya, my dear, of course." He had not quite heard all of what she said. "Tanya would be better leaving him. He might kill her . . ." But it was enough to start them off again.

Sasha held out the bottle, slightly aslant in his big hands, winked at Boris and filled up a tumbler for the girl and pushed it towards her.

"Good health!" he said, chinking glasses with Boris and motioning to her to do the same. She flushed slightly at his gesture, taken unawares by the formality of the toast and the unexpected gravity with which he performed it. Bending down, she brought more chocolate out of a large canvas bag at her feet; then some nuts, different cigarettes, a jar of caviare and a bottle of half-sweet Crimean champagne. Her face became pinker after the exertion and Sasha thought he liked it.

"Pushkin!" It could have been a question.

"What?"

"Pushkin, you know, your poet, wasn't this his favourite way of mixing, vodka and champagne?"

Sasha had no idea, so he replied decisively: "No. Are you English then?"

He had certainly read that the English drank more champagne than everybody else in the world. She held out her hand and introduced herself.

"My name is Roberta Weston from Rhode Island, in the United States of America. You can call me Bobby."

Sasha tried out the name, introducing her, in turn, to Boris. Bobby was easier than Amex. "And I'm Aleksandr Mikhailovich, but you can call me Sasha." Rhode Island meant nothing to him.

"Where's that, exactly?"

"Up from New York."

This didn't help much. The two women had not stopped.

"Of course I'm not writing, how can I?" cried Tanya, with a wide sweep of her arm. "Yesterday, when I got back, everything in the office had changed. For a start, the whole magazine has a new editor, a frightfully ambitious little creature called Kirilyenko who's a non-smoker, eats chocolate creams all day and has other disgusting personal habits." She shut her eyes for a moment and gave an exaggerated shudder. "He loathes women – on principle, I think. Especially professional women. And whose page does he want to take over? Mine. I mean, I'm not just *a* journalist on that paper. You know that, I'm the only journalist, I'm a writer, I'm an *institution*! We've always had a problem page on *Feministka*. He's already told me I don't fit the new house style and he expects me to adapt . . . write, write . . . well, filth, I call it. His word is modernisation."

Sasha took an interest: so that was what Tanya wrote about in her magazine. He felt round for the fragment of the *Moscow Evening News* which he had folded up small and hard and shoved down the back pocket of his trousers, before throwing away the rest of the paper.

A widow who lived in Rostov-on-Don wanted to set up house with someone in the Moscow area. "Friendship with a view to marriage." He looked at Tanya.

What sort of a view was that? He could ask, though: after all, it was her job.

Boris of course had been disparaging. "Thirty-eight, you say? That can mean anything from forty-one to fifty-five."

But Tanya wrote about problems and Sasha did not think he had one yet. Anyway, what did she know about anybody else's when she couldn't sort out her own? There was no hurry; the matter, as Olga Sergeyevna might say, could be safely postponed. Miss Weston's voice sounded in his other ear.

"I wish Momma could see me right now!" The liquor seemed to have got her going and she was trying to prise off the top of the caviare with a five-kopek piece. The pearls at her breast quivered. Sasha took over, rolling up his shirtsleeves with a grin, and the lid flipped into the air. Someone had told him that American women were frigid and for a long time he believed it signified something about body temperature. This cool, ashen-complexioned girl in her snow-white kit could make you want to test out the theory.

"I'm so at home here, in this place, in this country of yours, in spite of your wicked weather. I've never been so happy in my entire life."

"Who's Amex?"

She laughed for the first time. "That's not a *person*." Pearl-enamelled nails flicked through compartments in the leather bag: key-ring, driving licence with her photograph in colour, dollars and a small leather case with transparent pouches each of which contained a gaily-coloured card.

He knew what they were, knew what they were meant for but he had never held one in his hand before and he enjoyed feeling the rounded corners and sharp edges of the plastic. Meanwhile she went on, in her soft, pale voice telling him what she thought he could never have guessed. Amex, not Alex.

And he listened because of the cigarettes, for the fact she'd given them to him. Giving was always his job and giving had become a chore; women hardly ever reciprocated. The only present he had ever had returned was his own photograph.

"There's such appalling commercialism, back home," she continued, her violet eyes beaming naïvely, as if, in the length and breadth of his vast Soviet homeland, there was no newspaper which had not told him that countless times. Sasha let his gaze wander during the energetic prattle: small breasts, Len would like that, he thought smugly, remembering fat Natalie and how Len couldn't get anyone else. He'd always wanted a girl with small breasts.

He interrupted: "Are you married?"

She shook her head and made a face. "American men. Well, they're pretty disappointing when it comes to serious talk. They don't think a woman can be a woman and have ideas and opinions of her own."

American men, he thought, can't know they're born, with girls like this, with their serious ideas and their Amexes.

"I like a man to be, I don't know, kind of rugged, strong, more like the ones I've met here, men you can lean on, men who want to be men."

"I see," said Sasha, thinking of Andrey who might come through the kitchen door at any moment ready to break another nose. He knew a lot of those.

"What a comfort you have your mother." Olga was holding forth from her side of the table. "You can always depend on her."

The conversation had moved on, and Tanya had subsided into a pleasant calm which, with more champagne, would end in self-consoling tears. The pigeons fluttered in the crate. Three glasses were enough for Tanya to remember how much she loved Andrey and how handsome he had looked at their wedding twenty years before.

"Your Russian's marvellous, where did you learn it?"

"Oh, in school back home."

If only it had been at her *babushka*'s knee in Milwaukee or somewhere. Another intellectual; he might have guessed there would be a drawback. Breaking open one of the slabs of chocolate from its wrapping, he snapped the hard bar into lumps. The white nuts embedded in them gave off a distinct plummy smell. On the dark blue label was the picture of a Cossack galloping his horse over the snow at full tilt. The horse's front legs struck out together unnaturally, as in a serf painting.

"You mean, these men you meet, you think they're a bit like that," he said, nodding at the label, his mouth full.

"Do *you* think they are?" She smiled, touching his bare arm.

Unmoved, Sasha chewed reflectively. "I don't know about all that, but I could do with a bit of commercialism. Let it rip, I'd say, fine, wide and rampant." He gulped down his vodka. "Never mind fancying the horny-handed sons of Mother Russia. You come down the market one day with me, you find out what *uncommercial* potatoes look like, and see the old grannies queuing for them, too, *and* the meat, *and* the apples, even. Oh, not your market, not the ones in there," he broke off, impatiently, waving at her maps. "The scruffy ones, the backstreet places where old dears raise a rouble or two by standing round and selling an old bra or string vest – that's all they know about a commercial market – and frightened to death all the time because it's unofficial commerce, and they can get nicked for it. Do you want to see it? You really want to know? I'll take you, it's an ed – u – cation."

What did he have to lose? No point in letting her go on; next moment she would be rambling about saintly alcoholics, Holy Russia, beggars crossing themselves, birch-brooms, hearts as dark as forests, gypsies, troikas, the absence of bill-boards, how clean the Metro was, and the indomitable Russian peasant in his snow-shoes gazing at the stars.

"Toughness means things get tougher for us. And they're tough enough to start with."

"No, I've seen that, I know what you're talking about, but you're wrong. You only see one side, you don't know what I know about where I come from. There's no discipline, no idealism, no sacrifice."

Irina would have thrown back her head and laughed. She always said some woman, one day, would teach Sasha a lesson. But she could never have imagined her being this milk-fed cinema star American blonde in starched lace with a bagful of plastic money. He went on listening as she opened up about the big love affair: the vast, exotic city, the dust-red buildings, the barbaric Palladian façades of the palaces, stormy poetry readings, all those intense, fevered, professional relationships, which made communication so easy and uncomplicated with the most ordinary people.

"My head is reeling from it. Above all, it's the sense of energy and toughness I feel around me everywhere."

Mir, Freundschaft, Druzhba, hands around the table, hands around the globe. It was Irina again, proposing *friendship* in that teasing voice just after he'd bought the flowers; wanting chat when he was dying to put a hand up her skirt. That was supposed to be a love affair, supposed to be communication. Amex or Alex, he thought, they're all the same in the long run.

"Do you ever take off your spectacles?" asked Sasha, wanting to head off the topic of tough guys.

"Of course, now and then. Why do you ask?"

He wanted an unobstructed view of those startling eyes but, too shy to ask her if she would take the glasses off for him, he picked up the card wallet again and began fingering it.

"How would it be if I borrowed this thing, could I get things on it?"

"It can't be used without my signature. What would you want to buy, anyway?"

"Oh, things, things. There are all kinds of things, things I need."

"Let *me* buy them for you. That is, if you wouldn't mind my doing that, you wouldn't think I was . . . ?"

She had completely misunderstood; he only wanted to know how it worked.

"With that card?"

"Yes, and all the others, too." Smiling, she slid them out of the wallet and laid them out fan-wise, like a hand of playing cards. The signatures were in the same spiky writing: B. Weston; R. B. Weston; Bobby Weston; Roberta Weston.

He couldn't read any of them, or anything printed on the other sides.

"And every one of them is yours?"

"That's right, every one."

"How are they worth anything?"

"Worth? Well, you could say they're worth what I'm worth. I mean, what the people who give the cards think I can pay for. They go into all that before, and then they trust you to pay. Thousands of dollars, perhaps."

"Roubles, too?"

"Yes, roubles, too. And pounds and marks and francs and so on, all those."

Sasha was unimpressed but did not say anything. If you had thousands already, what was the point of messing about with cards? Perhaps they were just for Moscow.

"Look. I know I sounded off a bit just now, but you said you'd show me places," she said suddenly. "But I don't want those places you said. Are there others, you know, little places where only you can go? Places foreigners never see?"

The appeal was in her voice, not so much the clumsy words; there was a quaver. Taken by surprise, Sasha wondered just how much she did know about the place or its inhabitants. Tomorrow he had nothing to do except to clean his room and write to the widow in Rostov-on-Don. Tomorrow he could take the day off.

"Tomorrow?"

She took him up, instantly.

"But you'd better change those clothes, you can't be looking like that where we'll be going." Not that he had thought of anywhere yet but when he did it wouldn't be where there were girls in her sort of rig-out.

That was it: tomorrow he would be taking out Miss America incognito. He was entirely, unexpectedly delighted. This was going to be a story worth telling.

Roberta Weston took a tiny, expanding gold pencil out of her bag and entered his telephone number in a leather notebook with gilt-edged leaves. A whole page entirely for him. He rubbed his day's growth of beard, meditatively, and a concluding fragment of the women's conversation reached him. Tanya had started apologising.

". . . No thought for anyone else, and I've bored you all with my problems, haven't even introduced you properly. Bobby darling, won't you tell Boris and Olya about America? You could show them your snapshots." She smiled, forlornly. "Snapshots, yes," she repeated softly. "Bobby, I had one done for you to take home. Not bad, but not good, not very good."

4

There was a bumping noise in the hallway, then a muffled shout. Sasha, having been on the qui vive almost all the evening, had finally forgotten the terrible Andrey; now his hand gave an involuntary tremor as he put down his glass. The door burst open and an old woman, not quite so tall as Tanya, but with a bearing incomparably more elegant, and with the same white, thick hair, stepped into the kitchen, holding before her a round black cake on a square breadboard.

"What are you all staring at, for heaven's sake? Anybody would think I'd just stood up in my coffin." Her chesty voice was strikingly deep and she had a queer way of exhaling in time with the words, so that they emerged in bursts between sharp intakes of breath. To strangers, the effect was comical.

No one said that they were simply glad she wasn't Andrey.

The American girl pointed gleefully at the cake. "Marina Andreyevna! That's really the most wonderful . . ." Her voice trailed away when nobody took up her cry. The only sound was the scuffling and burbling of the imprisoned pigeons. The old woman picked up a long knife from the drawer by the sink.

"Well, thank God for the quiet, I suppose, nobody making scenes. If we did *that* every time someone died," she puffed, brandishing the knife in the direction of the front room where the television was blaring, "we'd be knee-deep in misery and floral tributes. Or I would be, at my time of life." She peered grimly at Boris. "Now there's a spectral visage, Boris Sergeyevich. Lord, Lordy, man, it was someone else that died and was buried yesterday. Thank God it wasn't you, thank Him for that lovely thing – *not yet.* Here's my daughter who's had a clout and she's metamorphosed into a tragedy queen. Don't go off the deep end, like her."

A great act, thought Boris. She wasn't really tough, not in the common way: all the pleasure she took in the performance came as the pleasure she gave came, from a delight in the contrast of her beautifully curved lips with the staccato breeziness with which she uttered the lines of her own part in her own play, across the long, seamlike edges of her mouth. Even her hands, wrapped round the knife-haft as she stabbed awkwardly at the cake, were thin-boned and tapering, unsuited to the work; the high line of her eyebrows was still discernible above her hooded lids. It must have been a joy to her once to whiten her hands, to pencil in those arcs. Boris knew the old bone structures, recognised the extinct refinement. Somehow Marina had survived, as his sister had survived.

They all, eventually, got a slice of the cake.

Miss Weston dripped cream down her blouse, and Sasha watched as she fumbled in her bag for something to sponge her lightly-covered breasts. He wanted to tousle the shiny blonde hair, cut back, which sprouted out thickly above her ears. The drink, by now, was taking effect.

The old *barinya* had sat down and was rolling a cigarette. "Come along then, all you intelligent people, entertain an old woman. Converse!"

Boris had hardly said a word the whole evening. At first he had listened patiently to his sister and friend but their monopolising of the talk at his end of the table became exasperating; and then there had been this American with her maddening, cockeyed Soviet fundamentalism; and it had been a hard day and he was not used to drinking. He felt sorry for himself, and spoke.

"Marina Andreyevna, today I found the answer to misery. Refuse to recognise reality, let the will stagnate, and to hell with self-discipline!"

This had less effect than he thought it merited. Olga snorted. "Borya, when will you learn? It's always the same with you, one or two drinks and you become a different person. In my time, God knows how many unique secrets of life I've had to hear you discover. Do be quiet. You're a dear man but about the least discerning I've ever known."

"'I've discovered *this*," persisted Boris, waggling the vodka bottle. "Don't let anyone tell me about happiness!"

"Borya . . ." Sasha tried to butt in but the older man was talking to himself.

"Miss Weston, you may think." His voice rose. "You *may think* I'm pathetic, but soon all I shall arouse will be curiosity and compassion and irritation. The rest of my life is going to be as simple as I can make it."

He was losing track and would soon fall asleep.

"Ignore the passing of time, straight from shop to coffin, no shop assistants, no cash desk, no doctors and no bloody priests!"

"Oh God, oh God," groaned Olga distractedly. "Don't begin all that again."

"But that's terrible," said Miss Weston, anguished.

"Nothing of the sort," called Marina Andreyevna. "Just unseemly, the indecorous bread of our daily lives. Look at this vile little cake! Miserable, are we, Boris Sergeyevich? You always were a hangdog little guttersnipe. Well, I'm relying on the kick I'll get out of my first drink. Go somewhere else and be dreary."

Olga came round to Roberta. Sasha heard the words: ". . . a letter, but I can't ask you in here." The American girl started and smiled bleakly.

Both women went out into the hall. A cold draught from the stairs welled through the warm kitchen, carrying the sound from a television set along the passage: drumbeats pulsed in the silence, heralding a hideous blare from the brass.

"Repeat after repeat," muttered Boris. "Dead but still not buried."

"Be glad if you go quickly," said Marina. "Can't imagine you really broken down, though. I'm sick of this place being like a morgue. Have a roll-up, darling." She held out a tin of black tobacco.

Tanya pushed her chair back from the table and went to shut the kitchen door.

"Bobby brought us all those pretty matches from the Beriozka, Mummy."

"What do I want those for? Dead men on matchboxes, indeed!"

Whispering was still audible from the passage. Marina smiled maliciously. "He didn't shoot people, at least that's something to be said for him. But, in the end, what sort of an epitaph is that?" She downed a thimble glassful of spirit in a single gulp. "Once I was a lady, then they wasted me." It sounded like a line from a song and Biryusov looked up, thinking she might go on, but she stared ahead piercingly, her clear black eyes fixed.

When Olga and Miss Weston returned, they were deep in conversation about women, something about their professional prospects, and Olga was unusually excited.

"I used to believe that once, too, dear, that it was all so obvious and reasonable, that merit was all that counted, that reasonable, good people will recognise the obvious, but in their day-to-day lives they don't think it applies. They're driven by other things, the things they know, the way they live and were brought up: all the tiny considerations of life swamp any kind of principle. What matters is what you have been taught to expect of life, and if you'd lived as long as I have, you'd wonder too, whether or not there'd be anything worthwhile left to you after you'd sacrificed those expectations, that deference and politeness, the humdrum round of that pleasurable, sexual conciliatoriness which decent men exhibit to women. I don't want the world that's offered me, I don't believe in it, we've lost so much already."

Miss Weston was unconvinced but her look was sympathetic and gently reproving, like that of a nun listening to a child who thought its discovery about a sudden loss of faith was a significant event, as if failure of belief implicated God in an appalling fraud. Why did she always seem so ready to involve herself in their lives but at the same time keep apart?

Marina Andreyevna was rolling long cigarettes and laying them out in a row on the dresser. "Every man wants his triumph, to square the world up to his own tidy scheme; break it up, eat it, digest it, assimilate it to the lineaments of his own being. My father knew the Okhotnii Ryad because you could smell it, smell the game from the Manège. You won't find that in my old Baedeker, not the reek of slaughter high in the Moscow air, not the debris of blood and down and feathers that stuck to your feet in the thoroughfare. We're honest; it takes a Prussian to sanitise a Russian shambles. Don't eat your snipe before you've gutted them, my little maid."

Boris stirred. "That's nearly as idiotic as a proverb," he said distinctly, without opening his eyes.

Marina picked up one of the roll-ups with black shreds of tobacco protruding from the ends and ignited it with one of Miss Weston's Yuri Gagarin matches. "Did you see how slow that funeral was? Running on the spot, slow as a nightmare. I've seen so many." She took a deep pull on the home-made cigarette without taking her eyes from Miss Weston. "Such a clean creature, you are, so clean, it's funny. Why can't my daughter be as clean as you?"

The American girl kept quiet, perplexed by Marina's manner.

"Don't take any notice of me, I'm an old woman, gone into the sere and yellow, sapless, your shrivelled immortelle," Marina muttered. "Tonight I'll read a detective story in bed with my tea. It's characteristic tactlessness in me to be here at all."

Sasha wondered how old she was; eighty or so, probably – the reminiscences would make her that. Rum old bird.

"*Babushka, babushka,*" murmured Boris, stretched out against his chair and in danger of sliding off. "What do you want us to do, do you want us to weep for *you*, or for ourselves? For what happened to people or for what *is* happening to people? Have you ever really wondered what happened to people? I remember that before the war there was some big do at Yasnaya Polyana – some centenary or other to do with Tolstoy. There were so many people – writers, critics, journalists and all the local party people as well as a lot from Moscow – that they couldn't be fitted in the house, so there was a great feast laid out in one of the barns. A journalist was talking to one of the writers (Olga knows who I mean) and whenever the conversation flagged, this fellow with a huge, white Gorky moustache, very old, shuffling along, came up to them and filled their glasses with wine from a great earthenware pitcher. At first they didn't take any notice, but he kept on doing it; every time they stopped talking, there he was, decrepit, whiskery, with his stone jug. The writer was intrigued, so after this had happened half a dozen times, he said to the old man: 'Tell me, why do you do that, why do you fill up our glasses every time there's a little pause in the talk?' 'Because the *Graf* told me to. He told me that whenever people at parties stopped talking, I was to give them more to drink.' '*Kakoy Graf?* What Count?' asked the journalist. 'Graf Lev Nikolayevich Tolstoy.' I've often wondered what happened to him. How much longer can he have lived in those times, talking about Counts? I know what happened to the writer; but perhaps the unreconstructed relic of feudalism survived and the wolves didn't come in and make a meal of *him*."

Sasha thought of his empty room; feet sounded in the outside area and a door slammed and then there was a sudden silence. Olga was finishing the caviare. Marina drained her glass and nodded at Boris, raising her fine eyebrows.

"Terrible drink, a filthy taste. Still, when you're unsettled . . ."

"I'm going home," said Sasha, suddenly. He'd had enough; the girl had taken his telephone number and they might be able to fix something for tomorrow, but the others were all a little bit mad, and it was a strain to follow the ins-and-outs of their memories. He wanted to be on the street.

"Winter has started," keened Marina. "Ice winds in a dream world, no refuge in sleep, Lord, Lord, deliver me."

Yes, he would wait for the girl to phone him. He would see if she meant what she said.

"Look at me, Granny, am I wailing? I've nothing to cry for because I never had anything to start with. Tomorrow is the first day of the rest of my life."

Wasn't it an American who had said that?

II

Miss Weston's Passion

5

Sasha Biryusov pulled off his fur cap and paused at the foot of the staircase. On the wall opposite was a gigantic poster of a rough-hewn woman grasping a baby to one hip and an assault rifle to the other. She was staring past him, her monumental face rigid in ecstatic contemplation of something very far away. "Forward into the Future" ran the legend.

Not with you, Lady, he thought.

0900 hours in the offices of *Feministka*. Squeals of laughter and the tinkle of cups filtered down from the first floor. Sighing, he began the ascent, smoothing down his unruly yellow hair. People raced past and along the distant corridors but he kept his eyes on the chipped and bleached lino in front of him, wishing he were invisible amidst all these women. A lot of high heels had passed this way.

Upstairs he heard voices, typewriters, and the clatter of indoor shoes as the girls from the typing pool scrambled from the cubby hole for smokers at the head of the stairs, before the charwomen came back up from their tea in the basement.

Did they believe they were going anywhere, *these girls*? In the back pocket of his trousers was a letter from a woman who believed *she* was.

Len had wangled him a place on this shift, in this area, far from the usual ward and he had cleared out office skips during the last week, getting closer to the right office – Tanya's. He had not seen her since the night of the party and he had not dared accost her in her kitchen, in front of Marina and, possibly, the violent Andrey. No, her office had seemed the best bet and this morning Sasha had found himself hauling enormous sacks of paper. The old porter whose job it was to burn all the inessential correspondence and papers belonging to the magazine had a living-room adjacent to the yard, and he had stood tremulously in the doorway, the long neck of an Andropovka a couple of inches out of his cardigan pocket, watching Sasha hump the bundles down to the furnace.

As he dropped the sacks a few letters fell to the ground.

49

"I stopped reading all those years ago," said the porter, smiling. "Depressing."

By the look of him he was hardly ever in a state to focus, let alone read.

They had shared a cigarette on the outside steps after the lorry went back to the depot. It was cold now and frost had scarred the paint on the water butts.

"I'm the only man in this building apart from the editor."

At night his job was to go round with a torch, inspecting the empty offices permeated with the odour of cologne and Parma violets, making sure the filing cabinets were locked and checking for smouldering cigarette ends.

The girls, he said, didn't count the editor, Kirilyenko, "unmarried, fifty-ish, head shaped like an onion," as a proper man, anyway, so perhaps he was the *only* one.

"I promise not to say 'boo' to him," said Sasha.

The emergency staircase had been the old man's suggestion. They waited an hour for the staff to get settled and the porter drew a diagram of the offices in the dust on top of his television. Tanya's was on the third floor. Just after the meal-break the porter climbed all the way up there to collect discarded letters and bring in new ones. "I've got a thing about lifts," he explained. Fat Masha, the editorial assistant, always sat by the door, sorting through the mail as expertly as a market fishwife gutting turbot. She was the only person who read about real problems, the ones which never got beyond her post at the door and were never published. She and the porter.

On reaching the first landing Sasha was confronted by a very old woman in a dark green overall, scarf and ankle socks, and a bright red armband. He bounded up the last few steps almost knocking her over.

A corridor lined with glass doors stretched ahead. On either side were dozens of women with typewriters. The clacking ceased as the old woman on the landing took fright suddenly.

"M-a-a-r-y-a!" she shrieked.

Behind him the ripple-glass panels of a door on the right showed silhouettes which bubbled apart and re-formed, and a red-headed girl swayed out of the office leaving a kettle on the boil steaming up the windows.

"My God, what do you think you're doing, creeping up on me like that?"

She stood against the light and to his surprise Sasha could see right through her skirt; that possibility was usually a summer-time bonus when Moscow girls went around without petticoats. He breathed more quickly, anxious that she might rumble him, and he'd never reach Tanya.

"Marya Fyodorovna, this young man hasn't got a proper pass." The crone's voice quivered joyously behind him.

Some clever hairdresser had razor-cut the girl's bronze hair so that the side-locks tapered downwards on both sides of her chin, leaving the edge as sharp as cut glass.

"I'm on the lorry," he said.

"The lorry left hours ago."

Maybe she was too good-looking to care. Some women were like that, he believed; it was a little way of distributing their sumptuous well-being to all and sundry. All down the passage women were looking out of their offices, giggling, glad of an interruption. He had never seen so many all together under one roof. In a minute he was going to dry up completely and they'd send for the militia.

"I have an appointment with Tatyana Borisovna Lestyeva."

The girl modulated the tone of her voice. "She's in conference." Then she stared at him, hard and curiously, her upper lip rising and tightening suddenly above her perfect teeth. It was almost a sneer, but she shooed the security hag away.

"Are you family?" She yawned and stretched as if she had just got out of bed and her breasts stiffened under the silk blouse.

He guessed it was silk although he had never seen anything like it before. "Well, yes, in a way."

"I thought as much." Clearly, nothing complimentary was intended. "At the moment she's with Philip Ivanovich. Under a cloud, actually. On the carpet, whatever you like to call it. I suppose you're in the picture, though, being *family* and all that."

Slamming to the door of her office with her foot, the red-head shrugged, gave Biryusov a sign to follow and started up the corridor. He came on behind, twisting his cap like a suppliant and trying not to look at the faces of the women who were sniggering sadistically on either side. What on earth was the matter with them? What was the matter with him, for Christ's sake? Didn't they have husbands or boy friends at home? Surely they'd seen a man close-to before. He glanced down quickly and was relieved to see that his flies were done up.

She hadn't said where they were going. The grey pleated skirt swished agreeably and he watched her waist rhythmically maintain its position relative to her hips.

"Aren't you a lucky bugger, then," she said lazily over her shoulder. "I could have got you into no end of trouble." Sasha hadn't expected the language, but she didn't seem to care about anything.

At the end of the passage were three steps. Marya Fyodorovna went down them and turned into a darker corridor where more doors and frosted glass panels, set over the lintels, denoted more tapping machines and more women.

"Lot of old cows along here," called out the girl brazenly. "Editorial secretaries."

He was beginning to feel scared: they probably had a place in the building where they put intruders like him and this sleepy little piece was going to introduce him to the resident big boys.

"Look, love, I don't want any trouble."

"That's his door," interrupted Marya Fyodorovna with an unaccountable leer. Through wobbly glass Sasha could just make out the lines of an extensive room, and before he had a chance to sidestep, the girl, without knocking, ushered him in, turned on her heel, and as she brushed past placed a plump hand squarely over the bump in his trousers and gave a manful squeeze.

Long windows ran down almost to the floor from the high ceiling. The effect was that of a studio, the principal concern being for light; almost an excess of it because it was apparent from the filing cabinets and bookshelves that no one painted in here. In spite of the windows slender fluorescent strips blazed brightly above the bald head of a small man who was seated facing the door behind a desk as big as an operating table. Across the desk, her back to the door, was the gaunt figure of Tanya, her white hair already unravelling beneath two immense black slides.

The little man was reading in a flat tone:

". . . kissed me lightly on the lips. Suddenly, as if lit by a warm flame, we kissed again, more intensely. Our love ripened as the weeks became months . . ."

He stopped and peered at the woman over half-moon spectacles, nodding his head like a pecking chicken. At first Sasha thought it was a *tic doloureux* but the movement stopped abruptly when he pushed out his lips, evidently weighing something up.

"She had a very tragic life," Tanya was whispering. "Her letter touched me, which was why I included it."

"Did they get married?"

Tanya shook her head.

"Did any of it ever happen at all?"

Tanya had no time to answer before he burst out:

"We're supposed to be educating them, *ma-dame*," he shouted lingering contemptuously on the foreign word. "Waking them up to reality." Out of the corner of his eye, Kirilyenko noticed Sasha who was edging round the room nervously twirling his cap, trying to look inconspicuous.

"Oh, it's you at last," he said, getting up from the desk and striding over to an area of the office partitioned off from the rest at waist height by banks of filing cabinets and bookshelves. "I'll show you what the trouble is. These stupid girls have been messing around."

Against a wall, and festooned with the trailing foliage of pot plants suspended from baskets which hung on wires from the reinforced steel joists of the ceiling, stood a complicated-looking apparatus. A small screen and a flat keyboard like a typewriter's were connected to another piece of equipment from which a long sheet of paper protruded, coiling down to the floor. Kirilyenko twiddled knobs, lights came on and the screen glowed.

"Everything is coming out either upper or lower case. Look."

He tapped the keyboard. A tiny red square flickered on and off at tremendous speed and letters followed its progress from left to right: *has harold had his hamburg hamster hung.*

"Aah," breathed Sasha, neutrally.

"Blasted nuisance. Do what you can. We need a first print-out by six at the latest," said the editor irritably before returning to his desk.

Sasha had seen one of these on television. He was intrigued. Perching his cap on top of a flowering cactus, he set to, imitating what Kirilyenko had just done. It was quite easy. *hit*, he began, *ler hated his happy home hat* – it should have been *at* but he didn't know how to change the thing once the word had appeared – *hannah hauptmann's as* – got it this time – *she hung her handbag on the hatstand.* For some moments he delightedly trotted out strings of aspirated words on to the little screen. By pressing a bar along the bottom of the instrument he found the capitals. Kirilyenko was right, it was either one thing or the other: *his hairy HANDS HOLDING her heaving HREASTS*, he tapped, running out of words beginning with "h", *hoisting his HUGE HOT.* He stopped, retrieved his cap and went back to Kirilyenko.

"That's all right," he said cheerily, remembering an arcane term of art from his spell in the motor pool. "The left axis is misaligned. I've put a grommet in."

"Thank God for that," sighed Kirilyenko. "Now we can get some work done round here."

"Love!" he resumed, twitching wildly, now roaring at Tanya. "Can't you ever think of anything else?"

Tanya murmured inaudibly. Emboldened by getting one over this nasty little man, Sasha wanted to say that the trouble was, from his point of view, that the women he knew wouldn't recognise love if it were gift-wrapped, but before he got a word in Marya Fyodorovna appeared again, sidling out from behind the bookshelves and flicking her perfect hair. In one hand she held a long sheet of paper.

Kirilyenko jumped. "I thought I told you to knock when you come in here."

"Yes," said the girl folding her arms across her chest, just below the nipples. "Yes, you did. Several times. But I'm bored."

He leant over the desk, threateningly. "I don't like your attitude, Marya Fyodorovna. In view of the circumstances . . ."

She ran a languid finger down the side of his desk, as crisply indifferent to him as a cat in a greengrocer's window. "What attitude? What circumstances? I've got better things to do than knocking on the doors of has-been old queens like you, you know."

Kirilyenko gripped his hands together and banged them violently on the desk top.

"Go on, dear, that's the idea, try to convince yourself you're a man," said Marya Fyodorovna.

Tanya was on her feet, clumsily assembling her papers and capping a leaky biro. Neither Kirilyenko nor Marya Fyodorovna took the slightest notice as she silently turned and crossed the room to the door. Tears ran down her cheeks.

As Sasha made to follow her, Marya grabbed his arm, waving the print-out at him. "And you're a dirty little bugger, too, aren't you?" she grinned lasciviously.

"What is it?" asked Tanya irascibly when Sasha caught up with her in the corridor.

"Me, Tatyana Borisovna. Sasha. Boris Sergeyevich's mate."

"Oh, go away, for heaven's sake."

She stumbled down the corridor ahead of him, dropping her papers. He followed, picking them up as he went. So far nine letters had arrived from the widow in Rostov, one of them sitting in his inside pocket now. She didn't want educating, didn't want reality; she wanted Romance and wrote the word with a capital R. What else would you want when you shared the living-room with your sister and brother-in-law and the bathroom with the children? *Love, Romance*, what you said to a lonely man you'd never seen while somebody else, in the same room was . . . They were all fragments of passion, letters like that, even if this Kirilyenko thought them pathetic.

"I've spent the last month trying to see you, Tatyana Borisovna. I want some advice pretty urgently."

"Please leave me alone. Can't you see I'm upset?"

She leaned back against the wall, her eyes closed and her jaw slackened in a long, choking sob. A lump still showed over the bridge of her nose but the bruises had faded.

"Look, here you are." Sasha brought out a small linen handkerchief embroidered with a flower in one corner. After she wiped her eyes he wondered if she had recognised it. She sighed.

"I can't advise anyone about anything any more."

"Look, I know it's no joke when the boss has got his knife into you."

When Zeldovich had been transferred to Gorky his wife walked out the day before he left. At the depot they said he'd started drinking over there and got into a real bother with a superintendent who was running some racket in surplus equipment. Zeldovich had got tanked up one night and taxed him with it. Since then his life had been a misery.

"Can't you fight back, give him an earful – like that Marya?"

"I could have done it once." Tanya shrugged and they went through the swing doors leading to a wide concrete staircase.

"Singlehanded I established femininity in the provinces. Now that moron has started to chop up my copy."

"What for?"

"I'd be the last person to be told that, but the sub-editors know why. And *they* never say."

Sniffing a little, she went up a few more stairs. "He proposed a new section to my 'Love and Femininity' page. A subsection." Her hands trembled on the banisters and she paused. "Bracketed: *Love* . . ." She lowered her voice and blushed. "*Difficulties.*"

Sasha had only a vague notion of what these entailed but they were probably concerned less with getting a woman than knowing what to do with her once you'd got her.

Tanya nodded. "I can't bear all those ugly medical words in Russian. But, that bully, that beast . . . He must think about it all the time." Her voice got louder. "Just like those oicks in the machine room who write dirty words on the print rolls at break time and put their empty vodka bottles behind the door of the women's lavatory. Animals."

Sasha made a mental note to curtail the extent of any advice he sought.

"All those ghastly letters Masha and I used to throw away he wants us to read. And answer. Not that Masha has obeyed so far. We still junk most of them, but Kirilyenko's getting worse. Well, you saw, just now."

He remembered the incinerator. "We must have burnt a lot of those this morning."

"Yes. But now we don't burn so many. And if I do what he wants and print that kind of stuff, I'll never be able to look people in the face again. It's hopeless."

They approached another landing where everything seemed quiet.
"That girl, Marya Fyodorovna," Sasha began.

"Ssssshhh! If you don't know whose daughter *she* is, don't ask."
She stopped and continued in a whisper: "Unreliable. Likes playing
games with people. She's wreaked havoc in this office."

It was all too complicated. Worse than the gossip at the depot. He
sighed.

"I've got this letter, Tatyana Borisovna. It came this morning and
I don't know what to do."

"Don't talk to me about letters!"

"It's this widow, Valentina Dmitryevna Afanasyeva, and she lives
in Rostov and she wants us to set up house together. But I've met
someone else, you see, someone quite different, and she says she
wants to marry me as well."

"Masha!" Sasha was startled; for a split second Tanya had called
out exactly like the hag in the armband.

"Masha, Mashenka, it's your job, tell me what to do."

Presenting a half-profile towards them from the top of the next
flight of stairs stood a woman so grossly overweight that for one
moment Sasha thought she must be jammed in the door frame. Her
almost flat face was perfectly circular but intersected by a line of
fringed hair which fell straight to her eyebrows, covering her forehead
and continuing at the same length all round her head. Looking at her
face side-on Sasha had the impression of one of those wafer-thin
watches he had seen in western magazines. In the up-draught, a
shapeless cotton frock billowed round her figure and she had not yet
taken off a pair of green galoshes.

"Dearest, darling Masha," said Tanya in a voice flooding with
relief. "This man's come for the wastepaper. Poor Grigorii's feeling
off-colour today."

Bewildered, Sasha stopped three steps down while the monstrous
Masha examined him.

"Getting more scruffy these days, aren't they?" she said in a
disconcertingly piping tone.

"Give him the dead letters. I'm absolutely exhausted." Tanya
disappeared leaving Sasha alone, his pleas for advice cut short, all his
efforts of the last few weeks rendered futile. He was further affronted
by the presumption of this awful woman who was dumping a plastic
sack at his feet – a sack almost as huge as herself.

She gave him a sweet, sinister smile. "Watch out, darling, don't
trip over your bootlaces and break your neck."

He clumped down three floors to the mezzanine with the bag and
then back down the little staircase to the furnace, past the radiant

Amazons on the walls, musing on the sexy Marya Fyodorovna. He stopped and delved into the sack. The letters might be fun. You never knew, girls like her might write up to the paper, like her they might be – he searched for the word – explicit; that was it, that was what he fancied about her, her explicitness; she didn't care. If they were good he could always read them to Len over a drink somewhere, augmenting the respect which Len now showed him when he turned up at the depot with a hundred Marlboro and a bottle of Gold Ring. He stuffed several handfuls into his jacket pockets.

Down in the basement he found the porter and two bottles of beer, which they drank watching the flames flicking over the spilled ink of a hundred different miseries. On impulse he threw the letter from the Rostov widow into the boiler. It flared up and burnt very quickly.

"I could tell you a few things," said the porter. "Life? Me? I've seen it all."

"You ought to edit the problem page, mate."

Outside the day was already subsiding into grey twilight though it was barely afternoon.

"You need to watch your step," said the porter gnomically. "Unless you know your way around. And even if you do, you can come to grief."

6

Rolling a cigarette that night in his room under the dim, unshaded bulb he remembered the old *barinya* in Tanya's kitchen cobbling shag and paper together with her stiff, arthritic hand. For a long time he had been trying to get the knack but the tobacco disintegrated and his blankets and mattress were dotted with shreds of leaf and fine dust.

The room, he had to admit, was a hole. That had first really dawned on him last week when the girl had put down her bag and stared around; nobody could make excuses for it – that's what that aghast look had signified. He knew people who lived rougher but he had made the mistake of saying so.

"How do you know what I expected?" Bobby had replied, eventually, picking at the newspapers over the window. "You don't have to defend yourself to me."

But she soon changed her tune. It wasn't just the windows or the mattress on the floor but the gap at the top of the ceiling between his room and next door: she could hear rustling from Lizaveta's room. He was so used to overhearing the old woman's solitary intimacies, her groans in the night, her disjointed conversations with the wireless and people who weren't there that he had forgotten all about her. Until, that is, Bobby found the proximity shocking; so shocking, she said, that sex was out of the question.

"I'd have thought you had more sense of decency," she whispered, pointing to the partition. "With her an old lady and all."

It was her first real visit to his room, the first without Olga or Boris or Tanya or any other member of "the gang" as she affectionately called it. They hadn't ever had much time alone and what they did have they seemed to spend in shopping.

She'd bought him a lot of clothes. The white shirt with red piping down the front lay in a heap on the floor; then there was the tweed jacket, the new woollen pullover in dark green, and the fur gloves. His new image.

Still, he'd given a lot away. They all thought he was running a fiddle or had knocked the stuff off: no one at the depot believed his story about the American girl. So he'd promised something more incontrovertibly exclusive to the USA (and a woman) than the unisex knick-knacks he'd been handing round. They suggested the obvious thing, but knowing him as they did, his mates gave that up as impractical for Sasha. What about a dainty something or other? A handkerchief – no problem there, surely? – something with a tag: "Made in the USA". Now he'd gone and given it to Tanya.

One floor down, at street-level, he could hear the noise of lorries churning up the banks of lying snow. A heavy flurry had settled that afternoon and already they were shifting it out of town. Lizaveta had predicted a miserable winter: muggy, not many frosts and no real snowfall. She was generally wrong about the weather.

Bobby had wanted a real winter: drifts, a room with a stove, and an ikon in the corner. She had already bought a mink hat for three hundred and twenty-five roubles. Next thing, she'd have him in a beard and *valyenki*. Americans mystified him with their energy and their queer priorities. One of his shutters (damaged years ago) hung loose from its hinges and he'd never got round to nailing it up. A few days before she had nagged him into looking for a hammer and had stripped further bits of newspaper off the window. If Bobby had been Olga, Olga would have . . . But what was the use of that? She'd have to have loved him and love came out in any number of ways. Bobby's way had its good side, and, anyway, Olga didn't love anyone now the Englishman had gone; except Boris, poor devil, who loved Galya who pretended to love him back.

The Miss Weston business had gone askew somehow; even the conversations were littered with mysterious hints which left him in the dark. What was he doing wrong? She seemed so keen at first.

"There are things you don't recognise in yourself, Sasha. Good things. Potentialities."

Potentialities, he gathered, fairly quickly, were what a woman expected you to realise. His shoulders, his cheekbones, his hands, his lips, they were OK but she stopped at his teeth and had given him an electric toothbrush with instructions to use it three times a day. And he had, to do himself credit, he had, every day, religiously.

In spite of the concern for oral hygiene, sex had still been out of the question.

"Lizaveta will drop off soon," he had said, but it was no good.

Then there was marriage. Not that *it* was out of the question. The very opposite, in fact, according to Bobby who had lifted her pink cheeks and limpid eyes to him on the train to Zagorsk and had actually asked him, right out loud, in impeccable Russian if he would like to marry her and go to America. He had tried to avoid the faces of the family sitting opposite who were listening breathlessly to every word.

Everything that day was daft. He must have been mad to start with, agreeing to spend his day off visiting tombs, with Bobby in her new hat lining up, waiting in turn to kiss the slab over what was left of St Sergius buried deep down there. He avoided that bit because anything to do with priests made him queasy, and anyway he kept visualising bones browned by the earth. The white walls and the pigeons and beehive shaped like a bear in the museum had pleased him more. He liked earthy things to be outside, exposed to the light.

"You can go to America. But we have to be married." They could always separate afterwards, she explained. Her grandfather could find a garage job for him in Rhode Island. He didn't want to go to America, but she couldn't understand why; he certainly didn't want a job in a garage – there were plenty of those at home.

By the time they reached Yaroslavl station that night he was enraged by her crude lack of percipience.

"There's no need to look so fed up. I'm so fond of you as you are, Sasha."

How fond was that? Len said women always set out to change you once you showed them an opening, but Sasha might willingly have undergone some less drastic self-transformation had there been something nearer home to get out of it. Not an exit visa, not ending up as a pump attendant in a garage somewhere in America unable to say "Good morning" in any language other than Russian. No, sooner rather than later, he wanted the girl to *let* him, properly, lying down, without all the sight-seeing and feverish conversations about life, all the *talking* which had so far got in the way of doing it. What was the point of ending up in Rhode Island beating about the same bush? Sex with Bobby was as hard and protracted and as faintly envisageable as Communism: always preceded by some lengthy and disagreeable stage where you were to earn your bright promise of tomorrow. Every day something new got in the way: a new present, a new idea, a new outing. Even the proposal put him off and in the end he couldn't kiss the reliquary any more than he was permitted to kiss Bobby with liquor on his breath.

Olga had been included in the largesse. She had new saucepans, a potato peeler, an apron and a blue and white porcelain teapot as well as lots of books. Sometimes Bobby could scarcely get up the stairs on account of the parcels and he would go down to the entrance to help her. Tonight it had been clothes for Borya's two sons, toy lorries, new exercise books, writing paper and a boxful of vegetables and fruits in glass jars. With all this munificent activity going on Bobby was impregnable.

Tonight she was eating upstairs with Boris, Galya, their neighbours the Lopakhins, Olga, the *dvornik*, and his wife Vera. One of those typical Russian meals Bobby raved about. He was not invited. The night before last he was helping Boris upstairs and Galya had put her head round the door and hissed:

"Don't you ever come up here again, you . . . you degenerate!"

No *shchi* or *pelmeni* for him and no Bobby either.

Lizaveta was excluded too, but that was from indifference – not animus. Poor old Lizaveta. She had started to collect up the fancy matchboxes, putting them in her memento tin where she kept the letters from her dead son and a photograph of her daughter's baby. Next door she was weeping because she had smashed her coffee-pot. Every evening after supper she dozed off and woke up in a panic in case something important had happened while she was asleep; it took her at least twenty minutes to calm down after a doze, and tonight it would be longer because in some tremor induced by nightmare she had knocked over the bedside table in her sleep and sent the pot flying.

Sasha looked up at the gap in the partition beneath the old stucco of the ceiling cove. Lizaveta was still whimpering and muttering and shuffling round, her skirts swishing against the furniture which packed the room. Soon she would start pushing things about, tapping glass vases, rubbing chair legs and lamps. A few of the things he had found for her, some had been Gran's which he didn't want to keep. Lizaveta had tried to do them up, sometimes rubbing them so hard that she cracked the glass or brought off the varnish.

A junkyard. Bobby had stood here, clasping and unclasping her hands, innocent and vulnerable as a naughty child, her previous assertions, opinions and persistent naïve questions about his daily life silenced by the brute austerity of his surroundings. Tonight she was in for a touch of luxury: Galina had washed the boys' hair, Boris said, scrubbed everybody else's floors as well as her own and had taken the day off to make those little pastry envelopes filled with meat and herbs that Gran used to make as a treat.

Last week Bobby had stood at the window and put her bag on the floor because there was no chair. She'd bought him some cushions since then but she hadn't wanted to stay in the room again.

His stomach rumbled and he remembered he'd eaten nothing all day. The letters from Fat Masha's sack were still in his jacket. He rolled over and hooked it on to his mattress. Maybe they contained some tips on seducing Americans. On second thoughts, he doubted it: not many people were likely to have his kind of problem. Fairly unique, probably, in spite of her saying he'd be a wow in Rhode Island.

The letters were without envelopes and many of the sheets were mixed up; most of the various handwritings were hard to decipher. The contents, as far as he could see, were illiterate and almost uniformly depressing: several described problems he didn't know existed and there were a lot from women complaining about men.

Sasha wondered if he were like any of these husbands. There were men who came to bed not only drunk but incapable, single men who couldn't manage to look after themselves, some who scarcely knew how babies were made. One woman from Kazan thought the drinking habits of men were responsible for the low birth-rate. That was an educated letter written from an institute of education, but it had gone into Masha's sack just the same. Never having read the magazine he wondered what they did publish, remembering what Tanya had said about the editor trying to destroy her by forcing her to select more sexually adventurous mail.

Well, Kirilyenko hadn't seen these and it was probably a good thing.

He found a letter which made him gasp. From a man and a policeman, too! Still, they had problems like other people, but what a problem this was, especially when he would have known what article in the Criminal Code it fell under. Funny, you always thought it would be a laugh to read things like that but when you did it was perplexing and sickening. Tanya was right.

Tanya? Tanya?

Interspersed with the letters was a number of long sheets of paper covered in large, educated handwriting. These were the sheets Tanya had dropped in the corridor and forgotten. They took the form of a report, but with something resembling an appeal about them, too – like the draft of a petition – addressed to the Director of *Feministka*, requesting Kirilyenko's dismissal and listing numerous accusations about his behaviour and that of Marya Fyodorovna who, Tanya asserted, was some kind of nark. What a carry on! All this mixed in with a lot of palaver about honour and Tanya's sense of dignity and then personal stuff about her old mother and her sick husband. What was her game?

Turning the pages he found a blank page where, evidently, Tanya's supporters on the magazine would be invited to sign their names.

He dwelt on the memory of Tanya in the kitchen with her mother and all that weird talk of social origins, those proclamations of what they once were, that pride in their bloodline. Was that what was showing through? A year or two before, Sasha had once found an old photograph someone had chucked out, stupidly, without realising dustmen often went through things. It had been taken one sunny day in the country and a lot of people in old-fashioned clothes were lounging about, and in the foreground was a man with heavy eyes, snapped as he put down his tennis racquet and reached for a cigarette. The Tsar had been a chain-smoker, they said. And a half-wit, as far as Sasha could tell, losing all that. Didn't he know what was what, know what *really* was going on? Didn't Tanya know when to shut up, know who she was up against? Surely she hadn't typed out her "protest" and sent it to the Director, Tomskii? Or would she have got as far as sending it only after she'd gone round the office, shown it to the staff and got them to sign it, too?

Unbelievable. Thank God he hadn't been born with a streak of refinement. He brought out a fragment of mirror from under his bolster and studied his face for the absence of noble traits: the blue eyes, very clear with a slight cast in one; his nose. It was a pity about his nose. It was flat and bore the mark of a blow from a *politruk* officer in Chelyabinsk who had kicked him when he lay mutely drunk on the floor of the gymnasium after pasting a cut-out of Goering's medal ribbons on the chest of the O/C Home Forces.

Having them all agog in the USA was not on with a mug like his, but, now, the Rostov belle, with her furniture, her optimism and her elaborately capitalised Romance and Love, she might not go so much for faces. Not that she didn't believe in utensils as much as Bobby: she had a fourteen piece tea-service, a set of handpainted wooden spoons, a picnic set complete with cutlery and folding chairs, and curtains and a big collection of dolls in national costumes. Just before he died her husband had made a case for the dolls and her cousin in Novgorod (who was still among the living) had painted the spoons by hand. Valentina turned machine tools and had won prizes for their quality but this, she assured Sasha, meant very little to her compared to those magic words towering above the lines of her fat letters – making them, as far as Sasha was concerned, almost unanswerable. Young couples had all the luck and wasn't Love just as important to the middle-aged?

Thirty letters he had altogether not counting the ones from the widow. What fools people were writing so ingenuously about problems you'd be better off burying. What risks they took! What a gift for someone! He saw why Kirilyenko was so anxious to get his hands on the problem department.

Better to leave off this correspondence business: not replying to the widow's last letter ought to have put her off. Bobby maybe was the better bet. He had written nothing gruesomely revealing to the widow; his letters had been careful, mostly about the flat and his work. Besides there would have been no point in misleading her and he had even listed a few of his minor shortcomings. Nothing peculiar, though.

Yes, Bobby might come round in the end; they might get down to things eventually. Love. His experience was so limited: he'd once or twice had a woman in the Army, not a young one and he'd paid her in vodka. Bobby could teach him all about the things he'd missed or didn't know; teach him *how* with all the subtleties he had never had time or opportunity to comprehend.

What would she be doing now? Listening to Olga or Galya or perhaps to Vera Grigoryevna, the *dvornik*'s wife, who could tell the dirtiest stories he had ever heard. Tonight, though, she was probably behaving.

Something grated along the passage wall and he tensed. Lizaveta had gone silent, too. Grabbing as many of the papers as he could hold he stuffed them under his bolster.

A car slithered down the street and stopped at the Embassy. The driver was arguing with the policeman.

Someone thumped at his door and he called out for them to wait, hastily wriggling into his shoes.

In the wilds of Byelorussia, he had learned from Tanya's male correspondent, you could do gypsies and factory tarts. But if you didn't fancy them or couldn't find them you did it with other police-men or high-school boys. He must burn that letter, once the visitor had gone.

7

"Only me, I'm afraid," grinned Boris, his arms full of parcels. "You thought it was *her*, didn't you?"

Carefully setting the parcels down on the floor at the foot of Sasha's mattress, he wrenched off his jacket and narrow, navy-blue tie and threw both on to the heap.

"Oof, what an evening! The wife and sister and other assorted females present assumed I was qualified to dissect their problems, being the only man there – apart, of course, from Lopakhin and the chap downstairs who don't count as male in that intellectual sewing-circle because they haven't got degrees." He looked round and retrieved a bottle from his discarded jacket. "Isn't it about time you bought something to drink out of besides mugs? Anyway," he went on, pouring out the liquor, "I declined, believe it or not. The worm turned. I said I wasn't competent to arbitrate on their psychic dramas any more and I walked out, just like that." He squatted down beside Sasha. "I'm learning, am I learning." Without the homburg he seemed abnormally exposed, his pink scalp glistening amidst the sparse hair.

Boris was right. He had expected Bobby, although he knew Galya's dinner party was bound to run on after ten o'clock and it was only twenty past nine now.

Boris was a bit worse for wear so there must have been plenty of wine upstairs. As was usual with him in this state, he tailed off into monologue. Sasha could picture him as an adolescent, terrified of girls, and practising devastatingly attractive looks which he never got beyond testing on himself in the mirror.

Nudging up to Sasha, Boris pointed at the parcels.

"Yours. She's bought you a Vietnamese silk bedspread and I don't know what else. I got this bottle."

"Why did you accept it?" asked Sasha. "You know you can't stand her."

"Because she wanted me to so much. She's amazing, that American girl of yours, anyone so infatuated with a foreign country deserves to be phenomenally indulged."

What did he have against her? Sasha had never known him become so rancorous about anyone. Galya, the neighbours, even Olga had all at one time or other been the objects of Boris's despairing ill-will – as if a sudden consciousness of his illness made him despise his previous, characteristically easy-going nature. That was understandable, but Bobby had become an obsession. Perhaps it was the condescension implicit in her generosity; or her infuriating habit of cross-questioning: how did they live, where did they go on holiday, what did your father do, how much do you earn?

"She's never happy without someone to patronise," Boris used to complain at the beginning, before he and Sasha had come to a pact about arguing over her. "Everyone she meets is so *nice*, and we're not all nice."

He knew what Boris meant: that someone like Bobby didn't spend money and time on someone like Sasha, just because he was nice. Sasha knew that, knew enough about women (or thought he did) to know that she wanted him, in some highly specific situation yet to be contrived, to be not nice to her at all but to feel very nice herself precisely because he wasn't.

He scrutinised the sick man. The collar of his shirt which Galya must have ironed that morning, flopped open to show the neck, longer, thinner and fretted with blue veins; the hands holding the mug had shrunk and they trembled perceptibly. He was losing his grip on everything.

Sasha turned and reached for a cigarette. Boris couldn't be blamed.

"She's so frightfully dull," Boris was saying, having forgotten their English-style agreement not to criticise a lady. "Tonight she almost ruined Galya's dinner party by going on and on about sociology and surveys and statistics."

"Well," said Sasha refusing to humour him any longer – after all, she was his girl in a kind of way – "she's clever, you know. She's got letters after her name, too." Olga and Boris had strings of letters after their names, and a few before come to that, because once he had overheard Olga excitedly telling someone over the telephone that she was now Dr Melentyeva.

Boris threw up his hands. "She's clever, all right: good at insinuating herself, making herself indispensable. Look at the way she gets you to dance round after her." He coughed and took another drink.

"That's rich, coming from you. What do you do, then, with Galya?"

At least I've got prospects of something which is more than you have, he might have added but did not because he was sorry for the other man.

Boris shrugged off the remark. He still wanted to talk about Miss Weston.

"Look, her problem is, she's never had to go out to work. Oh, I know she does a bit of language teaching, but tonight she announces that what she really wants to do is to write. Even to make some sort of living out of it as . . ." he wrinkled up his nose, "'a creative artist'."

That, as far as Boris was concerned, was the clincher.

"What's the matter with that, then?" asked Sasha, genuinely puzzled.

"What's the matter with it, I'll tell you what's the matter with it," Boris burst out, hammering the mug into his palm. "It means that all she wants to do is to mess about, mess about with writing, mess about with people, not do anything serious, do nothing properly, tell lies, get herself taken for something she's not, be *in-sin-cere*."

Something about her had already disturbed him profoundly. The idea that she might lay claim to being an artist as well struck him as sacrilegious.

This was all Greek to Sasha. One of the letters slipped to the floor as he shifted on the mattress. Picking it up he saw it was Valentina Dmitryevna's fattest and longest. He ran his eyes over the great, round hand.

Boris had begun to whine.

"I come down and I find you're by yourself and you're not at all pleased to see me. I suppose that if it came to a choice between drinking with me and not drinking with that girl, you'd choose the girl because it's gone too far now."

"Yes," said Sasha. "Yes, women do get in the way, but it looks like I've got two of them to cope with now. Here's the competition."

And he waved the fat letter containing the widow's inventory of her goods and chattels.

"You don't mean you've got one woman chasing you while you're running after another?" His face brightened. "That's more like it! Don't let one think she's all you've got, that way she'll end up despising you for depending on her. Keep them guessing."

Boris secretly admired the kind of man who, he thought, conducted his affairs according to the saw: "Love them and leave them", but had no notion of its inadequacy in real terms. Another was: "Keep them guessing", but neither principle had ever served him. He could never have left a woman in his life except when she told him to go, and his nature was so transparently deducible in the sexual context that he could never have fooled anyone, let alone a woman.

"Absolutely," said Sasha. "Absolutely." There was no point in explaining, when Boris was always getting hold of the wrong end of the stick. It didn't take him long to become fuddled these days.

The new bedspread from Bobby was thick. Miniature figures, houses and trees were embroidered in heavy relief around the border and the centre panel was formed by the intertwining silhouettes of two black cranes or herons. It felt stiff and smelt very clean. He pulled it over his knees.

"Borya, why don't you give this to Galya? It's not my sort of thing – no more than any of the rest of it is," he said pointing to the little porcelain lamp, the velvet cushions and the Cossack shirt which he wouldn't be seen dead in. With a pang he remembered burning the widow's last letter.

The older man smiled serenely. "Trouble with you is, you don't know what you want. As for Galya, she'll get nothing from me, as long as I draw breath. I've done with giving."

He talked like that more and more often now. They could hear Lizaveta shifting her old body, jangling the springs of her bed. Noise meant that she had fallen asleep, its absence that she was lying awake in the dark, rigid, hoping for a revelation.

Sasha leant forward. "Listen, Borya . . . Bobby has asked me to marry her."

Boris was dumbfounded. Sasha had to repeat the remark before he could take it in. Had Boris had time to compose himself he would have laughed out loud in contempt and disbelief but caught unprepared, his face sagged.

"So, Aleksandr Mikhailovich, we part company. Why do you have to tell me things like that? I don't want to know."

"I'm sick of being on my own, Borya, that's all there is to it."

"Know what she said to me an hour ago?" said Boris, sitting upright on the bed, his hands on his knees like an antique idol's, his voice echoing in the almost empty room. "She said, and I can remember every word: 'I am so weary of battling with the centuries of cold, of the grime and the apathy.' For her, we're not just a different species within a related *group*, we're a separate genus. We're not even the little man who looks back at you through the gorilla's eyes, the wizened inhabitant of the skull you can't get in at and un-imprison. No, she doesn't even offer us the consolations of empathy. We're what they longed to fetch back with a space-shot and handle with robot arms in a sterile bubble, we're alien structures, polyps in a bottle. This is the great life zoo, homogenised for her protection. Don't you see? She just doesn't get it."

"I don't care," muttered Sasha, doggedly. "Who cares about us anyway?"

"*We* do, you fool!"

Footsteps sounded outside Sasha's door, and they heard Olga's laugh. Boris quailed.

"Oh God, once my sister gets a couple of drinks inside her . . ."

Olga was wearing a green party frock with a low waist and a line of antique quartz buttons down the front. She was very flushed and her hair had lost its lacquered orderliness. Beside her stood Roberta as cool as ever in a wild silk two-piece, boldly striped in red and black. Her violet eyes glittered.

"Gracious, it's hot in here," cried Olga. Lizaveta, disturbed by the novel register of the voices, muttered and turned over. Olga and Bobby were too far gone to notice.

"I'm just bowled over at the hospitality," the American was saying.

"But a bit of a grisly encounter, for all that," added Olga, then realised that she was in the presence of the hostess's husband. "Your wife's a smashing cook, Borya darling. Why doesn't she like me?"

Whenever Olga and Galya got together for more than half an hour, neither managed to hit it off with the other.

"Nonsense, Olga. She adores you." With calculatedly superfluous politeness Boris got to his feet and held out his hand. Bobby responded coyly.

"Boris Sergeyevich, I guess I'll never really get to know you any better."

"My dear young lady, on the contrary, you have already divined all it is you need to know."

Sasha intervened. "Well, one thing's certain, Borya, your wife can't stand *me*." He tried to laugh.

Nobody contradicted and Bobby looked squarely at him for the first time. He reddened painfully. She had this trick of catching him out, making him feel foolish for something he was unaware of having done. Watching Bobby, Boris pulled a conspiratorial, pleading face at his sister.

"Olichka, can I put my feet up in your room for a bit?"

She knew he wanted somewhere to sleep it off and she nodded, fingering her hair and fastening a stray piece with a pin.

Sasha was alarmed. Now that Bobby stood in front of him he sensed obscurely that she had readied herself for a confrontation; that something was going on within her which was bound to make him suffer; and that she was determined to enjoy it.

"Don't go yet," he stammered. "It's still early, we can make a night of it." Who had said that?

Nobody listened.

She had paced the room several times from window to door, not speaking a word, before Sasha pleaded:

"Why don't you relax? Sit down, lie down, just stop doing that, you're making me nervous. I can't see your face."

The words were ineffectual and he went up to her and took her hands. She pulled away, arching her back and dropped her handbag.

"Look, Sasha, let's face it. I'm an understanding person and so are you."

Wiping his damp palms on his trousers he tried to touch her again, but she evaded him and moved over to the window. The bare patches, denuded of *Trud*, shone blackly. Before him Bobby's bespectacled face – the eyes widened by liner and mascara, the cheeks deep pink, the pearled lips – had a doll-like sensuality.

"I do like you, Sasha. I always wanted to get to know you more."

Her voice echoed the formality of her earlier remark to Boris and Sasha felt thrown. Something's really up this time, he thought slowly, grinding his teeth, and I am going to be dropped from a great height.

Her half-smiling, half-tearful expression was impenetrable, or perhaps she had too much light on her face.

"I'm not used to women like you," he muttered feebly. That was a laugh. "I mean, you talk about marriage, one week, before we ever had a chance to, you know, get to know each other, then you disappear for most of the following week. Now you're here and there's all this."

She moved a step closer and raised her thin eyebrows. "Don't think you have any claim to me. You seem to think you own me, but I'm free, always have been."

Own her? Freedom? This was incomprehensible, awful, women's twisted-up talk. A shot in the dark, then:

"So you've changed your mind about getting married?"

"Not just that," she said. "I don't know if I should see you again or not."

"Is *that* all? Well, you can just go to hell."

Sasha went over to his mattress and sat down. Better to live alone than have this sort of rigmarole. This must be her line with men – getting them jumpy.

She started to cry, came across the room and knelt down beside him. "There's no need to make a scene," she whispered provokingly. "You see, I've just realised that I don't own you either, and I've no right to ostracise you just because you've told me lies and you have relations with dozens of other women."

Have or *had*? Neither was anywhere near the truth but in the past tense it didn't sound so bad. In any case, what could it have had to do with her, *then?* If she meant *now*, where did she think he did it? On the lorry? But she was talking in a great rush, cutting him out.

He glowered.

"Of course, your promiscuity doesn't diminish you as a human being, Sasha, I'm not saying that." Christ, this was lunacy.

"But I must tell you how I feel, how it alters things. Not the fact that you *have* women, but the fact that you lied. I may not be able to see you any more, anyway. I mean, it's a great betrayal of trust. I can't take it, you see, being lied to, but I thought I owed you an explanation."

She fiddled the whole time with the letters which had spilled out on to the bed.

Snow was drifting up on one side of the window-sill. Lizaveta had had an earful tonight.

8

It dawned on him what had happened.

"Galina Semyonovna, that bitch! What's she said about me?"

"Ssssshhhh!" She was caressing. Now that the point had gone home, the better part of the pleasure was over. "All right, all right." She stroked his arm in supplication, anxious to maintain her control over the scene but curious to see how he would respond.

"And you believed her! That lying, dirty-minded old trollop, that grasping, snivelling, vicious old cat! She's obsessed with filth, with dirt – if she can't see it, she'll dig it up and if she can't find it, she'll invent it. That old man'd die to get shot of her. She's a killer that one, with her fawning and wheedling. She'd turn you in, she'd do for you! My God, if Boris had any balls he'd have fixed her years ago, brained the bitch. Can't you see that, can't you? Or is it you just don't understand the first thing about any of us, you're so wrapped up in yourself?"

She shifted, the black and red stripes of her suit realigning neatly as she picked up her bag and walked slowly to the door.

"If that's the attitude you're going to take I guess I ought to go, Sasha. It's getting late and I've a lot on tomorrow."

Still furious, he took hold of himself.

"Look, you mustn't credit Galina with anything, except lies. Honestly. Ask Olga Sergeyevna."

Jumping to his feet, he got to the door in front of her. "Think you'll ever come back?" It was more a threat than a query and she hesitated, still curious but a little afraid.

"All right, all right," he said. "You don't have to do anything you don't want to, but you can give me an explanation just for once. You owe it to me. Come on, tell me, I won't shout, I promise."

He wished he had a clean handkerchief to wipe her eyes free of tears, like the man he once saw in a film who always got to make love to girls after he'd stopped them crying.

"Galina mentioned letters," began Bobby quietly. "She said you wrote to women you didn't know and got them into bed with you. I didn't want to believe her, Sasha, but I'd never run into anyone like

her before, anyone so determined and persuasive. I didn't exactly
expect you to be a gentleman, living in a place like this, but . . ." She
looked round at the mantelpiece, and the debris of clothes and papers
lying on the floor. "Last week, Olga said . . ." She broke off. Sasha
shook her, but gently.

"Olga? What about Olga? What did Olga say?"

"Well, she said . . . Oh, this is embarrassing, awkward . . . well,
she said that you'd *advertised* for a woman. Is that right? And I
thought what a fool I'd made of myself all this time, and then there
was that business on the Zagorsk trip . . ." She was breathing heavily
now and Sasha pulled her close instinctively, and put his arms around
her shoulders, hugging her awkwardly, so that her chin dug into his
collarbone. Galina, Galina, he said to himself, widow's weeds are
going to suit you, they'll blend with that greasy black roll-mop hair
and your hairy upper lip, they'll match, they'll set you up. People
always made excuses for Galina but bags like her had always suited
themselves and got away with it.

"You mustn't blame Boris Sergeyevich, Sasha. He tried to change
the subject."

Her lips trembled and he could feel her rib-cage press up to his.
With a shock, he realised that her nipples were shamelessly erect.

Relaxing his grip, he took her by the shoulders and looked into
her eyes.

"You don't like me, really, don't like me at all, do you, Sasha?"
she said crossly. "I mean, I thought we'd have got somewhere by now
but you can't even bear to kiss me."

"It's this place," he said untruthfully, playing for time. How could
he believe anything she said? There was something queer about
needing to get sexed-up by lies. "Anyway, how was I to know you
cared for me? Really gave a damn. You've got a bloody strange way
of showing it. Why only now? I'm not a fortune-teller. Yes, yes, I did
write a letter, I did get myself a pen-pal. Lots of people do – here,
look at these, I'll show you."

Relieved at the idea of a diversion, he picked up a heap of the
letters and thrust them at her.

"Here, have a good look, read what you want. This is the kind of
thing Tanya gets every day, they're sent to her magazine. She . . ."
He paused, thinking up a pretext. "She let me look at these old ones
to get a few hints about how to go about it."

That didn't sound quite right. He swallowed.

"I'm not very well educated – you know that and I needed help
with the writing. If you think it's shocking because I wrote to a
woman – she's only a widow – well, this is a lonely room, and this

is a big, lonely town. How many people do you think write to *me*?"

He needn't have worried. Bobby was racing through the letters eagerly. He had never seen her so passionately absorbed, and he was thankful that he had palmed the policeman's letter before giving her the rest. Too late, he remembered about the others describing sexual quirks of one kind and another, and tried to grab them out of her hands.

"That's enough! And for God's sake don't tell Tanya I showed you. She'd be raving!"

Bobby frowned. "You're a strange man. So tough and down-to-earth but kind of sweet and silly, too."

If only she weren't so patronisingly wide of the mark, he reflected. But if he were ever going to have her (and by now he had decided that come what may he was) he would have to tread any line she drew.

"You don't think I'm a womaniser, then? I only wrote a couple and I burnt the replies this morning."

"Why did you do that?" she whispered impressed, coming nearer.

"Because of you," he replied. That cost an effort. Any other time it would have caused him to grit his teeth, but the rules were hers and he was learning to play the game.

This time he kissed her lengthily.

"I must go," she said at last, and began to gather up her things.

He wasn't going to let it go at that.

"Why don't you stay here? Nobody will know. Just tonight."

"We've all our lives in front of us for that," she said. Oh no, you don't, fairy-tale girl, he said to himself, you're not tucking that sweet little prelude into your handbag and making off into the night, you owe me.

"Never mind the rest of our lives," he said. "It's now I'm interested in."

"Men always say that." *I bet they do.* "I just don't know what to do, Sasha. I'm in a terrible muddle." *I bet you are.* "It's living here, meeting you and all the others, trying to keep my sense of proportion, my values, and not get side-tracked." *That sounded well rehearsed.*

"Truly, Sasha, I've had a rotten evening. I could have done without Galina and all the stories and now I'm upset and tired and confused. If only I could believe you're not making a fool of me." *It was going to be a long job.*

Lighting up a cigarette, Sasha had an idea.

"If I get a witness, will you believe me then?"

Her expression wavered and she took off her glasses.

"Oh God, we shouldn't need anyone's help. Why can't things be simple and natural, like they once were?"

"Just a minute, everything'll be fine." He put the cigarette behind his ear. "Olga Sergeyevna, she'll tell you the truth. She knows me and these days she's really quite friendly."

As he went out, refusing to listen to any more from Bobby, he couldn't help feeling rather proud of his new friends. This time last year Olga had been stand-offish and Boris only came out for a drink on special occasions. Now, with this new, sophisticated life he seemed to be leading, Sasha almost felt as if he could stand aside and watch himself with admiring eyes as he knocked familiarly at Olga's door, late at night but sure of a reasonable reception.

Olga looked grimmer and older than she had after the dinner, but she nodded him in to her main room. She had been sitting in a hard armchair working at a gros-point frame, still in her best green frock – although the euphoria of the party had evidently worn off. Stretched on her divan was Boris, fast asleep, and a small lamp glowed under a pink shade near her embroidery.

She put a finger to her lips. "Don't wake him up."

Sometimes, when Boris breathed in he would start to cough, and each time Olga involuntarily stiffened.

"He used to be such a fine man."

Sasha was impatient. "Do me a favour, will you, Olga?" he whispered. "It's no good crying over him, you know. It won't make him any better."

She shushed him again and took him out into the lobby where they could talk more easily. "Of course, people like you who don't love anyone in the whole world except themselves, just can't imagine how one feels." Then she went back inside the main room, picked up a big black and orange flowered shawl and laid it over her brother's legs.

"I've got a lot of time for him too, you know," he said when she returned tiptoeing across the parquet.

"I know, I know, I was a bit hard on you. So, what's the matter? Has Bobby been gone long?"

She gave an ironical little smile, knowing full well that the American girl would still be in Sasha's room. He blushed.

"You're a hard woman, Olga Sergeyevna. I've got things on my mind. I think I'm in love."

She absent-mindedly took a jar of white beans from a shelf and started to polish it with the sleeve of her frock. She was still smiling.

"In love, are you? My God, that's a laugh, if you'll pardon my saying so. Mind you, when Lizaveta said you weren't going round the beer-shops quite so much . . . But if it's that foreign girl, I should think she'll want more than just a reformed boozer."

"How do you know it's her?" he asked. Olga replaced the jar and came over, bit back her full lips and poked him in the ribs.

"What a situation! It's not bad, I suppose, but it's not good either."

"You do like her, don't you, Olga?"

"Of course." She seemed surprised that he should ask. "But what about you? Are you sure you're serious about her? Most people haven't an ounce of love in them."

Taken aback, he began mumbling about marriage, almost hoping that she would fail to hear, but she was listening carefully, and her face altered immediately, almost as if she were trying not to laugh.

"That serious? Well, if you're both so taken with each other, heaven help you. You must be dotty!" She shook her head gently. "It's got to be real love, Aleksandr Mikhailovich. Do you think she'll give up her country for you? I find that hard to believe."

She beamed a wide, toothy, schoolgirl grin. "*I* wouldn't marry you, not if you were the last man on earth. But you're not asking me."

For the first time he took notice of the slim waist between her rounded breasts and hips and realised, sweating a little, that he had never stood quite so close to Olga Sergeyevna and had never before smelt her characteristic smell of soap and lavender water so distinctly.

"I want your help," he said. "Galina Semyonovna's been slagging me off all the evening. You must have heard her, and Borya was hinting that something had been going on up there. Bobby's just told me and she's upset. So I said you'd back me up and tell her that none of it's true."

Olga raised her eyebrows. "What on earth do you need me for if you're both in love? Bobby doesn't believe anything that harridan says, surely?"

"You know what Galina's like." He remembered Boris, all those weeks ago, sitting in that bedroom upstairs, fingering the purple bedspread. Now he could hear the sick man's breathing: in and out, in and out, cough, rustle, cough.

"Bloody partitions," he murmured. "You can't even be ill without someone hearing you."

Olga looked through the archway at her brother. "I thought he had so much sense, too, and wouldn't squander every penny he earned, but what can you expect when someone's in that state? People make fun of him behind his back. Of her, too. He's set on this lunacy, this drinking business, this low life as she sees it, and now she's just waiting for him to die."

Sasha scratched his ear. There was no sound from his own room and he wondered what Bobby was doing. "I didn't encourage him, Olga Sergeyevna. The trouble was he didn't need encouragement." He could see the top of the line between her breasts through a gap in the row of crystalline buttons: one of the oblong quartzes was hanging by a thread. "Come on, won't you give me a hand? Galina's spilled the beans about my penfriend," he added ruefully. "You know who I mean."

Olga did know. So did everyone in the lane. The first time he found a letter waiting for him, his jubilation was so great that he had told the *dvornik*'s wife, podgy Vera Grigoryevna Baranova, who had subsequently informed anyone she met on the stairs or opened the front door to. He could see why Olga was grinning.

"What a half-wit you are, Aleksandr Mikhailovich. Bobby doesn't know you as well as I do and I'll try my best, but she'll end up thinking what she likes. A woman is sensitive over things like that."

She moved ahead of him, out into the passage.

"You," she said. "You're just a comical creature, lounging in the corners of beer-shops, dreaming. No, it's Borya I'm sorry for, and *her*, too, poor Galya. Being a widow won't improve her temper *or* her prospects."

When they came into Sasha's room it had been transformed. Bobby had tidied up, pushed the mattress over towards the mantelpiece, and tucked the new bedspread round the corners and underneath so that it bulged out slightly at the sides like a frilly valance. The old blankets were hidden away; the bare central light now filtered through a brand-new shade; and a tiny lamp, unplugged, stood on the mantelpiece. Red plush cushions were scattered round the room, like seats against the walls, and she had hung up all Sasha's clothes on nails behind the door, swept the floor and removed the last of the newspapers from the windows.

"Actually," she said, "it didn't take me very long, once I'd found a broom and somewhere to put the rubbish. I'll get you some curtains soon, Sasha, and I saw a darling little tea-set in that blue and white china, the other day."

Olga went into peals of laughter, forgetting it was the middle of the night for Lizaveta next door. "Look at that sloven," she gasped, pointing to Sasha who stood in the doorway struck dumb. "I wouldn't have missed his face for anything."

Bobby came up to him, anxiously. "You're not angry with me, are you? I suddenly wanted to give you a sense of perspective; I wanted you to see with new eyes. I mean, living like you do is a bit limited, a bit sordid, isn't it?"

The only thought which went through Sasha's mind was a query: why had this apparently meaningless operation taken place at all? There had been no warning of it when he went to see Olga, let alone during the past few weeks. Maybe, now, Miss Weston would feel it a more cleanly place to take her clothes off in. But he doubted it.

Olga stood by the window giving out on to the lane. "Just look at that snow! You'll have to walk a long way for a taxi tonight, Bobby."

Sasha scowled. For some reason she wasn't going to leave until she had separated them for the night. Perhaps it was just because the room was now so clean and tidy. Her sporadic puritanism might have revived at the sight of what she could take for heedful preparation. Last week, when Bobby might have been on the verge of submission, Olga had hammered on the door asking the girl to come to her room for a cup of tea. What a performance! Why should she want to protect an American woman's morals? Was it old maids' freemasonry?

They had started to talk about cleaning and how Olga scrubbed the passage with a bar of soap every three weeks. This could go on for ages.

"Olga Sergeyevna, what about, you know, what you promised? Bobby, Olga's on my side, she knows the truth about that old bat upstairs."

Olga retreated. "Do I? That's a grand way of putting it, Aleksandr Mikhailovich. Galina is my sister-in-law, and a good woman in many respects . . ."

Sasha threw up his arms in frustration.

". . . and a bare-faced liar, too," concluded Olga cheerfully. "I'm sorry to say it, but she is, my dear Bobby. You must never believe a word she says."

Her eyes drifted over to the little porcelain lamp Bobby had put on the mantelpiece and suddenly Sasha wanted to make a present of it to her.

Roberta was gesturing, making inchoate apologies. "You can't imagine how embarrassed I feel, how inadequate . . ."

Sasha went over and put his arm round her. Inadequacy was getting him down, particularly this trembling, American style with its stumbling excuses, deviousness and contrived sensitivity – all of which was designed, he could swear, with the sole purpose of putting him off. Surely, now that Olga had supported him he might be able to make some progress in the undressing line. One kiss had been fine but he didn't want to hang about for most of the rest of his life for

another, and he wanted to get in more than a kiss, in any case —
despite the thought of her being a bigger liar than Galya and rather
frightening, and the problem of where they could go.

"Oof!" Olga stretched. "I'm so lovely and tired I could fall asleep
here and now. I'm off. Stir yourself, Sasha, you two can't look at
each other all night. It's nearly morning and you've got a new room."

Hell and damnation, thought Sasha. This is like the Young Pioneers.

Bobby shrugged into a long dark cape which swirled round her
knees. She had left the raccoon coat at her hotel and Sasha wondered
why. He had hated the raccoon on sight because of the feel of the fur
when he put his arm round her. The cape was all right, though; it
was roomy, too. He remembered Len telling him that when you
walked girls home at night they let you do almost anything to them
because they felt safe standing up in the cold, far safer than sitting,
standing or lying in the warmest of rooms. But Len was a coarse and
callous soul and his women were raucous creatures. Len could never
have coped with Miss Weston, he decided proudly, unhooking his
old sheepskin from the nail behind the door where Bobby had hung
it.

"Perhaps I should come with you," teased Olga. A sleepless night
stretched ahead and early next morning she had to be at her translation agency. Unless Boris woke, she would spend the night on a
cushion in an armchair, listening in case he wanted something. She
and Roberta embraced with that tense familiarity of women who
were trying to rescind some subtle, playful rivalry while Sasha made
a quick survey of his refurbished room and switched off the light.

"That thing's not warm enough," he said, as they came out of the
big front door on to the pavement. He slid one arm underneath the
cape and felt her shudder. The policeman watched from his milibox
and Sasha grimaced in the direction of the Embassy. He urged the
girl to walk more briskly and they hopped smartly over lumps and
hummocks of snow until they were round the corner in a narrow
street. Sodium lamps turned the white mounds yellow and an occasional freezing gust of wind swept great clouds of powdered snow
into the air.

Bobby panted along, her exhalations hanging fleecily on the air.
He slowed down under a nearby lamp.

"Poor little thing," he murmured. "You need a good sleep." She
looked up at him, her figure hunched inside the cape against the cold.
A blast of snow hit them, making her stagger.

"Sasha," she said through chattering teeth. "Come back to the
hotel with me."

He shook his head regretfully. He had thought all along that she had intended him to do just that; but she had strung it out for as long as possible. She had given him to understand that he was only to accompany her as far as the taxi-rank; now she wanted to overwhelm him by an apparent change of mind. Right, he decided, she was going to work for this one.

"Why not?" she sounded surprised.

Why not indeed, he thought.

"At home," she muttered, inconsequentially but with a touch of pathos, "it'll be Christmas now."

He stalled. "We could go back to my place."

Bobby shook her head violently. "What, with that old woman behind the wall, Olga and Boris and God knows who else?"

Snow mottled her shoulders and head and her flowery Russian scarf. She looked so appealing, he could have taken pity on her there and then, as he would have done even last week, before he had begun to realise the games she played. Not foreign but female, was how slobs like Len viewed it, but, reluctantly, Sasha was beginning to admit to himself that Len and his kind, more experienced and considerably filthier in language and thought than Sasha, were all probably right. And it was her fault. Anxiously he stared at her through the snow, his resolution crumbling. Didn't she understand everything she was doing? Wouldn't she ever stop manufacturing difficulties for him, ever stop counting on the difficulties so that she could eventually bring herself to some mysterious, satisfactory conclusion?

Well, this time, somehow, he was going to try to be in charge.

"I'm freezing to death," she said. "What shall we do?"

He blinked away snow. A hundred yards away he could see headlights on the main road.

"All right, I'll give it a try. Your hotel, I mean." It was giving way too soon perhaps, but she was a clean girl who opened her mouth when she kissed you. Yes, he would try the hotel and be damned to the consequences. Something was always better than nothing.

9

A nocturnal blizzard had come on, and the lights of the hotel glimmered opaquely in the mist of snow. Inside, it was bright. Sasha was soothed by the restraint of colour: grey druggets of bleached canvas crossed the dark floor, and the cream-washed walls gleamed under obliquely-angled spots.

It was a clean place, run-down, and unmenacing. Nothing hung on the walls except some posters of Riga, a yellow aeroplane timetable, and a few faded shots of a sputnik. There was little furniture apart from ashtrays on tall stands, and four armchairs clamped to the floor.

A big man sat motionless in one of the chairs, his high boots stretched out in front of him, partly covered by his greatcoat. He looked up at them, gave an appraising glance at Roberta's elegant cape and thigh-length suede boots, then lazily shifted to Sasha. At the instant of recognition, he drew back his feet and put a hand to his belt. Sasha had already spotted the peculiar, lolling pose at the entrance. It was Legless.

"Hello, friend," he said softly. "Fancy meeting you here."

The vestibule was bare: no shady crannies, no potted palms.

These little places were chiefly for Russians on business trips, and the official nosiness was home-grown, pervasive. "We don't stop," he had told her. "We just go in and keep on going." Obediently, she had strolled through, past Legless, flourished her room card at the doorman and was now waiting for the lift. In the taxi, Sasha thought he had covered everything: "Nobody wants a row after midnight. The bloke at the lifts should be asleep by now. If you have to, flash him a few notes." He had pretended to know about such things and the girl had believed him.

No one could have anticipated Legless, or bribed him (openly, at least), or sorted him out — not with his warrant card, his walkie-talkie, his little automatic strapped to his thick waist, and the rest of his official paraphernalia. He was too big, anyway. Sasha had never seen him standing before. It was a shock: Len was big, but this one was massive.

"We're a long way from home, aren't we?" drawled the policeman. It wasn't a question.

He thought of Bobby. Bewildered at not finding Sasha beside her, she was looking back still holding her card aloft. Helplessly, Sasha grinned, in an attempt to reassure her.

"We've met before," said Legless. "I never forget a face." Bobby started to walk towards them, her cape swishing. That morning she must have taken her room-key by mistake and was now waving it at Sasha.

The huge policeman was puzzled; he had not yet grasped the connection between her and the Russian man and was pondering. You could almost hear him, in the silence, weighing up the possibilities. He might never forget a face but obviously faces took a long time to float up.

"I'm sick of running into you," he said at last. Bobby, he couldn't place.

"What's going on?" she called out sharply, in her almost accentless Russian, quite authoritatively free from fear and embarrassment. Legless eyed her carefully and turned to Sasha.

"English?"

"USA," answered Sasha very quickly.

"She paying you or what?"

There was no point in replying. "Put that down," said Legless, pointing to a little box containing some new make-up of Bobby's which Sasha had in his hand. "What's in it?"

"Nothing," said Sasha obstinately. He had no idea what was inside.

By now, Bobby was fidgeting nervously, taking off her gloves and opening and closing her bag. She avoided Sasha's eyes.

Legless walked heavily around the cardboard box. "Don't bullshit me," he said.

"Ask *her*," said Sasha, nodding at the girl.

Unhurriedly, Legless seized the shaggy collar of Sasha's sheepskin, bunched it inside his fist like collapsing a football and slammed him against the wall beside the aeroplane timetable. The doorman looked on, approvingly.

"Don't tell me what to do. I don't like it." Sasha felt himself choking as the policeman's knuckles pushed back his head.

"I might do you, I might," said Legless, ruminatively.

"What for?" Sasha tried to say out of the corner of his mouth.

"Breathing, friend. Just breathing." And he grinned. "Hanging round hotels? Harassing respectable foreigners, ladies? I could make a lot out of that."

"Not with me," panted Sasha, trying to twist his throat away from the ham-like hand. "I'm not that important. But *she* is."

Legless hesitated. "They all say that. It's not my job to judge. I just do the spadework."

"*She* won't like this. She's an American. They don't appreciate this sort of thing."

The big man let go suddenly, rummaged around in his pockets, took out a box of English matches and struck one against the wall. It left a charcoal streak behind, and he and Sasha looked at each other, aware of the significance of the minor act of vandalism.

Bobby Weston was shouting. "You bastard! I'll report you. It's disgusting."

Legless nodded. "Know something?" he said to Sasha. "You're lucky."

A tiny old woman in a man's slippers, her back misshapen from rheumatism, plodded up.

"We're ready for you now, Yuri Petrovich," she whispered. Legless nodded again, and for the first time, took notice of Bobby, saluting her:

"*Pardon, madame,*" he said derisively, mimicking foreign phrase and accent. "It's your boyfriend's lucky night. I haven't seen him. Nothing has happened at all."

"The elevator's broken," said Bobby tearfully.

"And I suppose you're on the top floor?"

"No, three, actually. But what happened down there, Sasha?" she asked as they began to climb the stairs. "Why did he hurt you?"

"I'll tell you later."

"Ought you to stay?" she said. "I mean, I don't want to get you into trouble. I've never seen anything so rotten in my life. Why didn't you hit him?"

"Me? Christ," he said, "I might have killed him."

The room was small with a window at one end and a washroom by the door. He saw a chair, a wardrobe, a fridge, a sepia-coloured elephant lying on the bed and a large notice behind the door which, in several languages, forbade the storage of perishables and smoking in bed. There was a list of every article in the room down to the wooden coathangers. An open trunk stood at the foot of the bed half-full of clothes.

Going into the washroom, Sasha threw off his coat and turned on the shower. There was no bath so he knelt down and put his head directly under the stream of water and filled the shower bowl in order to cool the sore and bruised areas on his neck. Standing up again, he examined himself in the mirror. There were no marks, he only looked tired. Legless was a professional.

"Should I report that awful man?" said Bobby with a frown, leaning against the door-jamb.

Sasha shook his head. "I don't think he works in this place officially. Probably he's just got some racket going here. He specialises in hotels. There'll be pickings — food, linen, light bulbs, lavatory paper and things guests leave behind."

He was aware of her intense scrutiny; looking away, he saw that the wash-basin was surrounded by stained tissues and marked with sticky rings from scent bottles and cream pots. Other objects seemed to occupy every ledge and horizontal plane and more tissues had been thrown into the corner by the shower.

"Len used to be in on a racket when he was in the building trade. No, our big friend will do the manager favours from time to time."

"What's your racket?" she asked, picking up a cigarette and lighting it with a tiny gold Dunhill. Sasha had never seen her smoke before, but she drew heavily on the cigarette before passing it over to him with the marks of her lipstick visible on the filter.

"I don't have one. I'm not in the right line," he muttered hoarsely. There was a short silence, broken only by the dripping shower. "Listen," he said. "It's better to keep your head down, like I do. You don't get noticed that way. That's the only rule: never get noticed."

He flicked ash on to the porcelain shower base feeling faint. His stomach was churning from nerves and hunger. "I've been noticed now. That's your fault, that is."

"I know, I know," she replied, almost inaudibly, and knelt down in front of him on the uneven tiles.

What she began to do was so unexpected and so uniquely, pleasurably scandalous that he lost his footing for a moment and put out an arm to steady himself. It fell across the shower lever. Hot water spurted out with a choked gurgle and then settled to a quiet, steady stream. Before the glass misted over Sasha glimpsed her in the mirror, plunging him violently, her spectacles still on, her pearly upper lip swollen and tight as she drew back fully and paused momentarily before her face disappeared again, and all he could see was her hair like a honey-coloured pelt twitching beneath his waist.

Clouds of steam, generated by the contact of the water, now almost boiling, with the cold surface of the washroom rolled upwards filling every available space. Condensing into a myriad of droplets it fell, drenching their hair, penetrating their clothing, running at blood-heat along the inside of Sasha's shirt. His boots were full of water from the overflow of the shower pediment and the gentle slop-slop of warm liquid was barely discernible above the hiss from the shower-nozzle.

It was all going too fast. He wasn't used to it and he couldn't last much longer taken over like this.

He arched back, taking her lips to the tip, slid his hands into the neck of her soaked jacket and grasped her breasts. The brassière came away, her glasses fell off and the coat burst open as his hands slithered upwards, desperately seeking a purchase. One after the other the buttons came away, plopping into the three inches of water which by now covered the washroom floor.

"Shit!" he groaned as he felt himself going and he hit the water with a splash, bringing her down on top of him, her arms caught fast in the ridden-down shoulders of her jacket.

After that, with the feel of her nipples rough against his palms and the sight of the slope of her naked shoulders, he wanted to laugh. He felt like the plumber in a silent film wildly casting about to plug leaks. Steam was escaping into the next room, whirling across the ceiling in great billows. It would soon be in the corridor and the *dezhurnaya* would think there was a fire and there would be hammering, shouting, bells and an axe through the door. Legless and the whole brigade in waders would be at the washroom door, knock-kneed with laughter, pissing themselves at the sight of him with his trousers down under a semi-nude blonde.

Christ, you've got to laugh, he told himself, and his torso began to heave and his belly quivered.

This she evidently took for something else because she clawed off her silk jacket and, wriggling her body to bring her head up to his, suddenly sat up astride him, the lacework of her bra hanging in tatters below her breasts. Vulnerable, blue veins ran to the points from under what appeared to be a paper-thin surface filmed by moisture. The dulled white and pink together reminded him of the puffy, overblown blossom of cherry trees.

"Hurt me." If a girl could be said to growl, she growled and groped in the water as she stared, unseeing, at him. Then she retrieved her spectacles, held them above her head and crushed the lenses and gold wire together. The crunch resounded sharply. Fascinated, he watched as she let fall the tangle of glass and metal, then slowly rotated her bloodied hands around both breasts, inwards and outwards and back again. Red streaks flared at the undersides.

"Do it to me. Kill me, use me like a fucking whore!"

Oh my God, thought Sasha, Christ God Almighty.

Her hands disappeared behind her back and a moment later the striped skirt was hanging half in and half out of the wash-basin. He was rather shocked; there was nothing left to come off now except the peach-coloured stockings.

"You great Russian bull bastard, do me, you fucking lout."

Christ. Her Russian was keeping up well. Through it all, he wondered which was the most extraordinary: that she knew what to say, that she said it, or that she could be serious about saying it. Obviously she wasn't just after a clout or two.

The blood merged pinkily into rivulets which coursed down her breasts as she finally found what she wanted and sank down over him, glassy-eyed, mumbling immaculate Russian: "Give it to me, you fucking Russian swine."

The shower hissed on. Around them the water was now so deep that he was developing a crick in his neck trying to keep it out of his ears. Soon the weight of the water would collapse the ceiling of the room below. Clearly she was in no mood for conversation, so, with a powerful effort, he raised his shoulders from the tiles and sat up, facing her. For a moment they locked, arms wrapped round each other like a mother bear and whelp.

"We've got to move," he said gently. Her eyes cleared and she seemed to wake up to their predicament.

"Oh God, yes," she said in a normal voice. "Look at the mess you're in. What a shame, I was just . . ."

By the time he had extricated himself, turned off the shower and slung all her enormous bath-towels on to the floor in a hopeless attempt to sop up the water, she had disappeared into the bedroom.

Irritably he followed her, stripping off his drenched shirt and singlet and draping them over the edge of her trunk. His eye was caught by a small handkerchief on top of the pile, its "made in" tag clearly readable, and he stuck it in his shirt pocket.

As he was pulling off his boots by the side of the bed, she spoke: "You will be careful, won't you?"

The laces had swollen with water and he was having a job to unpick the knots. Careful? Careful? A little while ago she was inviting him to murder her; now it was the way he did it. Could you do it carefully or carelessly? *Carefully* tear her apart? What sense did that make? He struggled with the boot, still feeling hungry. Perhaps he would faint and wake up in hospital, stark naked on the bed except for a size ten boot, a gaggle of nurses circling his body.

"You won't get me pregnant, will you?"

Successful at last, he flung aside the boot and looked up questioningly.

She was at the top of the bed, head propped up by several pillows, her peach-coloured stockinged legs drawn up, and, he thought, immodestly wide apart. One arm stretched down across her flat belly and she was doing something with the fingers of the hand, in front of him, which he had never seen, read about or remotely conceived as being done by a woman to herself. He gawped. She evidently intended him to gawp, too, because she did it faster as he watched.

This was a nightmare, even after the washroom shenanigans; he completely forgot about wanting her at all.

She was getting that look again and he glanced away. From a photograph stuck on the wall over the bed an old man waved to him out of a garden full of apple trees. In the background stood Bobby, her expression one of surprise as the camera had clicked. A bicycle with very small wheels was held fast between her legs.

Something hit the side of his bare arm. It was a small, slender package, prettily done up, with two hearts transfixed by an arrow ringed in gold on the front. He played with it, tossing it up and down in the palm of his hand, sniffing it as an ape would toy with a bar of soap.

"Thanks," he said, eventually. "Is it for me?" It seemed a queer time to be giving presents. "What's it for?"

"Of course it's for you, you fool!" She was starting on the language again. His heart sank. He couldn't make head or tail of the thing with the arrow and her legs were even less close together now, and she was doing it a lot more feverishly, screwing up her eyes at particularly satisfying passages and breathing harder through her perfect mouth. He thought of making a run for it, clothes or no clothes, shoeless and nude into the snow.

"Oh, hell! Give it to me! Haven't you seen one of these before?"

No, he certainly hadn't. Had he? Well, certainly not one like this, not black, not with all those knobbly little outgrowths. What, for Christ's sake, was he supposed to do with it?

She showed him. But it didn't work because whatever he had felt like at the beginning seemed as remote now as his last meal. In the end she made something of it, with her mouth, and they managed, but how long that would last, he couldn't have guaranteed. It was easy for her: the hand had never stopped.

Having made a quick appraisal of his readiness, she switched the pillows from the bedhead, and thrusting them, one on top of the other under her hips, she toppled slowly backwards, thighs outstretched.

This is it, said Sasha to himself and hoped that this time she would keep her mouth shut.

"Do it, do it in me, you horny, black Russian pig," grunted the voice. "Whip me, split me, spit me on it, you sadistic black bastard."

Now or never, thought Sasha, deciding to ignore the racial mix-up.

At the most vital juncture, he nearly stalled: not only was she stark naked, except for the miraculously-supported stockings, but her body was totally, entirely hairless. It was all shaved clean. Confronted by the gash he felt like a criminal.

"Do it, do it in me, for Christ's sake, do it," she groaned. So he did. She made a lot of noise and did a lot of wriggling and there was much more of the language. The rubber thing was a dead loss he reflected, bumping over the pillows as she writhed disconcertingly under him; he couldn't rid himself of the idea that it was already in shreds, she was so violent, and flapping around wetly, completely useless. Somebody had once told him that American products were tested to destruction but he couldn't see how you could evaluate the technology of this one, until it was too late. He pressed on, dreamily, desensitised by the foreign object between them but reassured of his adequacy every time she swore obscenely into his ear.

Then she started biting, nipping at his earlobes and the back of his neck. But when she sank her teeth into the flesh just above the collarbone, it was painful and he tautened his chest muscles, ready for the next onslaught. Sensing his recoil she started to bite indiscriminately – cheeks, chin and the points of his shoulders.

He reckoned this must be how women fight: all teeth and nails and pulling about. Rhode Island, Rhode Island chicks, Rhode Island reds, cock-fights in Rhode Island, squawking, feathers flying, steamy little cockpit, scratching and tearing, cries in the night: "Where's my little beauty, then?" "Gouge him!" "Get it in!" "Spur at him, attaboy . . ."

Without warning, she squirmed out from under him.

"You *bar-bar-ian!*" she hissed viciously.

What had he done now? Or not done?

"You filthy barbarian! What do you think you're doing?"

She righted herself and looked down from the heaped-up pillows, her legs still outflung, beads of foam clinging to the stiffly open gap which exhibited itself to him nakedly.

He passed his tongue over his lips.

"You're not servicing a peasant's cow! How am I supposed to manage anything when you go at me like a goddamned *bull*?"

"Manage?" He was lost. That was exactly the style he thought she'd asked for.

"Yes! Manage!" she nearly screamed. "What about me? What about my pleasure? Where's the fun in it for me?"

"What was it all about, if it wasn't about you, about what you wanted?"

"Wanted, yes. And I can go on wanting, can't I?"

"What are you talking about?" he asked, angry and belittled.

She inclined her head towards the shocking wound which, mercifully, now seemed to be closing up inwards.

"Look, I'll show you. You were doing it in the wrong place. You're suppose to . . ." she re-opened herself, cruelly, ". . . rub me here. And here. It doesn't take all that cart-horse whanging to get a woman off, you can do it with your *tongue*, for Christ's sake!" And she held herself apart, from front to back, indicating the spot with a vermilion-tinted fingernail.

"The hell I can!" He turned away.

"Oh, goddamn it!" she shouted, springing from the bed and grabbing her dressing-gown from the chair. "Can't you perform the simplest human function?"

"Simple? There's nothing simple about that," he said. "You don't learn that in school."

She darted about the room looking for her cigarettes.

"You're so hangdog, so crass. I'd have to be a sort of beast, a heifer, a sheep, to make it with you. Boy oh boy, I don't know how many women you've screwed but you're one big turn-off, a right let-down." She lit a cigarette, inhaling deeply. "I mean, one minute I'm a dainty glass flower, right? You open doors, you carry things, you don't look round for a drink every few minutes. Then the moment it comes to sex I'm just here to give you a thrill. I'm just a *body*, not a person."

He shuddered and silently began to put on his wet clothes. She started hammering at the bedside table with her fists. "I wanted a Russian. I wanted a Russian," she repeated over and over again. "I wanted to tell them back home I'd *had* a Russian."

He pulled on his boots, still wet from the shower room, and glanced at the trunk.

"When are you leaving?"

"Jesus!" she called out. "Just bloody work it out. Get out of my sight! Go back to fucking Mother Russia!"

The act of dressing revived him as if he had resumed his old identity with his clothes. Ahead of him lay a long walk. She had started to cry.

"I was mad for you . . ." Her voice tailed off into sobs. "We might have worked something out."

He opened the door, managing the goodbyes with a trace of his former jauntiness. "Never mind, love, better luck next time."

10

The hotel lobby was deserted. Outside it was pitch dark; the blizzard was over and a thaw had set in. There were no taxis. Sasha had no idea where the Metro was.

Not knowing the district he struck out in what he thought was the right direction and hoped for the best. It was hard to walk fast through the slush, but fearful amidst this wilderness of tower blocks and blank-fronted department stores, he set himself a smart pace back to the civilised Moscow of the Arbat, where, by now, parties of old women would be out with shovels, augmenting their pensions by clearing the pavements. Selling all they had left to the state, Olga had said – Our prostitutes.

He wasn't going to think about the débâcle with Bobby, but shove it into the glory hole at the back of his mind and see it wasn't ever re-despatched, even with the drink. He could do it; since the day Mum died when he was in the glasshouse he had had a technique for forgetting unpleasant things.

The dawn cold was a bonus; it stung his ears, distracting attention from mind and body. It was good for a space to be uncomplicated, physically diverted. Queer, that's what she'd wanted, and it took the street to give it to him.

By the time he lit on the depot Len was hosing down a lorry under the lofty corrugated roof of the maintenance shed. Pools of freezing-cold water lodged in the irregular surface of the concrete floor. He looked the picture of an old-fashioned slaughterman in his long rubber apron and gauntlets, breathing heavily in the vaporous air which reeked of gas-oil and paint-thinners. He limped up in boots borrowed from a smaller man; his had been nicked, Sasha remembered, a couple of days before.

"Well, bugger me, look who it isn't!" he shouted above the roar of the high pressure hose. "Been out on the tiles, have we? Christ, you look shagged, you poor bastard!"

A battery of arc-lights clamped to the roof joists invested his figure with an intense radiance, bringing his features into hard, electric monochrome. The unshaven chin speckled with white bristles stood

out blue-black and his eyes disappeared in the vertical down beam
beneath the overhang of his dazzling brow. He guffawed crazily,
towering over his workmates, a metal medallion flashing from his
neck like a heliograph.

"You silly sod," he roared at Sasha, waving his sinewy arms.
"What in hell's name have you been doing?"

Sasha's eyes had begun to stream and there was phlegm in his
throat. The sudden warmth and freakish smell of the shed brought
on a sneezing fit.

"Give us a drink," he gasped. "Think I'm going to croak."

Len hopped round the writhing hoses and fetched out a litre of
port wine from one of the inspection pits. Neither spoke again until
Sasha had taken two good pulls in the foreman's makeshift office at
the back.

"Cover for me, will you?" said Sasha. "I'm going down with flu
today."

Len grinned. "Flu, is it? Is that what you call it? Why don't you
tell me what you're up to? Like, how you get them running after you,
in tears, this time of the morning, howling? Judging by her face you'd
swear there'd been a death in the family."

Two young apprentices began to scrap over a wheel-brace and Len
broke off. "Stop horsing around, you little pimps, or I'll come and
nail your arses to your ankles!"

They grinned sheepishly and the smaller one let go of the brace.

Sasha's head began to clear. "Her face? What do you mean? You
mean a *woman* was here? Looking for me?"

"Well, she wasn't looking for me, mate, or any of that load of
randy little sods out there. No, it was you she wanted all right. Never
know what they see in you myself – not exactly a boulevardier, are
you?"

He began to roll himself a cigarette.

Sasha had a picture of Bobby running topless along the gutter, hair
flying, her blood-smirched breasts stiff from the frost. "Oh God – an
American?"

"Could have been an Eskimo for all I know," said Len. "Screwing Americans now, are you? Now what's a dozy piss-artist like
you doing with an American bit – improving international relations?"

Sasha felt too tired to explain.

"Oh, dry up, Len, don't you ever think of anything else? It wasn't
that. She's a decent kid, we were going to get married."

"Married? You? Talk about a spare prick at a wedding, you're
legendary, know that? Legendary. The limpest dick this side of the

Urals. The only thing you can pull is your own dong – never mind an American tart. Come off it, sonny boy."

Sasha did not want to argue. Len would never believe him anyway but he made a last-ditch effort to rescue his image.

"What about this?" He groped inside his shirt, bringing out Bobby Weston's handkerchief. "This is hers. Don't get these down the market."

Len threw his cigarette into the fire-pail before reaching over. "What does this prove, you cracked bugger?" he asked, holding the flimsy square of material up to the light. "Where's the frilly whatsits you said you'd had your hand in? This doesn't even say 'Made in the USA'."

"Course it does," shouted Sasha, and he half-rose to indicate the label. "There, it says it there."

"That says: 'Made in Brazil'." Len had learned some German when he was posted to the DDR and could read Roman script. "Where the hell's Brazil?"

Sasha thought quickly. "In America, thickie, where do you think?"

"Whereabouts in America?"

"Somewhere down from Rhode Island."

Len was unconvinced. "Well, if she's the one I saw today, she's a bit long in the tooth. No wonder you didn't bring her bloomers. What d'you want with an old bag like that?"

Sasha was puzzled. "Old?"

"Yeah, old, really old, wrinkly, not a drop of the juices left in her. Clapped out. If she had one, it'd be like an old walnut. No make-up either. Face looked like it hadn't been washed for a week."

Olga? Marina? Impossible. Sasha scowled. "Not taking the piss, are you?"

Len stood up and yawned. "Now would I do that with an old mate like you? No, she was here right enough, but if she was American I'm Mickey Mouse's auntie." He held Bobby's handkerchief to his nose as if trying to catch the smell of feminine perfume. "I'm off. OK, I'll cover for you, but for Christ's sake go out through the lavs so nobody sees you."

Who was running round Moscow looking for him? What had he done now? Pocketing the port wine Sasha left the depot by the route Len had advised. Near the river he found a taxi. The driver, who was reading *The Adventures of Sherlock Holmes* barely noticed when Sasha pulled open the back door and climbed in.

"The Dancing Men," muttered Sasha looking over his shoulder. "Good, is it?"

"So-so," said the driver morosely scraping the gears as he turned for the Arbat.

The big front door had been left wide open all night. The lift, as usual, was out of order. Sasha told himself to manage the stairs very slowly, one at a time. Perhaps he was really ill, perhaps he should stay in bed all day and get Lizaveta to make him some soup.

A woman emerged from the shadowy recess by the lift and blocked his way. A red scarf was pulled tightly round her ears and her brown flock coat was threadbare; her wide mouth looked blanched from the cold, almost as white as her hair. Sasha had seen her only twenty-four hours before, standing on another flight of stairs. That time she wouldn't listen. Now she was waiting for him.

"At last," Tanya murmured hoarsely. "Where have you been?"

Wondering if he were going to faint he dropped down on to the bottom step of the staircase and felt for the port wine. She descended a little way wheezing with suppressed rage.

"I want my papers, Aleksandr Mikhailovich. The ones you stole from me yesterday."

Sasha nodded dreamily. She was mad, he was comfortable on the step. Gradually he began to slide downwards.

"Papers? What papers?"

She came nearer. He could feel her breath warming his cheek.

"You know what papers. I dropped them by mistake when you came creeping into the office like a criminal. Perhaps you are a criminal. Come to think of it, you've got that sly, criminal look. We try to do some work, you come in, uninvited, steal papers from the office and disappear. I could have you charged."

Sasha went rigid. "Oh God," he whispered. "Oh my God. The letters."

"Not letters," said Tanya, beginning to cry. "My papers, my private papers."

Her *petition*. Sasha could just remember reading it last night, after he had read all the letters from the frustrated and miserable out in the provinces and before he had thrown his own letters from the red-haired widow from Rostov on to the floor with them. Then they had disappeared.

That was what Bobby had been doing: industriously sweeping the floor of his room; fixing the lampshade; straightening the bedspread; then carefully, while he was safely out of the way with Olga, picking up all the pieces of paper and putting them away, putting them away into the little box which he had carried back to the hotel, thinking it had her make-up inside.

That's what she'd done.

"You see," sniffled Tanya. "If those papers fell into the wrong hands it could be so . . . *awkward* for me." She loomed over him like a great, white-headed bird.

"I'm half-dead," he moaned. "My life's a mess, I've no energy left. Leave me alone."

Tanya was sobbing now. "If it were just for myself I wouldn't mind. But there's my mother and husband. You wouldn't harm them, would you? Look, I can pay you."

She brought up her hands together as if in prayer, and Sasha saw that between them were dozens of rouble notes.

He leaned his head against the wall. "I'm not up to this, I've not eaten for two days, and I'm in a bit of a state over a woman. I tried to tell you yesterday but you didn't care." He felt like crying himself.

"I'll help you. I'll help you, I promise," said Tanya eagerly. "Those papers I dropped, perhaps you did try to give them back to me but I was too upset to notice. You did hang on to them, didn't you? Because you see, if anyone from the office found those papers . . . it didn't occur to me until last night that you might have them. Masha and I hunted everywhere yesterday."

He remembered pushing the letter from the homosexual policeman up his sleeve. It must have fallen out and gone the same way as the others – as well as those from the widow, her box number in Rostov written at the top of each sheet and his own address clearly inscribed on each envelope. All of it a traceable correspondence fallen into someone's hands, along with Tanya's petition.

"I'm a dead loss, Tatyana Borisovna. I have been all my life."

Timidly she proffered her roubles again but Sasha's head fell on his chest. She tried to ease him into a corner of the stairwell, thinking he was drunk. Cold air gushed up the stairs every time the street door swung open from the wind. In the distance he heard the squealing of heavy truck brakes: the teams were arriving in the Arbat.

He stood up shakily. "Keep your money, Mrs Lestyeva. Don't worry, I destroyed your papers."

If Bobby had simply junked the letters they could have ended up in the Bakery Lane skip. Or in the box under the sink which Lizaveta took down to the yard every morning. With any luck they'd still be there and if he ran, he'd get to the box before Lizaveta and the five o'clock shift.

Unless the American girl really had taken the whole lot; but he didn't want to think about that.

"Go home," he told Tanya. "Don't worry and for God's sake put your money away."

94

She turned as if to leave, then paused as he started to climb the stairs.

"You did destroy them, didn't you?" she called out in her old, imperious manner. "If you haven't . . ."

"I've told you, haven't I?" he said. "And don't come bothering me at the depot again."

Bobby's voice sang in his head: "Barbarian!" and he put his hands to his ears.

The building was very quiet and no one seemed to be stirring. Perhaps Lizaveta was still in bed and not already poking around in the rubbish.

He pulled out his key with a shaking hand and made several efforts to insert it into the lock before the tongue slid into alignment. Inside the flat his door was shut, his room just as he and Bobby had left it five or six hours earlier. The lamp still stood on the mantelpiece; the Vietnamese birds wrestled on the bedspread; and the floor was clear of papers.

He checked the rubbish bucket under the sink in the kitchen. It was full of yesterday's garbage: Olga's apple-cores, a couple of tins the Kuznetsovs had opened for supper and Lizaveta's grits from her *kasha*; newspapers, a brown bag and an old, lined sheet on which someone had drawn a diagram; a lot of eggshells. By heaving himself up on to the window-ledge, he could just see the skips down in the yard. No one had emptied theirs yet but there would be no point in searching it. Bobby wouldn't have thrown the letters into the skip. She wouldn't have known where the skips lay or how to get down into the courtyard from the flat. So far this morning nobody here had taken any rubbish downstairs.

While he was at the window Lizaveta came into the kitchen, making no noise in her slippers.

"You had two women in your room last night. What are you doing now? Waving them goodbye?"

"Just checking the thermometer, Gran. There isn't a bag of rubbish lying around in the passage, is there? Papers and stuff like that?"

"You mean the lavatory paper? You're not to touch it."

"Let me look at it, darling. I've lost something. An important letter."

Lizaveta stored the paper in a cupboard next to the bathroom. He didn't want a quarrel but he'd risk one since this was an emergency.

"Don't you make a mess," screamed Lizaveta, furious at the thought of the chaos he would make of her neatly-packaged bundles. But he was already out in the passage.

The noise of the garbage trucks rose up from the lane. He flung open the cupboard door and ripped the bag apart, causing sheaves of unevenly-matched paper to cascade over the floor. Tremblingly, he began to turn over each sheet. They looked like letters all right but after a while he realised they were all rough drafts of a single letter, not one of Tanya's but a letter he had never seen before; and each draft began in a neat, upright hand with the same two words: *Lyubimiy moi*, My beloved, *Lyubimiy moi*, My beloved, *Lyubimiy moi*.

III

Starochersskaya and Pawtucket

11

"Disgraceful!" said Olga to herself, twitching the curtains across her window.

Seated on her divan she giggled, burst into tears and immediately felt better. Damned idiots, she thought, both making exhibitions of ourselves. I'm getting silly.

She had come home an hour early. Bobby had been waiting on the doorstep with a three-kilo jar of pickled tomatoes, a huge tin of fish, some grapefruit, onions and a cabbage. Olga was depressed and the girl could do nothing to lift her mood.

Olga had never imagined her as anything more than an acquaintance and her visit a faintly glamorous intermission, an interlude. But when she remembered that after today it was over, that Bobby was leaving, she had wanted to cry.

"I'll come back," the girl had promised.

"Thank you," was all the reply she could muster.

In her room the grapefruit had spilled on to the floor. She wept over them, shamefacedly, irritated at her sudden, futile tears.

Then she took out her best tea-service and started to lay the table, calming herself by spreading out the clean, pink cloth, and smoothing down the creases with the flats of her hands; and wondering if the man was still at the window, expectant and gleaming, staring into the dark.

"What a fool, what a fool," she intoned, and picked the onions and cabbage out of her bag. And who wouldn't be nervous? I'm an outsider, I don't even understand my brother's needs, or those of his wife, or Tanya's fears about her job or Marina's fatalism. Or why Bobby chain-smokes now, when she didn't smoke at all when I first met her, or why she and Sasha never talk to each other any more.

New Year had been a wash-out. Olga had had her party frocks dry-cleaned and bought a new set of hair combs but the parties were drab. Host quarrelled with hostess and the guests bickered, until finally she had seen the New Year in alone except for Marina who drank neat spirit as if it were water and talked incessantly about the old days. That was when Sasha disappeared for a week and had

miraculously avoided freezing to death after falling down in the road.
Boris had found him before the militia did, but Sasha pushed his old
friend away when they arrived home.

"I don't need any of you," he had said.

But, after all, Sasha wasn't her responsibility. He wasn't even
Lizaveta's though she fed him, but Bobby's.

What Bobby thought she could have given Sasha was not at all
clear, but, whatever it was, Olga knew it had finished. She found
Bobby on Russian men very hard to understand.

"They're so handsome in a chunky sort of way."

"Where are they, all these handsome men?" she had asked, exasperated. "Perhaps you'd point one or two in this direction."

"Chunky" was Bobby's word. It meant stocky, big-shouldered,
stubby-handed, square-chinned. Like Sasha, God help us, but the
night the *dvornik* came up and asked if anyone would help him carry
Sasha into the lift, Bobby had extinguished her cigarette and said she
had to go. Nothing Olga could say would make her change her
mind.

Evening darkness invaded the flat, suspending long shadows from the
old, high ceiling, blunting the outlines of furniture. Olga took her
bowl and vegetables into the kitchen. In the passage she turned round
and with her free hand released the catch on the inside, then heard it
click as she pulled the door to.

Locking her door was a new habit, and she enjoyed doing it each
time, meticulously, even if she were only going to the bathroom.

"You're becoming a fussy old maid," Boris said when he noticed
the key round her neck.

A broadminded fussy old maid, she thought, with an old faithful
in tow: tonight was the third time the man opposite had appeared at
his window. For three weeks he had been watching her but this
was the first occasion he had removed all of his clothes. She was
disappointed. For some reason she was curious to know if he were
circumcised. Wasn't that the difference between Jews and Arabs?
One of them anyway. But he had presented it to her as thick and
curved as a pump-handle and you couldn't tell with him in that state.

Lizaveta sat at the table, picking grits out of her *kasha*. "Good
evening, Olga Sergeyevna."

For years she had been saying "Good evening" in that inappropriately formal way. "Like a serf actress," said Boris.

The old woman sighed. "Nowadays I can't sleep. You can't sleep
properly when you're my age." She pointed theatrically to the hollows
under her eyes.

Olga put her mixing-bowl and wooden spoon on the table and tapped her clock above the stove just to check that it was still working. The Kuznetsovs had bought two new china cups, rather thick and clumsy-looking, and they had been placed ostentatiously on a shelf beside the door. The very sight of them jangled her nerves.

"Then I've got a long wait to see!" she snapped at Lizaveta. Bobby was late. Lizaveta stopped and leaned on her elbows.

"One day you'll remember what I said about being old. When you're as old as me, there's no looking forward." Her pinafore crackled with starch.

Olga began to sweep up the flour dust with a clean rag which she kept tightly wound round the legs of her stove. The movement seemed to incense her.

"You're obsessed with yourself, Lizaveta Ivanovna, it's nothing but yourself, gossip, complaints all the time. I mean, it's not as if there's anything really the matter with you."

Lizaveta was indignant. "I can't sleep. I hear you all at night, scurrying in and out of each other's rooms, doors opening and closing every five minutes!"

"Just do *stop* it! Don't be so nosey! If you had any idea what *I* have to put up with!" Olga dashed angrily at the dough. "You haven't a spark of discernment."

Water clanked in the pipes. Lizaveta wrinkled up her nose. "Having trouble with that woman, are you?"

Olga threw down her spoon. "One day, soon, I hope they come and cart you off to hospital. When I think of what happened to *me* ten minutes ago!"

Lizaveta was intrigued.

"That place opposite," continued Olga, "is turning into a sleazy hotel. I just have to open my curtains, and without a by-your-leave a man takes off his trousers."

"Was he black?" asked Lizaveta. "I've heard stories about black men."

"What's that got to do with it?"

"You should report him. Unless, of course, you want to make something of it in some other way. What was it like – black too?"

Olga gave a hysterical shriek. They both started to laugh and the old woman shook her head and wiped her eyes.

"Imagine!" exclaimed Olga. "At my age! He *showed* me! Perhaps that's the way they do things where he comes from."

"Spilled seed. God preserve us from the heathen and all his ways," murmured Lizaveta resuming her work. "Drink is one thing, but when the beast in them is roused . . . Now, your brother's a gentleman, through and through, in spite of everything."

"Oh, yes, he doesn't frighten old ladies, if that's what you mean." She was cutting up vegetables on a little hardwood block.

"I've done now, let me give you a hand," said Lizaveta, getting off her stool.

"I don't need your help, don't interfere. I'd like to find out who he was, all the same."

They might all start doing it. And she had a picture of a chorus line of naked swarthy men, each one with his thing poking out of his hairy fist, high-kicking on the balcony. "Upsetting decent people like that."

"Shush," said Lizaveta. "Have a glass of my daughter's home-made wine, dear." She pointed to a stone jar on the shelf. "It'll do you good, calm your nerves. It's your age."

"Oh, thank you for *that*. No, I won't, it's quite undrinkable."

Someone whistled on the stairs outside the flat but nobody rang the bell. Bobby seemed to have disappeared for good.

"Just because you spend your time pottering . . ." Olga began, still irritated with the old woman, but Lizaveta, too, was offended now. She stood up, put away her *kasha* bowl and took down her jar of wine. Hugging it to herself she began to hobble out of the kitchen. At the door she turned.

"I tell you, I don't like it, there are too many strangers hanging around this place."

Olga carried on kneading her dough, its texture becoming pleasantly springy. She remembered the sumptuous brown body against the rugs in the warm lamplight. His women would lie about in veils, waiting for him to take a whip to them, like a king with that great dark thing quivering. She smiled. "If only Bobby had been there! If only she'd seen!"

12

Lizaveta came back still holding her wine jar.

"There's a woman on the landing. One of *his*," she said. Lowering her voice, she continued in a whisper: "We don't want that sort here, do we?"

Olga straightened up and pushed one hand into the small of her back as if she had found a sore place.

"You've no idea who she is. It might be his sister. Let her in, for heaven's sake."

Lizaveta replaced her jar on the shelf.

"There's too many women in this place already without letting another in."

"Oh, *I'll* go. Really, what is the matter with you nowadays?"

She rinsed her hands under the tap admiring the elegant set of her long ringless fingers as they reddened in the hard water.

She found the woman sitting on the first granite step of the flight which led up to the second floor, her chin in her hands. She was crooning to herself quietly and her garish red hair, crimped into hundreds of tiny bobbing and jostling curls, quivered along the high collar of her full-skirted, purple coat. A pair of sturdy knees showed between the hem of her coat and the brown tops of her boots. Bags and boxes were strewn over the tiles; and a neat pile of suitcases, festooned with straps and twine securing yet more packages done up in newspaper, odd pieces of cloth and what looked like wire netting, was stacked up to the balustrade. A huge sack crammed with turnip tops and crinkly cabbage had been pitched in front of the door. Right at the bottom a bottle of kefir had smashed, the fragments of glass slitting open a bag of beetroots; a pastelly red stain was creeping over the doormat.

Olga gasped. "Is Aleksandr Mikhailovich expecting you?"

The woman picked her way through the luggage, held out her hand and smiled. Her teeth were small and yellowish; a solitary gold one glistened among her back molars. Her lipstick, the colour of dark apricot, was heavy on her round lips and her small hands were tipped with matching nail varnish.

"I should just think he is! I'm Valentina Dmitryevna Afanasyeva," she exclaimed in an attractively husky, lilting voice. "Am I glad to see a friendly face! I don't think I could have lived through the night out here."

A huge golden fish, complete with eyes, fins and tail, its head towards Olga, was squeezed under her left arm.

Without letting go of the fish Valentina strode into the hall and looked round, her nose tilted up between reddish, weatherbeaten cheeks.

"I was just figuring out where it could go. I didn't want to put it on the floor outside. Hasn't he got a fridge or anything? It is a bit big, but they were selling them cheap at the station – must have fell out of a crate or something!" She laughed loudly and slapped the fish, her multitudinous curls bobbling in all directions.

Olga went ahead, pushed open Sasha's door and switched on the light. The room had scarcely changed since Bobby tidied it all those weeks ago, except that the dust lay thicker, the bed was unmade again and seven or eight bottle tops were scattered on the window-sill.

The small woman who seemed so tightly bound in her heavy clothes that they threatened to burst at any moment peeped round Olga's shoulder.

"Is this his room? For God's sake, what a pig-sty." Her eyes roamed the empty space, populating it with non-existent furniture. "Men, I ask you, no chairs, no table, no wardrobe. Not a cup or saucer, either, I bet. Doesn't he ever eat?"

There was nowhere to put the fish.

"You'd better leave it in the kitchen," said Olga at last.

"Oh, but what about my luggage, dear, wouldn't do to lose that now, dear, would it?"

They started to pull the boxes and bags down the passage.

"Cardboard boxes, old tins, part of Grandad's hen-coop there, that's to stop the cheese from squashing, oh, but look at it, all grit and feather, he never cleans anything. They're all the same, men. Things I wouldn't normally be seen dead with. It's a long way from home, you need such a lot and with a man you never know if it's enough. Do you know him at all? A good friend is he? Doesn't drink, does he? Not a lot, I mean?"

There was no time for any answers.

"I wanted to bring a duck. Do you think I could get Vasya to kill one? That boy is so squeamish, how they had him in the Army I'll never know. In the end Pa chased it with a chopper right down to the river before his legs gave out, and those nasty Vassilyevs' dog got it in the copse. When Pa brought it back Ma screamed because it was her favourite drake. Trust Pa. None of us fancied it after that."

Puffing and heaving at her boxes all the time she was talking, she seemed never to have left home, and spoke of her neighbours as if Olga, too, had known them all her life.

"Still they wanted to set me up, give me a good send off. 'Another chance after poor old Ivan,' Grandad said, and he gave me a twenty-rouble gold piece from the orchard where he'd buried it in the bad times before the Communists. The stuff I've got: useless a lot of it, but how could you refuse, I asked myself. There's a horse blanket somewhere in all that, stamped 'Moghilyov Remount detachment 1915', and a snapshot album of Odessa, and the veterinary certificate for seventeen cows Grandad once owned. They just threw everything in."

Meanwhile a tremendous clatter was coming from the kitchen. Lizaveta in a fury had kicked over Olga's stool and was clanging saucepans together in the sink. If she heard, Valentina seemed to take no notice.

They made a heap of her baggage in the middle of the kitchen floor.

"You'll say I was a fool to have left my home, but there you are. It's always the same story. Love, I mean."

Lizaveta stopped rattling her pots, turned round, her arms still sunk to the elbows in greasy pan water, and stared jealously at the strange woman.

"Don't tell me you're in love with that Biryusov?"

Olga wanted to get on with her pie. Valentina watched as she took her rolling pin, an empty bottle filled with water, out of the cutlery drawer.

"Ah, now, pie pastry, I love that smell." She put the fish down on Lizaveta's side of the table and stacked some brown paper bundles next to it. Then tossing back her bouncy curls she took up Lizaveta's challenge. "Yes, Granny, if you must know, that's right, I am, that's how it's happened. Mind you," she added with an assumption of demureness for the benefit of Olga whom she had swiftly deduced was a spinster, and was now rolling out pastry on the opposite side of the table. "Mind you, he wouldn't agree for at least six letters. Then he told me this wasn't a posh apartment, not exactly a love nest. Love nest! That place of his is about as cosy as a mousetrap without cheese." She laughed again, uproariously, putting a hand up to her mouth to conceal the blemished teeth. A flush spread over her plump cheeks and down her neck, before fading away with the laughter. Her eyes continued to sparkle.

"What a lark this is, though, isn't it?" Breaking open one of the parcels, she sat down and placed a long white loaf on the table with a wooden-handled knife thrust into it longways, ready for slicing. "It's ages since I've had a fling. I dare say he'll be back soon from work and you'll all be fussing over him."

Olga gazed in wonderment at the plump hands flying over the parcels, ripping off paper and string. In Valentina Dmitryevna's world evidently any man, no matter who he was, would have been fated to be the only fact of life necessary to know.

This was too much for Lizaveta. "No we won't, that we won't," she said decidedly. "You daft lass, you don't know what you've let yourself in for, it's not like the country here, you know. He's no Grandad, your Biryusov, you won't be able to prop him in the kitchen corner shelling peas. He's a devil, that one, when he gets going. He'll have the hide off you if you're not careful, and *he's* not choosy who he goes with when . . ."

"We'll see about that," retorted the little woman, her wide black eyes firing up at Lizaveta's clumsy envy. "He may not be the Minister of Culture but he sounded a sight nicer than some of the wolves I've been around with who expect you to pay with God knows what bedtime acrobatics for a kind word." She blushed again, the skin mottling along her jaw bone. Her eyes went back to Olga's pastry. "Yes, pastry, meat, ah, the smell of those pies in the little shops where I got my taxi." She added proudly, "I had to get a taxi with me and all my things."

There seemed to be no end to her stores of food. Wine, cakes, biscuits and preserves were disgorged from the packages, tumbling out on to the table and half covering the fish.

Olga interrupted her rolling-out for a moment and smiled mischievously at Valentina. "I wouldn't like to be in his shoes when he gets back. You've killed the fatted calf already and he forgets the feast. Woe betide the little rascal, woe betide him."

Lizaveta stared from one to the other and her comradely femininity re-asserted itself: "You poor thing!" she said. "Men *are* disgusting. Of course he ought to be here. Why, it's nearly like a wedding where the bride is waiting for the groom. What a fool that man is!"

They could see that Valentina, beneath her thick make-up and tight corsets, was not that young. There were lines above the peaks of her cheekbones striating the soft underlay of her eyes, and creases at each side of the prominent mouth when her face was in repose. For all her gaiety and good humour she was clearly upset and embarrassed at Sasha's inconsiderateness. But the one thing she didn't want was female sympathy so she adopted a sulky, defiant expression, censuring Lizaveta without looking at her.

"Come off it, Granny. I'm no spring chicken. I've buried one husband so there's not much I don't know about men. They may all be pigs but I'm a country girl and I know there's nice pigs and nasty pigs – I've been over the sty-side and rolled about a bit, a tumble in the muck never did a healthy girl any harm. There's not much I wouldn't do for a few warm nuzzles in the ear. Besides, it was *me* that felt sorry for *him* when I read his letters about how worried he got, not being book-learned like the rest of you, no good at carpentry either or dancing and how shy he got with young girls."

"Are you sure you've come to the right address?" asked Olga, trying not to laugh at Sasha's unrecognisable self-portrait.

"All right," shouted Valentina. "He sounded a bit thick, I'll give you that, but he's a nice man. Anyone that shy," her outstretched fingers touched Olga's pie-crust making pudgy indentations in the plait arranged round the edge of the baking dish, "must be nice, that's what I think."

With this declaration she had recovered her self-confidence and moved round the kitchen singing under her breath. She went out for more boxes and when Olga passed Sasha's wide-open door on her way to the bathroom she saw the lights full on and objects strewn all over the floor.

The widow scurried in and out chattering the whole time. "Don't you get the idea that I'm hard up for men. I could have taken my pick at home, I can still twirl a leg, you know, and they don't all want skin and bone," she said giving her behind an approving rub.

Every thought was acted out or spoken aloud.

"You don't need education for *that*, do you? It's not there you need it then, is it? Not when it comes down to it. Let's have soup tonight. Didn't you know soup's the healthiest thing out? What it is, is I've always wanted to live in Moscow."

Normally, at this time of the evening, the flat was quiet. The Kuznetsovs were in but they hadn't stirred. Olga glanced at her clock. There was still no sign of Bobby.

"What time does Himself get home?" asked Valentina. She meant Biryusov.

Sasha's concept of time, Boris had once said, was susceptible of infinite variability. Olga couldn't tell that to the widow.

"He really does drive you to the limit," said Lizaveta loudly. "He'll be up to his usual nonsense, isn't that right, Olga Sergeyevna?"

But Valentina had lost interest and was very busy taking off her coat. Underneath she had on a short flounced dress in brownish green which fluttered around her knees as she dashed over to the stove to turn down the gas under the steaming kettle.

"D'you think he'll like my dress?" she called over her shoulder. "I made it myself."

Lizaveta looked round for cups. With a swagger Valentina brought out her own: deep, gold-rimmed, with violets stencilled on the sides.

"Lucky he's not here, really, because I want to get my best outfit on. It's mauve with a silver flower on the jacket. Of course, it was stupid not telephoning from the Kazan but you couldn't get near a phone at the station this time of night."

Lizaveta changed the subject. "This tea's horribly bitter. What about some of your special tea, Olga Sergeyevna? That stuff your friend brought?"

"A boyfriend!" shrieked Valentina. "I'll bet he's the brainy type. So you're the translator lady with the sick brother, am I right?"

Olga laughed out loud. "Heavens above, you learn something new every day – Sasha has lived here for donkey's years and this is the first time I knew he could write! That's what he's been scribbling about, is it? They must have been dull, those letters, nothing ever happens to us."

Lizaveta surveyed the widow's banquet, selected two white sweet rolls and, pouring herself a cup of tea, prepared to move off into her room for a snack and a doze. As she hobbled down the corridor, her false teeth clicked – a sign of forthcoming reprimand; she wasn't going to leave without issuing a warning to the new woman who, no matter how decent she looked, had a coarse way with her tongue which grated on Lizaveta's sense of communal proprieties.

"This is a respectable flat, dear. I trust you won't give us any trouble."

The widow said nothing and Olga pretended not to notice.

"Tell me about your husband," she said gently when the old woman had gone. "What did he die of?"

The widow blew her nose on a tiny handkerchief fringed with machine-lace. "Cancer of the stomach, it only took eight months. I really miss him. It's no joke being a woman on your own."

"I know what you mean," said Olga.

"Well, I'm sick of it," declared the little woman, her comely fist pounding the top of a jar of green and red pepper salad. "I'm sick of keeping myself nice and looking after my skin and hair and things and laundering my undies as if I were some scared little rabbit of a virgin waiting for Mr Right to knock on her door. So I thought I'd be out and doing, and grab one by the whatsisname. What's the harm in it? They can't eat you."

She gave a shrewd, appraising glance at Olga and shrugged her shoulders. Her overblown bust sat rigid in its stays. "Of course, you know how we started writing to each other, don't you? I felt like a silly tart putting that advert in the paper, but so what? I mean, you do want people to like you, don't you? You have to have them around, don't you? And you've got to get started somehow especially when it's the second time and you're my age. And I'm not frightened of chancing my arm – if you can call it that, what I'm chancing. Most lonely people are afraid, aren't they?"

Olga would not be drawn.

"Look dear, I don't want to pry," said the widow. "Let's talk about it another time. Now, can you tell me what time my man gets in?"

Olga went to put in her pie and came back to the table her cheeks pink from the oven.

"Well, actually, we've not seen much of him for a while. He's not badly off and he goes his own way. It could be tonight or tomorrow or next week, you can't tell." She stroked her upper arm. "I wouldn't have called him a marrying kind of man."

Valentina was eating cake, licking in the fragments from the corner of her mouth. "What would you know about him?" she retorted, stung by Olga's pointed qualification. "Or men like him? They've scrabbled round *my* skirts since I was out here." She indicated the region of her chest with a sticky forefinger.

"I'll wait here. If he doesn't come tonight I'll run up my curtains, it's lovely material, and then there's the pictures to hang. I won't be moping."

"Suit yourself," said Olga. Removing her apron she folded it into a small, round bundle, tucking the ribboned ties and yoke under the chintz panels of the skirt. "I don't know what anyone could make of a man like that," she added at length.

"Come along," said Valentina mildly. "You must be waiting for someone too, just like me. Is it the boyfriend?"

"No, it certainly is not."

The widow took a long plate and began to arrange her fish, inserting slices of lemon into its gills and sprinkling it with minutely-chopped chives.

The plate belonged to the Kuznetsovs but Olga said nothing.

"You've not got awful legs," said the widow suddenly.

"Should I have?"

"Everybody knows," said Valentina, pulling round the fish's tail, "that intellectual women always have awful legs. It's all that sitting down they do, works down from their thighs. Comes of keeping them too close together."

As Olga left the kitchen, Valentina was talking to the fish: "Aren't we the saucy madam!" she squealed, popping half an unpeeled lemon into its gaping mouth.

13

"Look at this old monstrosity," said Olga. "Could I cut the arms higher or would it be better without them altogether?"

She spun round very slowly in front of Bobby, leaning back to accentuate the fall of the shoulders. The dress was grey satin with three-quarter length sleeves. A grey satin jacket with a severely nipped-in waist lay across a chair; the cheval glass was half-shrouded by a tailored suit; and six dresses, three blouses and two skirts were scattered round the room, hanging from various pieces of furniture.

The American girl sat cross-legged on the divan, smoking. On the table nearby lay the remnants of a meal.

Bobby pressed a glowing stub down into a china plate, already overflowing with ash and crushed filters. "It's gorgeous, but so formal. So . . ." She couldn't find the word. "It's so *unspontaneous*, that's it – lovely, but calculated, rather restricting. Not a fun thing."

"You're being tactful," said Olga looking back to the glass. "You mean it's dowdy? Would I be such a frump if I showed a bit more leg?" she added, raising the skirt to mid-thigh and rolling her eyes.

"Darling Olga, you don't understand fashions, they change so quickly. You could never keep up. Fashion is money as well as lack of constraint."

"You mean they dye their hair with lapis lazuli and the razor-blades in their ears have to be gold?" Olga tittered and unzipped the frock. Her high-heeled sandals were silvery, her stockings clerically grey.

"I need at least two more decent frocks," she muttered to herself. "But I've put on weight. Perhaps I should do a few breathing exercises."

Her nostrils whitened as she valiantly inhaled. Bobby called out the seconds. Olga collapsed into giggles at sixty-five.

"What about the Embassy man then?" she gasped. "Now, there's a flat belly if you like. What kind of exercise does he do, d'you think?"

"Don't!" cried Bobby tapping a fresh cigarette so violently that the cork filter snapped. "He must be horribly depraved to stoop to that. I don't understand how you can be so light-hearted about it, Olga. That's intimidation."

Olga was admiring her figure in the mirror, caressing her thighs under a long, modest petticoat. "No, he's harmless. Perhaps he thinks he's got something to be proud of. Look, haven't I got a lot of clothes?" She waved a hand round the room. "But they're all so old. They only need re-cutting and fine stitching. Nobody recognises the old thing if the fashioning is bold."

Bobby blew a smoke-ring. "Gosh, I was sorry about your pie. I just couldn't eat."

Poor little thing, thought Olga. The girl seemed so apprehensive, all of a tremble, and so pale with that lovely skin it made you want to kiss her. Aeroplanes made Olga feel sick. She had only flown twice in her life and the memory made her queasy.

"Bobby, I'll show you my best dress. It's really classic."

She took a long box from under her bed, gently removed the dress from its layers of tissue paper and draping the skirt over one arm, held up the bodice.

"Chinese silk. I bought the material in Berlin with some of my foreign earnings." She laid out the dress beside the American girl. "Lectures in Dresden. I made it semi-antique with the dropped waist and long cuffs, like a 1920s flapper girl's. The lace belonged to my grandmother."

Bobby picked at the weave.

"The assistants in the shop were terribly polite and there were chairs by the counter."

Bobby was staring at her bag on the other side of the room.

"I've still got some packing to do and I'm very tired."

"I do wish you weren't going away tomorrow," said Olga. "And I have a favour to ask. You do remember, you said it would be possible."

She went to the bureau, opened one of the little cupboards and took out a thick pink, unsealed envelope. Inside were many sheets of the same pink paper, covered on both sides with minuscule hand-writing, part English, part Russian. There was no signature and the envelope was unaddressed.

Moistening the flap with her tongue she sealed the letter and turned, handing it to Bobby with a wan smile.

"Here it is. I did give you the name of his publishers in London, didn't I?"

Bobby gazed at the letter and sent more ash spinning over the plate. Some of it fell on the carpet.

"Oh hell, wouldn't you just know," the girl said. "I could have sent it out this evening with my research notes."

"You mean, you . . ." Olga gripped her fingers round the letter and smiled tremulously. "Well, I suppose there's nothing to stop me posting it here, actually. I expect it would arrive eventually. But it's rather . . . personal, you understand." She worried at Bobby's ash on the floor with the toe of her sandal. "If you do happen to see him give him my love. Don't make a special journey, of course."

"Honestly, my brain's going," said the girl. "All that queueing and hassle this evening at my Embassy. Everything's so complicated and bureaucratic."

"Does that mean you can't take it?" said Olga, a tremor in her voice.

"Oh, sure, give it here. I'll say it's a letter to me," said Bobby carelessly, slipping the envelope under her packet of cigarettes.

Olga was breathless from relief. "I ought to give it up at my age. I mean, it's not that you could really call it an affair."

At that moment a raucous female cry penetrated the room and they heard the whistle of a birch-broom on the lino in the passage. Olga shivered and began gathering her scattered clothes.

"It's an awful pity she had to choose this time to foist herself on us," she said. "Right on your last evening."

"He probably fixed it up on purpose," said Bobby, peevishly.

Olga pushed her head through the neck of a blue sweater and shook herself like a wet dog.

"Dearest darling Bobby, don't bother about him. I love you so much. You don't know how miserable I'll be when you've gone. Tanya, too. We all love you."

Nevertheless, Tanya and Marina had failed to turn up for the farewell meal. Something was wrong, but Bobby didn't understand what.

"Is Tanya having a breakdown? I mean, she just never wants to see anyone these days."

Olga rubbed hard at a ledge of the bureau, trying to dissipate a wine ring.

"Marina thinks it's her time of life," she said, without looking up, her lips pursed in concentration. "I'm sorry," she burst out abruptly, pulling away from the bureau. "It's a delicate subject I don't like mentioning, since I'm years older than you, my dear, but really, no, I don't know what's wrong with Tanya. She's always dramatised herself."

Bobby searched for her cigarettes. She had smoked almost the entire packet. "Olga, do you think I'll be able to say goodbye to Sasha before I go?"

Olga lifted her eyebrows questioningly, more than a little exasperated. The flat seemed to be full of wretched women who wanted

Sasha. Gone were the days of his fruitless telephone calling. She started to stack up the tea-things. Smoke filled the room, eddying turgidly round the lamp.

"He's been so moody lately," she said, finally. "He was in a dreadful paddy when he came back that morning, after he'd gone off with you." The girl looked down. "It seems a long time ago, now."

"Nearly a month," said Bobby through her teeth. She blew a long stream of smoke out of her nostrils and stared at Olga consideringly. "I guess I made a fool of myself over him."

"You did! We all did! I found him in the corridor, tearing up paper and cursing us all to hell," went on Olga. "I tried to stop him and he gave me such a look! It was terrible to see him in such a state."

"He was never in love with me, you know," said the girl. "I can't really explain but to a woman like me, he could be irresistible sometimes. But he was always so damned unsure of himself."

"Really?" said Olga, politely. She didn't want to be treated to details. "I've a cake nearly baked, dear. I'll wrap it up for your journey."

Bobby laughed. "Olga, darling, they do feed you on aeroplanes. Don't go. Tell me about your Englishman."

Olga stood at the door, baking-rack in hand. "'*Quand un Anglais est beau il est plus beau que n'importe qui.*' I wouldn't have wanted him to know more than was good for him, so I never told him, but he's very handsome. Dark, curly-haired, with a pale, olivey skin — like George Noel, Lord Byron," she added gaily, thinking of her favourite and handsomest Englishman. Bobby smiled.

"And don't talk to me about aeroplane food, Bobby. We'll have some fresh tea now and I'll take out the cake."

"Where I live you wouldn't survive," Bobby had said earlier on. That had hurt more than anything anyone had ever said to her before. Indeed, she thought; why not? *She does.*

The light in the passage was blazing. Valentina's luxuriant silhouette was outlined on the kitchen door. She was keening a wild dirge the words of which Olga had known since childhood. She paused to listen but the widow spotted her and came down the passage.

"Just look at that smoke!"

Olga shrugged. "My friend's a chain-smoker. What can you do?"

Valentina glared. "Your friend! I know about your friend! I was glad to get here but I'll be even gladder to leave if this goes on much longer! Something's got to be done!"

"What on earth's the matter?"

Sobs gurgled in the little woman's throat. "I knew he wasn't a monk, but that foreign hussy in your room, she's got her hooks into my man, she has. She has, hasn't she? You know she has." She wept noisily.

"What a poisonous creature that Lizaveta is," said Olga, guessing who had caused the uproar.

The door to Sasha's room was flung wide. Green curtains hung from a metal rod over the window; there were several good rugs on the floor; and a pile of furniture was stacked in a corner waiting to be fitted into Valentina's home-making scheme.

There was a sudden boom from outside, then a jolting crash. The lift has gone mad again, was Olga's first thought. The noise repeated itself, this time more shatteringly, and she hurried down the passage.

As she peered round the front door, she saw Sasha, leaning up against the lift button. Periodically the cage leapt from its seatings, jerked downwards, stopped, allowed the doors to crash open and shut, then shuddering like a tormented beast, began another futile upward climb. At the best of times the old machinery was temperamental and invariably violent in its operation, but now it seemed to have gone berserk. The shaft resounded with mechanical clashes and squeals.

Someone on the ground floor was swearing, and banging on the gate.

"For pity's sake!" Olga shouted over the din. "What's the matter with you? What do you think you're doing? Do you *want* to get arrested?"

His eyes were unblinking but he failed even to register her presence. One of his boots had vanished and his jacket was stained with dried vomit. Olga shut her eyes, overcome with nausea.

"I can't help you any more," she hissed.

Sasha drew one short, snorting breath before his knees buckled and he slid down to a squatting position.

"There's only Bobby," said Olga desperately. Sasha closed his eyes and began to weep. "I don't even like touching you . . ."

14

Bobby was doing her hair when Olga reappeared. The left side was combed smooth and fell sheer from the parting; stray filaments leapt out, galvanised by the static electricity which abounded in the heavy air and minutely disarrayed the severe, golden sweep. She sprang from the divan, the clubbed ends swinging back from her tilted face. Her legs were very long and very slender in the tight denim.

"What's wrong? Did Sasha come back?"

How typically knowing, reflected Olga. She has learned to read my face from my eyes, my thought from my gesture. Self-conscious at her transparency of feeling, and confused at having to describe the new, embarrassing state of affairs, she dropped her voice to the semi-audible antic mouthing of Lizaveta Ivanovna when something reprehensible had to be recounted:

"Of course. But you'd think he'd have some elementary acquaintance with the common courtesies, wouldn't you?"

The girl smiled at the Lizavetian mimicry. "Passed out, has he? To hell with him. He's a boor!"

The remark was too dismissive. My God, so she's nervous, observed Olga to herself, approaching the girl and brushing her mouth against the sculpted cheek highlit with blusher.

Taking Bobby in her arms, yet preserving a little distance as if wanting only their upper bodies to touch, she murmured to her as a mother would murmur a lullaby: "There, there, it's an unlucky day. I wanted to make such a lovely evening for you, but these awful idiots won't leave us alone. You're tired and you want a good sleep. There, there, hush, child."

She drew Bobby towards the door, all the time talking reassuringly in the same even tones. "The heart of a woman is so correctly promptable: he's got no manners, he's ignorant, brutish, but there's an unacknowledged splendour about him. It lies behind the shyness, the diffidence; there's some spring of action he wants to trace to a pure, unspotted source. But he's not for you, he's too unaccomplished, ineducable, remote."

At the end of the passage Valentina wailed a peasant song. She was scrubbing and her brush rasped backwards and forwards in time to the dejected whimpers of the quatrain:

> *Oy moy miliy*
> *Oy moy miliy*
> *Oy moy miliy*
> *Gdye ty, gdye ty?*

> Oh my love
> Where have you gone,
> My love, oh where?

Lizaveta would be out of her room any minute.

"We can't just leave him sitting there," said Olga and opened the front door.

Bobby looked back at Valentina but she was as lost to the world as the girl's lover in Voronezh. "Phew, what a smell!" was all she said as, in spite of herself, she followed Olga out into the stairwell and caught sight of Sasha stretched out by the lift.

His eyes flickered; bubbles of sweat had collected in the runnel of his upper lip. Bobby knelt down and touched his head as if to satisfy herself that this form of him was real. Olga administered a couple of stinging slaps to his face and got her hands under his armpits. "Heave ho," she said efficiently. "Give me a hand." They staggered back with him to the room.

Valentina was still scrubbing and chanting, her bottom moving resolutely as she gave the lino a good going-over:

> *Yesli, miliy*
> *Brosat stanyesh*
> *Nye rasskazyvay,*
> *Shto znayesh.*

> If you leave me
> Never kiss again
> And tell our love.

"God knows why I bother," panted Olga when they had got him into her lobby. She fetched a tin basin filled with warm water left over from the tea-kettle. Sasha lay supine staring at the ceiling, his eyes open.

Bobby passed a hand over his face. "He can't even *see*, for heaven's sake."

Olga realised this must be the first time she had ever seen Sasha completely drunk. "No, darling, he can't. He won't until he's vomited. Then, it'll be like magic – Poof! He'll stand up and be a human being again."

She had no grounds, from experience, for the assertion; but it might cheer the American girl.

But Bobby seemed to have lost interest. She wandered back into the main room and was flicking through Olga's books. "You like everybody, don't you, Olya?" she called out after a long silence. "I suppose that's why I'm so fond of you."

Olga found this inexplicable bent for the analysis of every trivial action perturbing and unnecessary. She went on laving Sasha's face.

"Nonsense," she replied, rinsing out the last suds and towelling his hair vigorously. "What else can you do? . . . All right now?" she whispered in Sasha's ear and wound the towel round his head.

She got up and stood by Bobby at the bookcase, wiping down her hands on her skirt. "If you saw someone being *destroyed* because they couldn't fit in, you'd try to prevent it if you could." Her voice shook.

Bobby played with the straps of her bag. "I think you're a really great person, Olya," she said overcome with the confusion and unseemliness of the scene they had just witnessed.

"Yes, sweet, can't you just see me turning into a saint?" She went back to the lobby.

Twenty minutes went by punctuated by Sasha's groans. The women had laid him out on the floor and Olga put a cushion under his head; he seemed to be asleep.

Her cigarettes exhausted, Bobby was testy but, it seemed to Olga, reluctant to leave. Before she had wanted to go but now something was stopping her. Perhaps the girl had some idea of reconciliation and needed Sasha to herself for the last time. There was that to consider. And Valentina, of course – she had noticed nothing yet, fortunately, and Olga had to have time to sober up Sasha before the widow was introduced to her Mr Right. Why she cared she did not know; Sasha was sure to put his foot through that relationship too.

"Tell me about the Kuznetsovs," said Bobby, for something to say. She stood under the archway between the lobby and Olga's room, her eyes averted from Sasha who had begun to snore. "I've never seen them, have I?" She went on idly worrying a fingernail with her teeth, restless as a bored schoolgirl.

Olga flicked Sasha's face with a wrung-out cloth; his head jerked reflexively and drops of water flew from his hair. He chewed his lower lip.

"Hardly any of us do, my dear. They're our creepmice tenantry, nocturnal feeders. Anna is nice but dull; her husband is mildly crackers. Whoops!" she exclaimed hurriedly putting her basin under Sasha's chin.

Bobby fled back into the main room. "Oh God, how revolting!" she stormed in English.

"What a crazy evening," said Olga to the wall. Sasha opened his eyes and seemed to recognise her voice. "Lucky you that I was the one to find you. Next time you can stay in the gutter."

"You're a wonderful woman, Olga Sergeyevna," he gasped with an alcoholic catch in his throat.

She covered over the tin basin with a fresh towel. "I'm just going out for a minute," she called to Bobby, her hand on the doorknob. "His wits are coming back to him."

In the kitchen Lizaveta and the widow were quarrelling. The air twanged with the soprano screech of Valentina's earthy imprecations. By the sound of it, Lizaveta had met her match.

Olga quickly ducked into the bathroom, locked the door and ran both taps. *I should have left him to his widow instead of trying to do the decent thing before they met. Bobby is no good at this sort of thing. Rural womankind with full bosoms, jam recipes, herb possets and immemorial spells is more in his line, silly motherless lad.*

She smiled. Sasha had no idea what was waiting for him at the other end of the passage. Sometimes it was fun to be a spectator.

Sasha came to without warning. It was always like that: one minute you're as rigid as a bone, the next you can see, smell, move and hear. The hearing part was excruciating: there was a voice floating above his head; an insulting voice, the sort of voice you might expect if you were a religious maniac coming out of a trance or a prisoner going off his head in a cell.

"Jesus Christ, I *hate* you!"

His body seemed to be made up of disconnected appendages. He sensed his head turn as if of its own accord, and saw his left arm lying, like a severed limb, flat against Olga's straw matting. Beside its hand was a pair of light-brown ankle boots and from them a pair of women's jeans ascended to somewhere beyond his range of vision.

"You never loved me, you just enjoyed hurting me, didn't you?"

It sounded crazy. He wasn't sure if he were meant to answer.

His eyes were isolating further resurrectional details: one disgusting foot poked uncleanly toes into his visual field, and further up he could sense some glutinous mass making contact with his chin. The voice wriggled through his insides like an exquisitely painful worm.

"I'm *so* grateful to you for being drunk tonight, I really am. You chose your moment. How much did you drink? Go on, how much did you put away? You sprawling great pig. I never understood your game, I wasn't clever enough. You went after me because you thought I was rich. I just got dragged along. Standing round, flapping like a starveling crow, terrified you were going on the bottle, miserable, always dreading you were going to have one too many. You great booze bladder, you spineless clown."

"Bobby!" He moaned and closed his eyes again.

"Get up, get up, you slob," she went on, becoming more and more excited. He felt a sharp crack in his knee. "Get off your back, creep. No man's going to leave me high and dry, halfway there, and get away with it. Try standing up. You bastard!"

Waving around like a stag-beetle on its back, stung by the blows, he managed to struggle up and get a stool under his right elbow. She was pacing Olga's room in her boots, her face distorted with passion.

"You're the one who had the fun." She advanced on him, and he cringed back, desperately twisting away his legs. They felt like broken stilts and he didn't know if he could trust himself to them enough to stand. "You didn't need new clothes or furniture but you got them out of me, didn't you? *And* slagged me off to your crummy friends. That fat, old hag, that widow . . . another pile of furniture she's brought you too, all that china, all that useless stuff. My God, I wanted you, but you only wanted my money. Your poky little existence had disintegrated so you thought my money would build it up again for you, didn't you? Did you never think it was *wrong* to use me like that? Or are you really the corrupt bastard I take you for? A creature of your own rotten system?"

He had an image of deep-frozen maggots writhing into life at the touch of a warm platinum electrode to their underbellies.

"All the time, there you were, plotting, scheming. All I wanted was you. I thought Russian men did it differently. I couldn't stand your sort of cruelty – just fooling around with me. The way you went at it was *abnormal*. Perhaps you ought to see a doctor. And take these filthy things with you."

There they all were, raining down on him, thick and fast: the pleas of lovelorn, dysmenorrhoeic virgins from Kaluga who thought they were going mad because they fancied women; requests for abortifacients, cancer cures, contraceptives that didn't make you sick; for help with addictions to drugs, home-brew, little boys. The unaired reptilian flanks of the shaggy Russian beast.

So she had taken them after all.

They whirled through the air, zigzagging over Olga's floor and he grabbed at them, recognising his own letters from the widow, and Tanya's petition.

"This is the end," said Bobby. "You're poisonous, you all are. I suppose you can't help it, Olga's the only one who's kept herself aloof. But even she's so submissive, so deferential. So *whipped*."

He found he could make it on to his legs. "Look," he said, weary of the vicious platitudes. "Your trouble is, you've never been afraid in the whole of your life. That's your good luck, and that's all it is. Don't think you wouldn't buckle under too, if you had to live like me, and her. Forget me, but shut up about Olga – she's got more steel to her nerve than the whole of the United States Air Force."

She smiled in contempt. "You're all so afraid, aren't you? There's no reason for it, it's in you, I've no idea why. This isn't my first time here, for Christ's sake, I'm not a greenhorn, no one I ever knew got into trouble. It's all play-acting, isn't it? A bloody great national farce. You're all too idle to answer letters so you say they've been confiscated. You want to get to America so you learn Hebrew and get yourselves sacked and whine about Jerusalem when you know it's only a staging-post for the fleshpots of the US. You pretend to be poor so that dim-witted outsiders will feel guilty and start digging into their pockets. You're all so feeble, broken-backed and subservient, begging for hand-outs. You make me feel sick."

"Well," said Sasha, bundling up the letters and papers. "That's that, then."

She wasn't finished. "A year ago I was one hell of a staunch defender: brave Russians, indomitable, unmaterialistic, making us look degenerate. That was before I met you, and some others, and set eyes on this ghastly dump." She flung out a hand, palm upwards, indicating Olga's room. "As if that weren't enough, you had to *hu-mil-iate* me on my last night, inviting *her* here, that moronic little peasant with beetroot hair."

His look of bewilderment enraged her.

"Don't come the innocent with me!" she screamed. "Save that for Olga, it's wasted on me! You knew, you knew, you crafty little faggot! She was on her way from Rostov all the time. I read her illiterate senile ramblings. I knew your game all along."

He looked around unsure that some other woman wasn't already in the room, hidden behind the furniture waiting to spring out and claw him.

"What do you mean?" he stuttered. "What do you mean? Invited? Who? Who's turned up now, for Christ's sake?"

There was no holding her. "Olga has a wet-dream Lord Byron. You get your dream girl out of an evening rag, up to the eyeballs in cheap rouge." She put on her spectacles, and looked him over. "She's probably in bed now, waiting for her clod-hopping Don Juan."

Olga was in the passage looking fraught but controlled.

"Was that you saying goodbye to Bobby?" she whispered. "Aleksandr Mikhailovich, you have a visitor."

So it was true. The widow had arrived. That was all he needed. Well, the sooner she turned around, packed up and went home, the better.

"Oh God, Olga Sergeyevna. Please, can you stall her for a bit? I can't face her this minute."

Olga brushed him aside. "Get out of my way. I've done enough for you."

15

The wretched confession of Sonya K. about the goings-on of her geography teacher Natalya M. lay face upwards on the leaky cistern of the communal lavatory.

". . . But she touched me first. We were alone on the platform, and I remember how cold it was, that winter of '78. We had our arms round each other to keep warm but suddenly she did something to me which I'd never imagined possible . . ."

I should think you didn't, thought Sasha. So that's what transpires in the murk of provincial railway halts. And to look at girls you'd never think . . .

He felt some sympathy, nevertheless, for the ill-starred Sonya's awakening in the backwoods wastes. Women never failed to surprise you: at one end of his own passage was a crazed American female with bizarre appetites; at the other some prying, rural widow who would want, in one way or another, to remould his life according to her bumpkin notions of domestic bliss. He hadn't yet clapped eyes on her but as sure as eggs she'd have some all-embracing vision of life that meant he'd be deprived of everything which made it worth living. Women like that went through your jacket pockets at night, smelt your collars for traces of alien scent or powder marks, looked under the mattress for stray items of other women's clothes and always got to the telephone before you.

He felt round for his cigarettes but he seemed to have lost them. Who had he been out with? Not Len, not Borya; neither would have let him come home in this state. What had he been drinking? It must have been distilled by a Japanese suicide pilot in a zinc urinal, to make him feel so bad. He was getting too old for the game.

The first job was to get rid of this stuff, then come to grips with the effects of the kamikaze brake-fluid.

The colours dizzied sickeningly from floor to cistern – blue, white, yellow and, worst of all, a fleshy pink. He was going to be very ill very soon. If the widow saw this lot! His hands were clammy, his head thundered. She'd already have it in for him. For some reason he should have been expecting her, met her here or at the station, God knows why. He thought he'd been so non-committal, so distant. Never mind that, all this had to be junked, otherwise he'd have another woman swearing he was some kind of pervert, a freak by correspondence. Tears of self-pity prickled his eyes.

Kneeling down he sifted out the foolscap sheets of Tanya's petition: ". . . raising the consciousness of female workers . . . harnessing the power of the under-privileged half of the working-class . . . organising structures of protest . . . working women's movement . . . achieving real power . . ."

A shiver crept up his spine. In his room last month he'd been too bored to read it properly. You could get hauled in for this, and no mistake. No wonder she had looked so scared when the thing went astray. What the hell was going on in that office of hers?

He never read anything properly, that was his trouble. What had the widow said in her last letter, the one he had burned? Surely there was nothing in it about coming to Moscow? There was bound to be an inquest and she would want to know if he had kept her letters. It took him a quarter of an hour to extract all of them from the pile before forcing them down the waistband of his trousers. Then he set about tearing up the others methodically, splitting the sheets lengthways, sideways and across so that the resulting fragments wouldn't block the waste pipe. The unusually thick pages of the pink letter were hard to tear. Two handfuls at a time he dropped the bits into the bowl.

"Are you going to be in there all night?" shouted Lizaveta rattling the handle. He feigned illness and gave out a piteous moan; then pulled the chain. The old woman's footsteps receded, but there was whispering audible through the door.

When he came out all the women were clustered in the passage. Bobby waited while Olga pulled on a pair of overshoes. Lizaveta was standing outside her room in anticipation of a scene. The air was thick from the smell of burnt cake.

A plump, diminutive woman with fiery red hair, a yellow bucket in her hand, was framed in the doorway of his own room. As their eyes met, she put down the bucket and dirty water slopped over the floor. Her eyes slowly moved from him to Bobby. The American turned up the collar of her three-quarter length camel-hair coat and stared back boldly. The light from the single bulb in the shabby hall seemed to concentrate over her; her thick hair scintillated, her pale lips curled back in a smile, baring strong white teeth. She turned into profile as she pulled on her gloves and flung her pigskin bag over one shoulder. The youthful suppleness of the movement pierced

Sasha: here was really something to be on the point of losing; someone like that he had briefly possessed.

She rolled back the cuff of her cashmere and glanced at her watch. "Better luck this time, sweetie pie," she called to Sasha in English. Only Olga understood. Touching the girl's arm she shepherded her across the hall. Bobby tightened her coat-belt, looked round at them all as if taking in a final picture and preceded by her companion, disappeared round the flat door.

"So that was her," said Valentina, addressing Lizaveta as if Sasha didn't exist. There was a touch of awe in her voice. "How do they get their skin like that, like a baby's? They must use something clever, that you can't notice. It can't be natural, that glow-worm shine."

"Of course it's natural," said Lizaveta. "It comes from the water and cornflour they stole from the heathen Indians. They mix it in the mountains and their black slave people pipe it to all the houses in America. That's why their teeth are so big."

"Like shiny pastry," mused Valentina, her great bosom cradled in her folded arms. The sight of Bobby radiant in her long-stapled wools and cottons had unsettled, but at the same time, vastly impressed her. She felt flabby and her ankles ached in the strap-over high-heels.

"They'd do anything to have big teeth," persisted Lizaveta. "It's a sign of getting on, like being a millionaire."

Sasha wanted to die from misery and embarrassment. One accompaniment of a hangover like this was that you developed the odd inclination to burst into tears and fall down at a woman's feet. With this pair, that was not an option — they'd probably sweep round his prostrate form.

He licked his lips and tried to speak. No sound came.

"Just look at that," said Valentina to the old woman, deigning to notice him for the first time. "That's what I gave up my lovely home for — an abandoned man, a profligate. Why, I could kill you!" she screeched, working herself up and turning to him. "You serpent in my bosom. You creeping little toad. You're no man to bring me to this, to make me despise myself for the true love I bore you." There was a mordant, Old Testament grandiloquence in her speech which simultaneously anathematised Sasha and yet retained her intimacy with him by its use of the biblical "thou". "You feeder with swine. You consort of strumpets! The brothel is your habitation!"

"Whoremaster?" prompted Lizaveta, as familiar with the scriptures as Valentina.

"Whoremaster!" they chorused in unison.

"God help me," mumbled Sasha, now actually on the point of tears. "God help us all, what a bloody shambles."

"Don't you dare call on the name of the Lord with that whorehouse talk," said Valentina with a prim pat at her temple. "No man uses *language* in my presence. Just look at you," she repeated mournfully. "You should be ashamed to be in such a state. Where is your dignity, your self-respect, your manhood?"

He could feel the sweat gather in the hollows of his breastbone. If he didn't get away from them, he was going to pass out. The noise and heat were stifling.

He tried to move but his feet felt miles away. The widow resumed, garnishing her harangue with flourishes of her dumpy arms: "What would my poor husband have said to see me so slighted and con-demned amongst men, cut off from my kind, discarded like a cut flower of the hedgerow, despised in the land of the living?"

He wouldn't have got a word in, poor sod, thought Sasha, bitterly. Remorse, fear and panic battled with the undissipated fumes of the hooch, and he slapped the back of his neck to invigorate himself with the pain.

"I'm sorry," he said throatily. "It's just not been my day."

He knew it was inept but it was all his brain could formulate at that precise moment. The front door seemed a long way away.

"*Your* day! And what, may I ask, do you think I have been doing — hem-stitching the Tsarevich's cloak at the embrasure of the enchanted castle? I've been *scrubbing*, yes, scrubbing my hands red-raw to make a cleanly dwelling for a man who reels home polluted from harlots!"

His feet began to feel intermittently closer to his legs and he started to creep down the passage hoping the widow would allow him past. She lunged at him with both arms. Locking them round his waist, she let her whole body sag.

"Where do you think you're going?" Her voice cracked. "Don't leave me on my own," she wailed pitiably.

He was far stronger but she was weighty and hung on almost dragging him to his knees. It was like drowning.

"I won't be long, for Christ's sake," he shouted, trying to comfort her and wriggle away but beginning to lose his temper.

"You won't come back, you won't come back, I know!" she howled.

At the door he succeeded in extricating himself. Valentina fell away, her démodé Sunday-best stilettos scrabbling on the lino like lobster claws; all her fury translated into blubbering impotence. "I shall die!" she screamed. "I know I shall die."

Sasha bolted down the stairs three at a time. Outside in the yard he could breathe. The skips lay glittering in the stars, their functional lines rimmed with hoar-frost.

Shivering, and shoving his hands in his pockets he found the remnants of the letters he had not managed to dispose of in the lavatory. With the joyous sweep of a wedding guest dispensing confetti he flung the pieces into the air, kicking up his heels in a wild dance of abandon, his face upwards to the steely night whence the paper-flakes descended, lodging in his hair and catching at his clothes like the first heavy snow of winter.

His protean cries echoed round the court and reached the ears of Lev Kuznetsov.

"What on earth is that at this time of night?" said Anna Kuznetsova twisting in the last of her curl papers.

"Oh nothing. The call of the undefeated," said her husband. "Old Russia. *Staraya Rus.*"

16

When he got back, Valentina was taking down her curtains. A folding garden-chair stood beside his mattress. Gratefully he sank into it.

"Oh yes, that's right, just make yourself at home with other people's belongings," she said, turning to him, her arms full of unlined hessian. "You might as well enjoy it because that's the last home-comfort you're going to taste for many a long day, my lad."

The speech and actions had been well practised in his absence. Her reproach was intended to have exactly that touch of the maternal which a man might not expect in such circumstances. While he was in the yard, Valentina had been busy restoring her composure by applying fresh lipstick, teasing out her curls and massaging her neck with attar of roses. She was shrewd enough to realise that it wouldn't do to persist with the dependent ploy. Not that she hadn't enjoyed the display of shameless clinging. That always made her feel how desirable she must be in a man's eyes, and the picture of her own submissiveness opened her up in excitement, but too much of it could demoralise him and he'd lose all his go. You had to be careful to get it right. She wasn't going back home and she wasn't going to sleep alone, but he'd have to appear to take the credit for bringing her round to both decisions.

It was a poor sort of tale, the one he told her – that he'd not understood what she meant when she wrote about "trial marriage", that he didn't know whether it was to be in Rostov or Moscow, that in the end he couldn't remember if she'd said she was coming at all – but it was enough. He wouldn't have believed a word of it himself, but she nodded understandingly.

"Why didn't you tell me before?"

"Not much of a chance, was there, with all them? Valentina Dmitryevna, you wouldn't have a beer, somewhere, in all that, would you?"

"You're incorrigible. Valya, it's Valya, now we're sorting ourselves out." She smiled and brought him one of the two bottles of wine which had been cooling for most of the evening on the marble sill between the inner and outer casings of the window. "Quite incorrigible."

Her brown frock was creased and there was a stain on the skirt. "What a shame. With everything going on today I haven't had time to try out my new outfit. Moscow's so dirty compared to home."

In the middle of the room she erected a collapsible table which matched his chair, and began to lay out the food.

The fish, its head and tail hanging over the rim of Anna Kuznetsova's bowl, was the centre-piece. Setting a plateful of black bread, butter, hard country cheese and small pickled cucumbers at his elbow on the mattress, she turned to the fish and started to slice it up with the blunt breadknife.

"What was your old man like, then?" said Sasha, feeling replete and emboldened after several gulps of the wine.

"Ivan? Oh, he was a big fellow. Up there, about up to here on me." And she stretched up on tiptoes marking an apex with her hands some two feet above her head. "Broad with it, too. Strong as an ox. He did a lot of boxing. His Ma used to think it got the aggression out of him, but I wasn't so sure about that. He was champion of his unit in the Army – light heavy. That was when he watched his weight, of course. But it didn't last after we got married. I couldn't stand to see him fight, and he wasn't good enough to make a real sportsman. Oh, lovely he was, though; a man is when he's that fit, I always think. But it's funny, you know," she went on uninterruptedly, tearing the flesh of the fish with the obtuse blade of her knife. "Ivan, poor soul, such a manly man, he was terrified of going bald. And it wasn't as if he was much to look at – you know, hair or no hair, it wouldn't have made a lot of difference. But he was obsessed with the idea that his hair was coming out in handfuls. Made my life a misery sometimes with the embrocations. All in his mind, of course. Men do have fancies, though, don't they?" She stopped and winked at Sasha.

"I thought you said he was a great reader," he said, trying to fit her description of this cauliflower-eared giant and his receding hairline with what she had said in her letters about her husband's interest in Roman history.

"Oh yes, he was all that too, but it seemed to go off with the boxing. I reckon he thought both things were a bit of a dead end. Never really made it, my man, if you know what I mean." She looked sideways at him, and blushed slightly. "Now you, you may not be an educated man, but you'll go far."

Sasha had started on the rest of the wine and was drinking straight from the bottle. It was a Don white and ought to have been halfway decent but it seemed tepid and sweetish. She tried to make him pour it into one of the plastic beakers from her picnic set but that made it fizzy and he preferred the cool of the glass neck inside his palm.

"You've eaten *nothing*!" she exclaimed. He stroked his belly with a circular motion looking at her pleadingly as she went over to the window. "What do you think of these, then?" she asked, planting herself to one side of the sill and extending an arm like a child self-consciously beginning a class-room lecturette.

A row of dolls, variously sized from a couple of inches or so to a foot high was ranged in order of height along the ledge. Their faces had the coarse porcelain texture of duck-eggs and the red lacquer applied to their cheeks shone luridly against the pitted matt. Trusses of hemp coiled round their heads in imitation braids. Each was dressed in the costume deemed appropriate to one or other region of the motherland.

"My collection. I never had any children you see – not Ivan's fault." She smiled tenderly. "But I've still got longings for baby woollies and ribbons, bootees, mittens, all that sort of thing. I know it's silly." She cradled one of the dolls, lifted its skirts to show him the layers of petticoats and a pair of long frilly drawers. "From Yakuta. See?"

He supposed he could, in a way, she was such a homely type but he was squeamish about unutilitarian grandmotherish underwear. A bit uncanny, that dolly-dressing at her age. In any case, he disliked folk costume, thinking it fraudulent to make out that any peasant girl ever dressed up in so many clothes when she was supposed to be starving and diseased at the same time.

The doll's face had a brutish squint. He looked at the widow's vast bosoms. "Why didn't you and him have any kids?"

She looked down modestly. "Women's troubles," she murmured. "Down there, they had to take it all out. Not that it stops your *urges*," she concluded with a gay chirrup, and dived into another of her bags which still encumbered the floor. In a twinkling she had produced a hammer and started to thwack nails into the side-mouldings of the door-frame. Soon she had arranged a line of ornamental wooden spoons down the architrave.

The wine bottle still in his hand, Sasha crossed the room to inspect her handiwork. The largest spoon showed the domes of the Znamensky cathedral in Novgorod, picked out in scarlet on a salmon-pink ground; beryl ivy leaves wound round the handle. Another spoon showed the Uspensky *sobor*, not at Valentina's Rostov but Rostov-Yaroslavsky north of Moscow. The remainder had secular themes of no particular epoch: vineyards on the steep river banks, men after crayfish, red wheat curvetting in the steppe wind.

She whispered nostalgically by his side: "On Saturday me and Dunya used to have cocktails in a place near the station. Really scruffy it was, and we thought nothing would ever improve and we'd die bored. She dared me to take the plunge and see where I landed up: 'Down a back-alley over the bread-shop is about your mark,' she used to say." She gave a startling screech of laughter which buzzed in his ear-drum. "Wasn't so wrong after all, was she, my Dunyasha?"

"It's getting late," he said, wanting to calm her down, but she was in full swing, giving him the benefit of her views of his fellow-tenants.

"That Lizaveta reminds me of my sister-in-law, always dishing out instructions before she lets you into the house: 'Take your shoes off!' Shoes? She'd have the stockings off your feet as well if she could. What do you expect with a kulak grandad? It always pokes through in the end."

"It's really late," he repeated and wondered what the sleeping arrangements were going to be. Her letters had made much of the word "love" but "bed" hadn't figured at all. Still, his room had been done over again – the second small plus from his wooing arrangements.

Valentina did not appear to be in the slightest way tired from her exertions of the day. She roved the room, fiddling with her dolls and spoons, complaining about the harsh light and trying to fix up Bobby's little lamp.

"I ought to get cleaned up," he said, thinking she would settle.

"Just a minute," said Valentina. "First I must put away the food. You don't want to catch your death in that old bathroom at this time of night. Plenty of room in here, it just needs organisation."

She wrapped up the fish, stacked it on top of the bread and cheese, sided the dishes on to a tray and went off with it all to the kitchen. He watched her down the passage. In a few days she would be running the whole flat.

17

Lizaveta was silent but no doubt alert behind the partition. He groaned at the thought of her invisible presence but decided to spare Valentina that piece of information about bedtime life for the time being. Fancying he heard a sob from Olga's room, he crept out and put his ear against the heavy panelled door: not a creak in the stillness. Under his breath he wished her unmaidenly dreams and his face broke into an affectionate smile.

Valentina nearly caught him at it; at what she would have called keyhole-peeping, but he slipped away just before she emerged from the kitchen with a kettle, teapot and two cups on another tray.

As soon as she had set it down on her folding table she was off down the passage again. The sound of metal clanging on metal came from the bathroom.

The last thing he wanted at this time of night was tea, but he made an effort to please her by sipping the scalding liquid. He was looking round for the sugar when Valentina came in again, this time backwards, dragging after her a very small tin bath, of the kind used by all the women in the flat for washing clothes. She had discarded the washboard and half-filled the bath with hot water.

"Right, young man," she said, hauling it up to where he sat. "Off with that shirt." Without pausing she deftly grasped the collar with one hand and thrust the other down the front, undoing the buttons from inside and pulling the grimy shirt over his head.

"It's the first time I touched the bare flesh of him," she chuckled. "How did you ever get to grow up? There's nothing but a baby's feel to this skin, puffs up between my fingers like a monastery capon. Ah, what a milky boy, skin as soft as a heifer's teat."

His shirt had been soon flung to the ground and he sat on his chair stripped to the waist while she pummelled his back lovingly. Then she did the front, twirling the hairs round his nipples and glancing up at him audaciously. It was a thorough drubbing up and down, under his armpits, with her every so often excitedly splashing the water over his chest and back and wringing out deliciously comforting dribbles from the red and white flannel glove on to the nape of his neck. He slumped forward unresisting.

He felt sure that had he been several times smaller and she several times bigger, she would have picked him up by one leg and immersed him head down in the suds, lathering away at his bottom.

It was pleasant, this second time in one day, being washed by a woman.

"Now, what about the rest?" she asked, running her soapy fingers round the waistband of his trousers. "Do you want me to do a proper job or are you going to finish it yourself? I'll face the wall if you're shy!" And she went off into a trilling squeal throwing down the rough, yellow soap into the bubbles.

"You can watch if you like," he said, but took care to slide off his trousers with his back to her.

"You can take a blanket and sleep out in the hall," she said afterwards, regarding him with interest over the rim of her teacup.

She had her good points, he thought, no doubt about that: waist pinched in nicely from the spread of her hips; a rotund bottom set a little too far back but she carried it well; her neck was rounded and pale, no sagging. *Sod it, Biryusov, you sound like a Cossack horse doctor, you're not selecting a brood-mare for covering.*

Best of all, he liked her arms: the way the blanched unsunned side turned in on your sight, when she put up a hand to pat her hair and her sleeves fell back to the elbows. It was something to do with how the long bone levered on the point of the elbow. A luscious mechanics that must last them to the grave. A pity she had such whopping tits.

He wiped his forehead with an end of the towel. "What's up? I thought you said this was to be a trial marriage. When do we start trying?"

"I don't remember saying anything about a trial marriage," she said airily. "Not about that side of things at any event. What kind of woman do you take me for?" Her cheeks brightened and colour traversed her neck precipitating a rash-like blush at the vee of her collar.

"If that's what you're after," she went on, her voice rising, "I don't know that I shan't be very put out."

"What, don't you like me then?"

She seemed even more confused. "I mean," added Sasha, recovering his aplomb, "you can't go home tonight, can you? You've been on your feet all day, and you did come fifteen hundred miles to give it a try. A bit longer won't do any harm, surely?"

"I don't know that I shall. I'm a respectable woman. This isn't what I bargained for." She seemed to be working herself up and he nodded, hoping to deflect her sudden anger by complaisance. "I'm no fool, whatever you may think. I've done some checking on your pranks. I think I know your sort – very rapacious." She did not know what the word meant, but evidently it signified to her a taste for rape and ferocity combined. "Good at swinging your fists and pulling girls about. You may pretend to be helpless but you're probably very good at helping yourself . . ."

Sasha was genuinely wounded. "Me? I've never hit a woman in my life."

"That's hardly the point," she said, illogically. "Physical attraction doesn't make a marriage."

Sasha could not fathom the reasoning behind the introduction of this old wives' saw. "My mother said you had to suffer men, and she had a right old time with my Dad. I don't doubt you've got qualities of your own, but where I come from," she continued with a proud toss of her head, "where I come from you'd be sent to Coventry for letting yourself go over a hussy like that."

Now the destination of her crabwise logic was apparent: he had not thought he would be so fortunate as to get away with the Bobby business.

"That expensive foreign slut may have rolled into bed with you at the drop of a hat but you'd have to work at it to get a decent girl in my village, I can tell you."

"Oh her," he said, sure that she was already halfway prepared to overlook his transparent guile in denying Bobby. "She meant nothing to me. I've told you once, I didn't give tuppence for her, or she for me. It was," he searched for a phrase from the lesbian schoolgirl's letter to Tanya. "It was *purely physical*. You know, just one of those things."

"Most distasteful, men's needs," said the widow primly, folding her arms comfortably, her eyes fixed on a point above Sasha's head. "They should be corked up!" She gave a tremendous belly-laugh at the implications of her own imagery then leant across to him almost choking with delight. "Mind you, to be honest there's thousands of women being knocked about every day, only you hardly ever get to know about it. Out there you can practically do your wife in as long as you keep on the right side of the neighbours."

"But I'm not like that, you've got me all wrong," he protested, annoyed at her reversion to the topic. "I don't even *know* anyone like that." He searched his memory for marital tyrants (Borya? Len?). He remembered Tanya and wondered if Andrey counted: being married to Tanya might be a reason if not an excuse.

"Well, it's a question of your standpoint. You see, you're not a woman, so it wouldn't occur to you. And just try to imagine what it's like. How do I know what you're capable of? A bit of tittle-tattle here, an innuendo there and a girl starts getting the horrors. That Lizaveta, now — has she got a down on you or what? She told me you were the next best thing to a hookah-smoking Pasha with some very unlikely kinks in your straight-grain: prowling around all night, coming home all hours, two women in a bed. Ivan the Terrible wasn't in it. What would you think?"

"I'd have the sense to see her for what she is, a lying old bag. And a jealous one, too, come to that."

"Ooh, there we are, you see, we do fancy ourselves, don't we? It's old girls and young girls is it, too?"

Sasha, beside himself with rage, picked up an empty wine bottle and threw it at the wall. There was a scuffling noise behind the partition. "Writing it all down, are you, Lizaveta Ivanovna? Having a treat?"

Valentina wriggled luxuriously in her camp chair. She had kicked off her shoes and was massaging her toes. Her tights were thick, the seams round the feet a lighter shade than the brown of the fine webbing over the calves. "There's no smoke without fire, is there? Now take that American girl . . ."

Sasha gazed enragedly at her swollen feet. "Look, missis," he gasped. "She didn't count. Can't you get that into your Cossack skull? It was a case of here today gone tomorrow, ships that pass in the night, hello, goodbye, all that sort of stuff. I only gave her a . . . For Christ's sake, it was a *fling*, damn it!"

"Oh, yes," said Valentina enjoying the row hugely. "Who flung themselves at who?"

Sasha was not generally unaverse to the truth but this time he went for the big, requisite lie. "Who do you think? I'm about as pushy with women as a . . . a . . . homosexual copper. It was *her*, she did the asking, I didn't know which way to look, I tell you. When women like that let their hair down, you need a meat-axe to stop them." He ran a hand round his neck. "They're forward. Some men like forward women. I don't."

There was a long pause. "You know what?" said Valentina at last. "I like you a lot. You're so honest."

She stretched out her hand and slipped the dry, hard fingers into his damp palm. Squeezing the hand he pulled her nearer, put his free hand on her arm and began to stroke the elbow, whispering "Valya, Valya, how nice you feel, let's be nice to each other now."

He avoided looking at her face. She brought her stool closer. The rounded metal legs nearly overbalanced as they caught in the knotted rug Valentina had placed in the middle of the room. She was projected forward slightly and he quickly moved his hand away from her elbow and ran it over her lap. As she slithered from her stool in front of him, he kissed her upturned mouth. After that he did not know where to go: everywhere on her body, under his hands, extended yard upon yard of seamless cloth ribbed with bone, the seemingly uninvadable work of some rural corsetière.

"If you break my zip you can pay for the damage," she said nervously.

Chance would be a fine thing, he thought. "Valya," he whispered, wishing he could ask her straight out where it was situated.

She squeaked loudly when his fingers pinched her midriff and stood up.

"It's more natural in the dark," she said, flicking off the switch by the door, glad to extinguish the sight of his white face, his barley-coloured hair falling lankily over the forehead almost down to the blond eyebrows, his mouth half-open and smudged with lipstick. When the room was in darkness he heard her tiptoe back, trip over a cup and catch her breath. Half-rising to meet her, he found her shoulders but couldn't immediately locate her mouth.

They carefully rolled over together on to the mattress.

"My frock . . . Just a minute," she whispered and held him off. There was a rustling in the dark, and then she pushed herself up to him again, her white nylon slip fluorescent against the blackness. "Don't just play with me, feel me properly." And straightening her back she offered up her breasts. "See, I've lost weight this last month, thinking of you."

At first there was no way in. After some minutes of fumbling he discerned a free inch or two between the lower rim of the brassière and the equally hard upper ring of the girdle. She quivered mountainously as his arms spanned her torso searching for some release device at the back. Nothing except more hard ridges and struts. He needed the light to extricate her from this armature of stays. Oh, for Bobby again, who undressed herself. All the time he was kissing her, the astringent perfume of toilet-water got in his nostrils.

"Not very good at this, are you?" she said at length, disappointed at her intactness after his umpteenth essay at stripping her.

His face burned. "Can't seem to . . ." He began pushing down her shoulder-straps in a final effort to get her breasts to disgorge from their bindings. He longed for them to spill out, enveloping his head in mammalian heat.

"That'll do," she said sternly. "You're being too rough. I can wait and I'm tired. Give me the bed, you can lie over by the door."

But she didn't move and at last he tracked down the fixings. With a loud snap the brassière coupling parted and the hook shot away from the eye, whizzing across her back as the weight was suddenly released. Valentina's breasts floundered apart into the capacious bodice of her slip. With a clammy hand he tore it down into a ruck at her waist, fastened his mouth at the nearest great swollen nipple and sucked. She fondled his head, whimpering, tugging at the hem of the hobbling slip in order to give free play to her legs.

Sasha was content to proceed no further than to the other breast, luxuriating in the hardness elicited as she grated the point on the tip of his tongue with greedy, aggressive squirms and muted juvenile screams. He wallowed in her as she flailed around the exquisite centre of his mouth, her arms and legs jerking spastically, her flesh rigid and runny at the same time, like a great gelatinous curd-cheese on the point of ripening.

Somewhere along the line she had divested herself of the girdle and all the rest of the articles which had given Sasha so much trouble and she was now spasmodically clutching at his right arm trying to encircle the wrist and force his hand down. He allowed the arm to go slack and with a grunt she thrust his hand between her thighs. She was wetter and shaggier than a Murmansk seal, and he let her trawl with his unextended fingers along the slithery inner sides, as gapped-open as a slit pumpkin. He felt himself declining from the peak he had felt at her breast; she, too, felt it, literally, sweeping him upwards and downwards with an experienced grasp.

"You're not ready," she said in a matter-of-fact voice as if she had been waiting for bread to rise. "This won't do. I'll have it out of you, yet, my lad. On your back with you. It'll take me three minutes flat that way, I shouldn't wonder."

She rose up before his eyes, but all he could see was the phosphorescent petticoat shimmying out like an ectoplasmic shroud from the insensible black of the lightless room. It flung itself this way and that, lifting and dropping, blue-white sparks spitting from the folds as it fluttered crazily like washing on a line in the still air of a vault. Somewhere above him the great breasts sloshed, oozing with the lactic serum his tonguing had expressed. His thigh bones were squeezing inwards from the pressure of her knees.

"Hell," he complained. "That bloody hurts."

But she had him pinned to the mattress, her arms fully extended and her strong hands athwart his shoulders, pressing him down. "I'm on top now," she said fiercely, and he smelt and tasted the olive and peppercorn of her sweat trickling along the deep gutter of her formidable bust. He tried to tell her that Lizaveta was awake on the other side of the wall, intent on every fluid squelch, every choked-back, lickerish whinny, but she was lost to sense and had him semi-engaged, crimped in the sticky furze, and head up, eyes to the unseeable wall, was riddling him, pitilessly, between her splayed verges.

He was engulfed: it was the opposite of falling into a crevasse — it was like being straddled by a chasm, having it bear down, the walls remorselessly straitening you until that unimaginable moment when ice touched ice through you and you flattened annihilatingly to a blood-hot squish.

"Get off, get off me," he yelled aloud. "You're killing me!"

Her body went limp, and the whole of her inert bulk shuddered above him like a stricken liner settling into the deep. "A-a-a-a-ah!" The shriek leapt across the silence like the electric bolt from a transformer, and for a millisecond after, thrummed in the viscid air. "Sweet . . . sweet . . . *my own* . . . sweet, oh so sweet." And she collapsed on to his chest, her upraised bottom thumping down, taking the wind out of his solar plexus.

He had thought he was due for his first heart attack. While he was recovering his breath, she offered him solace: "Poor thing, didn't get much out of that, did you? Here, let me. We can't have any unfinished business." And she took him comfortingly between her emollient breasts and tried to caress him up into some semblance of what he had been. "Poor sweet," she murmured after a few moments of ineffectual care. "He's gone to sleep without his dinner. Is it that you can only get to the end with younger girls — like that foreigner?"

"No, I'm tired, and there's the drink too, that doesn't help. It'll be better," he promised. "I'm just tired. Don't go away, that's all."

She lay beside him quietly and pulled the blankets over them both. "It'll be all right, dear, you see. I don't want you to be saddled with all that effort and not get any enjoyment out of it. I'll make it up to you, not to worry."

Sasha put out a hand to Valentina's genial thigh. She was warm and he snuggled up.

It would be the first whole night he had ever spent with a woman.

IV

OBSEQUIES

18

It was hot. Marina's Irish wolf-hound, the stud-dog she had bought two years before in the hope of making a few roubles on the side from mating fees, was trotting restlessly backwards and forwards, the full length of his lead extended from the running chain which had been linked to a horseshoe nailed to the door. No employment had ever been found for him: his temperament was too hysterical for untroublesome mating, and Andrey had sold his gun after arguments with the militia over his drunkenness, so the dog, once rangy and fit, had declined from lack of exercise and the evaporation of Marina's enthusiasm to an unpredictable foppish beast which ate too much and, in Marina's absence, had to be chained up away from the cats and pigeons in case he took it into his head to go for them.

Olga was very frightened of this dog and tried to divert him by throwing some scraps of meat which she had collected for the purpose, to the far side of the door. He snatched them up eagerly and she stretched a hand to the door knob, but when he caught the house-scent of fried potatoes and soup as the door swung open, he twisted round with surprising grace and bounded up, chain jingling. His back was level with her lower ribs as he sawed the air with his nose and wagged his tail hesitantly.

"Now, Jim," said Olga, terrified he would leap up and set his unclipped paws on the shoulder of her white spring frock.

"Now, Jim, be a good boy."

His name was another of those blind alleys up which Marina's enterprise always seemed to lead. She had christened him "Arion" but he would not respond to that in spite of intensive coaching. Finally, Andrey had gone back to the man who had sold him to her, a one-legged shoe-repairer with a kiosk near the Bird Market, and asked what his original name had been. As soon as the old man whistled and called it out, Jim had sprawled over him, licking his face and hands, knocking over the piles of boot polish and laces in the little box.

But today Jim was a model of deportment and kept his forelegs to himself, content only to paw Olga's skirt and whine. She gave his straggly hindquarters a pat and pushed the door open furtively. Around the knocker the dried-out splits and veins of the untreated wood were speckled with spring sunlight.

"There's a lovely boy, now, where's your mistress, Jim?" She escaped into the dark hall as tufts of moulting hair lifted along his backbone.

"You need to show that wretched animal who's who, lovey," said Marina coming out of the kitchen. "Jim – stay boy, lie – this minute!" The dog slavered copiously, his tongue uncurling; his tail brushed from side to side but he remained standing.

Marina slammed the door. "Dear, oh dear," she said, kissing Olga on both cheeks. "A fine house this is. Even the dog has a mind of its own. If Andrey had a chicken farm, the hens would answer us back. Come along in, my sweet, come along."

Olga stumbled around broken-open packing cases which littered the passage.

"His latest fad," said Marina. "Rabbits – but he forgot they needed hutches till he'd brought them home and now we can't get them out from under Tanya's bed."

"My watch broke," said Olga, pulling off her headscarf. "I must be awfully late."

"Time stopped here years since," answered Marina. "If anyone asks the time I always say 'a quarter past two'. That sounds a reasonable time to get stuck at, don't you think? A warm time, a sleepy time. Even the voracious birds doze at a quarter past two."

She brought out a bottle which had been hidden in the wood-shavings collected from Andrey's lathe for the rabbits' litter. "Thinks he can find a safe place for it," she grinned. "As if I'm not up to every man's tricks. And he never notices when I've topped it up with good Moscow tap water."

She held the vodka up to the sunlight which poured through the broad leaves of the shapeless lilac, its greenery almost obscuring the aperture of the back entrance, wands of unwinnowed stripling shoots making a *chevaux-de-frise* at the base of the trunk. "Enough here to set our knocking hearts to rest," she said. "Enough for a kick, more than a drop."

She filled two tumblers and raised her own to the ceiling, as if in a toast. "Absent friends," she called savagely, loud enough to intimidate the pigeons. "Here's to the precious blood, *aqua vitae*."

Olga nibbled a square of rye bread, the vodka flaming in her gullet. Jim set up a reverberating howl in the street.

Marina spread out her hands with the orderly gesticulation of one whom alcohol has already affected, and who enjoys the brief sensation of control over the objective world which it first brings. "These great hunting dogs, they need space, they want the wild moor to roam, not to have to cock a leg at the end of a tether in my backyard. I've grown to hate him, that beast. He can live in his own mess. Raptors, predators what good are they when they can't set beak and tooth through the hasp of their own chains?"

Olga stared past Marina into the garden, unanswering. One rainy morning last autumn workmen had moved in searching for a leaky gas main. Nobody said if they had ever found it or would return for their abandoned pickaxes and rolls of tarred paper. Now a couple of crows preened their tail-feathers on the deal shuttering boards spattered with hardened lime. A half-empty bucket of cement had set hard and the handle was sealed at a grotesque angle to the rim. Dribbles of cement lay everywhere like grey cow-pats surrounded by grass.

The mechanical digger which had devastated the little glade, once the last remnant of the spaciousness Marina so much prized, was embanked in one of the hollows it had dug, red soil flecking its scoop with bright orange spots of ore from the depths of the footings the workmen had put down. Bubbles of rust crumbled on the dry metal. The garden was devastated: only the lilac remained amidst the chaos of bindweed and ground elder creeping over tools and materials.

Olga took a small sip of spirit. "Didn't you used to write poetry, Marina Andreyevna?"

"As a girl, like all girls. All girls worth their salt, that is." She looked at her hands. "Why do they think it's only boys who do that? Why, at my school we wrote verses all the time, exchanged folders of the stuff, read aloud to one another under Pushkin's statue on the Tverskoy Boulevard in summer evenings. Now it's all men and dogs and that awful chess and newspapers. Women had the souls in my day. Have you kept yours?"

This was a conversation Olga did not want. She leant forward and tenderly placed her hand across Marina's swollen finger-joints.

"Does the spring make it any better, the rheumatism? Now that the cold's gone, I should think . . ."

"It's not rheumatism, that's an undignified complaint – for spinsters and old soaks. Arthritis, girl, arthritis! The fiery one! You don't creak, you burn, like a hundred unregenerate devils in hell. Purified by flames. Ha!"

"Yes, dear, but can't they do anything for you?"

The old woman raised herself heavily and reached for her tobacco tin on a shelf above the sink. "Do? Do? They offered me a place at a sanatorium. Do you know where? In Kislovodsk! What could an old cripple like me do of an evening, surrounded by fully paid-up crocks, on my own in a dead-and-alive hole like Kislovodsk? My Patience would have come out and they wouldn't have let me drink."

Marina's interminable game of Patience was a family joke. She was afraid of taking it seriously, believing that if it ever came out, she would die. It was Andrey's unacknowledged charity to disarrange the cards whenever she was on the point of a solution. Although he did this surreptitiously she depended on the knowledge that he would perform the favour but never referred to his doing it, and every time she resumed a sequence which he had disrupted, she complained that someone had spoilt the game. Normally an irascible man, he was patient with the charade, evidently counting it as a corporal work of mercy.

"Marinichka, darling, what an old grumbler you are! They only want to help. They can do such wonderful things now."

Marina heaped coarse tobacco strands on to a rectangle of semi-transparent paper. "With their chemicals, you mean, those trypano-somes and benzines and psoriasis, all that mumbo-jumbo bag of narcotic imps and tricks!" The words for diseases, microbes, drugs and bacteria were incomprehensible to her, but subsumed in her mind under the heading of "narcotics" – a word familiar from the TV and the gossip of her grandchildren. "The world is full of lotions and powders."

Olga sighed at the old woman's upsurge of anger and uncharacter-istically poured herself another measure of vodka but set the glass aside untouched. "Perhaps you're right, perhaps you're right. Some-times I feel we're all being quietly poisoned, even the best and the most dear."

She avoided Marina's eyes.

Marina perceived the hint. "Hasn't your man been in touch? Didn't he telephone or write?"

"No, not a word."

"Well, we had a card yesterday," said Marina, gulping the rest of her vodka. "So the post hasn't completely gone to pot."

"What on earth's he doing, writing to you?"

"Not from him, you goose, from that American girl! If her date's right it's taken four months to get here: I don't believe that but you can't read the postmark. Horrible, isn't it?" said Marina tossing over a view of the interior of the Museum of Modern Art in New York. "God protect us from painters and their catamites."

Olga had difficulty in making out Bobby's curvilinear hand.

"And God protect me from that kind of tasteless whiner," Marina went on. "I'm *so* sorry things are *so* rotten for her in America, poor thing, but whenever I clap eyes on my own daughter, I'm reminded which cat got the cream and which got its tail docked. I can't say it to my Madam abed upstairs, but that girl didn't exactly make a hobby out of the truth, did she?"

Olga gave up deciphering the card, having only pieced together the envoi "Miss you all terribly." "Tanya? What's the matter with Tanya?" She wanted to add "now" but guarded herself against an outbreak of the old woman's susceptibility by suppressing the word. There was no need, for Marina was already cross with her daughter.

"*The matter with her?* You heard her going on yesterday. God knows what the matter with her is, and He probably cares as little as I do. It's the effects that get me down: goes to bed at eight o'clock every night, gets up when it's still dark, comes in here for tea, sits in that chair," she pointed to a wooden caneback at the other end of the kitchen, "and doesn't say a blind word for hour after hour. Then, just when you're getting used to that, she bursts into fits of hysteria and we get tears and screams and mad cackling. I'm worn out with it. She has no energy – not that she ever showed much sparkishness at the best of times – and she doesn't even do the shopping and I can't get about like I used to. We'd starve if it was up to her, or kind folk like you didn't help out."

"She still holds down a job of work, Marina, and that's important."

"Work, is it?" Marina knelt down, swearing quietly at her stiff joints, and stowed the bread and potatoes which Olga had brought into a cupboard beneath the sink. "More like schemes and conspiracies all day with not a stroke being done by anyone except to thicken the Byzantine hotpot they've all got themselves into in that squalid office. God knows what they're up to, but it's killing Tanya."

Olga walked over to the open door. Beyond the garden stretched a wasteland of brick crofts and gutted nineteenth-century tenements; the pinkish evening horizon was jagged with crane-hoists and the naked beams of partly-demolished blocks. "Look at it, the Arbat," she murmured in English, recalling a line Bobby had quoted about the United States of America. "An old bitch gone in the teeth." Her attitude and intonation were sufficiently expressive for Marina to catch her meaning, as she tried to make herself comfortable in Tanya's hard-backed chair. "I'm frightened," she said. "One day soon, they'll come to scaffold us."

19

Olga gave a shriek at the touch of a hand on the back of her neck. Tanya had approached silently, her slipper-socks noiseless on the kitchen floor.

"Olichka, I sensed you were here!" she said in a faint voice as the other woman whirled round. "How wonderful to see you."

In the black shawl wrapped tightly across her chest she looked breastless; she had aged, the hair was sparser, her face was yellow and moist, the teeth more prominent. Under the shawl she wore a chemise which stopped above the calf to reveal spindly white legs.

Marina spat out a hard piece of tobacco leaf which had escaped on to her tongue from her cigarette. "Look at it," she shouted. "Repulsive! Slopping around like a wall-flower in a bordello, all camisole and dirty garters. If I were hale again, I'd take a rod to your back, miss!"

The younger women embraced, then stood apart, but close, face to face. Outside, those sides of the lilac leaves unpresented to the sun blackened in the declining light.

Fingertips at the declivity of the temples, as if seeking the nerve root of an incipient migraine, Tanya seemed to be on the point of swooning and she breathed shortly and deliberately.

"He took my papers, I know he did," she said, round-eyed. "I swear he did. He must have given them to someone, given them away when he was drunk, or telephoned the militia for a practical joke with a story about a political movement at *Feministka* led by this immoral journalist on a women's magazine who had foreign contacts . . . and an anti-Soviet mother. My God, we all spoke so freely in front of him."

"Don't you dare call me anti-Soviet," cried Marina. "I've done more time as a Soviet woman than both of you put together."

Olga was more uneasy about Tanya's ghastly appearance than what Sasha might have got up to. "That's quite impossible, my dear one. Sasha Biryusov knows better than to play hoaxes on the authorities. He's a good-hearted drunk with not a trace of malice in him."

"Is he?" shouted Tanya raising her arms ceilingwards. The shawl unravelled to disclose a row of indigo rosebuds worked into the fabric of the upper part of the chemise. These tiny islets of femininity were so incongruous in the wastes of Tanya's utility polyester that Olga smiled. The other woman did not notice and continued her obsessive berating of Sasha.

"*You* say he is, you would with your peculiar ideas about his type. To hear you talk you'd think drunks were put on this earth to do all our drinking for us – like monks do their praying."

"Tanya, you're not yourself, my darling. He's changed, he's a changed man."

"Oh yes, I've heard about that, too. These days he might look respectable, snoop round the Arbat in Levis and sports shoes, talking about kitchen gadgets. But do you know what he's doing, have you any idea what he's doing all the time? I'll tell you what that slovenly good-for-nothing is doing " She dropped her voice like an actress in the part of a lunatic escapee. "He's writing everything down, putting in reports on us, taking wages for denouncing us. Why did he suddenly turn up at my magazine last winter? Answer me that! Why did he get so friendly with your brother? There's an unlikely friendship! Why did he conceal the fact that he had kept my papers and tell me that he had destroyed them? Blackmail! Blackmail! That's why!" Her eyes were bloodshot from agitation of soul; her big face blotchy from the energy of speech.

"This is sheer insanity," Olga protested. "You have nothing to go on at all. I've lived in the same flat with him for years. He knows all about my views, my foreign friends . . ."

"Ah, Ah! But he never met *me* before, did he?" cried Tanya, pouncing on a fact she thought Olga had overlooked. "That evening. Remember? He couldn't look me in the eye. Now he's got a new suit. It all adds up. Something's happened. There's something in the air. Kirilyenko knew what it was."

"They sacked Kirilyenko, they showed *him* the door, not you," said Olga, unconvinced that reason was entirely to be abandoned. "Biryusov is settling down, thinking of getting married, turning over a new leaf."

"The only leaves he's turning over are those in the standard-issue Manual for Informers. You listen to me, Olga Sergeyevna. I know what I'm talking about."

When her daughter flung herself full-length across the table, her screams jarring with the crash of broken cups and the flapping of the pigeons' wings, Marina had fled.

After an interval in the street, long enough to smoke two cigarettes, she returned with Jim at the end of his lead. As soon as he saw Tanya he dived under the table to the side where she was sitting and put his nose up her skirt.

"You scabrous animal," said Marina gently, with a tug at his collar. "Have this." She offered him a large gherkin which he wolfed in two bites. His leash unfastened, he went over to a dish in the corner and drank the cat's milk.

"It's a disgusting world," said the old woman. "But the least of the vices is gluttony." She squeezed her daughter's shoulder but Tanya's ire had been extinguished by her wild fit and she did not move. "My mother was so lovely but she never danced. They were brought out too young in those days. She was just a child in swept-up hair and unseemly décolleté – no man was as interesting as the champagne sorbet at the buffets. The taste for sweeties kept her straight for ever afterwards – no woman can cope with *two* appetites."

The old woman pressed her nose against the window glass and confronted the pallid spring night, as withdrawn, for a short space, as her daughter. Unalarmed by this apparition from the lighted kitchen the garden crows stumbled along their branches, cawing in the haze which rose from the Moskva.

"Well, I've got to eat if no one else has," said Marina, and she began to peel some of the potatoes Olga had brought, bathing her hands in the flow of sweet Moscow water which gushed from the sink tap. "How's that booby brother of yours?" she asked, pulling a face at the back of Tanya's head. "Now that's real suffering; he looked to me like one marked down to perish, that pitiful man."

"Borya," said Olga quietly, gladdened by Marina's relieving presence. "Borya will never recover. He looks so old now, so harrowed. You'd never recognise him. He's just over fifty but he behaves and looks like a man of seventy. It's a question now of what will kill him first – *her* or the drink."

"I've never seen Galina," said Marina. "Is she some kind of recluse or what?"

"That's partly the trouble. She's so possessive that they never go out in case she gets jealous of someone he meets. He was such a sociable man at one time, made friends wherever he went. Now he's a prisoner in his own home."

"A booby, I said so. What kind of man puts up with that? Try doing that to Andrey." She detested her son-in-law but would defend him, even take a pride in his boorish maleness. Tanya sniggered. "Thank God you've got a man, my girl!" called Marina, slicing chunks of peel haphazardly from the potatoes. "What a spectacle you'd make trying to bag another."

"Tell that to Galya," Olga went on. "She's never realised what misery she inflicted on the poor wretch with her penny-pinching housewifery. That worrisome, repressive drive would finish anyone off, man or woman. He'd have been better with a trollop in curlers. She used to rouse him out of bed, nagging about being late for work. He never even had enough sleep. Now he lies there all day, coughing, his lungs in tatters. She can't bear his being sick any more than she could bear his being well. She wants him to die."

"A kind of ill-wishing commoner than any Christian would suppose," said Marina, scowling at her handiwork, a heap of mutilated potatoes with half their skin intact. "Don't talk to me about the torments we devise for one another."

"Here, you take the weight off your feet," said Olga taking a pinafore from a hook on the wall and rolling back her cuffs. "Let me finish those."

The old woman sat on a corner of the table and watched, unheedful of her daughter's savage face at her elbow. "My, my, what an old witch I've become. Hands like claws."

Olga splashed the water about, pleased to be active. "She's a very odd woman. I can't make out whether she hates him because he's ill, or hates him because he's done her some terrible wrong just by being a man, and she is frustrated because his illness prevents her punishing him enough for it. She gets ill herself and harries him for not taking enough notice of her. Last month she said she had a prolapsed womb, undiagnosed since her last pregnancy. And she was at the clinic every day accusing the doctors of incompetence while he struggled around trying to feed himself."

The Sunday before she had made a rare visit and found Boris semi-delirious on the sofa, his breath shallow and irregular, yellow mucus crusted at the corners of his mouth. The children were huddled in a corner watching ice-hockey on television. He was trying to write something in a notebook with a red ballpoint.

"Getting something down for the boys . . . doing their marks . . . it's dreadfully late."

There was nothing but scribble. She made the boys carry him down to her own bed and rushed out to buy some delicacy or other to tempt him to eat. When she got back he was gone. Galina had returned and forced her sons to take him upstairs again.

Tanya stirred at the end of this recital. "Why should she be an unpaid nurse? What has he ever done for her, except get her pregnant and let her give herself airs because she was married to an educated person? That won't get her through the long nights when his choking keeps her awake."

"Tanya, you really are impossibly selfish! Where does your spite come from?" Olga was outraged and Marina snorted with laughter. "Do you really think you mean more to me than my brother? I won't argue. That's the last time I'll tolerate your stupid, menopausal fantasies!"

"What a forthright creature you are, Olga Sergeyevna," said Marina staring into her daughter's eyes. "Very strong, very unflustered. Quite the reverse of our frail vessel here. Who is to keep night vigil with her? My force is spent." Her voice thrilled with malign tenderness. "Behold. Beloved daughter of mine. How she shrinks from her own shadow."

"Mother," whispered Tanya. "It's not shadows which affright me."

"Heavens!" exclaimed Olga disconcerted by the quasi-liturgical responses. "Come out of it, both of you – next minute you'll be spell-binding."

Tanya collapsed into giggles, the tension loosed from her body.

"Listen," she said in a collected voice. "I must tell someone again or I'll seize up. Things *have* been difficult at work, it's true. I wanted to get rid of that Kirilyenko horror and I built up a sort of anti-Kirilyenko beach-head. At first I thought I had it under control but as time went on I felt it was spilling out beyond me as if some other person were directing it and my role had been eliminated. Then, yesterday, something did happen: Kirilyenko was sacked."

"Yes, I've already said, wasn't that just what you were after?" asked Olga, fearing another rehearsal of Tanya's *idées fixes*.

"You don't understand." Tanya covered her face and rocked to and fro. "It had nothing at all to do with me. Tomskii, our Director, arrived in the morning." She paused as if this in itself were significant. "Generally, he's so idle, he's brain-damaged. He never goes anywhere if he can avoid it. Well, seeing him puffing round the office yesterday, I knew something big was going to spring – and I wasn't the only one. The atmosphere couldn't have been danker if he'd been preparing to shoot everyone." Carried away by her own excitement Tanya moved into her habitual journalistic overstatement. "Absolutely humming with the threnody of dread, the whole caboodle. I could tell by her face that that lecherous little sneak, Marya Fyodorovna, was hugging some nasty secret to herself. Meanwhile, Tomskii and Kirilyenko were in deep conferral. At the end there was no shouting, but after Tomskii left the secretaries reported that Philip Ivanovich was clearing his desk, and packing away the photographs of his old mother. Then he came upstairs. Masha was flabbergasted. 'Here he is,' she said. 'Your ex-boss, large as life, coming to see you up here for the first time ever.' 'Don't worry about me, Tatyana Borisovna,' he said, doing that horrible pecking with his head, like a clockwork chicken. 'Don't think you've got away with it. You've dug a pit for yourself. They'll be coming for you soon.'"

"He was lashing out, trying to get his own back," said Olga.

"As soon as he'd gone I got on to Tomskii, I needed to know the lie of the land. That's when things became really scary."

"A lie! You were born looking over your shoulder," interrupted Marina.

"Over the phone he couldn't have been nicer. Quite terrifyingly so. Not only did he know my name but everything about me. Normally he's such a slouch that he wouldn't recognise his own hat on the hallstand, but he knew me – names, age, length of service – just as if he had read it off from the personnel files. And all the time the charm *oozed*. Somebody must have put him up to it, frightened him into not frightening me, if you know what I mean."

"Lord help us, how many more times do I have to hear this?" said Marina. "I want my dinner." She got up and put a match to the gas ring. "They're a gang of crooks. It's as plain as the nose on your face. Very cultured, sensitive, ingratiating and criminally insane. People who write for magazines are bound to go mad because no sane person can have opinions once a week for a living."

"Aren't you going to put water in that saucepan?" asked Olga, wishing the old woman would keep quiet and cook. "You've done nothing wrong," she said to Tanya. "Try to keep some sense of proportion and don't let men like that talk down to you."

Tanya rapped the table with the back of her hand. "I can cope with the men all right, it's that smug bitch Marya Fyodorovna who really puts the wind up me. Today she barged into my office, waggling her behind in that gross way and inspected the place, just as if I were her sweeping woman and she wanted to check it was free of rubbish before moving in."

"Some columnist will slit that doxy's flawless neck one day," said Marina putting half a filterless cigarette behind her ear and lighting up another. "He'll rejoice to have found a practical way of alleviating evil."

"Oh God, Mother!" screamed Tanya. "Can't you go and read one of your thrillers or something. This is serious!"

The old woman grunted impassively and closed her eyes.

"A lot of people are going to be sacked," Tanya continued. "Kirilyenko is only the first."

"But, surely that's not too important, is it? There are plenty of jobs for a woman of your experience and you've not done anything . . . imprudent, have you?"

Tanya was silent.

"Well, have you?"

"That depends," said Tanya. "Tell me, is it true that that rough fellow in your flat has suddenly acquired new furniture as well as a new suit?"

"Oh dear, Tanichka, do try to control yourself. We've been over all that already."

"He has, hasn't he?" persisted Tanya.

"Yes, but that's his widow again. She's new to Moscow and her husband left her some savings. She's always buying things. You know the type – up from the country with a wallet, five string bags and a man."

"How do you know she buys the things? How can you be sure?"

"Well, he tells me and I see her. I can't ask for the receipts."

"And he's altered, you say? Respectable, now? Sober?"

"I couldn't swear to his being teetotal yet, but, yes, he's more restrained. He looks more prosperous – fatter, certainly. A car is next on the list, I think."

"My God, that does it!" shrieked Tanya. "I knew! The swine is on the take!"

"That's not it at all," cried Olga, incensed at the conclusions Tanya was drawing from her unwitting co-operation. "That's a terrible thing to say! If you must know, they do nothing but quarrel about money and he's always accusing her of being tight fisted. He wouldn't have anything to do with your affairs." She appealed to the old woman. "Marina Andreyevna, you should know him like I do. He's a *lump*. No one could trust him to remember to feed the budgerigar. He couldn't plot his way across the road. Do make her see sense!"

Olga was embarrassed. Spying on the neighbours was foreign to her but nowadays she was always on the lookout for Borya and the postwoman; and Sasha's quarrels with Valentina were noisy.

"These set-tos," said the old woman. "Do they start at night?"

Olga knew what she was getting at. Marina had a low opinion of the sexual competence of Russian working-class men. "As a matter of fact, they do, but that's irrelevant."

"Not at all, absolutely the very kernel of the matter. I always thought he was a tusker in heat, the way he looked at women. He must take her like a Viking."

"Really, Mother," said Tanya. "I know old ladies have bees in their bonnets, but don't you think that at your time of life . . . ?"

". . . they shouldn't think about such things, eh?" exclaimed Marina finishing the sentence. "I've had enough time on my hands since Stefan died to replay every bout I've ever had with a man. Wonderful early-morning reveries they make."

"There's nothing wonderful about their mating," said Olga blushing at the infectiveness of Marina's phraseology. "They just go bump in the night."

"No frills?"

"No frills, I'm afraid, Marina Andreyevna. It's really rather sordid."

Her knowledgeability was presumptuous. In truth she had seen little of Biryusov and his woman over the past few months. Whenever their paths crossed in the hallway or passage he looked the other way and reddened, for no reason Olga could fathom. "Of course, he still takes a drink, that might account for the occasional row," she went on. "That's part of her straightening him out, like his clean shirts and the polish on his shoes. The upheaval in his life simply arises from that. She's knocking him into shape."

Tanya seemed mollified by these details, which fitted her own sense of the predominance of the domestic in life over the professional aspect. "I wish I had the knack," she said, remembering her state of mind that morning when she stood in the bathroom ankle-deep in the welter of Andrey's dirty washing.

"It's quite amusing until she starts on me," said Olga frowning. "I have to put up with her without the compensations of being a bedfellow. Women like that seem to think you by nature incapable of man because you live alone."

Marina stroked Olga's back reassuringly. "Make yourself some memories, my dear, then you can participate again when you're my age and all the men are shades. I am peopled now by the revenants of a well-spent youth. I doze off amidst the hurly-burly of flashing limbs."

"Mother!" called Tanya from the other side of the kitchen where she was taking things out of Olga's shopping bag. "Mother! When are you going to do something about that dog? He's peed all over the eggs!"

20

Valentina Dmitryevna Afanasyeva had eight thousand roubles in the Savings Bank. Her husband had been a parsimonious man whose chief pleasure in life had been watching their money grow, and she was a careful manager with a delight in domestic economy. Most of their vegetables and fruit were supplied by her father from his own plot and there was so little worth buying in the country that most months she and Ivan could add at least half their wages to their stock of cash.

Only in Moscow did she begin to query the virtues of accumulation: what was the point of having money tucked away when every bright shop window invited the opposite?

Sasha had wanted a car, but that would have meant more cheese-paring and a long wait, and she had had enough of both, so he was dragged from store to store, his opinions canvassed about carpets, wardrobes, kitchen equipment, porcelain and glassware, none of which he wanted. There were exhausting trips to out-of-the-way shops which advertised some new gadget on the morning radio, where, on arrival, they were invariably told that it was a one-off item only and sold a quarter of an hour before; or was for demonstration purposes; or where the assistant denied that the item existed at all.

None of this deflated Valentina whose eyes lit up at the prospect of a renewed hunt the next day. Sasha, on the other hand, was depressed.

Two women in Biryusov's life had spent money. As an activity it had its interesting side. With Bobby it had been an expression of power, her cards conjuring something apparently out of nothing, a transmutation which reminded him of the only chemistry lesson which had held him rapt at school, when his teacher had described the fixing of nitrogen from the air. He had forgotten about the goods Bobby had produced as quickly as he forgot what nitrogen was for: the lovely simplicity of the technique was its all.

With Valentina's methods of shopping, there was no magic: her joy resided in the awkwardness of the problem and the inelegance of its solution. On those long-drawn-out expeditions by bus and tram, often involving visits to parts of Moscow he did not know and where they tramped for miles never seeming to find a passer-by who gave them accurate directions, the business was finally done – after jostling and elbowing first to get a sight of what she thought she wanted, queueing more than once to pay and then collect – with bundles of notes so dirty that they seemed to have been passed back and forth from hand to hand from one end of Moscow to the other.

The crush of folk all bent on the same exchange, distributing their re-usable vouchers for parcels that they tied up themselves, bumped up against one another, had to keep an eye on on the escalators, in the underground trains; which split from their inadequate sugar-paper wrappings, and weighed heavier and heavier the nearer they got to home – the whole gimcrack system of commercial intercourse inspired him with dread. As for the products, he was dead to all sense of them: quality was neither here nor there – it was the sheer quantity of encumbrances to his life which goods represented that caused him to cry out in hatred and despair every time Valentina pounced on him after work to show off some coveted knick-knack which, against all the odds, she had secured that day.

"And you know a woman *begged* me to sell it to her, the moment after I bought it."

Today they were to make a withdrawal from the Savings Bank as soon as Sasha had got back from work: she had planned an extensive foray to the plushier shops for a white wedding gown and veil.

He did not want to go home and wandered up and down the Arbat stopping now and then to gaze into the shop windows. Nothing attracted him except a rubber plant in a florist's on the corner. He watched as the young shop assistant dusted its unnaturally green leaves. The plant was priced at thirty-five roubles and had been there for nearly two years.

During that time Sasha had come to know it better than he knew some people, overseen the first vivid splodges exfoliating into fat jungle weed, glossy from the overheating of the shop and the assistant's lavish watering. She was bending over now, scrutinising it for mites, as delighted as he that its hideousness in the eyes of the buying public had formed a bond between plant and keeper. Sales resistance on the part of the goods themselves was something Sasha had learned to value.

"If she's going to take charge of you like that, you take charge of her money *before* she gets the ring on." Len was one of those tedious people who knew what everything cost; the kind of person Valentina would have been better suited to – with her "cash-on-the-nail", "no-questions-asked", "what's-it-worth-to-you?" kind of morality.

Len despised him for not extracting his price for the residence permit Valentina would receive on their marriage. The time had come, he said, for Sasha, in a manner of speaking, to "capitalise on his resources": "Get something out of it, you twat. If you can't use your brain, for Christ's sake use your cock. Who are you waiting for – Marina Vlady?"

Over the way was the beer-shop he had avoided ever since the incident with the empties. At midday there was no queue and he soon bought three bottles of Moskovskoye and was hidden behind the arch of an alley-way nearby swigging the first and looking out at the girls who were swarming from shops and offices for their lunch break.

In the shade it was chilly. Spring was always a flawed season, carrying over the bite of a winter not quite overcome. The real warmth would bloom in June, July. Their honeymoon time, Valentina had decided. At the end of July (the exact day had not yet been arranged) they would be married. Ahead of him loomed the absurdities of a ceremony which he knew Valentina was anxious to experience for a second time. Half of August would be spent cooped up with her on a boat, for she had booked them on a Volga cruise beginning shortly after the ceremony.

He watched the girls unlongingly. It was still early to leave off tights and jumpers: only high summer would fetch them out in white blouses and shirts, their legs bare, the sun sweetening the colours of their densely made-up lips and eyes. But even the memories of the diaphanous cottons, the soft, unmuscular arms, the smell of face-powder everywhere under the American maples in blazing afternoons along the Gogol Boulevard failed to incite his lust.

For most of his life women had thrown down a challenge which he had picked up mechanically, without hope, but with a comforting sense that he was doing his masculine duty.

They provoked; he responded, and something might come out of it; the play was fair. With Bobby, he noticed for the first time that the rules could be changed, unilaterally, and he could be expected to conform to an image which she had of him but which he could never have developed himself. Subsequently, with Valentina, this image could be varied again to suit her requirements. All women, presumably, had their ideas about a man. Those ideas had nothing to do with the man himself, and he could never predict what aspect he was required to produce at any particular time. The terrible feeling was that whatever he did could be right or wrong for reasons quite outside himself, and depended on another person's idea of who he was.

Observing the women in the bright street, he speculated that each one had her own, individual idea of a man, and the chances of the man he felt himself to be coinciding with the manikin she carried inside her head were practically nil. If, in that case, one woman was the replica of another, what was the point of getting rid of his widow?

She wasn't much to look at – there were no two ways about that. Most blokes wouldn't fancy her. He didn't himself. But that was a side-issue: he *couldn't*, even if he did, and that was the problem. Increasingly he thought he couldn't with anyone, ever again. Perhaps he was undersexed; perhaps they had been right about him all along at work; perhaps he lacked some essential drive; perhaps, even, it was the drink. None of these explanations did he believe. No, it was all much simpler – in some fundamental way, the desires which he had, which he once thought were the desires which made him an ordinary man amongst ordinary men, were, in fact, quite the opposite: this feeling he had to be himself, to set out his own impulses, to do what he liked, was a property of others, not of his.

"And I thought you were a real man!" was Valentina's refrain. "A real man would stand up to me." What sense could that make? He felt himself to be real enough – at one time man enough – without having to take a stand on or against anything, person or principle; he had hoped that he would eventually, without too much searching, find a woman to fall in with, agree with, stand together with. Why should she want him to quarrel? He hated the rows which Valentina seemed to thrive on. So far she had got her own way over the colour scheme for the re-decoration of his room (he had done the stripping, painting and papering); the moderation of his drinking habits; and his customary slatternly habits of dress. Not satisfied with easy victories over him, she had clashed with Olga about the use of the kitchen. Olga would not budge from her set hours and a rift had opened between her and Sasha. Though it was none of his making, Olga blamed him: as the man he ought to have been able to control Valentina.

Olga then tried to enlist Lev Kuznetsov on her side but he backed off, refusing to complain about the widow's high-handed ways with his wife's crockery and saucepans. Although the cosy harmony of the communal kitchen had been destroyed by one domineering, energetic outsider, Anna Kuznetsova took her husband's part and ceded to Valentina what, for no reason anyone could see, the widow asserted to be her rights.

If Lev, Anna and Olga, with all their degrees and education couldn't master her, how could he?

Then there were the nights. Had he been capable of exercising some dominance over her then some of it might have been transferable to the daylight world, but he could only blush at the recollection of his own failures in bed. As with everything else nowadays, she took the initiative there; often did it all herself. A real one-woman band.

He shivered in the sunless archway. Time was running out. There would be hell to pay if he were late. Dreamily he stood the three empty bottles in a neat row, walked backwards along the edge of the pavement and with a running kick, sent them crashing into a handbarrow parked at the end of the alley.

Sprawled midway up the first flight of stairs in the flats was a human figure. Blinded by the change of light from the open street to the murk of the interior, Sasha took several moments to take it in. A hat lay on its side on the bottom step; an empty bag and a pair of soldier's woollen gloves on the next up. A snore whistled through the sleeper's nostrils. There was a strong smell of spirit.

"Not again," groaned Sasha, picking up the hat and dusting it off. "Borya! What do you think you're playing at?"

An empty bottle rolled off Boris's chest as he struggled up, banging the back of his head on the stone steps. He rubbed the side of his neck.

"Hello, old chap, fancy meeting you here," he said vaguely with no real sign of recognition. "I've had a good time . . . I've had a good time, you know." His voice rose defiantly as he laboured to put a name to Sasha's face. "All good times . . . Al . . . Ale . . . Dreams, too, dreams . . . narrow, hard dreams, Alek . . ."

It was a matter of days now, not weeks, thought Sasha.

"Come on, old fellow, let's get you up these stairs," he said, ramming the hat on Boris's head and gathering up the rest of his things.

Several floors above, there was a clack-clack of a woman's shoes, the noise of the lift-gates crashing together and a whirr as the current engaged the motor.

Sasha watched the cage on its leisurely descent, curious to see who had been on his floor. When it was still some distance away he could see through the open mesh side panels that a woman was coming down. A woman in white leather slip-on shoes with almost flat wedge heels. Although she was not wearing a skirt, her ankles were exposed because the bottoms of her khaki trousers started higher up the leg than would be acceptable in a man's. The material of the trousers bagged out from a tight belt at the waist, obliterating the line of the thigh. This disfigurement ceased temporarily at the narrow waist which was encircled by a white leather belt matching the shoes, but began again at the midriff where more khaki stuff engulfed breasts and shoulders.

Marya Fyodorovna's hair had been re-styled. Gone were the sixties flick-ups brushing the slant of her cheeks; a frieze of auburn curls quivered along her white forehead like the fillet of a pagan vestal. The untight curls reached back to the crown of her head where the natural straightness, bushed by step-cutting, piled downwards to wisps flared out by careful undercombing.

She greeted Sasha as if he had walked out of the sea on to her desert island. "If it's not my unwashed Mr Wonderful! So this is where you pay your service calls." She turned to the moribund Boris, tapping the side of his nose with her forefinger. "You look after him, matey, he's the best equipped fitter since Potyomkin. A real stoker, that one."

Sasha lurched under Boris's weight. "Couldn't give me a hand, could you?" he mumbled, overcome by the same sense of fear and shame mixed with desire which had intimidated him at his first meeting with Marya Fyodorovna. He was slimy with sweat and she sniffed at the open collar of his shirt.

"My God, get that," she said. "Chock-a-block with pheromones!"

She had no intention of helping, so Sasha undraped Boris's arm from around his right shoulder and deposited him gently in the middle of the flight of steps. As he sank down, Boris twitched at the coldness of the stone. The girl pushed aside his feet to make room for herself and patted the step inviting Sasha to sit down beside her, but he remained standing, Boris's head resting against his knees.

"Holy Mary, Mother of God, pray for us sinners now and at the hour of our death," began the sick man, his mind wandering. He could get no further before coughing; the paroxysm seemed to tear at his vocal chords.

"Nobody's ever called me that before," tittered Marya Fyodorovna. "He'll be expecting me to wash his feet next."

Boris could still hear. "Oh no, dear. That was another lady altogether," he gasped between spasms.

"Lady-schlady," said Marya. "Who cares as long as the boy loves his mother?"

Boris's head flopped to one side, his mouth hanging open.

"Never had much time for all that kind of stuff," she continued, taking a very long cigarette from a soft pack and lighting it with overdone panache. "Most mothers are like mine – cows. Wouldn't get much change out of my prayers to her." One hand fending off the overplus of smoke burgeoning out from her amateurish drags she focused on Sasha through slit eyes, holding the cigarette away from her and allowing a grey line to plume upwards in the foetid air of the stairwell. Her nails were bitten down to the quick.

Sasha remembered what Tanya had said about her and the fear in her voice when she said it, but he weakened pleasurably at the unpractised simplicity of her pose and the candour of her malice, as one might when confronted unexpectedly by an untamed, elegant beast.

"The heat's done for him, darling, best let him uncrinkle in the cool. You must be flaked out, too. I know I am. I've done nothing but run errands all day and I'm soaked to the gusset." Resting the cigarette precariously on the banister rail, she unzipped a small glazed leather handbag of quite noticeably foreign manufacture, and withdrew a brown bottle of Caucasian mineral water.

"Here, take a sip of this. It won't put hair on your chest but then I shouldn't think you'd need it." He accepted gratefully, struck off the cap on one of the metal supports of the handrail, took a long drink of the water and handed it back down to her. Without touching the neck with her lips she poured about a third of the liquid into her mouth, gargled as if it were antiseptic mouthwash and spat it out over Boris's shoes. "Can't stand the stuff myself. Plays hell with your insides." Sasha shuffled on his step, wanting to sit down and rest his legs but nervous of doing anything that might rouse her to further acts of appealingly sinister unpredictability.

Lighting two cigarettes at once, she inhaled both till they glowed, then passed one up, at the same time indicating the empty space once more and hutching up to the wall encouragingly. After carefully setting Boris's head against the balustrade, Sasha ensconced himself alongside her thigh. Marya Fyodorovna rubbed her upper legs together like a little girl anticipating an outing.

"That's right, that's lovely. There's no hurry, no need to rush off. Let's have a nice heart-to-heart. I've had a perfectly ghastly morning. The stink of these flats is indescribable in the summer."

Sasha, feeling more and more awkward at his own inability to think of anything, said the first thing which came into his head: "Are you collecting for something, then?"

This she found wildly funny; and as she threw up her hands to her face, her alto laugh carolling from wall to wall, she unsteadied the bottle of mineral water and it rolled away, chinking from step to step before coming to rest on the landing below.

The noises woke Boris who, with his head askew could only glimpse the side of Marya's head, the lobeless ear presented to him nestling amid the flaming locks.

"Child, I know you," he said in a gravelly voice, his throat unresponsive to his lips. "You stood with me once at Kolomenskoye, unbedecked, the water in your hair salt from your own tears, in a cleft where the women from the orchards go down to bathe, your innocent eyes cleansed from the dust. I know you in your nakedness."

Sasha turned his back on Marya Fyodorovna and stretching out an arm, laid his head against the side of Boris's face. With his thumb he caressed the quivering eyelid. "Soon, Borya, Borya, you'll be home soon."

"He's gaga," said Marya Fyodorovna. "They get like that with the DTs – seeing floozies dance round in the buff."

Sasha felt irritated at the response but was nevertheless too nervous to risk her annoyance. "It's not really that," he said mildly. "He just wants us all to be saved."

Marya was nonplussed. "From what?"

"Don't ask me," said Sasha. "He only talks like that when he's drunk and when he's not drunk he can't remember what he's said when he was. Sounds quite nice, though, if you're in the mood."

"Suit yourself, it takes all sorts," said the girl. "Thank God I'm not moody." She yawned, put a hand under her khaki top and adjusted the shoulder strap of her brassière.

Sasha, having watched Boris off to sleep, recast his original question. "What *are* you doing here, then? Visiting?"

This question, too, was evidently a scream, for she laughed again louder and longer. "Paying my respects to the folks at home, to the salt of the earth, the backbone of the nation?" she said, suppressing her mirth with difficulty. "Is that what you mean? No friend of mine lives here, my dear . . . or ever will. Unless, of course, you decided to get chummy. Even then, it'd have to be a case of *my* place not yours. What a thought, though – slumming for it!"

With a shake of her curls, she suddenly cut off the jokey talk and resumed a matter-of-fact voice. "No, darling, I've been talking to people all morning. That's what I do, you see, most of the time. Just talk to people. They like talking, so do I, and so we get on famously. I had a marvellously instructive conversation not long ago with one of your neighbours. A dark little woman with a problem of superfluous hair . . ."

"Galina," said Sasha, involuntarily.

"Know her, do you? You should. She certainly knows all about you. A wife and a half, she definitely was, too. All rings and aprons. She flew about with the dustpan, the whole time I was there. My God, how the other half lives. A treasure, though, a treasure. She tracked through you all like a computer. We ought to have her on disk. A live catalogue of the locality with instant recall. Press the right button and she couldn't stop."

Some years before, the authorities, considering it uneconomical to collect household revenues for the newly-abundant Siberian gas, had removed the meters from the flats. Recently, with the energy crisis, there had been talk of re-introducing them. The truth dawned on Sasha.

"Oh, yes, you've got the right one there. She could take you to every single one in the whole block."

"Every what?"

"Every meter. Haven't you come about the gas?"

"Not the natural kind," said Marya Fyodorovna grimly. "Are you really a moron or do you only put it on for the ladies?"

"What's going on? What the hell is your game?" shouted Sasha, completely foxed.

The girl leaned back her eyes sparkling with malice. "I couldn't tell you if I knew myself. All I'm authorised to do is offer you a little something on the side, put a few drinkies your way. We could have fun together, sonny. Wouldn't mind working under me, would you?"

"I've got a job already," said Sasha defensively, now thoroughly alarmed.

"That's not a job, that's purgatory. Mine'd pay twice that *and* you'd keep your hands clean."

"I'd rather dig in my own dirt, thanks very much," he answered.

"Look, there's nothing to it," said Marya Fyodorovna, patiently. "One phone call a week with a few tit-bits about this stuck-up lot that fancy themselves your betters. A story or two, that's all."

Sasha's knees shook as he stood up. "What kind of stories?"

"Keep your hair on, I'm not on militia business. You can have a dozen vodka stills in the bath-house or run a brothel for all I care, that's not my line. Just a watchful eye is all I'm asking – who's who, coming and goings, odd friends, funny postcards, little meetings that aren't birthday parties or barmitzvahs. Come on, duckie. You've got the idea."

He had got the idea all right.

Boris was twisting his body from side to side, brushing feebly at his blue suit as if to ward off things which were climbing up the lapels. "Lucifer!" he shrieked and sat bolt upright, his eyes round with terror. "Bearing the lights before him, his vesture the raiment of angels!"

Marya Fyodorovna looked at him stonily and then roared with all her might: "Oh, why don't you dry up, you pathetic old soak! You wouldn't recognise him if he gave you his name and address. They'll come for you with a bucket and shovel not pennants and swords!"

Boris was momentarily silenced and sat uncomprehending, like a drunkard whose last order has been refused. They both watched with interest; neither would have been surprised had he levitated, such was his state of exaltation. But he sank back on the granite edge of the step, his horror at the apparition ventilated by baffled outcries: ". . . retinue of Belial . . . princes of the void . . . swallowing the light . . ."

Switching her glance back to Sasha, she became the lewd-eyed teaser once more. "Don't want to do a little jig with me, then? Think of the after-hours goodies in it, for both of us."

She saw him as an opportunity to be taken. He saw himself as a man with a price on his head: with women, he was learning, you were nothing if not an encashable, spiritual chitty.

"Look," he said confidingly. "You've got the wrong bloke. It's not that I don't fancy . . ."

Disdainfully, she threw away her cigarette. "I should have known. No balls for it. What are you bothering with half-wits like that Lestyeva for, anyway? She's on the slide, you can take that as gospel." She stood up facing him, the white bag under her arm. "Do you know who the next editor of *Feministka* will be?"

"Masha," he guessed.

"Masha! Me! Me! You fool. I'm making my own way without Daddy's help."

He walked down to the lobby with her and out into the sunlit street. On the corner, near the café, a black Chaika was parked. Two men were playing cards on the bonnet.

"A couple of my suitors sweating it out," she said, giving a wave in their direction. The younger one smiled back and scooped up the cards. "Pigs," she said, feelingly. The sight of them worked to restore her good-humour with Sasha. "You could have been my consolation, you know that? For a while, at any rate."

There was reluctance in her parting from him – as if she had been a man to whom the girl had said "no" and who had taken the refusal philosophically and still liked her.

"All right, darling," she said, one foot on the pavement, the other in the gutter. "You're a fool to turn it down, but I'll tell you what you would have found out soon enough. There's some bother coming. Take your fat old girlie and clear out. Don't stay around here."

"I live here," said Sasha, mystified, his mouth dry. "I can't just up sticks, we've nowhere to go, we can't disappear into thin air. What can I tell her when I don't even know what's going on myself? What's it all about?"

There was a clatter from the stairs. Boris had taken off one of his shoes and thrown it at the glass door of the entrance-way. Sasha looked distractedly from him to the girl as she moved away. "What is this?" he called after her. "You can't leave us like this."

All morning an asphalt-laying machine had been trundling along the lane squirting tar and chippings over the surface pockmarked from the frosts of winter. The gang's meal-break had just finished and the vehicle started to roll forward again with a deafening screech.

Marya Fyodorovna turned towards Sasha from the camber of the road. "Christ, love, you don't think they'd tell me, even if I asked? They think they're on to something! Keep your mouth shut if they come!" She gave an elegant shrug in Boris's direction, the khaki fatigues wrinkling up on her chest. "*He's* as good as dead and *you* can pretend to be pissed. A pair of clowns like you aren't a threat to anyone! *Ciao!*"

The nearside rear door of the car opened as she hopped on to the coping stone of the kerb made higher now by the stripping of the old layer of tarmac from the road. When she got in, the arm of a male companion came across her lap to slam the door to. Hot grit rattled on the wheel arches as the car slowly moved off.

As it came alongside, the driver, a big man with a silver earring and blond beard, turned deliberately towards Sasha, winked and shouted through the open window, "What's your problem – couldn't you get it up today, sweetie?"

21

Sasha's key lay deep in the back pocket of his overalls, quite inaccessible while Boris was slung across his shoulders in a fireman's lift. He managed to reach out to the doorbell of his own flat.

Olga answered the ring in her office dress, a dark blue shirtwaister with long sleeves and stiff cuffs. She might have been a nursing sister except for the coppery gold rings dangling from her ears.

"Oh Lord, just when I'm already late for work!"

She stood aside believing them both to be drunk as Sasha staggered past into the hall, but a look at her brother's face convinced her of the truth.

"He's feverish, feel him shaking, be careful, careful."

"Get your door open," said Sasha, shifting under the weight like a coalman with a full sack. "Jesus, I nearly fell getting him out of the lift."

The floor was wet and his feet left smears as he stumbled into her room. She darted ahead, whisked a pair of shiny black high-heeled shoes and black stockings off the divan, stuffed them anyhow into the bottom drawer of her bureau and then taking her brother in her arms, laid him out full-length.

"How can I go to work now?" she said. "I must ring the boss, and the doctor will have to be called. How long has he been like this?"

"Search me," said Sasha. "I just found him down there. That woman's no good to him – he should be in hospital."

"Not hospital, Olya," panted Boris, twisting about on the divan. "Not hospital . . . couldn't endure it . . . the indignity."

Sasha turned his back and sank into the only armchair, immensely weary. For a man who hated scenes, he found his life was becoming a torment. Now, everywhere, suddenly there was storminess and temperament; even Olga was surrendering to feeling.

Since Valentina's arrival he had not been inside her room. The widow had characterised his friendship with the Melentyevs as unequal and their attitude as patronising. Now he looked round affectionately, renewing his acquaintance with the orderliness of the interior aspect of their lives, enjoying its airy spaciousness. No awful dolls or trashy knick-knacks, but good quality furniture and books and books and books. The window stood open and a cheerful blur of shouts, whistles and honking traffic floated in from the street. How fortunate they were to have that ten-metre drop to the roadway; always a current of air, even at that modest height, ruffling the stuff of the curtains, exchanging the stale heat in the warren of apartments with the cool winds circulating from the river. Boris was sucking in his breath like a man who snored but could not draw up sufficient air to satisfy his lungs and began to catch for more, knowing that however deep the craving he could never have his fill.

Sasha wheeled the chair round. Olga was on her knees beside the sick man, stroking his gaunt neck. "Borya, Borya, darling."

Out in the hall the telephone began to ring. "That'll be Matvey from the office. I'd better answer it."

He heard her firing questions with increasing impatience, until finally she slammed down the receiver. "Some idiot with a wrong number."

"Where is everyone?" asked Sasha, remembering that he had been supposed to meet Valentina over an hour ago.

"How on earth should I know?"

Going to the bureau, Olga pressed a brass stud concealed amidst the carved tracery of a false drawer-pull. A flap fell away above the central recess of the desk and half a dozen long ampoules tumbled out. She stood over Boris, prised off the caps of two of the containers and teased out some round tablets with her thumbnail. In her other hand was a glass of cold tea.

"Well, something's got to be done. You can't leave him in this state – he's going to cough his guts up any minute. He needs a doctor quick."

"You don't understand," she answered, hovering by the sick man, awaiting the opportunity to slip the tablets into his mouth.

"Understand? I bloody understand all right. I may be all kinds of a twerp in your eyes but Borya's not the first bloke I've seen in that state. He's got cancer, you know it and I know it. My CO had it and my Grandad. He needs a lung re-section. Morphine's no better than booze – it'll just make him dopey. His lungs are shot to hell. Can't you see?"

"My brother," said Olga slowly, her body rigid as if she were stifling a scream. *"My brother will die a graceful death."* And she raised her arms above Boris, holding them still for a moment in the gull's-wing posture of a sacrificial hierarch about to administer a ritual benison. "In this we are one."

Boris spluttered as the pills adhered to his tongue, and closed his mouth. With surprising strength she unclenched his teeth and forced down the tea. After a while the stertorous breathing subsided and he slept.

The immediate crisis over, both Olga and Sasha reverted to normality. She relaxed enough to ring her boss and the doctor. As she wound down, and the problem of Boris temporarily lessened, Sasha's fright at his queer encounter with Marya Fyodorovna reasserted itself. He was anxious to tell the story, partly to warn her, but mainly to have the assurance of a clear interpretation.

". . . So someone's making trouble. My bet is on Galina Semyonovna."

Even though Boris was unconscious, she dismissed any discussion of Galya in his presence. "He might hear you. She's his wife and he's too ill for this kind of thing."

"Well, someone's got Lestyeva into a jam. That crazy Marya didn't leave off polishing her behind on the office stool to come down here for nothing. She wasn't even snooping – somebody in this block has been doing the snooping for her."

Olga was sceptical, but listened, pale and motionless, her hands clasped over her brother's.

"But there's no connection, no link at all. I know she works at Tanya's place but there's no reason for her to take an interest in anyone who doesn't. I do think you exaggerate, Aleksandr Mikhailovich."

The big green eyes travelled speculatingly over Sasha. "I've heard about Marya Fyodorovna. But Tanya isn't well. She imagines things. And you, you're a bit of a romancer too, aren't you?" Releasing Boris's hands she removed the long pins from her chignon and shook out her hair, unloosing the tight strands with the tail of a pocket comb. Her gaze was comprehending, familiar. "You and Tanya," she said softly. "Just the same, seeing phantoms in the air, frightening people, portraits of enemies, cloud horsemen . . ."

"But Olga Sergeyevna," protested Sasha, aghast that she failed to believe him. "She warned me off. Told me to clear out of Moscow."

"You've already said everything there is to be said about her. She's in a world of her own. *Crazy Marya.*"

There was nothing he could do. For some reason she was determined to make light of his fears. God, how sick he was of women. He couldn't name one who had ever told him the whole truth.

"Ask Borya, ask him when he wakes up. He knows it all happened."

"Just look at him," said Olga. "What condition is he in for interrogations? Go away and stop worrying the both of us."

His boots rumpled the sheepskin rug as he stood up. "There's something you're keeping to yourself and it's not about him. What's up?"

"Nothing, nothing at all." Wearily she flapped a hand at him. "It's an unlucky day and you look dead tired. Go and sleep it off."

Sasha wanted to shout and tell her that in some way it was all her fault: she shouldn't have been so clever or fallen for an Englishman; or been born with a straight-boned face and the heavy-lidded eyes that you sometimes saw on the frontispieces of nineteenth-century novellas, or had friends like Marina who lived on memories and wouldn't die. They had drawn him into their lives, contaminated his innocence. Once he had believed in them, envied what he had thought to be the glamour of their complicated feelings. Now they concealed themselves from him and the feelings had developed into secret actions, the consequences of which had involved him, but which they had kept hidden.

"Tell Borya I'm around – if he wants me, I mean."

Olga saw him out. "He wants no commiseration. Just to be let alone. That's what I want, too. Here, take this," she said, handing him her brother's bag which contained two full bottles of strong vodka. "I don't want to see alcohol near him again."

In his room there was no sign of Valentina. Both windows were fast shut and it was stuffy. Undoing the catch of the larger one he swung open the inner and outer panes. A stream of cold air flowed in as he searched round for a glass. The vodka bottles were carefully wrapped in white, shiny paper.

On the inside of the paper there was print and the small round stamp of the Lenin Library. That was where Boris had often spent his afternoons. The paper was a set of photocopies, the type immediately recognisable: they were part of a newspaper obituary. Sasha ran his eye down the columns. The usual boring recapitulation of civic and Party worthiness:

... Osipyenkyo ... (b.1918), member Politburo (to 1978 m. of Presidium) Central Committee of Communist Party of Soviet Union from 1974; sec. CC CPSU from 1978; twice Hero Soviet Labour (1968 and 1978). Member CPSU from 1943. Fitter by trade from 1937. Grad. Military Aviation School 1942/3. 1943: fighter pilot during Great Patriotic War, Moscow NW Front; Grad. Rybinskii Aviation Inst. 1945; 1945–53 air attaché, various foreign postings. 1953–7 mem. Military council 18th Army. 1956–9, 2nd Sec. Zaporozhskii dist. party; 1959–62 Ist Sec. Sverdlovskii dist. party.

Mem. CC CPSU from 1956; 1974–8 1st dep. chairman CC CPSU Bureau for Russian Soviet Federated Socialist Republic. Candidate member Presidium CC CPSU 1969–73. Dep. Supreme Soviet CPSU from 1950.

He stood his empty tumbler over the top of the first sheet. The weight of the heavy, cut base flattened out a crease over "Osipyenko". The name, Christ, Osipyenko *Fyodor Pavlovich*, Christ . . . *That's* whose daughter . . . *Marya Fyodorovna* . . . That's Daddy!

22

When Valentina came back, he had finished off one of Boris's bottles and was drifting into sleep pursued by a Chinese doll in a red wig and a militiaman's cap. She woke him by pulling hard at the short hairs at the nape of his neck.

"You don't love me. You're nothing but a brutal, callous man!"

There was no sign of any shopping. He wondered how far she had walked in the heat, dressed up in her short-sleeved, ice-blue best summer blouse. It was transparent but the most prurient onlooker would have been deterred by the sight of her medieval underwear with its snap-catches and toggles chafing the flesh.

With the empty bottle in her left hand she teetered over the mattress in her platform shoes. "You earn too much, that's the trouble." He ducked but she dropped it on his shins. "You might think you can go on taking me for granted, but I've got a bag packed. One more time like this morning and I'll be off into the wide blue yonder."

The threat was standard, and unenthusiastically delivered. Leaving him was the last thing she wanted to do. There was no place for her back home and if she arrived on the doorstep with her traps and bags they would probably shut the door in her face.

Contented by the ritual expression of abuse, she parked her great bottom by his feet and smiled at him indulgently: "It was good of you, that, to bring him back here."

After reading the obituary, all thoughts of Boris had fled from his mind. The flat was in semi-darkness, the window had been shut again, and dark clouds were rolling up behind the cupola of the church on the highroad. He must have been asleep for ages. It was late, or it was morning, or tomorrow evening.

"He's dead! I knew it! I told her she was killing him!" He reached out to grip her arm but she pushed him off.

"Now, now," said Valentina shaking her head. "Of course he's not dead. Or he wasn't a few minutes ago." Her voice was subdued, almost the voice of a stranger. "He's my friend too, isn't he?" This was said quickly as if she were ashamed of herself. It was quite untrue.

"Is or was?" asked Sasha, disbelieving and afraid. Valentina dabbed her nose with a pink tissue.

"I've just come down from upstairs. He's had a bad turn and they've put him to bed. The doctor has come and his sister's sent for the priest. I fetched his wife a while ago." This last seemed to have upset her more than anything. "She didn't want to leave the washing. Does she care, that one? Or has he got a fancy woman? He kept on apparently, about some girl he'd seen in the altogether."

"Talk sense for once, woman, if you have to talk at all."

"Oh charming, I must say," said Valentina reverting to her normal tone. "I'm wasted here informing you of your friend's approaching demise while you lie blotto, in creased clothes, and he's up there, back home, drawing his last with that Galina woman and all the whited sepulchres milling around, complaining about how terrible they feel. His sister looked about all in."

"I'm going to see him," said Sasha, rooting around for his shoes. "Borya, Borya . . ."

"They won't let you," said Valentina resignedly, raising herself with a grunt and straightening the line of her skirt. "There's a priest there now. *She* didn't want to let him in but Boris Sergeyevich kicked up a row, threatened to throw her out of the window. You never heard the like of his language." She rubbed her knees and breathed heavily like an old woman.

Valentina's newly-bobbed hair looked unwashed and sticky when she switched on the little lamp. The sheen on her dolls' faces was glassy at the edge of the pool of light. Everything else in the room was lustreless, and their colour attracted her. Picking them up one by one, she arranged them in couples, nose to nose, flat on the ledge; then began to heap up the pairs into sixes, dusting down their hollow cheeks and piggy eyes. For the first time he noticed that she had put out their cherrywood box and polished it. Perhaps, after all, she did intend to leave, without a word, on the sly.

"Can't you stop fiddling with those bloody things!" he shouted, glad to have a target for his frustration and guilt.

Without a flicker of acknowledgment Valentina laced up the bundles with lengths of blue and white ribbon and made parti-coloured rosettes at the pot napes of the topmost dolls. In a sing-song voice she began to repeat the childish incantation: "Betimes he loves me, betimes he loves me not."

"What's love got to do with it?" he said and burst into tears. It was the first time he had ever cried in front of her. She turned away without a word and left the room, carrying her box of dolls as if it were the coffin of a dead baby.

Lizaveta Ivanovna had a collection of stories about genies which got stuck in bottles: the bulldozer in the basement of a tower block at Krasnaya Presnya which had been bricked up by mistake; and the crane in the hotel boxed in and immovable with four floors concreted around it.

After the jokes staled, his mind retained the image, as if he had been entombed with the machines and was witnessing the extinction of light when the last brick was mortared in.

Thunder rumbled in the hills to the south-west.

He held out his hands against the window glass, sizing up the townscape through the gaps between his flat, square-ended fingers, measuring the dimensions of the gutted blocks to the north in comparison to the stone lintels, beams, heaps of stucco fragments and splintered brick tossed down a long chute from the staved-in window casements to choke up the narrow streets. There seemed no way in which those little rooms, just like his own, could have accumulated so much lumber and still not yet be picked clean.

At a noise at the door behind him he braced himself for Valentina's sulks or a resumption of bickering. Olga came in without knocking.

"He wants you – now," she said and turned on her heel. The stuff of her blue frock clung to the line of her spine where sweat had accumulated in a wet patch spreading across to the shoulder blades.

"How soon will he . . . ?" he asked but she had gone. "Olga Sergeyevna . . . Olga Sergeyevna . . ."

The lights in the passage were off. The scent of her unwreathed before Sasha like an invisible presence as he felt his way up to the landing. They collided at the door to Boris's flat. Not a soul was about.

"Aleksandr Mikhailovich," she whispered, turning and placing her hands flat on his chest. "That girl . . . he told me something. Does it make sense to you?"

"To hell with her," he said and pushed past into the bright hallway.

Inside it was as busy as the entrance to a beehive. The flooring of coconut matting susurrated beneath the concourse of feet as well-wishers, co-tenants and the simply curious formed and reformed, conversing in subdued tones like a congregation on the church steps after a wedding.

There were familiar faces: Lizaveta and Valentina stood by the telephone, speechless. Having both spontaneously abjured gossip as *de trop* in the face of such a solemn eventuality they could find nothing to say to each other, and faced the crowd with the condescension of ticket-holders affronted by strangers gate-crashing a rout.

Boris's eldest son was sitting on a low nursery chair outside his parents' room, scuffing the heels of his new school shoes on the skirting board. Their neighbour, Mrs Lopakhin, in a hairnet and cretonne overall, was at the bend of the passage, a long tray of teacups in her hands, staring malevolently out of tiny eyes at the newcomer. A young man, possibly a tenant, but unknown to Sasha, with hair down to the stiff collar of his shirt was holding forth, cigarette in mouth, to a little group of onlookers, about the medical details of Boris's illness and the deficiencies of the Moscow ambulance service.

At his shoulder Vera Grigoryevna, the *dvornik's* wife, was handing round a box of chocolates. "Past ambulances, he is," she said, a *langue de chat* nipped daintily between finger and thumb. "It's a stroke. I always said he'd have a stroke. Drinking like that. Here, have a praline, dear."

The young man was in full spate. He had developed some curious knack of working the cigarette into the corner of his mouth where it lodged securely no matter how loudly he spoke. False teeth, deduced Sasha stopping to take the chocolate. He just clamps them on the fag.

"Not a stroke," said the young man with a grimace, expertly revolving the cigarette. "You're confusing cerebral haemorrhage with cardiac arrest. It'll be a coronary. It's not the cancer that kills you, you see, but what it brings on. The heart in the end can't stand the strain and just packs up. It's merciful really. A wonderful thing, the human body."

Sasha thrust his head forward and the young man stumbled.

"And what does Mummy call you when you're at home, sonny?"

"I know what I'm talking about. I've been studying for . . ."

"And I know *who* you're talking about," said Sasha. "That's my friend in there, the one you're sewing up with your mouth, not some down-and-out on a clinic slab. You save your chin-wagging post-mortems for the other butchers down the city knacker's yard. Why don't you just fuck off, you pimply little sod, before I lay you out too?"

The catch of the Melentyevs' bedroom door was faulty. Caught in the draught which Lopakhina had manufactured by propping open the kitchen window and keeping the flat door ajar to cleanse the sultry interior, Boris's door swung outwards at every ripple of storm wind. At each gust Sasha caught an image which froze for a moment on his retina, dispersed when the catch banged impotently to, and was almost instantaneously replaced by the onset of another. The effect was of primitive, vivid cinema. A priest – how did they get him to come? The succession of pictures jerked him to attention: round specs, grizzled beard, long hair – odd, no trace of grey; but not well-washed. Pectoral cross swaying like a plumbline from a thick neck. Some business had been done. There were the instruments (or whatever they were called). There on the dressing-table, a white metal goblet, a nasty-looking ikon, a cloth. Away they went into a dinky little box. It packed away beautifully. That was the most engrossing part; folded up to a cube. Lovely, like a kid's hollow, hinged red building block.

Another image of a skinny young man, also in black, slid over the figure of the priest like a blob of dust in the projector gate.

"Ah, now, doctor," beamed Mrs Lopakhin as this man emerged trying to shut the bedroom door behind him. "It's no use, such inferior workmanship nowadays. Won't you have a cup of tea?"

Her seven best cups were on the tray.

"Haven't you anything stronger?" asked Sasha. The doctor was even thinner than Boris and looked exhausted.

"I can't do anything more here. We'll have to take him in. You haven't got a drop of brandy anywhere, have you?"

"For him?" cried Lopakhina, staring at the door incredulously. "I thought that was what had caused . . ."

"Not for him, woman. For *him*," said Sasha, nodding his head at the doctor.

"And for the wife," added the doctor. "She's taking it badly."

Sasha got up from his seat and let the doctor sit down. "She's not in there with him, is she?"

"I've not set eyes on her at all," answered the doctor, yawning. "Some old woman told me she was having a lie-down in her place. Nerves. No, the sister is with him at the moment."

"Not so much of the 'old'," said Vera Baranova flirtatiously. "Poor soul, I've left her on my bed downstairs. She's prostrate . . ."

"How long will he last?" said Sasha. The doctor had barely started his prognosis before Lopakhina returned clutching two tumblers filled to the brim with cognac. "My husband has gone off with the cupboard key. These were all I could find." She looked askance as Sasha took the two glasses, handing one to the doctor who smacked his lips at the taste of the drink. "First of the day," he said.

Lopakhina hung around, morbidly inquisitive as he resumed his account of Boris's collapse. "It's simply a matter of time. We'll do a blood gas analysis when he's taken in but I can't see his respiratory system coping for much longer. Even if we get him on a ventilator, the kidneys are on the point of packing up. He's already jaundiced. When one organ goes, that'll be it. His blood pressure . . ."

Lopakhina was rapt at the disquisition. For one time in her life she was privy to the unfolding of a mystery. That the words could have been Swahili for all she knew was quite beside the point. The language of decomposition had the orgiastic timbre of juju and this occult naming of inner parts made her sense them within her own body, joggling obscurely awash in their bags of fluid.

"A wonderful but fragile thing, the human body," she sighed, elaborating the words of the other young man, glad to have fastened on this philosophical *tout ensemble* of man's mortality.

"Holy Mother of God," said Sasha, looking at the dumpling arms crossed over her tremendous bosom. "Who told you that – your husband? Being married to you must be like going to bed with an inflatable life-raft."

"Oooh!" whinnied Lopakhina. "You horrible, uncultured man! It's my glands, you see," she said, appealing to the doctor, her eyes filling with tears. "They're the downfall of the women in my family."

The doctor lay back wearily, his head against the wall. "I'm so tired, I haven't slept for twenty-four hours." Sasha handed the empty glasses to the fat Lopakhina. "Time for a re-fill," he said. "We can't have the driver asleep at the wheel."

When the priest came out he was embarrassed at the hush which greeted his appearance. The dull boom of thunder, gone practically unnoticed by the throng in the hall as they bent themselves to eager discussion of impending death, now crackled vividly in the clouds sailing aloft the tenement and came closer and closer into synchrony with the lightning as it raked the deserted courts and back alleys with gigantic flash-fire.

Peering timorously through his spectacles, he fixed at random on the conceited young man with the cigarette and the long hair and addressed him: "Brothers and sisters in Christ, the servant of God, our Boris, is departing this life. Let us now entreat the intercession . . ."

In an unexpectedly orotund voice he began to pray aloud in the face of the startled company.

In a very short time it became apparent that no one, except for Valentina and Lizaveta Ivanovna had any idea what to say, so they mumbled haphazardly, losing much of what the priest had said as the building quaked under the bolts of thunder unleashing themselves at the roof at intervals of a few seconds. Without losing track of his prayer, the priest surreptitiously withdrew a bundle of cards from the side pocket of his cassock and nudged Lizaveta Ivanovna who passed them around from hand to hand. When Sasha's card reached him, he nearly dried up altogether: the prayers were in Old Church Slavonic and the only word he could make out was "God". It was a word which, as far as he could see, occurred pretty often, so he cleared his throat, and joined in, *sotto voce*, trying to introduce as much variation as he could into his private litany, "God, oh God, God, oh, God . . ."

Rain crashed at the open kitchen window; the lights surged into brilliance then dimmed, as the obsolete wiring of the flats took the shock of the outbursts from above.

Having devised a satisfying metrical scheme for his lone word, Sasha was still chanting absorbedly when the rest of the makeshift congregation had stopped, and he looked up to see Valentina kissing the priest's ring and handing him an umbrella and a packet of sandwiches done up in brown paper. As he passed down the hall, the crowd divided, and he moved from side to side while people, mostly the women, except for Boris's son Anatoly, bent low and touched his ring-hand with their lips. At the door, Sasha noticed, money changed hands; Lopakhina gave a valedictory cringe, and the priest prepared himself to disappear into the night.

"Hold on a minute!" Sasha's shout rang in Valentina's ears and she put both hands up to her face as if a dog were about to be run over on the road. The umbrella was of the telescopic variety and the priest was pushing down so hard that the spokes shot into a reverse canopy. He looked up gratefully, anticipating help, but Sasha, as Valentina had guessed, was not interested in the umbrella. "Look, your . . ." he said, suddenly feeling stupid because he didn't know how to address the priest correctly or even if priests had any kind of special title at all. "Excuse me, but is that all there is to it?"

"All?" asked the priest.

"Yes, all. Do you always knock off before the end and go home to your wife?"

They stood toe to toe. The priest was unoffended at the vulgarity of the insult. "My son," he said. "I have anointed him, he has been shriven. The Church has prepared him. There is no further act beyond that private opening of his soul to Christ's grace. A man makes his own peace."

"No, I don't mean . . . I mean . . ." Sasha was lost in the tumult of words inside his head.

"What is it, then, that you think I should do?" asked the priest patiently.

"Isn't there anything else?" Sasha burst out, irresolutely, now only half-convinced that his first question had any meaning yet baffled that he could not express the truth of his enragement of feeling.

"What more can I do?"

"You could hold him, you could be with him. You know what it's about, you could take him there — part of the way, most of it — you could take him."

The priest put his fingers to Sasha's cheek. They smelt of chrism and sweat. "'But they slept'," he said, and kissed Sasha's forehead. "We, too, shall know Gethsemane."

"What *is* that?" he said to Valentina, after the priest had gone, anxious to gauge the usefulness of the advice and humbled by the priest's perfect manners.

"Oh, that," said the young man who was sitting on the table by the telephone checking the doctor's instrument case. "I'm surprised a man-about-town like you doesn't know where that is." He began to draw lines on the dusty surface. "Here's Malaya Bronnaya Street, there's the little market, and there's your place, just off the corner. Old mother Bessmertnova's run it for years. It's the only squaddies' knocking-shop for miles, Gethsemane . . ."

Sheer incomprehension restrained Sasha for that fraction of a second the young man needed to leap from the table with the box and tear out of the flat. With a roar Sasha launched himself across the hall and down the stairs, his steel-tipped boots skittering and sparking on the invisible steps. For all his squat bulk, his job kept him fitter than the young man's, and he floored him on the bottom landing with a flying dive. The case burst wide on impact with the mains' junction box showering bandages, syringes and hundreds of tiny pills into a pool of rainwater. In the reflected light from the street lamps, a scalpel glistened. The young man's eyes were circular with terror as Sasha wrenched back his head by the hair and pricked the point of his jaw with the horribly functional knife.

"If I ever see you again," he panted, "your shrunken little balls will be where your mouth is."

Sasha's own flat was deserted. He jumped as the telephone buzzed, and shouted down the mouthpiece: "Yes, yes, yes." Tears streamed down his face. "Who the hell is this? What do you want? Leave us alone! We've had a bereavement."

From a long way off, through a hiss like the far-out roaring of sea-shell breakers, came two metallic clicks. Someone sniggered; and a male voice said: *"And I don't like that either."*

23

With a confection of spirit, milk and white breadcrumbs, the recipe for which had been handed down from mother to daughter, Lizaveta Ivanovna had cleaned her shoes. Her best frock which was usually stored away in the bottom of her press, to be taken from its wrappings no more than once a year at her private celebrations of Christmas, now lay airing, straggled across the two bolsters from her bed.

It was time to lift out of its box the only hat she had ever possessed: a velvet toque, unadorned, with nap like black baize. Whenever she touched it she remembered the burial of her son; the barked commands, the harsh tearlessness and rigour enforced upon her, that colourless March afternoon, so long ago, by a ceremonial which with its final parade-ground rattle of musketry had placed him for ever behind the unassailable parados of the secret life of men. Black it is, black it was. Black for passion, black for the unendurable pangs of love. Black it will be.

In the top drawer were her gloves and the paper ikon which he had carried in the pocket of his field tunic, and which was returned to her, without reproof, with his watch on the back of which she had had engraved "A son is a son" for his twenty-second birthday (simple, so as not to embarrass him with his brother officers). Everything came back. Even his soldier's unwitnessed will, pencilled at dawn before the assault, and the pre-war photograph of them all at the pool at Sochi beneath an unclouded sky.

Moth had burrowed a line through the Virgin's face. She slipped the ikon between the pages of an old prayer book and placed it on one side, took a tiny packet of rice for the deceased and three one-rouble notes for the candles, arranged them neatly in her jet-beaded bag, and looping its chain-link handle over her left wrist, slowly made the sign of the cross.

There was a sharp breeze and the brilliant sky was rippled with creamy streaks of high cloud. The white minibus was outside, drawn up close to the kerb, its motor running. Climbing into a good seat, near the front, she felt for her clean handkerchief and throat pastilles, rehearsing the words of the responses.

Lord God Himself knows them no better. Today is mine, and his, and his, and his. Mine and theirs, and the untold faithful dead, standing forth with the living to vivify the mystical body of Christ.

Valentina hitched up her skirt, spat on her fingers and rubbed at the ladder which was about to run up over the knee of her tights.

"Drat, you wouldn't credit it! That's eight roubles gone to glory."

Sasha was hopping across the room trying to get his left leg into the tight trousers of a blue suit.

"Come here." She caught him round the middle and held him fast while he waggled his free foot out of the seat and finally succeeded in thrusting it down the leg. "I don't know what you'd do without me. Here, you're forgetting something," she said, stuffing the material of his shirt down the waistband. "Tails are being worn *inside* the trousers this year."

She stood back to survey him. "My God, you look like a fish in combinations. How do I stand it?"

There was truth in her candour. Sasha felt awful. The suit had been run up for him ten years before by an aunt, and she had skimped on the backside. Even then it was a wriggle to get into. Now every time he relaxed, the zip of the fly ran back halfway. "It'll do, it'll do," he said, holding his breath and trying to jam the zip fastening at the top.

"Well, keep an eye on it for heaven's sake, we don't want you obtruding your personality at an interment. Thank goodness there's me to keep up a good front."

After Boris died, her dolls had been partially re-instated, but for some reason, never explained to Sasha – who, in any case, had taken little interest in anything after the death and had been practically silent for three days – only a selection had found its way back to the window-sill. She fingered the knees of the bedraggled Romanian milk-maid into whose pails Sasha had dropped matchsticks, and sipped daintily at a thimble-glass of vodka, her little finger poised.

"How much longer I can stand this slum I've simply no idea. Oh, remind me to bring a handkerchief. You never know how it might take you."

Down below she saw various of the Lopakhins running in and out and giving orders to the driver. Several people were already inside the bus: fat Vera Grigoryevna next to Lizaveta, the *dvornik* in front. His dog, Bootik, had been locked up and muffled barks could be heard from the basement.

"That widow of his," went on Valentina, while Sasha hunted for his tie. "She'd do anything to get herself noticed. Fancy not coming to the church, not paying her last respects. Whatever they got on like, there's common decency in these things. The kids can't be up to much either, falling in with her like that. I'd be so *ashamed*. Still, that's where education gets you, I suppose."

"Why should she be any different now from what she's always been? Death alters nothing, otherwise we'd all be saints."

"You're a gloomy devil," said Valentina with grudging respect. "But a consistent one, I'll grant you that. And I'm thankful you're a man. We're running short on those in this place. You never know who might get in here, now the men are fleeing like flies in winter. Some maniac might climb in one night to rape her and take her money."

"One look at her and any self-respecting rapist would be down the drainpipe before she had time to get her knickers off. What money, anyway?"

"I thought he'd put a bit by," said Valentina, surprised.

"That went a long time ago – mostly to doctors, but the rest he drank, thank God."

Valentina had bought a new coat. A distant cousin had found out her Moscow address and called on them one day in the winter. With an eye to business he had bought along a bundle of kidskins and offered them at a knockdown price. Valentina had had them made up into a coat by a craftsman introduced to her by Lizaveta Ivanovna. Although it was absurdly unseasonal she was determined to wear it at the funeral and it now hung behind the door, lustrously black, a tasteful departure from her usual brilliant colours. To match its solemnity she had bought a pair of black stiletto-heeled, toeless sandals in which she could walk only by holding on to Sasha's arm.

He looked at them, and the coat, and her and thought of Olga whom he had seen an hour before dressed for the service in a navy frock, gold ear studs and black scarf looped back and tied gypsy-fashion behind her ears. He opened his mouth as if to speak, thought better of it and unfolded the newspaper as she put the finishing touches to her toilet.

"Trust a friend of yours to die in a heatwave. Well?" she demanded. "Am I dowdy enough?"

The red mound of curls surmounted by a gauzy black scarf, the prickly fur coat and the toe-gapped high heels gave her a wholly accidental resemblance to an elderly procuress stepping out on the razzle.

He mastered his feelings. "It means you care, I suppose."

She blushed and took his arm with dignity. They processed into the hallway where the Kuznetsovs were assembling.

Little Xenia, her white forehead curving out from her piled-up hair which had been scraped back in a style resembling Lizaveta Ivanovna's, was holding a posy of artificial violets. For a moment Sasha saw the child grown not into a girl but an old woman with a shawl, her breasts as flat as they were now.

Lev Kuznetsov's face was as pale as his daughter's. He nodded to Sasha and Valentina.

"Them too," said the widow in his ear as the family formed up in the doorway. "The charms of your Boris were scattered wide indeed. Do you think they'll know what to do? In the church, I mean. Can't have had much practice, can they, being as how they're . . . ?"

"They'll hear," said Sasha.

But she continued to whisper, clinging to his sleeve as they followed down the stairs. "I'll tell you something: I think he must have been a bit touched, that Boris, a bit holy. How else to impress the infidel?"

"Oh dry up."

The minibus was crowded but the *dvornik* and the fat man from opposite made room for them. When Tanya and Marina arrived Sasha got up to give the old woman his seat. She accepted without a word or glance. Tanya ignored him completely, and wriggled over to the window side and stared ahead over the driver's shoulder.

The church was off the Ring Road and its low domes had been re-burnished for the Olympics. Their richness was set off by the concrete stanchions and grey sweep of the roadway carrying the Moscow traffic high above the uppermost cross.

First out of the bus came Lizaveta Ivanovna, her back very straight. She marched up to the gate which opened on to a little path leading to a side-door of the church, then held back for the other mourners to assemble behind her.

Inside the church it was dark, cool and spacious. Here and there, banks of slim candles on breast-high stands set before the ikons at the walls and pillars, diffused a brassy, hazed glow.

Sasha's trousers were so tight that he had handed his wallet to Valentina in the minibus and he felt left out when all the women bought candles at a little counter just inside the main door. The steel tips of his boots rang as he trailed after them to a huge ikon of St Michael the Archangel, where Valentina shared out her candles with him. He stood awkwardly, holding them like a child with sparklers at a firework party, nervous at the gloom, the smell of incense and the prospect of the inevitable foolishness of his actions – since, if he ever knew, he had long forgotten what it was that would be demanded of him. The ikon was hideous: the Archangel grinned inanely from between a pair of wings so inadequate for the wooden solidity of his body that they would have given it no more levitation than a box kite. Lighting his candles dutifully and placing them amidst the hundreds of others on the little holders, he stepped back as Lizaveta Ivanovna first, then the rest of the women, kissed the ikon's hand through its yellow metal cladding.

When Lizaveta knelt, lay face down then kissed the stone flags, the hair stiffened at the back of his neck. When Valentina, too, began to heave herself down, he walked backwards a few steps, coughed and turned away. They had lost him, and frightened him. He wanted to go home. At least, to get out.

As his eyes accustomed themselves to the dimness surrounding the clumps of votive lights, the bass voice of one of the celebrants rumbled along the nave, and a handful of choirwomen took up the melody, singing out, unaccompanied, the first bars of the Office for the Dead. The odd thing was that until that moment Sasha had forgotten he was at a funeral. Nothing up to then had seemed to have anything to do with death. At the makeshift bar where they had bought the candles, a roaring trade was now going on in holy water. Medicine bottles, vodka bottles, zinc dixies, porcelain pie-dishes and anything which could be filled and stoppered or covered was being passed across the counter to complete strangers, people who didn't know who he was, who Boris was, didn't seem to be aware – or were quite unconcerned if they realised – that at the other end of the church one of their number was stretched out stiff as a plank, being bustled over more extravagantly than a virgin on her wedding-night.

What were they here for, he thought, these rheumy old biddies, sparky enough to hold their places and fend off queue jumpers, with time enough to gossip, their soft-jawed talk crackling with reproof of the weather, their daughters, shortages, the cost of things, the price of life, stars in their eyes at the crudely-lithographed mass-produced pocket ikons of Christ in Majesty hanging like seaside postcards from a rail above their heads? Faith, perhaps, or age, habituated you to every débâcle, even your own; rendered you as inconscient as an abattoir cat licking his chops in the glut.

Why hadn't Borya taken it like that? Was it because he knew he was going to die? But don't they know – these old men and women who clog the antechambers of death? On the street you might have understood; there was no place there for this nearness and ordinariness, not outside. There you couldn't tunnel through the years knowing beforehand that the earth kept up with the hole and closed up behind you as soon as your feet inched forward; and that in front of you a moment would come when your head hit solid rock and you were banged up for ever.

Out there you were an individual, your fate seemed handleable. Whatever happened to him or her, or them, you fought as if you had a chance. But these old dears, camped out here, like the rag-tag-and-bobtail of a defeated army, ready, as soon as one body was carted away, to swab the flagstones and scoop up the dead heads, this lot seemed inoculated to the mortality which swashed around them. It was grisly, this feeling of clocking on at a bone-yard.

Borya, according to Olga, had spat at the priest. At the end, or nearly the end, that was. The doctor consoled Galina and said it was a muscular contraction common in the dying. If that were so, Sasha hoped that he could work up a good gob of spit for his muscles to shoot at any prissy bastard who told him, as his number came up, that it was a blessing.

People said that the dead look different. He'd never thought that. To him, they looked like what had happened to them; they'd been stopped in the middle of doing something. They looked – not exactly angry – but shocked, disbelieving. The expression was so familiar to him from his Gran, and his Mother, that at one time he had thought about it a lot. Perhaps everyone, however far gone he appears to the nurses and doctors and the relatives round the bed, however gaga he might have got, perhaps he sees it coming and sets his face to take a last swing at the God Almighty outrage it is. What it was his Gran saw in the distance he'd never known; only, that if she'd got there before it, she would have murdered it, whatever it was.

The only trouble with Boris was that they'd kept him too long. His lips had that blackish, corrupted tinge which came from an overlong stay, this hot weather, in a mortuary where they were too obsessed with energy norms to cut in the thermostat at the right temperature. In the candlelight, a viscid line gleamed along the crack of the eyelids. The dead face didn't bother him. It was Boris all right. Somehow they'd managed, thank God, to iron out the awful, inappropriate smile and he lay with his nose to the roof-vault, looking only a little worse for wear than Sasha had seen him often before when he waddled home from a drinking bout, full as a barrel.

The coffin was too small. Boris was wedged in, his shoulders crushing the white upholstery of the lining. Trust Galya to make it a tight fit, thought Sasha. There'd be no getting out of that, even if they turned it upside down and tried to shake him out. A grey-bearded acolyte knelt beside the body tucking in the little packets of rice which people brought as last favours. Then he encircled the brow with a long ribbon of paper bearing some scriptural text. He was deft and respectful. Not a bad old chap, reckoned Sasha, considering where his vocation had led him. Poking rigid limbs about for a living wouldn't exactly make you the life and soul of the party.

Tired from the noise of the choir, the braying priests and the unnatural darkness of the church, he made for the door and, once outside, sat down on the grass, leant back on his arms and flung out his chest to the sun. It was good to breathe expansively in the light. He decided to wait out there until the service was over.

Across the road a young man in a black suit and open-necked shirt was doing up his shoelace under a tree.

The words of the liturgy brought out the fight in Olga. She made the responses spiritedly, breathing in hard during the lulls between phrases to give full force to the plosives and sibilants which abounded in the chant. Inside her pocket she fingered a small travelling ikon of antique brass, its two wings unfolded from the central panel of the triptych: Ascent, Crucifixion, Descent. She had no need to bring it out. Every detail showed to her touch.

The voice of Boris calling her "Olga . . . Olichka . . . Olga," was quieted by this full-throated intercession. Everything had been and would be, properly accomplished. The dead must be given their dues. A Mass was promised, a Mass was given him. A settlement come to; ordered and delivered. Trim and on the nail; finished now, for her.

She blew her nose on a handkerchief moist with lavender water and tried not to think about going home. She might move.

Sasha left the church, noticeable as ever, head down, his hair brilliant in a shaft of light. The dereliction pained her. Fairweather friends. She thought of James. Gentle, tall James; James the doubter with perfect manners, who believed only in charms and had a vulgar medal of St Christopher on his key-ring. A mix-up of dimensions. Wearing the clown's trousers with a frock-coat, she had said when he showed her.

If only she could weep here. Oh Lord, how dreary is the recitation of Thy names. Why do I believe that I must submit to disciplines?

James was afraid of flying but had flown. Borya was afraid of dying. And had died. A pity there was no credit to be gained from not having the choice. If there were, you could do it for a dare and enjoy the pomps of triumph, and revile your own fears at the other side or behind the door or under the hill or wherever it is.

James had never written. It was six months now.

Marina looks silly in that pill-box hat, a ridiculous survival. Why couldn't she have worn a scarf? Tanya looked as if she had been taken from a suitcase and shaken out.

At the flat Galina will have laid out the food, gratified to be the hostess, to have a job to do. She was always better out of the way. There would be squabbles over the meats. Who had paid for what and will the wines run out? Lopakhina will speechify and the men will lose their tempers and become drunkenly argumentative.

Why is Sasha so frightened? Why can't I sleep? It was only the telephone. All wrong numbers. Nothing has happened.

One kiss now. Save the last for when they close him up at the burial ground on the other side of the city.

V

IN THE FAMILY

24

The day before his wedding Sasha forgot to re-set the alarm clock and woke very early, in time for the first shift. The sight of Valentina's dress at the back of the door, its white satin petals clustered modestly over the voile bodice reminded him that he was on holiday and he sank back.

Last night's stag party had fizzled out when Len started crying. It took a lot to start him but once he was off, he didn't stop until he had regressed, past toddlerdom, past his infancy, past the breast, his mother's pregnancy, his own conception, back to her father, a patriarchal giant from Oryol who had felled a Uhlan in 1916, bringing him down by slashing his horse's hocks with a barley-sickle. Len still had his St George medal in a shell-case. At each step down memory lane Sasha grew more numb from boredom and dread. Long ago he had come to hate every sprig and off-shoot of Len's appalling family tree.

When the obligatory roll-call ceased in the early hours, Len required consolation. The week before Natalya had left him. One day there was soup on the table; the next, no table. She had taken everything, even the tin-opener. It was like burglars. He felt at that moment, he said, like an amputee whose missis had sawn up his wooden leg.

"But what a woman!" sighed Len.

For the next quarter of an hour they drank stolidly and in silence. Skeletons of dried fish lay on newspaper all over the table, flakes of gristle adhering to the white bones.

"Natasha, Natalie, Natalya. What a woman, my woman."

Sasha reminisced privately. That wide, flabby smile, that excruciating forlornness (not surprising when all you had to look forward to the whole day was the re-entry of this hypertensive gorilla), and that sickening way she had of crushing lumps of flour into the casserole with her fingers.

"Never answered back," Len was saying. "No fuss. Just got on with it."

And just buggered off, thought Sasha.

Walking back in the pale light of the small hours, he felt himself to be a lucky man. He had a future. Everything Len had once had but affected to despise, he now had himself, or could look forward to. Len's loss had made him see sense about Natalya. Sasha was not going to let it come to that with Valentina. There was nothing special about her, as a woman. On your arm in the street or at a party she was just about passable; in bed, a little more tolerable these past weeks; but she had, Sasha knew and appreciated, those more important qualities which Len mourned in the passing of Natalya. She was chaste, houseproud, and content to serve him. What more could he, what more could Len ask of a woman, at their ages and situations in life?

In this mood of optimism, solace at Len's disaster, and unusual sobriety, he strolled in the uncool night relishing what was to come: a ten-day break, a wedding-feast at which he would star, the Volga cruise.

Not even Valentina's scolding, when he got into bed, choked back his anticipations. Before turning out the light, he frizzed up her scarlet locks and kissed her on the ear.

"Cuddle up, country mouse," he said. "It'll be official soon."

Early as he had woken this morning, Valentina was up before him. About now, very likely, she was storming at the manager of the hotel where their reception was to be held tomorrow evening. She had been keyed up for a set-to after he rang late when Sasha was at Len's to say that there had been a muddle over the music. The little string band she had wanted could not play that day. Would half the restaurant rock group do, or should they make do with tapes?

Valentina had shot out of the flat at crack of dawn to sort him out.

A great gang of her relatives would be arriving today and tomorrow from various remote parts. In her absence he had been ordered to entertain any or all who turned up.

The water in the bathroom was deliciously cold. He slurped mouthfuls at the tap before sluicing down his puffy face and throwing on his clothes.

My God, that's early, was his first thought when the door bell sounded. No one answered. The flat must be empty except for him. As he pulled open the bathroom door and shook the water out of his ears he could visualise them, the numberless Afanasyev clan, pullulating in an uncouth gaggle, nut-dark, leathery elbows into each other's ribs, huddled on the landing like a pile of toads croaking at a mill-race, clambering to get a sight of the intended and deluging him with their rustic first-fruits of castrated cockerels, birch bark flip-flops, *samogon*, holy water and blue crawfish.

The in-laws.

Compressing his features into a suitable rictus he opened wide the door. Not a sign of them. For one delirious moment he had the idea that they were hiding and would come tippling out of the brickwork, sun-baked faces jiggling, all agog for the hullabaloo of a surprise party. But no hide or hair of them. The place was desolate.

As he was about to shut the door a burst of sunlight from the dusty landing window illumined the head of a man; an odd head, the hair cropped at the sides but on top long, so long that it almost had to be coiffed and it lay up stiff like the peaks of black egg-whites. The head bobbed at the sight of Sasha and the rest of the body emerged, as a slight young fellow in a bumfreezer flying jacket skipped up the stairs two at a time.

"Hi. Thought you were on the lav," he said with a lopsided grin. He carried a toolbag and was very out of breath.

The hair came closer, crumbs of dandruff visible in the black side stubble. The face smiled, the lips curved behind a kingsize cigarette. As the man moved towards Sasha a loop of blue smoke spun away neatly in the air, above his head. He spoke out of one corner of his mouth. In the other was the cigarette, sending up a thick haze which completely obscured one eye. This was no Rostov hick.

"You come for the wedding?" asked Sasha, uncertain.

The man continued to smile and raised an eyebrow. "Drains," he said.

The Bakery Lane pipes had been defective for years. They were laid in the late nineteenth century when jerry-building was rife and Lizaveta Ivanovna swore they had blocked annually since the death of Aleksandr III. The *dvornik* and the fat man opposite had a stock of rods and brushes which they plied most summers after heavy rains while conversing for hours about T-junctions and male and female connections.

"Where's Baranov then? That's his job, isn't it?" said Sasha, meaning the *dvornik*. The stranger was nonplussed.

"Don't know anything about a Baranov," he said. "All they told me was, your drains were bunged up and here I am."

"Big problem, is it?" asked Sasha. "My missis, you see – she'll be wanting a bath when she gets back and we're expecting company."

"I wouldn't call it that," said the young man. "Nothing I can't sort out."

Once inside he lost much of his cheeriness.

"Always something going wrong with these old places. Cattle sheds, really. Look at that," he said, pointing to a long split in the plaster of the corridor. "A retaining wall, too. You'll be up to your neck in rubble one day, mate, this lot is sinking." He went on into the kitchen. "See, it's settling, that's what it's doing, settling. Should be condemned."

Sasha was nettled. "Hold on a minute, we can do without the survey, just stick to the drains. You can demolish the block afterwards."

The young man was oddly got up for plumbing. His shoes, jeans and snazzy jacket were more like a disco-dancer's than a tradesman's. He stood in the centre of the kitchen, gawping up at Lizaveta's jars of pickled cabbage along the top of the dresser.

"What did you say your name was?" asked Sasha.

"Ivan Ivanovich Ivanov," said the young man flatly. "I've come to give your little nest a seeing-to."

"Here," said Sasha, thinking by now that Ivan Ivanovich was some kind of speculating odd-job man who called on folk at random looking to make a bit on the side. "I'm not a policeman, I don't want to see your driving licence, OK? If you do a good job I won't quibble over the price. Only, be quick about it, the family's on their way."

"Oooh, I *am* sorry you're not a policeman," said Ivan, coming right up to Sasha and staring into his eyes. "They can be brutes, can't they?"

A diamond, its claw setting heavy with gold, flashed on the little finger of the pseudonymous Ivan Ivanovich.

"I think we'd better make a start, don't you?" said Sasha, taking a step back, anxious to be in movement and at a distance from this odd character. They walked up the corridor again, Sasha enumerating the rooms they passed: "And that's the bathroom, and the lav next door."

Ivan Ivanovich switched on the light in the windowless lavatory, peered up and down the back wall following the run of the pipes and shook his head.

"There's no trap," he said dolefully. "You haven't got a trap."

"What do you mean – trap? Bloody thing's only blocked at the end. You don't need to tap into the soil pipe."

"Engineer, then, are we?" said Ivan with a giggle and he lit a fresh cigarette from the embers of his old stub.

"No, a cowboy spotter. I know your sort. You'd saw out the waste-stack and leave us on buckets while you looked for a nice pipe length to nick from a site. I've done a bit of that myself, so I know. Come on, it's a ten-minute job, that is."

"You're a hard man, citizen Biryusov," said Ivan, flexing an arm and making a clenched fist salute. "You know a thing or two, you do."

"Hey, how come you know my name?" asked Sasha. "Never bumped into you before, have I?"

"Well," said the young man, giggling again as if he were a comic struggling against the humour of his punch line. "We haven't exactly been *introduced*. A hairy woman upstairs gave me your calling-card. Seems she's got sewage problems, too."

"Trust Galina to shove her nose in. All right. Let's get on with it."

"At your service, your excellency," said Ivan. "I'll just get my plunger."

He retraced his steps to the kitchen and bent over his toolbag. Sasha took the chance to clear off and leave him to it. Before he had reached the end of the passage, a voice stopped him in his tracks. It was gravelly and lisping but the speaker sounded as if he had too many teeth for his mouth comfortably to contain and the words came out half-chewed and slobbery.

"I don't know how to tell you this, kid," it said.

Like a man with night-nurse's paralysis, dreaming but open-eyed, unable to move any part of his body except for his head, Sasha turned his face towards the kitchen.

Down at the end of the passage, dark against the morning light from the kitchen window stood the figure of Ivan Ivanovich, a trilby hat pulled down over his eyes, his hands thrust into the pockets of a cream trench coat.

"What in God's name do you think you're playing at?" began Sasha, thunderstruck.

Keeping his hands in his pockets, Ivan slouched towards him, puffing hard on a cigarette at the end of which a long worm of ash stayed miraculously intact. He stopped a couple of feet away, planted his legs astride in the manner of a soldier standing at ease and blew a cloud of smoke into Sasha's face.

More words came out as a kind of spillage from the overfull, masticating jaws:

"In all the joints, in all the cities, in all the world, she came into mine."

Sasha recovered his wits and swung round to face him. The man was mad. He had heard about this sort of bloke before. They were harmless, like flashers, but with them it was their obsessions they wanted to dangle, not their privates.

"Look, mate," he droned, in what he hoped was the prescribed fashion for sedating crackpots. "We've all got our problems. Normally it wouldn't bother me if you came in here in a tutu and wand and pretended to turn me into a chocolate mouse, but don't you reckon you'd be better off at home, wanking into a glass slipper? I mean, I've nothing against you personally, but you're not exactly dressed for sorting out the main drainage, are you? Now, why don't you be a good lad and go back to where you come from and have a nice bikky and cocoa."

Ivan's cigarette had gone out. Bowing his head to an imaginary wind he turned up the collar of the trench coat, cupped his hands round a match and lit another, all the time watching Sasha out of the corner of his eye. With a world-weary smile, he blew out more smoke and continued to stare, his features screwed into an affectation of immense cynicism:

"*Never mind that, let's talk about the black bird.*"

"Christ!" shouted Sasha, dropping the therapeutic approach to lunacy. "Who in hell's name do you think you are? I never even sent for a plumber in the first place, never mind a loopy wire-puller in a rubberised mac. Shove off, get on out of it, some of us have got lives to lead!"

Ivan took off his hat and gave a petulant shake to his disarranged hair.

"Not really on the ball, this morning, are we, dear?" he said in his ordinary voice.

"You can leave the question of balls to me," said Sasha. "What I want you on, is your bike, and pretty bloody quick too."

"That's not very nice, is it? I mean, for you I put on a *performance*. I'm the image of him, don't you think?" he said, smoothing down his hair.

"The image of who?"

"Oh, go on, have a guess. Let's sit down in there, we can have a cosy little game, guessing, and that."

Sasha followed him into the kitchen thinking that once the young man's pretended identity was established, he might find out who he really was and then he could blow the whistle on him with the Street Committee.

They sat at the table.

"Go on, then, don't be shy," said Ivan Ivanovich, crossing his legs and bunching his hands under his chin. "I'll give you three goes."

Sasha couldn't believe that what he had witnessed in the corridor bore any resemblance to a human being. While he puzzled, Ivan tapped his fingernails against his teeth, delighted to have drawn him into the game. "Come on," he said, eager from anticipation. "I had him off to a T."

"Gromyko!" said Sasha, working round from the broad jowls to the scarcely-moving lips and thence to the hat.

Ivan was offended. "Him? What on earth made you think of him?

Oh dear, that's *awful*. They have to jump-start him to get him out of bed in the morning. Oh no, love, you're wrong there. Anyway, he doesn't smoke. Go on, have another go." And he cocked his head to one side, giving Sasha a further hint of the sophisticated image he had to project. "Forget about the living dead. Concentrate."

Sasha felt bereft of all inspiration. "Not a politician, then," he said. "Give us clue. Is he still alive?"

"No," said Ivan.

"Dead a long time?"

"Well, not that long."

"Big fellow, was he?"

"What do you want, his sock-size?" said Ivan. "No, not big."

"Not big," repeated Sasha. "Not Stalin, though, because he was a sort of politician and there was the moustache. I know, I know – *John Lennon*!" Ivan Ivanovich groaned. "You're not playing properly. Seriously, have you ever seen John Lennon in a trilby? Not his style, was it? He was more into caps and sneering. I'll have to tell you. I can see you're not a devotee of the silver screen."

With that he stood up, put the hat back on and did a final turn: "*You played it for her, you play it for me*. Get it? An American actor, thirties and forties films."

Sasha only knew one American film actor from the 1940s.

"Oh," he said, relieved at his identification. "But I don't remember the hat. You're Ronald Reagan."

Ivan sat down slowly. "What do you do for a living?" he asked.

"I'm a dustman."

"Yes," said the young man. "Not the most horizon-broadening type of employment. You're to be pitied really. That was Bogart, Humphrey, star of the best gangster movies ever made. You *must* have seen him."

"Not up my street. Now let's get something straight: that's a silly-bugger name you gave me. What's your real one?"

"*You* can call me Bogat – rich by name, rich by nature. Reminds me of my Humph."

"Bogat," repeated Sasha awkwardly. "OK, Bogat, get spannering in that bog, before my constipated in-laws roll up."

"Right-ho," said Bogat, stripping down to his cerise shirt. "Lead me to it. I'm a devil for work when the fit takes me."

He was as good as his word. For half an hour there was no sound in the flat except for the crash of metal as he set about the water-works with gusto. Occasionally Sasha looked in to see how he was getting on and Bogat smiled his knowing smile and went on about the lay of the pipes, the correct drift of the system and the drop from the header tank. He seemed to know his stuff all right, thought Sasha, the gurgle of water and the scraping of steel pleasant to his ears as he did the domestic round of his own room, dusting and tidying things away as Valentina had instructed. Perhaps he wouldn't report him. He was harmless. A bit cissy. Those bastards on the corner would be bound to give him a kicking. Better not.

As he was sweeping under the radiator with a hand-broom, Bogat popped his head round the door.

"Like your pinny!" Valentina had given him an apron for his birthday and although she had tried to buy one masculine enough to spare his blushes, Sasha still felt daft because Bogat had caught him in it.

"Yes?" he said, standing the broom in a corner and straightening up.

"Got a little problem," said Bogat. His hands were smeared with grease, and strands of caulking stuck to his shirt. "I want to stop-off the down pipe, only the sealant is rock hard in the joint. My van's downstairs. Think you could run down for my big Stilsons and bring up my taps and dies set at the same time? Can't go myself because I've just rigged up a temporary overflow from the main and it won't hold for more than a minute or two if I'm not there to pack it. Don't want to be flooded out, do we? Sorry to be a nuisance."

"All right," said Sasha reluctantly. "But how will I know what to look for?"

"No bother. My mate's down there, he'll show you. Big fellow – called Rocky. Tell him I've hit a snag, but I shouldn't be much longer."

Still in his striped apron, Sasha made off down the stairs. Bogat leaned over the landing-rail and shouted after him. "A long box for the dies – fat as a copper's thingummy!"

His whinnying laugh descended the stairwell.

"Blast you," muttered the dustman, undoing the waist strings of his pinafore as he half-slid and half-ran, his heel backs glancing the steps of the second flight. It was shadowy, but enough summer light had filtered through the windows for him to see his way without resorting to the electric light.

A tall man stood smoking a pipe at the side of the main door. When Sasha appeared on the first-floor landing, he took the pipe from his mouth in a leisurely fashion, knocked it out against the side of his shoe and pushed it, bowl upwards, behind the row of ballpoint pens in his top pocket. As Sasha thrust out his hand to push open the glass door the man smiled and stepped back a pace, folding his arms.

On the street an ambulance was parked. Two of its wheels were on the pavement in front of the entrance. Except for a lone militiaman strolling up and down in front of the Embassy compound there was not a soul to be seen. No van, no plumber's mate.

Sasha was about to call over to the militiaman to ask if he had seen a van drive away, when a powerful hand gripped the neck loop of his apron from behind and yanked him out of the sunlight into the shade of the ground-floor lobby, nearly garrotting him. Wheezing and arching his back against the apron-strings which cut into his throat, he felt that he was on the point of swooning. Suddenly, the grip relaxed but the hand maintained sufficient hold to prevent him from turning. A wrist-watch tick-tocked loudly under his ear and there was a smell of stale tobacco-smoke and sweat.

"Now, aren't we just the duckiest little home-help?" hissed a voice. "Keep absolutely still and you can have your head back in a minute."

A hand moved swiftly, lightly brushing his body, judiciously patting for the areas where pockets might be. The hold at his neck tightened agonisingly as his spine was forced back to allow a similar search of his legs and arms. Apparently satisfied, the unknown assailant gave a final violent wrench and shoved him on to the tiled floor.

"All right, frilly knickers. What have you done with him?"

Sasha unwound the ligature and tried to speak, but his throat burned and his croak was unintelligible.

"I can wait," said the man with the pipe. "You're going nowhere and I've got all the time in the world." He sat on the bottom step, took out his pipe and rubbed it slowly against the side of his nose. The bowl shone darkly as he twirled it in his fingers. From the pocket of his tweed jacket he took a silver container resembling a round snuff-box and placing it snugly in the palm of his hand, applied pressure to its sides. A lid flicked up and he began to stuff the pipe with *Zolotoye runo* tobacco, tamping down the excess with the flat of his matchbox. Stretching his neck from side to side and caressing the tenderest patches of skin with his fingertips, Sasha followed the whole process from the floor. At last the stranger lit up and the air filled with an agreeable, sweetish aroma. He puffed on his pipe. He was right. There seemed to be no hurry at all.

Besides the tweed jacket, he wore a blue shirt with a white collar which might have been detachable – from his angle, Sasha could not tell – maroon jumper, reminiscent of one of Bobby's cashmeres; an obliquely-striped white and black tie; beautifully-creased grey flannels, and brown shoes of a type Sasha had never seen before. A sort of half-shoe, half-boot, with leather laces. The man was hard to place. A long haggard face with deep rings under the eyes, a fine, aquiline nose, wide-set grey eyes and ginger hair, brush-cut. He looked like an over-elegant Russian imitating what he thought was a foreign style of dress. Like someone who appeared in those language-lesson playlets on afternoon TV where all the Englishmen had umbrellas and waistcoats and sat about in parks discussing the weather.

Working the saliva round his mouth, Sasha swallowed, several times, until the fluid had sufficiently lubricated his voice-box for him to try out a question.

"Where's Rocky?"

"Rocky? Oh, Rocky knows where he is. Here's Rocky. This is him," said the man, pointing the stem of his pipe at his chest. "What Rocky wants to know is, what you've done to his friend."

"The drains man?" said Sasha, his throat easing.

"The drains man," said Rocky. "Have you been interfering with him?"

Sasha was unsure how to take this. "I let him get on with the job, if that's what you mean. I don't know anything about drains. I never touched him."

Rocky surveyed the crumpled figure on the ground. Brown stains splashed on to the wall as he shook his pipe stem free of moisture. "I bet you didn't," he drawled, smiling for the first time since Sasha had passed him at the door. "Too rich for your palate, I imagine. Still, you make your own fun round here, or so they tell me."

"I don't know what you think you're playing at, you two," said Sasha getting to his feet. "But do I get to take your pal's taps and dies and stuff or do I piss off before the pair of you get together for another thumping session?"

"Now, laddie," said Rocky quietly, not budging from the step. "Do yourself a favour. Just stay there and keep mum until I indicate that you are to open your mouth. That way we can transact our little business with the minimum of inconvenience."

Sasha had never heard anyone speak with such an odd blend of condescension, pedantry and threat. With the bits of street talk mixed in, Rocky sounded part pickpocket and part newspaper leader. He remembered Marya Fyodorovna and fell silent.

If she and Rocky weren't related, they were close enough to use each other's toothbrush; they had a slangy insolence which must come from being in the know. They made you feel helpless.

"You've never played cricket, I expect," said Rocky.

This was true. For all Sasha knew, cricket could have been black-jack, a stage role, or a perversion. Perceiving no signal to speak, he followed Rocky's advice and listened.

"Cricket," Rocky went on, hitching up the knees of his flannels and inspecting the sides of his miniboots, "cricket is an English game, nowadays played mostly by negroes. Or rather, I should say, played *best* by negroes. It is a very elegant game. Even what we might call a *classy* game. You follow me?" Sasha nodded dumbly. "They dress up for it, all in white. Every person in a cricket team is clothed in white."

Sasha saw a troupe of black men in tailored burnouses limbering up on the touch line, whirling like dervishes and uttering strange cries.

"The ball is very hard, the cricket bat is made of solid wood. Cricket is the most dangerous game in the world. Yet, to look at the players, you would think that they were dressed for a tea-party, so cool and unflustered do they appear. Games of cricket occupy several entire days." Rocky went on to explain some of the nastier aspects of the play so that Sasha thought it sounded rather like ice-hockey played on grass with a stun-grenade for a puck. "So beneath the surface lurks a terrible violence. People are killed at games of cricket. Not only the players, but spectators, too. They are drawn in, as it were, and struck down. Are you taking my meaning?"

Sasha was damned if he were, but he wasn't surprised that black men had come to out-do the white. The only black man he knew had once thrashed Len in a fight over a woman. They were tough.

"You mean, it'd never really catch on here? Too primitive?"

"Oh no, it's caught on all right. Except the likes of you never see it being played, do you?"

"Ah," said Sasha, accepting the further permission to speak. "Like porno-movies – you know they go on, but you never know where."

"Excellently put," said Rocky. "While the show goes on, you're always knocking at the wrong door."

"I get that," said Sasha. "But what has this cricket got to do with me and the drains man, and you down here and the strangling bit?"

"You," said Rocky, drawing himself up, and standing nose to nose with Sasha, the pipe still between his teeth. "You, laddie, have walked into a porno-movie cricket match and the in-field is zinging with very many, very, very hard, totally invisible balls. So what do you do?"

Sasha knew. "Keep my head down."

"Here's a laddie who doesn't need to be told twice. He keeps his head down." Rocky dug the fingers of a well-manicured hand into the flesh of Sasha's shoulder. "Now, you and I will have to continue our discussion at a more convenient time and place. To our mutual benefit, a colloquy, filling in the gaps of our inadequate education. Instructive for both of us, don't you think?"

"What about?" said Sasha.

"Oh, this and that. In my line of business you never know what you're going to find until you start looking. I bet you've seen a few sights in your time and heard a few things. The sort of things a man in my position is never privileged to see or hear – at first hand."

Sasha watched him, transfixed, like the pilot who sees the ground coming up at him but can't pull out of a dive.

"I just mind my own business," he said trying to draw away from Rocky's hand. "I'm no good to you."

Rocky stiffened and his nails dug harder. "I'm your business," he said in a whisper. "Mind me."

Without another word he inserted a flannelled knee between Sasha's legs and gently rubbed it up and down in a way that Sasha himself had often done to girls in the opportunistic fumbles preparatory to a good-night kiss.

He had time to say: "Hey, I'm not . . ." before Rocky struck him neatly on the delicate bone above and behind the ear. Had Rocky been a boxer it would have been a beautifully-angled, very short punch, but instead of his knuckles he had used a sap the size and shape of a small avocado, leather-covered and filled with small shot. As Sasha went down, clutching at the tweed jacket, Rocky selected his moment and with a similar economy of effort sprung his knee upwards and fractured Sasha's left cheek as neatly as a cosmetic surgeon snapping a nose-bone.

From the Embassy side of the road, the militiaman watched impassively as Rocky polished the instep of his right boot against the back of his trouser leg to buff up the scratch that came from the last kick to Sasha's mouth as he lay on his back behind the glass door, blood darkening the white stripes of his apron.

"Pissed as a newt," he called out as he brought Sasha round to the back of the ambulance, managing to hold him semi-upright with one immensely strong forearm while he unbunched the keys to the tailgate. He had difficulties with Sasha's feet which straggled brokenly over the bumper but he eventually bundled them in, slammed the door and locked it. Curtains round the windows of the rear section obscured the body from the view of inquisitive passers-by.

Rocky brushed himself down, turned and went back through the glass door.

When Sasha came to, the militiaman was fiddling at the aperture of the ambulance window from the driver's side, his walkie-talkie clattering against the door pillar. It was a squeeze but he forced his arm through the quarter-light and unlatched the door-handle from inside. His face was very near to Sasha's; he was the one whose money Boris had never repaid.

"Are you all right, mate?" he said. Sasha groaned. The cheek had swelled up and he could only mumble. "What does it look like to you?"

The militiaman explored the cheek with his index-finger.

"Definitely not cheerful," he said. "You've lost a tooth as well."

"Only one?" said Sasha, his mouth filled with blood and what felt like granite chippings: "I never thought coppers could count."

"Look," said the policeman confidentially, indicating the entrance to Sasha's block with his eyebrows. "I recognise the bugger. He does it for fun. He ought to be locked up."

"I ought to have known," said Sasha. "He's in it for the kicks."

"That's right. They take all kinds of scruff these days. Whatever happened to standards? Makes you wonder what the country's . . ."

Sasha was fighting off the pain in his face and jaw, while he dragged himself to a sitting position and tried to think. "Here, can we talk about national decline some other time? Give me a hand to get out of this."

The militiaman hesitated, partially closed the door and looked round the street.

"Or is it more than your job's worth?" cried Sasha, his hand on the inside catch.

"Bugger that. I don't like his sort any more than he likes you. It's a question of standards," repeated the policeman.

Over the way the bull-horn in his milibox began to parp with a low insistent tone. "That's the station. I've got to go — they won't stop till I've answered. Come on, he's only done your head, your legs still work."

Sasha could hardly stand. The militiaman hustled him across the road.

"I'm going to drop out for a couple of days," said Sasha over the growl of the horn. "Get a message to my missis, will you?"

"Who's your missis?"

"The red-head."

"The red-head? Ah, the red-head, I know. The red-head with the big . . ."

"That's her," said Sasha. "Tell her I can't get married tomorrow."

"Tell her you can't . . . ? Hey, I know you, don't I?" called the policeman.

Sasha staggered away towards the nearest side-street.

"You never came back with the beer. You owe me two roubles!"

"Don't worry!" Sasha shouted back. "I'll put it in the post."

25

Arriving at work, Olga found a note from her boss in the in-tray. He suggested a meeting at twelve.

The director of her literary agency, Matvey Yakovlyevich Shkiry-atov, was a huge man with freckly face and prominent ears whom she had known for half her life. His tempers, jokes and unsuccessful but agreeable flirtatiousness were part of her daily round. As chief translator and editor she had achieved a certain degree of freedom and she enjoyed it because Matvey encouraged her to do so. He respected her as the cleverest woman he had known and often said that she should be running the agency herself. Olga had become his office friend, his confidante, but never, as she had once told Bobby Weston in a rare access of pride, never his mistress.

Shkiryatova still telephoned most days although they had been married for almost thirty years. The girls on the switchboard listened to the quarrels, tickled by the spiritless way their huge, blustering boss gave in to all his wife's demands. That in their own home the Shkiryatovs led a perfectly amicable existence, only Olga knew. They quarrelled in public, over the telephone; in their roomy, almost luxurious flat they barely exchanged a word.

Today she wondered what problem had cropped up. Private or professional? There had been occasions lately when she had entered his office to find him startlingly drunk, practically speechless with his secretary pulling warning faces to Olga in the direction of the girls in the typing pool. Olga and a trusted porter had waited until the building cleared in the late afternoon before calling a taxi, rather than using the official driver, and bribing the cabbie to help him out and as far as his own elevator. The precautions were excessive: most of the agency workers were fond of Matvey Yakovlyevich, a kindly man in spite of his bark, but they saw less of him than his private secretary, a generally uncomplaining girl who was sometimes at her wit's end when he was bad. Then she could not file his reports without checking them for errors – his grammar deteriorated with his state of mind – or had to write his letters when he was too drunk to sign his name or clear his filing cabinet of empty bottles and keep Shkiryatova out of the building should she decide to call.

Instead of roaring out a greeting, letting fly one of his glorious laughs, putting an arm round her and coaxing her to sample some of the rich or intoxicating titbits laid out on his battered desk; instead of performing any of the teasing little rituals which had coloured her office life for so long, he kept to his seat, not even looking up but staring at the wide, gold ring on his third finger, a present from his dead daughter whom he had idolised.

"Take a seat, Olga Sergeyevna, take a seat." The formality of the naming made her uneasy. From the top drawer of the desk he took out a long, slender Havana cigar, lit it, and swivelled round to face the window, his back towards her. Had he lost his job? They would never sack him surely? Had somebody complained about him to the Ministry – or worse, to Shkiryatova? His desk was very bare and exceptionally tidy: no piles of galleys, off-prints, dirty glasses and half-eaten chocolate bars. Even the floor was clear of litter.

"I've never been much good at this sort of thing." He swivelled back again and gave her the ghost of one of his old, energetic scowls. Why did hair only seem to flourish in inappropriate parts of his head so that whereas his nose and ears were fuzzy, his head was almost completely bare and his moustache pathetically sparse?

"No good at all, blast it." In the stock-room next door was a stone sink. Olga heard splashes as he drew off some water into two of the cardboard cups he kept on the filing cabinet. "If you weren't such a tedious little prude I'd offer you something stronger," he said, lumbering out and pushing a cup towards her.

She took the cup but did not drink or reply. There was a bleak restraint in his manner which she did not like.

"I don't know how to start," he muttered. "Never thought I'd have to do this."

It must be the sack. A pain started in her throat and for the first time in her life she knew why people smoked cigarettes.

"Today is Tuesday, isn't it? And I know that on Tuesdays you pop along to see that journalist friend of yours, Tatyana Borisovna Lestyeva."

This was odd. As far as she could recall, she had never mentioned Tanya to him. But if it were about her, Olga found she could breathe again, since Tanya existed only on the periphery of her professional world. And if she had had an accident surely no one would have briefed Shkiryatov to break the news.

"Yes, well, what about her?"

Sweat shone at the sides of his fleshy nostrils. "I am bound to tell you, to warn you. I have been instructed to warn you . . ." His voice was high and expressionless and the words would not come at his bidding. ". . . not to visit her again."

"You've been *instructed*?" said Olga, rattled but incredulous. "By whom have you been *instructed*?"

"By a friend."

"And which of your friends issues instructions to a man in your position?"

"You bloody well know who!" he spat. "A friend who has friends. These things have a way of percolating downwards without the formality of orders. It's quite clear what has to be done."

Her contemptuous, unpitying, fearful gaze irritated him and he cursed, using obscene slang which she was amazed to hear from his mouth but before long he seemed to lose heart.

"I can do without that old-fashioned look, my girl," he mumbled, as much to himself as to her. "You know it's not my fault, those bastards do what they like. Don't worry, I've kept you out of it. I can still take care of you." There were tears in his eyes but Olga hardened, refusing her sympathy.

"What will happen to Tanya?"

She had to strain to catch his words. "They're taking her in tonight. There'll be charges, serious charges. Exactly what, I don't know yet."

If anyone had accused Matvey of cowardice, she would have agreed that, yes, he was a coward but his cowardice was irrelevant. In his professional life he had no need of courage. The freedom he gave her was not the concession of a brave man, but the politic act of a lazy and clever one. Had she been as unprincipled and ambitious as he, their collaboration would have been that between overseer and slave. As it was, he could pride himself on being a liberal master. In reality he was capable of selling himself, her, and them all.

Tanya was different, she loved Tanya. Tanya was out of his moral class. The association of the two women irked him precisely for this reason.

"Couldn't you have put in a word for her with those friends of yours?" she said. "Or are you quite devoid of conscience?"

"Conscience?" he bellowed, knowing that the secretaries were listening in the ante-room. "Conscience? I will have no talk here of irresponsibility of that kind. You cant to your priest about all that if it makes you happy, but I recognise no individualistic humbugging higher authority here. Can't you see I'm trying to help you, you idiotic woman? You have no loyalties to her or to yourself. None! None! None that go beyond that loyalty which embraces us all. You have some idea that you can stand aside, make judgements on the merits of the case. There is no *private* life like that, and your pretence that there is, is an old maid's delusion. All I want is that you don't walk out of this room broadcasting that you knew, the whole time, what she was up to, and you think that because of it she's some kind of admirable and wonderful person."

Olga stood up. "Tanya had enemies. People on that magazine were jealous of her talent, people who would lie in order to ruin her . . . Time-servers, idlers, backbiters, rascals . . . Oh yes, Matvey Yakovlyevich, and cowards, cowards like you!"

Long conditioning by similar abuse from his wife rendered him easily speechless and guilt-ridden. He blushed like a girl and tried to take her hand, as if he could only regain his composure by the contact, but she was too upset to keep still.

"I always pick the wrong women," he groaned. "Do you think I'd have been different if I'd married you?"

"To have married me, Matvey Yakovlyevich, you would have needed to be a man," she said with a smile.

"Oh, God, Olichka, this is turning into a lovers' quarrel. Let's start again."

She listened quietly as Matvey talked quickly, fluently, outlining the extent of Tanya's lunatic schemes, schemes she had never told anyone about, not even Olga, schemes that Fat Masha alone had known.

"A talented journalist she may be, my dear, but she has no other talents. At least, not for clandestine politicking. Nobody at *Feministka* conspired to trap her. They didn't have to. She was right out there, in the open, inciting subversion and political mayhem. Even then, they were so dozy it took years for them to rumble her."

Olga shook her head. "We're talking about another person, not my Tanya. That sort of thing is just not her style."

"Listen, Olya, listen. Do try to get it straight. Take that wretched problem page she established . . . apparently it was a front for some daft women's political movement."

Olga blinked rapidly, fighting down her disdain for his easy way with the in-built, perverse grandiloquence of this language. "Movements indeed! You and I make a 'movement'. You, me and the office-cleaner criticising the quality of the floor mops are a 'subversive organisation'!"

"Oh, I know it sounds like a story from a militiaman's notebook but there must be something in it. No one is going to waste time and personnel on office chit-chat."

"Them! They've nothing to do."

"Listen, Olya, I said you knew nothing about it yet!"

"All right, all right, persuade me. Go ahead."

He cleared his throat and spoke even faster than before, as if the story were a draught of nasty medicine to be got down quick.

"She and that fat assistant, Masha, they tampered with the numeration code on the Xerox, got supplies of paper on the black market and dished out some rubbishy feminist manifesto to all the women who'd written to them."

"Ha!" said Olga. "Dyed-in-the-wool revolutionaries undermining the state with cake recipes."

"It was serious, I tell you. Hundreds and thousands of these things have gone out!"

"So what? I fail to see anything more in that than stealing State electricity and engaging in a little underhand commerce. You do both every time you ring up that smut-peddler Krasyenko about those horrid books."

Krasyenko was a speculator whose speciality was eighteenth-century French pornographic book engravings.

"Don't you? Don't you? Well, that's just where the mouse is blind to pussy when he thinks they're equals because they both preen their whiskers, have four feet and long tails. It's a question of motive that separates them. That, and scale. Are you following me?"

"Periodically, Matvey Yakovlyevich. You know how I abhor quaintness of speech."

"Damnation, woman, I'll spell it out, unornamented. She has been issuing open invitations to the female all-and-sundry of our great land to create groups, cells, circles — whatever you like to call them — with the object of 'raising their political consciousness' and establishing contacts with like-minded females abroad. I ask you! And all this using State property, even stamping the envelopes with the official franking machine! Are these the acts of a good woman, a woman whom you trust, confide in, respect? Is she in her right mind?"

"There you have your answer, Matvey. That's clockwork politics in the electronic age. She's very, very sincere and obviously quite hopelessly incompetent: in the war she would have dropped leaflets on Berchtesgaden imploring Hitler not to bomb us for the sake of his immortal soul. Have you lost all your sympathy and imagination? Those are the acts of someone terminally innocent."

He took out a fresh cigar, ran the whole length of it under his nose and then began to unroll the leaf, making a little pile of bits in an ashtray.

"Bah!" he snorted. "You should have been here when they came. Perhaps they'd have taken it from a little old lady."

"Here? You mean, they came here?" asked Olga, looking about her as though some physical taint had been left on the furnishings.

"No, no, only the errand-boy." The memory evidently disturbed him. The cigar was almost destroyed and he gave the inner packing a vicious rip which showered his desk with the remnants. "They're a bit odd nowadays, those people. Odd, definitely odd. I never expected it."

"Unpredictable, you mean? Well, they're not running their own show, are they? They're probably as hazy as you about why they have to do things as they do and when they do — someone hidden upstairs is pulling their strings."

"No, no. It's more a matter of *demeanour*, if you take my meaning." Matvey gave her a shifty glance to see if she had taken his point.

"What then, for heaven's sake?"

"*They're a bunch of screaming pansies.*" His roar could have stopped a clock. Outside the door the cleaning-woman, broom in hand, froze with delight, glanced sagely at Matvey Yakovlyevich's confidential secretary and tapped the side of her forehead. They settled to for the sequel, but Matvey, exasperated at his own outburst, dropped his voice to a whisper. "Absolutely, the God's truth, I tell you, as queer as a bear in georgette knickers. Horrible, horrible. It's a disease. They ought to be put down."

Matvey feared homosexuals as some women fear spiders. It was a phobia which years of intellectual considerateness for strange clients had left unmastered.

"Poor boy," she said sweetly. "Did he try to get off with you?"

"Olga Sergeyevna, I had to shake his hand. Things aren't what they were. These creatures have *power*."

"You mean there was more than one?"

"That's the whole point, you see." He leant far across the desk. "The one the first one took me to, *he* was worse."

"How *worse*? Aren't they all just as bad as one another as far as you're concerned?"

Matvey considered this for a moment. "Well, different, then. Yes, there was a definite difference. The first one was the tough kind — the cropped-hair kind, with hands like a gas-fitter's and ghastly boots. You could only tell about him from his voice. But the other, he wore scent, he was like, he was like — the girl-half."

"Matvey Yakovlyevich, aren't you forgetting something?"

"I don't think so, honestly, my dear, that's how he was. You know, the mincing variety, waving his . . ."

"Forgetting what you were there for. Which is presumably why I am here now."

"Absolutely right, Olya, absolutely. That's why we're here."

It took a little time for Matvey to come down from his high point of fascinated outrage but Olga gradually led him up to the matter at issue.

"Apparently," he said, clearing his throat, "in the course of their investigations of Lestyeva they had stumbled – that was the word, stumbled – on a few irregularities." He stopped speaking and waved a hand vaguely at the walls of the office.

Olga was determined to drag it out of him. "Irregularities," she prompted.

"Some . . . irregularities, Olya, yes."

"What, where, when?"

"Oh, irregularities, various things."

"For the love of God, Matvey, *where?*"

He snapped out of his trance-like state with a shout that made her jump. "Where do you think, woman? Where do you think – *here!*"

He had the upper hand now. Shamefaced but defiant he floundered on, not daring to meet her eye. "I hire people who have too many contacts, with foreigners, he said – that's what. And not only that, but the same people have a direct line to Lestyeva."

Olga flushed a deep pink. "I thought we'd get down to me in the end. Now, look here, Matvey Yakovlyevich, you can just take a message back to your little invert: nobody tells me who I can and can't be friendly with. I've done nothing, nothing at all."

His face seemed to have shrivelled from exhaustion. Letting his body sag against the back of his chair he glared at her. "You go and argue the toss with them yourself. I'm sick of it all."

At this she realised that matters might be more serious for him than for her.

"Let's try to work it out, Matvey. Right . . . Tanya has committed some indiscretions. Tanya is a close friend of mine. And I work for you. Aren't I the weak link in the plot? My life on the whole is so extremely dull and respectable, not exciting, not political. A few questions here and there would establish that. How could anything I do be a problem for either of you?"

"God knows," he sighed. "Neither you nor Lestyeva are the types to give the jumpiest policeman nightmares. It's the simple fact of a connection. But I think there's more in it than that. You've told me yourself that your flat is an open house for interesting people, from here and abroad, and I rather admire your lack of discretion. But there's no denying the risk. And some of our work here, as you well appreciate, has its sensitive aspects. Your neighbours might take a less sophisticated view and it would only take one disgruntled individual to make a lot of trouble for you, over what is essentially a harmless desire to be open-mindedly sociable. They want to cover themselves, want to be one step ahead if you really are up to something. The same applies to the lads with the after-shave — their job is to lop off the branches if there are no buds left to nip. What seems to have happened is that someone has offered you up as a sacrifice — either because he or she makes a bit extra by doing a little social watchmanship or — and this is the more tiresome — they have got it in for you for some personal reason. All I can tell you is that the information which has been gleaned about your life and habits is pretty extensive, intimate and accurate. Do you have any enemies as close to home as that?"

Olga's mind flew instantly to Sasha and she saw him, as though for the first time, revealed in his true colours. James, Sasha, Roberta, Sasha. Sasha had been everywhere then. Still was. Had wormed his way into their lives. Sasha, how could you?

The view of the city through Matvey Yakovlyevich's great plate-glass window was drenched in brilliant light. Suddenly the little office seemed stiflingly hot. The posters of pretty girls advertising French wine, his maps of the London underground, were all missing from the wall, and the photograph of his daughter lay face down on his desk.

"Matvey," she said slowly. "Matvey, I know they have done something to you because of me. What is it? Tell me."

"Me?" he growled, opening the bottom drawer of the filing cabinet. "Oh, they *bribed* me. Look. Caviare, Finnish lingonberry vodka, books, sturgeon. A load of sickly muck I can't stand. Even the Tsvetayeva. Relieve me of it, my sweet. It'll only make my wife fat and discontented." He piled it all up on her side of the desk. "Now what a lot of junk, not my taste at all."

"Matvey," she said sternly. "You *never* take bribes. You bought it this morning, didn't you? For me?"

He blew out his cheeks in pretended self-disgust. "Well, what the hell else could I have done? I had to make some kind of splurge after listening to that little swine. Instead of taking a poke at him, I listened. Typical. I never get it right. There was caviare in his office, too, that's what gave me the idea. Caviare, I thought, is for ladies, not catamites. So I lashed out — afterwards, with roubles."

A few soft words from her and he would break down. She knew him of old: he was always moved to tears at the prospect of his own generosity. If she yielded too far to her own inclinations of pity and gratitude (he had tried, in his clumsy way, to help her, hadn't he?) he might make a spring. Men needed watching all the time. So boring. Did they ever think of anything else?

"Matvey, thank you. You are a dear man. But what about the agency? Are they going to leave us alone here, not bother us, I mean?"

The agency had been Matvey's bolthole, the only place where he was cherished, loved and understood. He felt safe in his office, just as she had felt safe working for him.

"No problem about you, Olya. That's been fixed. One or two other changes, though – trifling adjustments, you know, a little restructuring. Administrative stuff."

"So they're making you do the dirty work for them? How awful – sacking people who'll hate you for it and not know why it's being done and you can't explain. Awful."

"All part of the job," he said briskly.

"I don't know how you can do it, I really don't."

He caressed the stitching of the edges of the lapels of his English-made suit. "Oh, it's a knack, my dear, you develop it. This time, however, I won't need it."

The window saturated his figure with noon-day light. Every fleck of colour had drained from his great moonface, and she thought of discs of unleavened bread. Making love to that. Fancy. Straddled by a chapati in tweeds.

"Second nature by now, I imagine," she said automatically, wondering how long it must take him to undress, swaddled as he was in all that excellent cloth.

"Yes, but I won't be doing it. After today, I won't be here."

"Why not?"

"Why not? Why not?" he said, irritated at her naïveté. "Because moving me on is part of the deal. I go. You stay."

Olga sank down white-faced on to the hard Bauhaus chair. For a few moments the only sound was of a typewriter a long way off, tapping softly and irregularly. Some junior was practising her speeds during the meal-break. Matvey fiddled with the neck of the red vodka liqueur bottle.

"They don't like the way I run things here," he said. "They reckon I'm too familiar with you all. Unvigilant is the word, I believe. Then there's the drinking. Everything comes out in this kind of wash. An opportunity has been seized to tighten things up, that's all."

The idea of a drink was distinctly appealing to Olga at this very minute.

"But what will happen to you, Matvey, after all this?"

"Oh, there'll be no scandal, if that's what you think. They're *promoting* me," he said with a queer, unhappy grin. "Moving me onwards and upwards – a thousand miles from Moscow. My wife calls it transportation and I think she's got something."

For Olga the swiftness of these transitions was bewildering and terrifying. Before she had fully taken in the unpleasantness – to put it mildly – of the exposure of her treasured privacy to God knows what little uniformed ragamuffins with their preposterous suspicions of her relationships with many of her friends, he had jollied her along by assuring her that her job was still secure. Now, apparently, he had lost his; lost his because of her; ruined his marriage (Shkiryatova would barricade herself in their flat rather than move to some provincial hole). She had lost her freedom with her boss, he had lost his job, his privileged Moscow existence and, probably, his wife.

Matvey Yakovlyevich had not yet finished with her. Animation had returned to his round face as he watched her confusion with all his old, fond malice.

"I wonder how the staff will take to my successor?" he said, knowing the anguish the question would cause her. His deputy, Mikhail Ivanovich Gudzii, was an elderly bachelor.

"If it's Mikhail Ivanovich, they'll revolt, Matvey, I swear it. They can't bear that old shellback namby-pamby. He feels himself as they take dictation." She shuddered.

"Don't concern yourself, my dear, this is not Buggins' turn. I have the nomination. I have *made* the nomination." His smile broadened as he remembered his skill in pulling his crowning diplomatic *coup*. "After some persuasion, they saw the advantages. Warmed to them, eventually, slapped me on the back for my brilliance. I may be an old dog, but I'm not a done dog, not yet."

Olga's restraint broke, tedium overcoming her fear. "Merciful God, Matvey! Where is all this leading? Get on with it!"

He stood and flung his arms wide in a gesture of embrace. "Olya, my love, the job is *yours*."

"Oh no," she whispered, like a girl faced with a proposal of marriage from a man who up till then had always behaved as an uncle. "Oh, no, no, no. That simply cannot be."

Her collapse appeared to excite him and he began to shout. "Damn it, woman! Doesn't that solve everything? Don't you know what you're being offered, what it *means*? A flat in Co-operative Housing, no more living cheek-by-jowl with drunks, access to a few luxuries in life, a bit of travel thrown in. And – *authority*!"

Crouching on the low chair, she steeled herself for the onslaught, hands over her ears.

"Well?" He was raving; wild at her rejection of this last, and finest present he could make her. "Well? Well? *Well*?"

She took the opportunity to broach the vodka and pour him out a large measure in a paper cup. He drank it down in a single movement, shook his head and whistled.

"Ugh – sweeter than Pepsi."

"Never mind. It'll calm you down," said Olga.

"How can you expect me to keep calm under all this . . . this provocation?" he muttered in his old, hoarse voice, as if her refusal had been not totally unexpected, but, on the contrary had cleared his mind, even reassured him. "I'm getting old. I can't convince women any more."

"You always feel old when you can't get your own way." The relationship was nearly back on its old footing.

She knew she had not disappointed him if he could sulk.

"I've never got my own way with you, have I, dear?" he said, coming out from the desk to stand behind her, his hands pressing down on her shoulders. "What I went through to fix that up for you! I pulled every trick I knew. And do you know what persuaded them in the end? That they could keep an eye on you better, if you were in some sort of relationship to them. I actually used that frightful word 'relationship'."

Shkiryatov detested the mildest scientific terms of art, preferring to see both public and private connection as a furtive grappling of soul with soul, its drive originating in the murkiest recesses of an ineradicable human need to dominate.

"You would have to report – on yourself and on the others. It was thought, after I had elaborated the 'relationship' for them, that that bit of stick, together with their bit of carrot in the shape of a fancier life-style, would do the job nicely. They never reckoned on your unholy zest for buggering things up. Neither did I, this time, but I can't say I'm surprised."

He ran his fingers as far as he dared down the front of her frock, balancing the liberties which her succumbing to the emotionalism of the scenario conferred on him, against her known testiness at his advances. This time, however, she did not shrug him away and his hands crossed over her chest lightly enfolding her breasts. Bending low, he rubbed his nose against the lobe of her left ear and whispered: "Why are you such a stiff-necked little bitch, Olichka?"

"Because, Matvey," she said, slowly, enjoying the warmth of his breath and the solidity of his big hands, and relaxing in the knowledge that it was all over, and that he could have no more surprises for her, "because there are so few people whom I want to want me, and if I were not what you say I am, they might still want me, but I wouldn't want them."

"Mmmm," said Matvey. "That's a captivating little moral fly-trap. Does it mean that you'll go to bed with me if I pander to you, morally? Accord you, as they say, grudging, but admiring respect?"

"What it means, Matvey, is that although I might love to be ravished by an old fraud like you, an old fraud like you will reach no further than he has at present, because he's an old fraud." She turned her neck and kissed the tip of his nose. His hands fell away.

"Seriously, Olya," he said, back at his side of the desk. "Church-going should be no bar. There are plenty of people in much bigger jobs than mine who have a devout side. Well, I suppose that's what it is. They manage to pay their devotions even-handedly, anyway: 'Unto Caesar the things that are Caesar's', isn't it?"

"I know. That's Christ's Judaic temporising – an appearance of equivalent formalities. But one always has precedence over the other. It's like speaking several languages and being so proud of your fluency that you say you are equally at home with them all when you know you're not, and cleave to the mother tongue and swear, natively, in a crisis."

"Belief can make you as direct, as uncompromising as that?"

"It can, it does," she said. "And I don't want the *angst* of anticipating a collision between that and what every good Director has to trot out as his guiding Party lights, every moment of my working life. I'm too old as well. You forget – I am a Stalin child. That bit deep into my heart. I could tell you where all the busts once were in the vacant niches of MGU or the Gosplan building. We ought to have a sing-song occasionally; I have not forgotten one word of all the songs we learned at school. To disillusion me with the world of men was cruel and irreparable. My innocence was taken young. The Church permits doubt because without it there is no fault. These are simple things, Matvey. All you offer is the pretence of certainty, a conspiracy of the factitiously right-minded."

"I don't understand you, Olya. I never have."

You liar, she thought. He understood but preferred the fake to the real, as most men. For him, faith ought to accommodate the world, make the most of it, not confront it with its own inadequacy. Look on the bright side was his watchword. It was a social ritual, decently enacted and kept under wraps.

"And what you say you understand is not what you do understand, Matvey, you old fox. You're a romantic bubbling in his own stew of Leninist catchphrases, State Publishing's Five Year Plan, and genuflections to the wonder-working ikon of Our Lady of Kazan. All the contemporary Russias rolled into one. Damn Byzantium, be a Roman, be pitiless about your fate. Be a man, like my brother."

He saw her to the door across the ante-room and into the lift, handing over the pile of presents as she stood with her finger on the "wait" button. "You won't forget me, Olyonok, will you?" he muttered, using the pretty diminutive with a hint of peevishness.

"No. You will forget me."

"Ah," he said, in a squeaky voice, hand on hip. "Nowadays, my dear, don't you think that falling on one's sword is so frightfully *passé*?"

26

There was no reason to feel afraid. Matvey had assured her that refusing promotion would bring no reprisals. Yet, as she took the long way home, Olga shivered in the hot afternoon sun. She needed time to think, and the chance to be alone among the crowds thronging the boulevard.

Matvey had gone. For the last time she had heard him pass her door, breathing heavily and shouting for his driver. At some time during the afternoon he would have telephoned to report on the outcome of their final interview. There was a moment when he had come to her again; stood for a long while outside her office, his hand on the door-lever. But it had quickly sprung up again as he evidently changed his mind and abandoned any hope of forcing her to reconsider. He had accepted defeat.

Now she was without a refuge. No longer could she rely on that solid, reassuring presence to keep at bay the thousand and one petty irritations which her day-to-day working life threw up. From now on she was to be isolated. Isolated and exposed.

Under the still limes and elms of the broad walk, the heat was dense. Red dust filmed her shoes as she drifted slowly through the masses of Muscovites who bumped, paused and twisted round her, anxious to be away to train or bus, to be home, to be quiet, to be out of the humid bustle and into the breeze which, summer or winter, never ceased to sweep between the great tower blocks on the outskirts of town. Threading her way through the swell, lost to the world about her, she seemed to have been walking for hours. At an intersection of the Tverskoy she stopped and waited for the lights to change. Out of the shade, the approach of evening brought little relief. The sun blazed and her flimsy scarf clung wetly to the throbbing pulse of her neck. Underfoot, the kerb was scorching.

Ahead of her was a wiry little woman in black. A white-faced man panted up behind, almost pushing them into the road. Without apology he pressed himself between the women and turned to wave to a fat old lady in a floral dress, who was struggling with a small boy.

"Mother of God, Fyodor!" she shouted. "I can't bear another moment of this!"

On the other side of the road, row upon row of swaying, swerving figures hovered between pavement and gutter, anticipating the red light at the opposite junction but fearful of the militiaman's whistle. As the cars stopped on each side the mob broke and rushed across, avoiding midway collisions by weaving expertly in and out.

For a second or two Olga could not move but stood in a dream as if she had been planted naked and lost amid this respectable and determined citizenry. But the onrush carried her off and she crossed, panic-stricken at the contagious haste.

Safely over, she found her hand held by the little wiry woman who was looking at her with concern from beneath greened eyelids.

"It's this awful drought." She made it sound as if it were someone's fault. "Take it easy, my dear, you don't look well."

She has been weeping, thought Olga. Her eyes are bloodshot. That's why she has so much make-up on. Does that make a difference? Painting away sorrows, varnishing over the cracks. Should I colour myself up, restore myself?

She nodded to the woman, dismissing her compassion. Why the paint? What kind of strategy is that? One needs to put on more than a brave face. But there is something terrible about the sun, the way it flays out the very lineaments of pain. How long in coming is the merciful winter light.

Calm, calm, she told herself. You can go back, rest, think. These others have commitments to fulfil: one day starts when another is over. If they knew how I live, they would follow me home. And if they came to me, would I let them in?

Let only princes come to me. Only they shall be unconsumed. Blood smokes beneath the uplifted trees, uncurling against the dust. *I smell Russian blood.* The Tsar's bird is uncaged, its liver-red tongue flicking at the ochre walls; Baba Yaga is plumping for the un-elect, the uncrowned, the dispossessed; settling on the creatures of the street with their bundles and their humps, their gap-teeth, their stumps, their wounds, their flat, triangular cheeks, their shaven skulls, their thickened, laborious hands, their immemorial, misshapenness wire-drawn from one brute ancient ingot of miscegenation, paganism and fear. Morsels for an insatiable crop.

Who among us is unafraid? It was foolish to apportion blame.

If submissiveness were a crime, as a woman she was doubly guilty. Her nature shut her away even from token defiance, and she doted on a freedom which no man would distinguish from slavish obedience to the dictates of her sex. She could not throw it off. Matvey knew that by instinct. They were all, the women she knew – friends and colleagues – they were, all of them, absurd and self-deceiving and, most deadly of all, happy, because they were expected to be so. Men knew about women in a way that women never knew about men: they knew what they were incapable of. With a man you could never tell. And they *were* absurd, these women, retreating like herself, further into their shells as they grew older, choreographing the retrogression with pretty back-leaps of memory, as if there had once been a time and place where they were themselves, whole and free, and could unlimber without constraint.

Marina lived in a past which had never existed: where the lily pond had never been fouled and the great black carp mooned agelessly, fronding the courtyard pool like spokes in a translucent wheel. Her lovers had never lived so cleanly and erect, unblemished, zooming at her beck and call, stately and naïve. Industriously she had worked up her past in appliqué and stretched it, edge to edge, upon an incongruent world.

A group of young girl construction workers passed her, laughing aloud, oblivious of the heat, their blue dungarees grainy from splodges of cement. Tanya knew the recalcitrance in the nature of things. For all her faith in the perfectibility of women, she knew they lay down to sleep, as she did and would do, with monsters and creatures of darkness. Belief, ideology and nature were all of a piece; between them they got the future born.

Behind the far line of trees the sun was declining, its corona fuddled by dust-haze, and the birds hopped across its radiant diameter squawking for roosts. Now she had not far to go.

The crowds thickened as she made her way past the department stores lining one side of the wide street. A few yards from the Metro stop nearest to her flat someone made a grab at her heavy shopping bag. Wrenching it back instinctively, she twisted round to face the attacker, determined to let fly with a mouthful of abuse.

Before her stood Sasha.

Knowing what she now knew he was the last person she wanted to see. She dodged out of his reach, turned the wrong way into a shop portico and found herself trapped by a pair of massive glass doors, padlocked for the night.

The voice behind her was pleading: "Olga Sergeyevna, Olga Sergeyevna. Olga, I've been waiting ever so long outside your office but you must have come out a different way. I thought I'd catch you on the way home. Are you OK?"

"How dare you speak to me after what you've done? Get out of my way, you *creature*. You drunken, brawling, spying, mendacious creature!"

Rocky's knee and two nights on Len's floor had done nothing for Sasha's appearance. The shirt and jeans had been slept in and his unshaven face was blotched with scabs and bruises. He followed her down the steps and through the subway to the opposite side of the road.

"I know I've done a dreadful thing, Olga Sergeyevna. I know, but I can explain."

"Aleksandr Mikhailovich, you're a proven liar. Explanations from you are not required. Now, stop pestering me. I am very tired and it is very hot."

"Yes, you look all in," he began, with a feeble attempt at sympathy. "You must have had a hard day. I expect Valya gave you a bad couple of days before that, too."

Olga could scarcely believe her ears. "You have the cheek to think I'm upset because you didn't turn up for your own wedding? And your female accomplice was broken-hearted? Leave me be, I tell you. Don't bother me with your sordid concerns! Merciful God, you'd see us all in hell, if you could."

He had wrinkled up his forehead and was staring, unaware. Was he really such a cretin not to have imagined how she felt? He had betrayed her.

"It'll soon be dark," he said irrelevantly. "You must listen."

To ensure that she did, he wrested the heavy bag from her numbed fingers, threw it into a big tub of flowering shrubs, hoicked himself up after it and sat on the concrete rim, his boots dangling on a level with her waist.

"I want to know something, Olga Sergeyevna. What happened in the flat – yesterday and the day before?"

"You callous brute," she whimpered. "You follow me, bully me and take my things. None of us has seen you for three days and you ask about the *flat*!" Her upper lip was twitching uncontrollably. He held out the bag but kept a grip on the handle farthest from her.

"Didn't you notice anything unusual when you got back from work on Tuesday? Workmen about the place? Strangers?"

"Strangers? It was nothing *but* strangers! Don't tell me you didn't know she had invited every single relation she ever had to the wedding? You never saw such a miscellany of tattered hobbledehoys in your life. And the racket! Downstairs were banging on the ceiling in the middle of the night to stop the screeches and the music. On the second day, half of them went missing. She never got out of bed. An old man in his underwear was phoning all the hospitals. Someone fired a shotgun at the bath. They drank everything, ate everything, and gambled away their clothes. They were strangers all right – like you are, like she is. I curse the day I ever set eyes on you!"

"Oh, God," he moaned. "I knew there'd be mayhem when that lot got a foot in the door."

Heavy clouds had rolled up. Darkness made the heat even more unbearable. Olga's voice was reedy in the gloom.

"You've got a fantastic cheek, Aleksandr Mikhailovich. I've said too much to you. My brother and I were too open. Tanya as well. You began it all, didn't you, that day you waylaid Boris in the street last year? You deliberately ruined our lives. And now he's dead and Tanya's been arrested and I've been drawn in. Andrey will have gone. Marina is alone. What a despicable, unfeeling wretch you are. Why did you do it?"

"Me? Do it? Do what? Olga Sergeyevna, do *what*? Valya's yokels are one thing and I admit my part in that, but what's all this about destroying you? That's not me, you know me . . ."

"Oh, I know you. *Now* I know you. Your girlfriend may have no pride and still be waiting for you with stars in her eyes. I can't be fooled so easily. How did you do it without letting on? Come on, you can tell me now. A phone call to the local police station? A letter? My God, you must have been convincing."

She waited, expecting him to say something, then dropped her voice. "Tanya said you were untrustworthy. Like a fool I dismissed her fears as hysteria. Now she's in prison. My boss has lost his job. I'm being investigated. Marina is alone and helpless. If I were a man I'd kill you!"

Sasha gaped at her like a bullock stunned by a captive-bolt. She tore the bag from his grasp. "And what are you going to do now? Manhandle me again? Bring in your policeman cronies to harass me?"

He swayed on the ledge his square frame sagging. When he spoke, the anguish throbbed in his voice. "God help me, I thought such a lot of you all. I cared, I really cared. I never cared for people like I cared for you. *For the first time in my life I put myself out.*"

Nothing he said could move her. She shrugged. "It's terrible to see what a man can be brought to. All for a few drinks and a new suit. What did we ever do to you? Was it Bobby's fault because she spurned you? Did I get on your nerves with my old-maidish ways? Are you jealous of the little we've got?"

She began to cry and stumbled into the road, blind to the honking traffic. He watched her white blouse bobbing between tail-lights and bumpers. The subway was quicker. When she reached the far side he was waiting for her.

"All right, Olga Sergeyevna, all right, if that's what you think I am, I won't bother you much longer. Snobs, that's what you are, all of you. You don't think someone like me is a human being. I've been with my friend Len. He hid me for the last couple of days. He might be what you call a lout, but he doesn't think I'm a nark. He does a friend a favour, when that friend's in trouble. You and your bloody boss," he shouted in the darkness of a side street. "I suppose you think he must be all right because he's clever. Clever enough to shop you, too, or hasn't that crossed your mind?"

Olga increased her pace.

"You'll learn," he cried desperately. "One day you'll be sorry. Now listen to . . ." Listen to what? He had no explanation for what had happened. Whatever he said, he knew that it sounded guilty. He felt guilty himself – as if he had actually ruined Olga and all the others, only could not remember how he had done so. The feeling was not new – alcoholic amnesia had landed him in many a scrape.

At the doorway of their block she turned and raised her arm after the manner of a policeman halting a line of vehicles. Sasha glared at her miserably.

"Listen," she said very clearly and slowly. "We share a flat. Inevitably we will meet on the stairs or in the corridor or in the kitchen. In future, or until I move out, you will make sure that those are the only places we do meet. I forbid you to enter my room. I forbid you to address me on any matter. This is the last time we shall speak together, Aleksandr Mikhailovich. Before some gang of hooligans lynches you, or your so-called workmates shove you off a moving lorry, take that frightful, vulgar little female of yours and clear out. That's my advice to you. Don't worry, I'm no tale-bearer. I won't betray *you* to those you have betrayed. But things have a habit of getting out, and a lot of people live in this block and some of them might not be as nice as me to a person whom they suspect of setting the dogs on them. If I were you I'd make myself scarce."

In order to follow her up at a respectful distance, Sasha hung around for two or three minutes. After pressing the lift button several times, he noticed that the safety gates were jammed against the side of the shaft. The cage, as usual, was stuck between floors.

Far above his head he heard a woman's squeal.

In spite of his sinister experiences on these same stairs, Sasha was too weary for prudence and climbed steadily, slouching like an old man, not caring if ten Rockys lay in ambush at every sweep of the balustrade. As he turned up to his own landing someone was stock-taking in a loud, carefree voice: "Caviare, chocolates, poetry. All fixed up for a comfy evening, eh?"

A powerfully-built man in pale green linen slacks and matching sleeveless shirt was itemising the contents of Olga's bag. A yellow-metal watch glinted on his wrist. His blond hair was very short. Sasha recognised him at once and turned back to the stairs.

"No need for that," said Legless. "I'll think you don't love me any more. We're all friends now, as I was telling the lady. Can't leave one another alone, can we, sonny?"

Olga was huddled up against the wall. Out of uniform, Legless was bigger and a lot smarter. He smiled broadly at Olga and tucked her bag under one arm. "Don't you worry, I can take care of all this for you. Ladies need a helping hand with the shopping now and again." His icy blue eyes caught Sasha's and the grin rigidified into a leer. "Return of the Prodigal, is it? Come and join us in your kitchen. You're not too late for the feast."

Inside, he bolted the door.

"Who are you?" demanded Olga, her courage reviving a little in the familiar surroundings. Legless smiled again. His teeth were massy and even. "*He'll* tell you who I am," he said, pointing to Sasha. "We're chums from way back."

Olga let her shoulders droop, drew back her neck and with a vibrant hiss, spat into Sasha's face.

27

At the head of the kitchen table sat Bogat.

"Come in," he said, neatly placing his knife and fork at twelve o'clock on the empty plate in front of him. "Take a seat. I was talking about the old days."

At the other end, as far as it was possible to get from him and still be at the table, was a clump of very subdued figures: the three Kuznetsovs at one corner, Xenia on a low stool at the apex; Valentina sat apart, rocking morosely on an uneven-legged wooden chair. Lizaveta, as usual, was at the sink. Everywhere hung the stink of fried onions.

Whether out of consciousness of rank or simple awkwardness, Legless hovered around Bogat, uncertain how to proceed. The arrogance which he had shown outside seemed to have gone. "You staying here all night?" he said at last.

Bogat raised an eyebrow as if at a waiter with his thumb in the soup. Sasha was conscious of an edginess between them which exceeded a merely professional distaste. The contempt was mutual and personal, beyond the bounds of duty.

"I've not finished my supper. You know how I hate to hurry my meals."

His petulance was aggressive and confident. Sasha wanted to laugh, until he caught Bogat's eye and was quelled. He realised for the first time that this absurd little man with his nancy-boy act exuded a power which, if it caused Legless to submit, could utterly crush him. He sat down. Bogat was a man who could hold court.

Legless had similar thoughts. "Sorry for asking," he murmured, eliminating any trace of resentment, and went off down the passage, whistling.

Bogat talked a lot.

Wistfully, nostalgically, he comfortably unbuttoned in surroundings which previous to Sasha's arrival he had somehow rendered congenial. Fed, satisfied, an audience at his feet, he resumed his discourse, picking his teeth meditatively with a tiny silver prong in the shape of a half tuning-fork.

"Twice a day from the Head GPO. In those days we drove a grocery truck. Assigned to us on the quiet from the Sokolniki Co-operative."

As he drew out his memories, the staccato manner gave way to flowing sentences and he built up his narrative, varying the tone, and pausing, conscious of the necessity of exact timing. It was the performance of an actor who had spoken his lines many times, loved them and each time wanted to remake them, afresh.

"Of course the run-out was all right unless you wanted to smoke. My friend Vanya was left-handed and he had to grip the security chain. Tensioned brass, it was, I remember, and ran all along the inside of the tail-board. If anyone tried to fiddle with the lock on the outside you were supposed to sense the faintest tremor."

As Bogat lisped on soothingly, Sasha felt safer. He liked stories, and for all the sordidness of Bogat's life, it had brought him adventures. They had that in common, Bogat and he. Although Bogat might be a purely nominal male, he had enjoyed his life among men as Sasha had enjoyed his in the Army. They had both been in something together – belonged – and for the time being that sense of camaraderie which Bogat's stories evoked, lulled Sasha into dozy reminiscences of discomfort, dangers shared, and careless youth.

"That was before we had radio. You know, I've seen that same truck since, stuck in a traffic jam near the Kamenniy Bridge. I knew it was our old one because Vanya had stencilled it and the Es and Os of GROCERIES were blodged. You see," droned on the imperturbable voice, "in those days we all had a go at everything. Even spray-painting. In those days it was all make do and mend, get your own this, do your own that, like the old Cossacks rolling up with their own horses – one mount, one re-mount, and all your basic equipment supplied from your own pocket. Now we have professors over us. Professors and accountants . . ."

A sound of splintering wood came from one of the rooms off the passage. Lev Kuznetsov closed his eyes. Xenia tried to get up but Anna grabbed her sleeve. They heard objects being rattled in a container, then a tinkling crash as they hit the floorboards. Sasha winced. On her rickety chair Valentina seemed ready to explode.

Bogat stopped and contemplated his listeners. Like pupils guilty of welcoming diversion during a boring lesson they avoided his disciplinarian eyes.

"Boys will be boys," he said apologetically. "Now, where was I? Ah, yes, professors, *academical gentlemen*. The cross we have to bear."

His cheeks already rosy from wine, became darkly flushed. Evidently the thought irritated him.

"Some of you worthy folk are book-learned, skilled in logic-chopping. Quick as a flash, I bet, with the old intellectual repartee. Where's the cut and thrust then? Where's the backchat? Surely we have some champion who can take me on, can trounce me? Isn't anyone going to ask me for my papers, enquire ever so politely, knowing his citizen's privileges, what right I have to lecture him in his own home, exactly what I think I'm doing here?"

Sasha reckoned that this left him safely out of things. Bogat's gaze was settled inexorably on Lev. Even Olga, the one real intellectual in the place, was excluded. By the look of her, any thought of contention had long since gone. She sat with elbows on the table, her hands over her eyes.

When they come, pretend to be daft. Lev could have acted on Marya Fyodorovna's advice. Instead, he returned Bogat's gaze, staring him down with dull, impenitent persistence. They both knew he would say nothing. For years, in like situations, from playground to squaddie messroom, wherever there was space and leisure for any old quasi-authoritative gibe to be directed at his sallow face framed by the frizzy hair and whiskers, he had held back and simply stared, twiddling his plump fingers and waiting for the moment to pass.

Nobody helped. Sasha was ashamed, and felt his bruises.

Bogat's native sense of decorum rescued him. This was neither time nor place for a punch-up, verbal or otherwise. He condescended to reply to his own questions.

"I'll tell you why you daren't state the obvious. You don't need a degree to work it out, or a witness from the street to vouch for my correct demeanour when I choose to pull you in. He'll know who I am, won't he? And he'll lose his tongue, and lose his eyes, and his memory will go, won't it? Because he knows, like you know, who I am, and that I know who he is and who you are."

He threw a flat box of cigarettes across the table.

"See that?" he said, indicating the picture on the front. A huge figure of a man clad in a Norman hauberk was scanning an invisible horizon from the back of a war-pony. He was armed to the teeth. "You think he's gone away, don't you, like my professors do. Closed over by the antique mists, with his corselet and nose-piece and Tartar bow. Well, he's not, he's here and now, up-dated and fresh as a daisy. Only now his chainmail fits him like skin and his arrows are re-feathered and barbed, and in inexhaustible supply. There always was a man on a horse, scattering all before him like sheep. There always will be. Because he is a representative, the outrider of the horde, the picket at the far line, the outrunner and guard. I am the

man on the horse. I ride at you, belly-high, exultant and whooping. Have no truck with me."

Holy Christ, thought Sasha. This is carpet-chewing stuff. He remembered Arkady at Vladimir who went stir-crazy after three months' solitary and broke a guard's spine with an aikido kick. They hosed him down from the roof and Sasha had met him when he was doing a stint as ward-orderly and Arkady was in the sick-bay with his legs in traction. He knew they were going to shoot him because the guard had died but that was his only contact with reality. Every morning he woke the ward at 0400 hours screaming that he was Lenin's son by Eleanor Marx. Sasha tried reasoning with him about the dates not fitting but it was no good. Arkady said he had a mission to exterminate all Communists who weren't related to his mother. For some reason Brezhnev was in on the plot, and they had nightly meetings under Arkady's bed tracing the pedigrees of the Central Committee. Brezhnev apparently sat in his braces eating pancakes the whole time, crossing off names with an indelible pencil. The psychiatrist put it all down to wanking and class-deviationism – Arkady's grandad had been a master shoemaker in Vologda. They shot him in the bath-house one morning, before reveille.

Everyone was stunned by Bogat's rhapsody, except Lizaveta. The wildest of speeches sailed past her ears as long as there was no hint of moral deviance. She had taken to Bogat. He was a nice boy. He had manners.

"I've done what you said, it's all there and I've kept a bit aside to make yoghurt, but it looks unhealthy to me. Silly fads and fancies, you young people go in for these days."

Bogat smiled expansively. "It's health-food, Granny. No preservatives. Try some."

He spooned up a liquidised mess of nuts, raisins and fruit. The old woman backed away. "Pig-food," she said, shuddering.

Bogat ate greedily. The concoction seemed to act as a psychic restorative, for his previous exalted mood evaporated and he looked around him, smilingly, apparently unaware of the effect he had just produced. The tenants, so recently scared out of their wits, were only too ready to comply with his new mood.

"Shall I tell you what interests my friend Rocky about England?" asked Bogat.

This was Sasha's chance to shine. "Cricket," he announced, pleased to have retained the queer word in his head after all the buffetings it had received. Bogat was taken aback.

"What do you mean – cricket?" he said, clearly not as well informed as Sasha.

"It's a game," said Olga wearily, uncovering her eyes. "A game the English play in the summer. A gentlemen's game. Is there to be no end to these insane disquisitions? I must rest, my head is going round."

"Hold on," said Bogat, alarmed at the possible implications of Rocky's involvement in some exotic practice which had been kept secret from him. "A *gentlemen's* game?"

"A black gentlemen's game," corrected Sasha. "They wear white cloaks and throw balls."

Olga groaned.

"Well they do," persisted Sasha. "It's dangerous. Ask his friend with the pipe – he knows the rules. They hit one another a lot."

"Ah," said Bogat. "I must take it up with him, we never discuss sport, only literature. Sport is so unsubtle."

Valentina stirred. "There's art in it. My late husband was a sight to behold, weaving and ducking. Co-ordination is everything, he used to say."

"I shall scream in a moment," said Olga. "Can we get this over and done with – what other benefits has this Rocky person derived from his study of the English?"

"Natural morality," said Bogat with an arch smile.

At the mention of morality, Lizaveta Ivanovna pricked up her ears. "This isn't going to be a dirty story, is it?" she said taking up Bogat's plate and wiping over the oilcloth. "Because if there's one thing I can't abide it's smut. I had more than enough of that when I was married. A bit of fun is one thing. But downright filth . . ."

"Don't worry, Granny," said Bogat, watching with distaste as Xenia continued to pick her nose. "This is fit for the ears of babes."

Olga guessed what was coming. The rest were flummoxed.

"Rocky took to it as an infant to the breast. Natural morality, good people, is a principle enshrined in the verses of the bourgeois English poets of the eighteenth century: *Know your place*."

In a flash Sasha divined its applicability. It was like the verbs you rote-learned in the baby class but which, when you graduated to the wickedness of the world, went funny after the first person plural: we know our place, *you know your place, they know their place*. A slight twist and you had the key to the whole system: THEY KNOW YOUR PLACE: YOU KNOW THEIR PLACE. That's how it figured.

"So that's why you've got your feet under my table and I don't even know your telephone number?" said Sasha flatly.

"Exactly," said Bogat. "Your place is my place and everything in it is mine, including you. Get it?"

"Oh, I get it. I got it at about the age of five: there's always a

strapping cuckoo to feed, and the kitty can always be divvied up to provide the ponce with his silk underwear. You're going to squeeze us, aren't you – for a percentage of the knick-knacks and our take-home pay?"

Bogat nodded kindly. "I know just how you must feel," he said in the conciliatory tone of a hangman fingering the noose of an unco-operative prisoner. "Rocky got a bit over-excited about you, didn't he? He's what you might call over-protective. It's concern for my welfare. Don't take it to heart so, I'll have a word in his ear."

As much maddened by the silence of the other tenants as the insolence of the man's manner, Sasha lost his head and began to shout at the only person whose help he would need to eject Bogat and his colleague. The women were useless.

"Come on, Lev, you're not going to sit there waiting to have your cock snipped by this fucking parasitical fairy, are you?"

Snatching the wine-bottle from under Bogat's nose he threw it into Lev's lap and grabbed Lizaveta's boning knife from the sink top. The blade waggled an inch from Bogat's shagreen eyes. "I'm not done yet, you arse-licking pouf minion! Let's hear you whoop!"

The bottle rolled down Lev's knees and clunked to the floor. He continued to stare straight ahead. Bogat removed his toothpick and holding it like a tiny sword, gently pressed down the knife, crossways.

"Look," he said, considerately. "I know it's a shock, but we must be reasonable."

Xenia looked up at her father. "Daddy, what does he mean?"

Lev spoke for the first time. "You see that noisy man with the knife, darling? Well, this one," he added mildly, raising his eyebrows in Bogat's direction, "this one can kill him."

Valentina screamed. Sasha put down the knife.

"Now, when I've gone," said Bogat, "you must all ask your percipient friend what experience had yielded up such insight."

Valentina stretched out a hand to touch Lev's shirt. "Can he?" she whispered.

"He can," said Bogat yawning and stretching his legs. "He can."

Legless came pounding in, his ears scarlet from exertion.

"It's all trash," he gasped. "Nothing but trash. Women's trumpery. I've been through the lot."

Suddenly he noticed the square-cut cornelians at Olga's ears. "Hey, that's a bit of all right. Nice and dusky, just the job."

Bogat raised his eyes to the ceiling. "He has this thing about jewellery, dear. Show him an aquamarine pendant and he positively drools."

Legless went sheepish. "Well, you know what she's like. I've got to keep her sweet."

"Of course, you have. He means his *intended*," said Bogat confidentially to Olga, whose face was white with fury. "She makes the most outrageous demands on the poor boy. You'd better take them off, dear. You know what ladies can be like."

In her haste to avoid being touched by Legless, Olga tore at the earrings and one of the fastenings ripped through a lobe. Tiny spots of blood spattered on to the oilcloth. Angrily, she rejected Bogat's offer of a handkerchief.

"Oh dear," sighed Bogat, pushing away his pudding bowl. "Don't you think, Olga Sergeyevna, that promotion would have been better than all this . . . this unpleasantness?"

But Legless hadn't finished with her yet. "And the keys," he said. "That big desk's yours, isn't it – the one in the front room. Unless you want me to kick it in."

Olga detached the bureau key from a gilt chatelaine at her waist. For a moment she held it to her bosom then let it fall to the table where it plopped noiselessly into Bogat's muesli.

"You silly bitch," exclaimed Legless peering into the goo. Reluctant to sticky his fingers, he poked around with the pencil from his diary. Both key and pencil were minute.

"Having problems?" said Valentina coming round to his shoulder. "Here, let me, my fingers are more nimble."

Legless grunted and wiped the pencil on a piece of newspaper. Valentina plunged in her hand. "Got it!" she cried after a single turn of the wrist, held up the key dripping with sour cream, and dropped it down the cleavage of her frock.

When he realised the trick she had played on him Legless was breathless with rage. "You give that back," he yelled, choking on the words. "You don't do that to me!"

He lunged at Valentina but she was too quick and skipped round behind Sasha. Legless lost his balance and fell across the table, upsetting Lizaveta's dessert. When he got up there was a patch of what looked like gritty whitewash spreading across the green of his safari jacket.

"You cow," he howled, surveying his front, aghast at the horrible constituents of the pudding. "That was clean on this morning . . ."

Bogat was giggling helplessly. "He's only telling the truth," he sniggered in delight. "His Mum'll be livid."

Valentina fluttered behind Sasha, amazed at her own audacity in taunting this vile fellow but not quite knowing which way he would take it. There was not long to wait. Heartened by Bogat's laughter, Sasha said the wrong thing:

"Don't talk to her like that. You're not in the station now with one of your poxy whores."

In his astonishment, Legless unflexed his fist and the earrings fell to the floor. He wasn't used to being cheeked, and Sasha was making a fool of him in front of Bogat.

"You talking to me?" he asked, plodding round the table, his tiny bull-elephant eyes aglint with ferocity. Valentina screamed louder and Sasha stepped back flattening her against the wall.

"Now, Yuri," muttered Bogat, half-rising from his chair and trying to resume control.

Legless was too quick. Sasha had tucked in his chin, but the policeman went for his body. The punch doubled him up and he crashed on to a stool. His sudden weight shattered the matchwood seat and the legs flew outwards under the table. Valentina collapsed on top of him, wrapping her arms round his head, and bared her teeth, foaming and gnashing like a sow in heat.

"You dare, you scumpig!" she hissed. "I'll strip the flesh off your rotten bones!"

Warily Legless circled the wriggling heap of limbs, saw his opening and kicked out at Sasha's kneecap. But the steel-tipped boot only glanced off Sasha's right thigh. He had time to slither away and get to his feet. The knife was still on the sink top.

Bogat was on his feet shouting. The Kuznetsovs scrambled to the safety of Lizaveta's store-cupboard and locked the door behind them, leaving Olga and the old woman, stock still, witless from terror.

Valentina scurried across the lino on all fours, dribbling with rage and snarling bestially whenever the policeman sought to close the gap between himself and Sasha. Legless was not one to give up once he had scented a victim, but kicking a woman was something to be kept for more private moments, so he contented himself with answering her, snarl for snarl, while grappling with the problem of attaining his quarry. Bogat had ceased to shout and stood to one side, like a referee, arms akimbo.

Legless was a good judge of distance. With a wild yell he hurled his body in a high-jumper's roll straight over Valentina's head. For a split second he was completely airborne from head to toe, one hand outstretched a few inches from Sasha's nose. As he rose in mid-flight, Valentina arched her neck and bit him neatly right between the legs. The scream was horrible.

Bogat dropped to one knee beside the stricken policeman. "What did I tell you, Yuri Petrovich?" he whispered vindictively. "There's a time and a place for everything. You've completely ruined the atmosphere."

When his writhings had subsided, Legless hobbled to the bathroom, where, shortly after, Bogat joined him. The policeman sat on the edge of the bath, his linen slacks round his knees, surveying the damage with the help of Olga's hand mirror.

"Bloody bitch," he mumbled. "Look at that, that's a puncture mark. I'll catch something. It's gone right through."

He poured disinfectant down the front of his underpants with agonised tenderness.

Bogat looked away and proceeded to lecture him. "This is a family place, a *home*. Get that into your head. You've got to drop this head-banging Mr Universe stuff. Authority should be sensed by these people, not thumped into them. We could have a good thing going for us here – I want them to see us as friends."

Legless was still truculent. "What are you talking about – a *good thing*? You and your waste pipes crammed with gold coins, old dears with diamonds under the mattress. They haven't got two kopeks to scratch their arses with. We're wasting our time."

"Don't be in such a *rush*," said Bogat. "You've got to be patient with this sort of operation. Jolly them along. I know what I'm doing. Be nice to people for a change. It'll pay off in the end. I'll leave them their instructions."

Olga called out from the kitchen: "Oh, Mr Bogat, have you a moment?"

Bogat liked the way she spoke. "For you, Olga Sergeyevna, I would always have time." He grinned in the doorway.

"Will you be seeing Mr Rocky this evening?"

"Yes, probably. Why? What is it?"

"I have a message for him." She handed over a strip of cardboard torn from a tea packet and written on, end to end, in block capitals.

"But this isn't Russian," said Bogat.

"No, it's English. He does know English, doesn't he?"

"Of course he does," said Bogat. "So do I, a little that is. But this looks hard."

"It's a suggestion for a motto for your unit, for your section."

Bogat was touched. Educated people were surprisingly pleasant. "Isn't that nice."

"It would look nice engraved on those pretty identity discs you fashionable young men wear."

"Do read it aloud then. Hearing English always gives me a *frisson*."

"Very well. It's a verse by an eighteenth-century English bourgeois poet:

"I am his Highness' dog at Kew;
Pray tell me, sir, whose dog are you?"

28

The two men had left the flat unnoticed. For a long while no one said a word but sat wondering if they had really gone: Bogat could still be padding about somewhere in his crepe-soles.

The Kuznetsovs, sensing from the quiet that Bogat and Legless had at least left the kitchen, began to hammer on the store-cupboard door. Xenia was crying loudly. Weeks before, Lizaveta Ivanovna had removed the only light bulb in response to an appeal on the radio for economy in the consumption of electricity. Xenia was afraid of the dark and her sobs mingled with Lev's muffled banging. The door could only be opened from the outside and when Lizaveta, in a frantic state of nerves amidst the wreckage of the kitchen, could not remember where she had put the key, Sasha had to force the mortise with a cleaver. Xenia emerged first, her plaits tacky with cobwebs. Sasha bent down to wipe the tears from the little face.

"You're the ugliest man I've ever seen," she said and stuck out her tongue. At that moment Sasha would have loved, more than anything else, to give her a thick ear, but he responded in kind by sticking his thumbs in his ears and twitching his fingers.

His face, he reflected, must have been an absorbing sight for a kid. The turmoil with Valentina and Legless had split open the legacy of scabs from Rocky's boot. An entertaining mess for such a nasty child. Sasha remembered seeing her at the cockroaches. She was the kind to enjoy trying to replace beetles' torn-off wing-cases.

Repairing him was going to be like lacing up a sandbag.

"There's not a pot they haven't smashed, nor a cupboard they haven't ransacked. Not a drop of drink in the house, neither. The locusts have stripped us bare," said Valentina standing before them, her face aglow with the bad news, a dishcloth and two bandages unrolling over one arm.

With typical hooligan pointlessness one of her young cousins, Vanya, had rifled a first-aid box the day before yesterday, on the line from Rostov. The liniment had been drunk but since he could find no use for the dressings he had brought them along as a wedding gift. The bandages were a godsend since they gave Valentina a renewed sense of purpose. She sat Sasha down and began to probe the cicatrices on his cheeks with soap-smelling fingers.

"Oh, I'm forgetting," she said, swabbing out the longest wound with yellow ointment. "That son of Cain – that little one – he left two notes on the hallstand one for Lev and one for Lizaveta Ivanovna." She thrust out a hip so Olga could extract them from her pinafore pocket.

"Now you, my lad," she said, chiding the woebegone Sasha. "Why am I so nice to you?"

He relaxed: she was not going to blast him immediately for his sins of omission during the last three days. Giving Legless some lip had sent up his stock. That wouldn't last but for the time being he might as well make the most of his grotesque allurements. "Because I'm so goodlooking."

"Ugh!" said Valentina yanking up the ends of the bandage she had swathed round his face and pressing down one length with her thumb on the crown of his head to make it knot tightly with the other. "You just need a monocle to make you like one of those sabre-scarred Hitlerites on TV." Valentina's favourite programmes were serials about war-time partisans. "But I'm sure even those paragons of beastliness turned up . . ." She gave a series of vicious twists to the dressing. "Turned up . . . for . . . their . . . weddings."

For all the notice the others took of their conversation it might have been pillow talk. Lizaveta Ivanovna was peering short-sightedly at Bogat's note. In the confusion she had mislaid her spectacles. The letters fuzzed before her eyes. "'Don't boil it,'" she read. "'I like the skin crisp.' What on earth does he mean? 'Don't worry about the tr . . .' about the, ah, 'trimmings'. Trimmings? Trimmings for what?" A thought struck her. "Heaven preserve us – he wants me to make him a frock! Oh, no," she exclaimed with indignation, slapping the paper with her grave-spotted hand. "Health food is one thing, perversion quite another!"

"Give it here, Gran," said Lev gently, looking up. "No, no, this isn't a dressmaking pattern. You haven't read the other side, it's a menu." He went back to his own note.

"A menu, now, think of that, a menu. I suppose that's harmless." She read on, painstakingly. "'You can get me a chicken.' Oh yes, chickens are delivered once a day with *Pravda*! . . . 'And a couple of bottles of champagne.' Are you sure this is addressed to me? 'I am entertaining a friend here tomorrow and I want you out of the kitchen by eight.' We'll see about that!" A post-script was appended, but in such tiny writing that she had to ask Lev to read it. He did as she asked, racing through the message. "'Here'stwentyroublesyoucan-buyyourselfsomethingwiththechange.'"

"Where's twenty roubles?" Lizaveta Ivanovna turned the letter over and over, felt round and looked under the table. "Where?" she muttered. "Where's twenty roubles?"

"Gran," said Lev with a wry smile.

"Yes?" said Lizaveta, hopefully, thinking he had received Bogat's cash by mistake.

"There it is." He pointed at her tea-caddy.

"But that's where I keep my pension."

"That's right. He's just subjected it to a twenty-rouble deduction for services rendered."

"I don't owe him any services, Lev Davidovich," cried the old woman, nearly in tears. "I made him a meal tonight out of the goodness of my heart."

"I'm afraid you do, Gran. His service is only taking out twenty — not fifty."

At the sound of Lizaveta's sobbing, Olga gave a shuddering sigh and drew her fingernails down each side of her face, gently clawing her cheeks. White marks showed on the flesh. "We must change the locks," she said to Lev. "What did he want of you?"

Lev flicked over his note. It was less chatty than the old woman's: "Vacate the main room and the child's alcove by noon tomorrow. Leave everything as it is."

"That means you three will all live in the bedroom. Are you going to do it?" asked Olga.

"Anything he says, anything he says," murmured Lev, and led his wife and child from the kitchen.

"What was that all about?" said Valentina. Olga told her about the contents of Lev's note.

"Just let them try it on with us! I'd rend them limb from limb!"

Olga's answering look of contempt unnerved her, and she faltered, suddenly aware that she was excluded from some secret, ignorance of which rendered her behaviour foolish. "Well, you wouldn't give them half of your living space and say nothing, would you? They wouldn't get it off me, I can tell you!"

Olga simply asked for the key to her bureau which had lain forgotten in Valentina's bosom. As she closed her fingers over it, the metal felt warm. She looked round and picked up her earrings. "No one will be asking *you* for anything," she said. Sasha fiddled with his bandages and looked at the wall. "You have no need to defend yourself – *he* has already done that for you very effectively. You're insured."

After she had gone Sasha was grateful for the ambivalence of the remark. It retained sufficient connection with known realities almost to persuade Valentina that Olga Sergeyevna was just talking about his brawl with Legless, albeit in a typically high-flown way. But the coldness with which it was vouchsafed nagged at her. After all, she argued to herself, it had been she and her man who had stood up to the swine. Before she had time to give voice to these complaints, Lizaveta Ivanovna cut across her thoughts.

"It's the wife, you see," she said in a hollow voice.

"Which wife?" said Valentina, vague about the marital status of all the women in the flat.

"His. *The Jew's.*"

Anna Kuznetsova was the kind of woman who, although you had known her for months on end, was hard to recollect the moment she had gone out of the door. Valentina sought to reconstitute Anna Georgyevna in her mind's eye but caught nothing physical, except for her eyes which were too large and always seemed to be swimming with tears. As for the rest, she had never noticed. Perhaps, once, she had been pretty, but Valentina's dominant impression had been that such a thing would never have mattered because when you parted company with her it was a relief – as if a drearily commonplace phantom was just slipping off to its tomb.

"What about her?" she asked without interest.

Sasha was pottering about the kitchen, gathering up the bits of matchwood which had scattered under the gas-stove and cupboards.

"Not that tale again, Lizaveta Ivanovna. It's got bugger all to do with anything."

"It has, it has," urged Lizaveta.

"*He* thinks it has," said Sasha. "That's all. And what goes on in that poor sod's head is anybody's business."

He had had enough for one evening. The revelation of Lev's secret fears could scarcely add anything of note to the situation. "Valentina doesn't want to know."

"Oh, but she does," cried Valentina excited by the glimpse of forbidden fruit. "You speak for yourself. Come on, Gran, let's hear. Is it about a man?"

"Men!" exclaimed Lizaveta Ivanovna scornfully. "There's other things about men besides what's inside their trousers. There are men and men. Yes, it was about a man, but not the way you think."

The story was a long one. Kuznetsova had been in prison; and in prison had given birth to Xenia.

There was an older child – not Lev's – a boy, who now lived with the grandmother in Krasnodarsk. Ten years before when she was living at Yugo-Zapadnaya Anna had taken to travelling down on the tube to Karl Marx Prospekt, wheeling him in his folding buggy along the subway to the corner of Gorky Street and then patrolling the sidewalk from the Hotel Natsional, past the old university building down to Hertsen Street and back again. The child's pram seat concealed a wad of flysheets. Every so often she stopped a likely-looking person – usually young or very old – and if they proved to be sympathetic slipped out one of the sheets and handed it over. She had been making this trip every morning for three weeks in the depths of winter, when one freezing Tuesday morning she stopped a young man in a windcheater and Norwegian ski-hat who took a pamphlet, chatted amiably for a quarter of an hour and left. On her way home he got on the train at Park Kultury with another man and a young woman – all dressed, like him, in the sort of clothes then fashionable among juveniles. The men followed Anna up the escalator at Universi-tetskaya and bundled her into a corner by the payphones. The young woman fetched a policeman from his militia post by the exit. They laid a complaint which was apparently so serious that neither she nor the baby got home that night because they were taken off to some-where near the centre. Later on, she went to court and got five years. The child was going to be taken away at first, but a friend telephoned her mother and she came up for the trial from the south and made a deposition that she would take full responsibility for the boy's upbringing.

"I always knew there was something funny about those two," said Valentina. "Is *this* kid his?" "Kid" was her epithet for Xenia whom she despised for her sneakiness and lack of high spirits. Like Sasha, she thought the child had a cruel streak.

"Trust you to ask that," exclaimed Sasha. "A pregnant woman is sent down for five years and all you want to know is who put her in the club."

"'The fathers eat sour grapes and the children's teeth are set on edge'," quoted Valentina complacently. "It's in the blood."

Lizaveta lost her temper. "Just what do you mean by that?"

"You know very well what I mean. That sort spells trouble and always has – they're discontents by nature."

"Don't talk to me about nature!" shouted Lizaveta. "You farmyard bamboozler, coming here from God knows what sordid country midden. It's the blood of the likes of you that could do with some disinfecting. You think people are no better than your village hens that can be marked off with a dab of paint. Don't think I don't know your sort – Soviet Russia isn't enough for you, with your hankerings after the good old days. My father was in the Ukraine in 1919. He saw what village-pump witches like you did to those dismal, persecuted people like Lev Davidovich. I'm ashamed of my country when I hear you talk such sinfulness."

Valentina was shaken. Up to now, she had assumed that Lizaveta Ivanovna shared all of her most intimate prejudices. They both knew their places as women; ikons stood above their beds; they crossed themselves at the name of God and all His saints. But Sasha gave her an imploring look, and she had the grace to prevaricate.

"Oh, my dear, *that's* not what I meant. I'm sure that doesn't make Lev Davidovich a bad *person* – it's the political business I was talking about. It must have been something like that, mustn't it? Five years is a bit steep."

"Politics? What are you talking about?" grumbled Lizaveta quietly, disinclined to provoke a shouting match in view of Valentina's adroit submission, and anxious to get to the end of Anna's story. "She was defending someone, a man, some kind of writer. A lot of lies had been told about him and she wanted to put things straight."

To Valentina this bald summary made the matter even more obscure.

"Well, she chose a queer way to go about it. Why didn't she write to the papers?"

Lizaveta had no answer to this. "Ask her," she snapped. "Perhaps she did. Once upon a time you petitioned the Tsar. Fat lot of good that did, I should imagine."

"That's a point," mused Valentina. "What was his name?"

"Whose?"

"The writer's, of course."

"No idea. Why ask me? I haven't read a profane book in thirty years."

The conversation threatened to become strophic. Sasha intervened as Valentina was on the point of grasshoppering to Lizaveta's selective reading habits, and whispered something to her.

"Ah," said Valentina. "*Him*. Now him I've heard of."

"What I can't understand," whispered Valentina, hesitating on the threshold of their room, "is why it took that dim lot of ours three weeks to pull her in. What are they doing all day – polishing one another's buttons?"

"You know your trouble, don't you?" said Sasha, his voice muffled by the bandages. "You can't keep your mind on anything for longer than two seconds. The point isn't whether or not they spend their time pulling one another's dongs in the snow to keep warm, but what happens when they leave off and start justifying their wages. Anna has a black mark down against her, a blob as big as a house. Once they get your number, Lev reckons, you're in the book for keeps. So when those two strolled in and started to help themselves, he thought it was his fault for being associated with her, because she knows you-know-who. And that it was his fault for introducing you, me, Lizaveta and Olga and poor old Borya to her, knowing that she knew you-know-who. Got it?"

"Is he right?" demanded Valentina.

"No. But that makes no difference."

The place was a shambles. When the incentive was there Legless was an enthusiastic worker. He had used system: anything loose, unfixed or withdrawable – pots, boxes, bags and packages, drawers – had been heaped at one side of the room, emptied on to the large close-piled white rug in order to show up the smallest item of jewellery, and then sifted through with the bamboo cane of Valentina's feather duster. Once the containers were empty he had thrown them with great force against the far wall where they eventually formed the heap which now threatened to crash down at any moment. At a country flea-market it would have been a totter's paradise.

Valentina stood amidst the shards of her dolls' limbs like a salvage-master on the poop of a wreck, not knowing where to begin. Somewhere in it all were her wedding presents. With a howl of dismay she dragged the fichu bodice of her wedding-frock from underneath a blood-stained crate from Rostov which had once held four sucking-pigs ready for the spit. Guessing that the sight of it could well be the prelude to a night of hysteria, recrimination and blows, Sasha decided there and then to broach the subject of the non-wedding. She'd be sure to get round to it sooner or later and while he still had a good conduct mark for facing up to Legless, soonest was best.

"Thanks for lending a hand out there," he whispered giving her a reminder. "That was real guts."

Silently and grimly Valentina contemplated her wedding dress. "Look at it," she said at length. "Despoiled. As stark as a combless cock."

"We can get you another, Valya. I'm sorry, I really am. I did send a message, you know, I tried."

He avoided mentioning weddings – the very sound of the word might drive her into a frenzy. But Valentina was too fatigued for a scene.

"I know, I know," she sighed resignedly. For the first time Sasha noticed what the past few days had done to her. Her spirit was nearly beaten down; even the verve of her speech was flagging. He beckoned her over to the bed, heart-sick at his own misdeeds: it must have been rotten to have fought off single-handed the malicious solicitude of a posse of freebooting hayseeds, only to have had to defend your bridegroom-to-be from official marauders with your teeth before he had a chance to make a proper apology.

"Come on, Valya, have a little lie-down, let's give ourselves a treat."

The invitation was unperspicuous. With glowering eyes she pitched the rent bodice to the ceiling where it clung vaporously round the light fitment, the filigree work scorching on the naked bulb.

"I got your message all right," she panted, re-vitalised at the memory of her humiliations. "Was it your idea to send it round with that hobnailed Quasimodo from opposite? You know what he did? You know what he *did*? That leering bulbous snail –"

Sasha closed his hands over the gap in the bandages which Valentina had left for his eyes.

"He touched me up."

His response was automatic, misguided but well-intentioned: "Where?"

Dolls' legs, fragments of vase and a framed chromolithograph of a peasant wedding scene underneath the legend "Where there is love there is God also" rained down upon him.

"*Where?*" she screamed, her throat quaking with outrage. "*Where?* I'm not a geography globe with my zones banded! Isn't it enough that I told you – a man of character would defend his wife's honour!"

"But we're not married," giggled Sasha. "That was what I thought he came to tell you – that the do was off. No, what I meant by 'where' was over *there*," he went on, pointing to the Embassy residence through the window, "or over *here*, because I thought he wasn't allowed to move off station, even for a bloody massacre. Never mind, never mind, it was stupid of me, I apologise."

Valentina accepted this rare admission of blame with magnanimity, and sat down on the mattress beside him.

"Had his lugubrious eye on me for months," she said not displeased at the memory of the devouring glances her magnificent frame had evoked in the lovestruck policeman. "Didn't seem to care about getting into bother though, because he actually came right up here, cap in hand. Is he married?"

"One wife, two divorces and four assorted kids," lied Sasha. "Why couldn't you call it off then, if he passed on the message all right?"

"He was too late, wasn't he?" she replied glumly. "Couldn't face

239

me until he'd had a few drinks after he came off duty, and then he had one too many and couldn't find the block in the dark, in the state he was. You won't believe it but he had to ask a policeman the way. The upshot was he knocked up Baranova at six a.m. and she supported him up the stairs. Until she smelled his breath she thought it was a dawn raid because at the time Vanya was playing Cowboys and Indians in the bathroom with that blunderbuss of his. Anyway I gathered what wasn't going to happen, even though your messenger was full as a tub. He also said you owed him money. That's when he got familiar and said he knew he wasn't going to be paid, so he might as well take his pound of flesh there and then, on the spot. He nearly did me an injury."

"I tried to ring, but the phone was always engaged," said Sasha, circumventing the topic of male lechery.

"Hardly surprising, was it? Nobody had a wink of sleep the whole night except Pa. And when the gunfire started he shot out of bed to find that my covetous menfolk had emptied every drinkable item of the wedding-breakfast down themselves, and set off into the town rip-roaring for more. There wasn't a drying-out station he didn't ring, nor a hospital. And then there was me, all of a doodah, hovering on the brink of insanity, sure that you'd been carted off to be murdered. Never again will I wait for any man."

What Rocky had done to him – even though he embellished the account, and she had seen his cuts and warped cheek – seemed to leave her curiously untouched. The most stupendous blow had been inflicted on her pride, that much was clear.

"I only escaped because your mucky copper helped me. You were right, they might have murdered me if I'd not cleared out. That mad Bogat was in here taking the drains to pieces and making jokes like a pantomime werewolf."

"Yes," said Valentina dreamily after a long pause. "Vera did say something about a repair man. I wasn't exactly in any condition to listen at that precise moment."

She got up from the mattress and shuffled about the room, picking out slivers of glass from the grooves of the floorboards and collecting them in a saucer, indolently, with only a pretence at clearing up.

"Weren't you surprised when they turned up again while I was away?" he asked, impatient at her desultory reply.

"Not really. I knew by that time something was up. That big one, he rang the bell tonight. Fawning as a Ministerial dogsbody. I let him in, thinking there might be news of you."

"But Olga Sergeyevna said there'd been no sign of them. When I told her she accused me of being in cahoots with . . ."

The specks of glass danced in the saucer. "Olga Sergeyevna! Olga Sergeyevna!" shrieked Valentina, without warning. "I'm sick to death of hearing that snooty female's name! She's got the morals of the hen-roost. You came in with her tonight, didn't you? I knew it, long since, the first time I clapped eyes on you together – you're snuffling round her like the lickerish hound you are."

Sasha had borne up under too many similar attacks of her ground-less jealousy to do more than groan with weariness. "That's rich, that is. She spat at me not a minute before. She thinks I'm a spy."

"Oh, she would! Women like that would do anything to inject a bit of glamour into their dried-up lives. Ask her what other guises you appear under in her maidenhead fantasias. Very orchidaceous, the blooms under single beds. One minute you'll be a gladiator, the next a tamer of lions. Don't you know anything about women yet?"

"Get away with you, Valya. You know you're not making sense. We'd be a right funny couple, her and me."

"That's just it. She's class and you're a ruffian. Some women who eat off silver dishes love being rummaged by creatures like you. They ache to feel the calluses sliding down their bellies. I know a thing or two about that type."

He absorbed this in silence. Sometimes her shots were much wilder. Bobby shared the torn-silk syndrome, certainly, but Olga had never given him a sign. It was simple. She hated him. Whatever her incli-nations towards the rough, a woman wasn't going to come on for a bloke she swore was going to land her in clink.

"She despises me. She thinks I'm some kind of layer of information to the militia – or worse."

Valentina giggled spitefully. "I told you: she's got a yen for crooks. She wants to be jemmied by a burglar who violates all norms – legal or otherwise. Fancy picking you! That'd be like having your bottom pinched by a shoplifter."

After a final scan, she decided that the planking was free of glass and got painfully to her feet. The big job of clearing away Legless's smash-up was still to be tackled and she went straight to it, first extricating her cherry-wood doll box which the policeman had tossed aside intact. It was covered in glitter-dust from a box of crackers which he had ripped apart, one by one. As she dusted off the box, she directed a mean, hard glance at Sasha.

"Seriously, Aleksandr Mikhailovich, that woman you think so grand, she's as mushy as pie. Do you want me to put in a word for you?"

In any other context this might have been sarcastic, but the use of his public name brought into the open that hostility in her which he had sensed at the outset. All along she had been planning something which could only be to his detriment. He watched as she took her box over to the waste-bin just inside the door, shook out the residue of sparkly trash, and started to line the satinwood interior with the choicest articles of her range of queer underwear. Even Legless, thought Sasha wryly, had drawn the line at ripping up that armoured lingerie.

"Men," she said, caressing the elasticised ruches and inset panels of a flesh-tinted pantie-girdle. "Men I can do without. This was my last adventure."

Without looking at him again she shook her head from side to side like a wet-nurse reproving an infant which had declined the breast. "You could have asked my sister-in-law how easy I can lay off. Back home there were oodles of men every week, calling, cajoling, in blue suits and white shirts and clean fingernails, bowing and scraping, all for a word from me. It's no different here either. Only the other day a man rubbed up an acquaintance with me on the tram – a most distinguished-looking individual, a painter. He wanted to paint me, kissed my hand. Said I'd the most sumptuous figure he'd ever seen, was I a model, had I ever posed nude?"

All the time she was trying not to cry. Not, he realised now, from the shame of her being made ridiculous in the eyes of her relations but from grief at having once more, in her tenacious but luckless existence, failed utterly to secure even a particle of undiluted happiness. She had come to him, as she had come to many a man before, persuading herself against all reason and experience that this time the bastard wouldn't let her down. The net result was that she was shacked up on the poky first floor with a down-and-out and five thousand roubles-worth of debris.

"I won't stop you going," he said pulling her round to face him, her cheeks slobbered with tears. "You've had enough, duck, more than enough."

He ran through a gallery of women's faces: Olga, blanched as vegetable flesh, Anna's lips riddling with terror, Lizaveta's false teeth chattering, out of control, when she dug into her cash box to pay for Bogat's spread. Every one of them effectively abandoned by the men to whom they had once looked for protection. Even Tanya and Marina, the brave ones, those who cast themselves as ladies of spirit, even they had only one another to cling to.

Thank God he had been born a man.

Valentina could not put reasons to her misery, but fell back on events. "I wrote you a four-page letter yesterday and I ought to have long since departed. But it's no good," she sobbed. "It's no good with them, any more. They didn't want me in the first place and now they've barred the door to me for ever. I can't stay here and I've nowhere else to go."

Respectful silence was all he could afford.

"It was a bear-dance with Pa and my brothers and those idiot men-cousins, swilling and gorging. I sat here for four hours in my dress like an undertaker's mute, in spite of what your police-messenger had said. When you didn't come, the women started on me because I'd let their husbands drink. I had to pay them to go back home. Pa threatened me with a larruping. Simple murder didn't figure in what they were going to do with you if they caught you. My brothers cursed me for a wall-eyed witch and said I'd never set foot back home till I'd squared them all up, cashwise. Sasha, Sasha, it's all gone, I've not a kopek left." At the mention of her depleted savings her voice rose to a wail. "All gone, all gone!"

"Never mind that," he said. "That's a detail. The first thing to do is to get you out of here, somewhere quiet and safe. I think I can fix that. Now shake yourself down and we'll get organised. Where's your powder compact and your comb? Put on a fresh face and you'll feel better. I'll help you pack."

Valentina blew her nose violently and groped round for her make-up bag.

Decisive and confident, though with little idea of what to take or what to leave, Sasha grabbed at what came nearest to hand. In ten minutes he had filled his old carpet bag with the relics of their communal property.

"Where are you taking me?" asked Valentina, in the street.

"You'll see, you'll see," he said, hurrying her along. "It's not far."

But Valentina, now she felt more secure after escaping from the flat and realising that Sasha might after all be as good as his word and not be about to throw her to her lupine relations or leave her in the gutter, was keen to show her gratitude by convincing him what depths her kinsfolk could plumb.

"Look what they left you," she said, stopping at the roadside to unclasp her handbag and taking out a square of paper folded over many times.

"Later, later," he said impatiently.

"No," insisted Valentina. "Let the fresh air blow through the names. There they are, all of them, the whole sackful of snot-nosed goats."

Sasha took the paper to a street lamp, undid the folds into a long, greasy sheet and peered at the list. The family he had forfeited, the family he had never known and never would, there they were, exhibiting their primitive existences in rude agricultural hands, the great tree-stump letters forming up into the Mityas, Praskovyas, Palashas, Egors, Grishas, Vanyas, Fedyas and Yashas whom he had never seen, and whom Valentina despised with all her soul.

At the end of the list someone (it looked like Pa) at some time during the hellish two days had cracked, and blocked out a last message to Sasha in vast geriatric capitals:

LISTEN YOU SCUMB BASTERD YOU MESS WITH MY LITTLE GIRL AGAIN AND MY LADS WILL DO YOU UP SO GOOD YOU'LL FORGET WHAT YOUR COCKS FOR PS PLEASE RI-MIT R200.95 K FOR EXPENSES INCURRED

29

When Sasha pushed at the street door it swung as if hinged from the bottom, toppled back slowly against the through draught, and settled with a little crash on to the hall floor.

"Merciful God!" whispered Valentina. "What is this place you're taking me to?"

Grasping her arm Sasha pulled the widow into the passage, put down his bag and blocked up the entry with the hingeless door. Apart from the noise of something which crunched underfoot, an uncanny silence hung over the building. The air was choked with a fine dust which smelt of slaked lime and gypsum.

Dustmen remembered entrances and Sasha knew his way in the dark.

"What's happening?" said Valentina in the blackness, scarcely able to breathe, terrified by a hissing sound which grew louder as they felt their way along.

"They've had visitors, too," said Sasha in his normal voice. "We weren't the only ones."

He felt for the kitchen door, found it ajar and reached behind for the light switch.

Whoever had been there before them had had a grudge. White dust was suspended above their heads, swirling down the corridors behind them in the electric light. An axe, or a long pole with a cutting edge, had been taken to the lath and plaster and there was a deep, irregular gash extending the length of the ceiling from the kitchen to the street door. Periodically, whoever had done it had rested his arms by attacking the hard seraphite plaster of the walls, and scabbed long chunks from the unpapered surface. It had been a leisurely affair, to judge by the cigarette butts heaped by the skirting.

Much energy had been expended on the kitchen. The lead piping to the taps had been levered from the wall and thrown with great force into the sink, going right through it, making a jagged hole in the flat bottom. Hot and cold water was gushing in a vertical fan against the wall from the severed network of exposed pipes. Along the far wall were gaping scars where shelves had been wrenched from their brackets, and the curtain in front of the lavatory hung crazily, half its rings torn away. The missing ones had been dropped, with grim humorousness, like hoopla circlets over the legs of the overturned table. Only the lavatory and wash-basin had escaped attention. In the tiny wash-place the bulb swung gently in the faint breeze of evening coming down river from the hills.

The first thing that occurred to Sasha was to find some means of turning off the water. He knelt below the sink in a milky puddle, scraping his knuckles in a frantic search for the stopcock. Unable to see what his hands were groping for amongst a mess of rusty cans and floor cloths, he spreadeagled on to his belly and lit a match. The flame burnt down just as he located the biggest of three brass taps. It wouldn't shift. Twisting half on to his back to obtain greater leverage, and with one arm at its fullest extent, he gave an anti-clockwise jerk to the tap wings. There was some play. As he gathered himself for one more twist he bumped up against Valentina.

At that same moment she screamed, as he had never thought any human being could scream. For an instant his body went as rigid as a bar of pig-iron, and the thought hit him, quite illogically, that the wiring circuit had somehow been punctured by the fractured pipes and he had become a conduit for the mains current which was jumping through him to her. But no such thing had happened. The cause of her scream stood in the kitchen doorway.

An unrecognisable figure, white hair streaming and muddied with blackish red patches, dragged heavily towards the widow. Neither its face nor its body could be seen. From hairline to toe it was entirely covered by grey, curling tresses – resembling, in Sasha's terrified imagination, a giant hairpiece which had somehow come dislodged and was draped over a stumbling child.

The figure lost its footing in the rubbish strewn over the floor and the chevelure slipped from its face. It was Marina.

On to her shoulder flopped the open muzzle of her dog, blood congealing round a powder-singed hole which had once been his left eye.

"Look," she said tenderly, fastening her arms tighter round his ribs and brushing her chin against his ear. "Look what they did to Jim."

The dead weight of the animal was so great that she fell to her knees and Jim, as yet unstiffened, rolled off her like a scalp and lay, paws outstretched, in the acrid plaster slime which was foaming in the gaps of the floorboards.

Valentina who had remained throughout in the posture her first sight of the apparition had induced – arms flung out as if to ward off a blow – recovered quickly. She dragged the old woman away from Jim, righted an up-ended chair and sat her down.

"Cleanse me, cleanse me," mewled Marina in a catatonic sing-song. "Cleanse me from the stench of death."

Rusty flakes of blood glistened on her skin, drying out along the flaccid clots which caked her face, neck, and the loose ends of her hair. Her skirt and thick lisle stockings were fronded with pinkish drops salivated by the mortally injured dog. Sasha, his heart in his mouth, felt over the old woman's chest and back, looking for entry wounds; but having swiftly assured himself that they had restricted themselves to the slaying of animals, he seized an enamelled bowl from the floor and held it up to one of the gushing pipes until he had collected enough hot water to begin washing away the blood.

Valentina mopped up some of the water with her handkerchief, swabbed Marina's forehead and lips until the material was filthy, then lifted her own skirt and tore off a long strip of petticoat.

With clear, untearful eyes Marina looked at the widow as if it were the most natural thing in the world to be tended by her.

"They pierced him once, my valorous boy, and then they thrust him through," she intoned in a playground lilt.

While Valentina was administering first-aid, Sasha had managed to shut off the water. The ensuing trickle from the pipes was now the only noise in the room. He looked round and saw the mangled carcase of the dog. A shiver rippled through his body and he moved closer to the women.

"Who did?" he asked. "Who are *they*?"

"They shot Jim once, they shot him twice and then he went away."

"Ssshhh!" said Valentina. "She's taken it bad. Let her take her time."

"I must know," insisted Sasha. "Unless it was thieves, they could still be around. Judging by the level of water they can't have done this damage more than about twenty minutes ago."

He cosseted Marina's hand between his palms. "Be a dear, Marina Andreyevna, it's important. Can you remember what they looked like?"

"Bang!" softly exclaimed the old woman. "Once in his great stove chest. Jim came on, like the Irish boy he was, and slashed the puppet's leg. Marks, marks he'll have to show himself tonight. Bang! Out went that bold eye."

"Yes," said Sasha, falling in with Marina's talk in the hope of bringing her to specifics. "Yes, Jim was magnificent. Now, who did that to your lovely lad?"

"Ah, the perpetrator?" cried Marina, perking up. "The villain of the piece, the guilty party?" She gripped Sasha's hand and craned towards him. "Well, I can tell you this – this time, the butler didn't do it!"

"No," said Sasha patiently, knowing Marina's fondness for detective stories. "This time it wasn't the butler. Who do you think it was?"

Valentina interposed herself between him and the old woman. "That's enough," she said. "Leave her alone."

Sasha pushed her aside. "Marina Andreyevna, who do you think it was?"

Marina went on staring. "A Nazi," she said. "A Gestapo."

"I see," said Sasha wearily. "And what was he here for, this Gestapo?"

"For my daughter, of course," cried Marina. "For my firstborn."

"Listen, dear," said Sasha, leaning over her. "Think carefully. Did he have a gun?"

From what he had seen of the dog, his wounds were not necessarily from bullets. The fog in Marina's brain seemed to clear instantaneously.

"A pistol!" she rapped. "Nine millimetre Walther – blued, with walnut grips."

Sasha didn't know that much about foreign pistols but this one sounded authentically lethal.

"I see," he said limply. "And did you notice anything else?"

Marina scrabbled in her skirt pocket. "This!" she shouted theatrically, holding up a spent cartridge case.

"Yes?" asked Sasha left behind by Marina's technicalities.

"Hollow-nosed parabellum. Have you seen the back of Jim's head?"

Sasha wanted to be sick, but Marina was by now totally in command of herself.

"An expanding bullet! You wouldn't use it on a dog." And she laughed at her own joke. "Unless," she added, "you were a very common little man, like he was. You never saw such clothes. Too well cut for anyone but a scoundrel, good but out of place, like father's cast-off tweeds on the gardener. He kept fiddling with a silver case."

"He gets about, does Rocky," breathed Sasha to himself.

The old woman's voice once more relapsed into musical waverings: "Damn, damn, damn the enfeebled flesh, the ichor desiccates in my womb, my entrails wither."

Suddenly her head rocked in spasm and her lips brimmed with spittle. Valentina, thinking that she was having a fit, forced the soaked wad of petticoat between Marina's teeth and sprang at Sasha.

"There now, look what you've done with your heartless inquisitions!" she shouted, thoroughly alarmed. "You've given the poor dear a stroke! Stop gawping – I can deal with this. Go and dig a hole for that great beast before it putrefies on us."

By the light from the kitchen window he searched for some implement with which to dig the grave. At length he stubbed his boot on the haft of a pick lying among the yellow stalks of the knee-high seeding grasses. Propped against the outhouse was a sheet of plywood which he took off with the pick to the far end of the garden.

Before he had done more than clear a shallow trench in the matted soil, Valentina came puffing across the hummocks dragging the carcase behind her by its hindlegs. The dog was shrouded from Sasha's sight by some white material.

"Befitting, isn't it?" said Valentina sardonically. "In the space of twenty-four hours my wedding veil is become grave clothes." The cemetery humour was lost on Sasha who, too squeamish to touch the animal with bare hands, was edging it on to the plywood shutter with his instep.

She nudged him. "Cheer up. You have to laugh. You can't have the miseries on our honeymoon. Where's the stomach to you, man? Why, I lost my virginity among gravestones!"

"Valya . . ." he began, but didn't know what further to say and turned to his digging.

"That's a very crazy old girl in there," she said, lowering her voice. "She wanted it to be a proper Christian burial. Here's doggie's monument."

She handed him a cross of ceiling laths knotted together with twine. "Don't forget the prayer: 'Earth to earth . . .'"

Half an hour later he staggered into the kitchen, wiping the sweat from his eyes. Valentina had already made inroads on the kitchen rubble. The table was the right way up, and on the stove water was bubbling in a saucepan.

"There was just enough from the taps to make tea," she said, handing him one of her best china cups. He was grateful for the drink and curled his fingers round the bowl.

"Where's Marina Andreyevna?"

"I've washed her and put her to bed. They seem to have kept their depredations to this floor. She keeps calling for liquor but she'll nod off soon, I expect. Would you believe?" she added, pleased to have acquired Marina's confidences and eager to share them with Sasha. "They carted off her son-in-law as well as the daughter. The rest of the inmates made a run for it when they heard shooting and left the old lady defenceless with her dead dog."

Sasha wasn't surprised. "What else do you expect? It's called not getting involved."

"Well, you're getting involved," said the widow decisively. "I'm not staying here alone all night with that doolally old lady. You can find a spot to doss down, you've had enough practice these last few days. Another night sleeping rough won't cripple you. Tomorrow we can start getting sorted."

"Why don't we go back to the flat?" asked Sasha. "At least there's a bed."

"I'd sooner sleep on my feet in this charnel house than go back to that hell-hole. It's six of one and half a dozen of the other. In any case, we can't leave *her*."

"They won't come back here," said Sasha quietly. "Not now they've taken everything and everyone useful. She's no good to them – they would have bagged her years ago if she were. You're right though, it's worse back at the lane. We haven't seen the last of them there. There's money in it for them. They're going to pick us clean."

Valentina shrugged. "I'm well out of it, then."

What she did not tell Sasha, was that after that half-hour which she had passed tête-à-tête with Marina Andreyevna, she had no intention of returning to him, his bed, his flat or his friends. Marina had told her that she was epileptic. No one knew except Tanya and Andrey and no one knew when they might return. Tanya's absence was bound to be measured in years, not months. Andrey was a ne'er-do-well who had tangled with the authorities too many times ever to be able to stand up to them. No, there was a task for her here, thought the widow. And though it might not be an easy one, and she was under no illusions about Marina's eccentricity, a rapport had already been established. Marina liked her. She could tell that from the old woman's attitude. She liked her in a way Valentina was happy to be liked: as someone upon whom one could become securely dependent. Men were too suspicious, too self-conscious, too wary, to esteem the dependability which Valentina offered. Not so a woman, particularly a woman such as Marina Andreyevna. For the early part of her life she had been brought up by servants and the relationship of mistress and maid was one which, although it had long ago disappeared, still exerted a sway over her personality. She wanted a confidante, a handmaiden, a companion and, from time to time, a butt for her discontents and queer humours. All that required an inferior, for the proper accomplishment of her role as a lady; but she knew, as Valentina had naturally grasped, that the inferiority was only an outward semblance. Privately they would be equals, the one relying on the other for confirmation of a dependence which each found mutually beneficial. The maid needed her lady and the lady needed her maid.

Before Sasha, Valentina preened herself on her secret avocation. To be indispensable gave her heart ease. She had found her ultimate lodging. In her voice was a new vibrancy.

"There's dignity for you. *That* only flowers in long-stemmed kith. Bred up in her. You can keep the reach-me-down graces of your Olga Sergeyevnas. Blood speaks."

"And spills, and stains and contaminates," said Sasha. "It might be a nice cherry-red to you, but on the inside it pumps good and black. So you reckon you'll stay?"

"I'll have a dabble," said Valentina, as stubborn as a woman with an untried lover. "Perhaps her past is better than my future. At least there, there are no unwelcome knocks on the door."

She had given up but what did it matter? Her new-found exultancy sailed over him. She had mounted herself among the sepia-washed flummeries of Marina Andreyevna's vast album of photographs, where madam would unfadingly lounge, the hammocks still swung in the orchard, and the parlourmaid smirked up at the lens. Good luck to her.

As for him, they hadn't done for him yet.

30

The style of the house was a puzzle. At first sight Bogat was reminded of a castle: there was a medieval keep built over the stable block, complete with arrow slits and machicolations. The front door was set at the foot of a square Romanesque tower; but as one moved from the flying buttresses and decorated pinnacles to the family's living quarters, it was obvious that interiors must have obsessed the builder as much as the external configuration. The Caen facing of the main block was pierced by cosy mullioned windows, their glazing starred by medallions of thick, sweet-shop glass which would once have warmly distorted the scarlets of an autumn sunset or the fires of great rooms.

Inside, there had been apartments as variegated as the architecture of the building itself. A room, decorated *à la Chinoise* with wall paper showing bamboo groves and long-legged birds, complemented by furniture of miniaturised chinoiserie, had been favourite among the children allowed to handle but not to play with the contents of this grown-up toy. An ebony bureau, its folding doors decorated with German oriental exotica of floating landscapes where straggle-bearded Chinamen strayed between lagoons, had fascinated Olga's grandmother. Not because the scenes were so distant from the buttery haycocks, dark fish pools and willows of the Central Russian summer, but because the cabinet was fitted out with tiny Bramah keys. These, even when full-sized, required the slightest of pressures to turn the noiseless locks; but here, in this house, they could only properly be manipulated by craftsmen or the delicate fingers of a child.

All Olga had since learned about the English had confirmed her grandmother's perceptions of them as a race which paid minute attentiveness to the apparently trivial. The barrel of the dolly key was turned as finely as the propeller shaft of an ocean liner, and the tumblers of the lock yielded only when the precise amount of energy was applied against the spring loading.

Olga's great-grandfather in the breakfast room, after coffee, smoking salty Trichinopoly cheroots, had instructed the little girl in the devious intricacies of the English mechanical bent. The child was less interested in what lay inside the cabinet. The drawers were boringly dissimilar and wood, it seemed to her childish mind, had no possibility of the delightful exactitude of metal.

Left alone, Olga's grandmother would have played all day with the Chinese room – that, and the model dairy where the hand-churns cried out to be whirled – but the family was strict. When she played she was to be instructed. Someone, probably her father or his factor or, at a pinch, his valet who, for some reason understood engines, upholstery and furniture styles, would superintend her examination of the interior and exterior of the house. It was like her study of English, French and German: a process in strict rotation to be charted and timed. On Thursday the Renaissance hall, on Wednesday the Romanesque tower and so on. In that way she came to know every detail of the house which had, long ago, been christened Sherwood's Folly. And she had passed the knowledge down to her daughter, who had passed it to hers.

"There was once a landscape surround," said Olga. "That would have been the view from the ha-ha, a quarter of a mile from the main façade."

Bogat fingered the Gothic letter-press at the bottom right of the folio-sized photograph: "Quaas, Stechbahn 2, Berlin", indented within a quaint, Wilhelmenian cartouche. "Like the undersheet of a telegraph pad," he muttered. "The positive superscription entirely disappeared."

At the edges, the photograph was peeling from its cardboard mount. Moistening the ancient glue with a finger, he pressed back the image. "It was all to scale, then?"

"Oh, precisely," said Olga. "It was Germans who made it. All that remains of the building is this." And she handed him a large fragment of papier-mâché over which newspaper had been pasted. "This was part of the base which used to fit over a marble-topped commode." At the masthead of the newspaper ran the legend: *Berliner Lokal-Anzeiger*; next to it a circular reading room stamp: "Offentliche Bibliothek und Leschalle, Alexandrinen-Str. 26."

"Ah," said Bogat still poring over the picture, disinclined to relinquish a whole house which no longer existed, in favour of a lump of its footings which did. "That un-Russian *détaillisme*. There the cages would be open but the tinplate nightingales would still sing their mechanical songs, fizzing with clockwork, but unmoving, claws round steely roosts. What shapeless, organic creatures we Russians are, Olga Sergeyevna, don't you agree?"

"Un-toylike bears, if you like," said Olga. "But who is to draw our teeth?"

"Not Germans," said Bogat with a laugh, gently laying down the photograph. "Now, what else have you to show me? I feel like a boy again, foraging in a bran-tub of unbelievably precious things."

Olga's divan was strewn with tiny objects: two clouded amber necklaces, as big as a grown woman's bangle, a Dresden dinner-service and an ivory paper knife and malachite blotter, a gold watch chain and seals, all proportioned to the size of the jewellery. Bogat's trench coat lay nearby, with his plastic carrier bag, *Rive Gauche* italicised on its sides. He picked up a porcelain tureen, rotated it in his palm and read off the manufacturer's label: "'Hengstmann, Leipziger Strasse, 39'. Exquisite! Germans everywhere. Did they make everything?"

"The house itself was their work – the shell, that is. The fitments for the rooms, the door furniture, the brasses, the hinges, anything remotely mechanical – even the lead weights for the sash casements in the bedrooms – the machine-like aspects of domestic life – they were all catered for by the English. And all that disappeared, of course, with the house itself. The Teutonish things are accidental survivals. Once the spread was more European."

"Baltic amber from Unter den Linden," said Bogat slipping one of the necklaces over his thumb. "Artificial flowers from Leipzig. Did we do nothing, had we not yet awoken?"

Olga had hidden the most valuable of the Russian works under the refrigerator, a diadem of topazes and enamel, its diameter only the width of Bogat's big toe nail, the work of the Moscow goldsmith Ovstchinnikov. Now it was lodged amidst the mouse droppings and the fluff from the rugs in the lobby.

"In the 1860s? Perhaps by then we were feeling our feet, I think." Fearful that he would unstring the little ambers she led him over to the bottom drawer of the bureau which stuck three-quarters out into the room, packed with balsa wood cartons.

"This was in the housekeeper's parlour," she said. The lid slid back, and taking up one of the boxes with her little finger she hooked out a long sofa with a half-oval wooden frame carved with cinquefoils and upholstered in chintz. "That material ruins it, but my great-grandfather thought chintz homely. For servants, at any rate. And this," she went on, her voice as toneless as a guide's, bringing up another box, "this was the harp from the drawing-room."

The instrument was shrouded in a white leather case with bone fastenings. As Bogat gently drew it from the wrappings, his fingers touched the wire strings and they ping-ed tinnily.

Olga looked away. To watch Bogat's groping her things was like watching a man slurping tea from a saucer. She could not remember the last time she had unparcelled the dolls' furniture. Well over a century ago her great-grandfather had commissioned the model on the plan of a monstrous, imitation Gothic castle, which was further deformed by the addition of an English Elizabethan wing. Now the only record was a photograph and a few account books which gave details of the work let out to sub-contracting craftsmen and recorded their purchase of silks, tapestries and rare woods.

Bogat's polite foray into her room (preceded by her insistence on several days' notice and the absence of Legless) was almost a relief. The dolls' bric-à-brac held so many unwelcome memories that she would be glad to get rid of it. Bogat, however, was more interested in the house than its contents, and, encouraged by her uncharacteristically complaisant manner in displaying its treasures, unloosed his sensibility to atmospherics.

"Imagine one winter afternoon, being curled up in a library chair with a good book, the log fire blazing."

"I can't imagine anything more trying," she said languidly, bundling the packages back into the drawer, "than burying oneself in such a dismal hole. You do realise nobody ever lived there – or ever could. It was not a real house, only the miniaturised plaything of an idle, silly old man, who could think of nothing better to spend his money on."

Bogat was not stupid, merely romantic. He wanted to inhabit the place, stroll around its avenues, slash the tops off the cow parsley at the edges of the gravelled drive, poke in the chests in the muniment room on rainy mornings, to be simply in sole occupation and flourish in full view of a demesne.

Yes, thought Olga, so did my great-grandfather, but his mad languishings after total possession – that, to her, was what the house represented – were never put to rest. He was tormented by the threat that after his death his claims would be disputed and his tiniest properties ransacked. Thank God he was right, and that this last burden might slip from her to his worthy inheritors.

To ridicule the longings of this awful little man who sat before her, mesmerised by covetous respect, she lectured him with the authority of vanished privilege.

"The nucleus is sham Gothic derived from prints in an English book of architectural designs, dated around 1840."

Bogat, understanding almost nothing of this part, was ravished, nevertheless, as she recounted the history of the building and the constant refurbishment of the rooms to take account of the latest domestic advances: the flues had been so designed that the hearth fires of log twigs would actually draw; in 1910 the rooms had been wired for electricity, and running water installed. There had been a doll-family, headed by a grandfather with a long white beard like Tolstoy's who sat in a huge carver chair in the dining-room; a smooth-jowled father, overweight, to whom a disgruntled housemaid set light in 1891; and the mistress of the house in black silks and pelerine who dwelt in the morning room, seated at an embroidery frame stitching a petitpoint counsel, "Bear the Cross and Wear the Crown".

Bogat drank in the words reverentially. "There," he sighed absently, when she paused to struggle with a box, the top of which was snagging the pull of the drawer. "I knew about you by instinct. One look was enough to tell how much you were out of the common run. If you only knew how much one craves refinement and civility in my line of business. People are so crass, generally, so *rude*. You see, I'd like to feel I could just drop in on you, occasionally, for the cool refreshment of cultivated talk and we could muse on the past, esteem your exquisite properties, give ourselves over once in a while to art, life, and things of the mind."

Olga, horrified, wrenched out the drawer so that the handle end tipped on to the rug. "What? You mean you're going to come back? Aren't you going to take all this away and sell it?"

Bogat was mildly scandalised that she should class him with Legless. "Oh dear, that's not my style at all, Olga Sergeyevna. I recognise quality when I see it, and realise when I am confronted by a very superior human being. Consumerism is for the likes of that dunderhead policeman." He crossed his legs elegantly, smoothed the cloth of his denims and glanced shyly at her. "I'll tell you what, Olga Sergeyevna – do you think I might call you Olga? – His sort, creatures of that ilk – they're scum. I don't steal – not from people I admire and respect. Even if I bought some nice article from you, what sort of home would I be taking it to?"

Olga had no idea.

"Irredeemably," he whispered, "*irredeemably petit bourgeois*. There, I've said it. I feel it, so I've said it."

"I don't quite understand," said Olga. "How can you be *petit bourgeois*?"

"How can *I* be?" he said. "I'm not – I said 'home' – it's the kind of flats they give us – but *they* are. You should see them – they've got shopkeepers' souls and shopkeepers' three-piece suites."

"God preserve us from the *nouveaux riches*."

"Exactly," breathed Bogat. "Exactly."

Two hours later, Olga was still entertaining her unwelcome guest. She had suggested tea, in the hope that after tea he would consider the afternoon to be rounded off and take his leave. But he drank the tea gratefully and stayed. Neither her outright yawning nor refusal to sit down during the last half-hour made the slightest impression on him. When he had introduced some prosy reflection on the nature of existence for what must have been the dozenth time with an "After all, Olga Sergeyevna, what is life all about?" or a "This is just it, Olga Sergeyevna, where is it all leading?" she was ready to fall at his feet in a dead faint.

At last, he dropped philosophy for personalities and brought up the subject of friendship. In particular, that of his own with Rocky.

"A loner," he explained. "An individual much misunderstood. His type broods on the chances he's never had – educationally, I mean – and it comes out as aggression. You'd get on with him, I'm sure, and he'd love to see your collection. He's taught himself about antiques and he has this anglophile bent. Friends everywhere as a result, knows all the connoisseurs from a trumpeter in the Circus who collects Bibles to the most illustrious members of the *corps diplomatique*."

Christ have mercy upon us, thought Olga. It's enough to make you want to set fire to anything over one hundred years old. That's what they call culture. Where have all the *common* criminals gone? How can the Kuznetsovs bear his conversation, now that he practically lives with them?

"My English is really quite good," he said, going up to her bookcase. "Not as good as Rocky's, of course, but I'd love to borrow one of these. I love books and reading, especially poetry. At night sometimes I lie awake weeping about the sadness at the heart of things. That's my inborn lyricism coming out, I suppose."

"But don't you find poetry in other languages hard to understand?"

"You might say that, Olga may I? You are, of course, Olga, as a linguist, entitled to say that. I approach verse from a professional point of view. By that I mean, that the first thing to identify is the information being conveyed, the subject matter, and having, in my time, appreciated the work of numerous poets from all ages and lands I have concluded that they have only two concerns – one being love, the other being death. Topics with which, you might say, I am not unacquainted. So in that way we all speak the same language."

"Doesn't the unique form of the words matter?"

Bogat thought for a moment and thumped a volume of Fet with his fist. "I wouldn't say so, Olga Sergeyevna, not really. After all, it comes down to the same thing in the end."

Olga went over to the window and looked out at the crows perched on the roof of the café. If I were forced to live with such a man, she asked herself, would it be a mortal or a venial sin to dream of poisoning him?

By now Bogat was sure they were on the same wavelength. "Art makes life worthwhile," he called softly. "Fancy waking up in the morning, looking out of the window of that house and having an idea for a poem."

"How many times do I have to tell you?" said Olga through gritted teeth, sensing the onset of a liberating hysteria which might, at last, free her of her guest. "Nobody ever lived there. It never existed except as a pretence, a joke, a fraud, a folly, a sham. And it wasn't a house. It was a castle, a lunatic, bad old man's dream of a *castle*!"

"That's what Englishmen call home, isn't it? A castle?"

It was no use. She shut her eyes and rested her forehead on the window-glass. The soft voice rambled on. There was no way of stopping him. No doubt he was insane.

"Yes, I think I am correct in saying that we owe that concept to the English. One time lords of the earth. I've learned a lot about the English from my stint in the post room. Great writers, the English, so many letters from Englishmen. People say they're a cold race, but in my experience . . ."

The blood was pounding in her ears. "Mr Bogat."

He smiled at her. Empathy suffused his features. "Yes, Olga Sergeyevna?"

"Mr Bogat, I must ask you to excuse me."

"Oh dear. A headache? A little tummy upset?"

"Mr Bogat, have you ever heard of the concept of pre-menstrual tension?"

He hadn't and he didn't like the sound of it.

"Well, I shan't explain. Suffice it to say that it has just stopped and I am about to have a very heavy period."

Those he had heard of. With a furtive movement he reached for his hat and his *Rive Gauche* bag and began to make for the door. As Olga was on the point of ushering him from the room, he turned, hat on, bag under his arm.

"Oh, by the way, I was coming round to it a few minutes ago. But . . . I don't quite know how to say this, Olga Sergeyevna. I believe I have something belonging to you."

Olga thought he must have pocketed one of the dolls' house pieces and wanted to return it.

"Oh, don't give it a second thought. I hate all those things, I told you."

"No, I mean . . . Look, what I mean is that *it* – rather *them* – don't belong to you, and I don't really have them, but I can get . . ."

"What is it you're trying to say, Mr Bogat?" asked Olga sweetly, taking pleasure in his confusion.

"Letters. Letters from abroad, letters to you, all from the same person. Copies are on file but I can get the originals. You've been so nice. A favour, between friends."

"Letters from where?"

"From England. From . . . John? was it? Jack . . . or J . . . ?" Olga's voice faltered. "James?"

"That's the one," said Bogat. "Was he a friend of yours, too?"

The answer to Olga's question about how the Kuznetsovs tolerated Bogat lay in the character of the husband. Over many years Lev Kuznetsov had schooled himself against displays of feeling; from his parents he had inherited an innate discretion; and self-discipline had bled all passion from his bland, plump features.

Early in life he had learned to pass unnoticed, to engender neither admiration nor anger, never to make people remember him more than anyone else; never to stand up to an adversary, never to leave by gesture or word the lightest imprint of his individuality on the outside world.

The one incautious act of his life had been to marry Anna. And that had destroyed him. Now the enemy was camped in their midst.

Bogat had commandeered their main room and Xenia's alcove. Behind the flimsy partition he entertained at their table, using Anna's mother's candelabra to impart an air of taste and intimacy to those assignations which Lev knew from the infamous noises which penetrated the wall, were a prelude to unspeakable deeds committed on his daughter's bed beneath his wife's patchwork quilt.

Bogat liked to play host. "You can't beat family life," he had once confided to Anna. "My place lacks atmosphere – one needs a woman's touch. We bachelors are so deprived."

At times Anna could even find this love of domesticity rather touching. The things around him were always neat and scrupulously clean. A row of brightly-polished brandy glasses was arranged on top of the bookshelves next to his foreign cookery books. His knives were always sharp. Every three days he changed the water of his flowers, and every week he bought new ones from the street-sellers at the Kiev station. Once he had presented her with a great bunch of purple gladioli beautifully done up in cellophane.

With Xenia, he wanted to be friends. "Children and dogs always take to me." But Xenia was reserved, plain and disconcerting. She threw away the doll he gave her. Lev's spirits soared.

"Give it time," said Bogat, unabashed. "Give it time. They always come round in the end."

Legless was different. To him Bakery Lane was no home, simply somewhere to park his TV on nights off when his girl was working late and he needed a quick snack. Lev found him more tolerable than Bogat. He was neither companionable nor interesting, but his criminality was banal. You knew where you were with him. Besides, Bogat detested him.

"I can't stand that individual," said Bogat in the kitchen one evening, watching over a saucepan of wine, brandy and spices which he was mulling for punch. "It's the way he talks. 'Bloke told me this, bloke told me that.' Really gets me down."

Lev wished there was more animus in Bogat's whine. But thieves of his kind, they never fell out.

A fortnight had gone by since that terrible day when Olga had found Bogat presiding at the kitchen table. Now he and Legless had the run of the apartment. Late at night Bogat might want to play Mahler very loudly on his Japanese stereo, while Olga lay in bed, her head under the pillows and her hands clamped over her ears. Or Legless would watch seemingly endless games of football on his portable, urging on his team with choleric, uncouth bellows in the kitchen. Sasha gave them both money. She had witnessed that one Thursday. Lizaveta was similarly mulcted, and deprived of the peace of her kitchen, cried and cried. Only Olga had been spared. Until today's visit, but even then Bogat had demanded nothing tangible; rather, he had wanted in his unpredictable fashion, to give, to do her a service. The man was adopting her – after today's performance she felt like a kept woman. Had Borya still been upstairs and Matvey still her boss, she could have asked for advice. With the defection of Sasha, and the pusillanimity of Lev, there was no man to turn to.

Her grief for her brother was unabated. For that reason she avoided Galina. In any case, Galina was untrustworthy and Olga suspected her of being embroiled with Bogat in some way. The younger of her nephews might come downstairs to borrow tea or bread, but he was either morose or embarrassed and never stayed. At work they were still without a Director: all she knew about Matvey was that he had left Moscow.

Of Tanya nothing had been heard for ten days. In desperation Valentina had taken Marina to a side-office at the Ministry of Home Affairs. They waited in a queue of people who, like themselves, were ignorant and afraid. After two days they were given a date for Tanya's trial, told that until then she was not permitted to see anyone, but that she could receive a parcel.

That night Olga had raided her store cupboard and next day, a covered basket of chocolate, fruit, fish and cigarettes on her arm, went in search of Marina. At the back of the house she found Valentina, in overalls, superintending the redecoration of Tanya's vandalised kitchen. One of the upstairs neighbours, a pot-bellied taxi-driver with peculiarly short arms was white-washing the ceiling. When Olga appeared in the doorway Valentina pretended to be giving instructions.

"There's a patch over here you've missed, and here, and here." The man meekly descended his stepladder and began to drag it across the floor. In the corner sat Marina, drinking tea from a glass, engrossed in a thriller.

Valentina took one look at the basket and knew why Olga had come.

"We can look after our own, thank you very much," she called out. "Tatyana Borisovna can do without parcels from you." Above her head, rolling his eyes, the taxi-driver dabbed inexpertly round the light fitting.

Marina calmed her down with caressing words. Behind the widow's bluster Olga saw a genuine terror: if she could not, at every point, demonstrate her fitness to be in charge, Marina might dispense with her. Olga's own position was little different. Were she to lose her nerve, Bogat would be pitiless. But Valentina's possessiveness was irritating. At this rate, she would be nabbing the last of Olga's friends.

"Why don't you go and paint Aleksandr Mikhailovich's room?" Olga had shouted back, making it clear to the taxi-driver that his new girl had a past. "He's let things go to pot since you left."

Valentina held herself back until Olga was on her way out. At the front door she caught up with her. "Sorry, Olga Sergeyevna. I'm a bit touchy these days, and you know what men are like. This one is manna from heaven to Marina and me, now that Andrey's done a bunk. I don't want him thinking I broadcast myself to all and sundry."

"That's very quick after Sasha," said Olga in surprise.

The widow winked. "Oooh, there's nothing like that in it for him, however much he longs. I've done with men – in that way. Like yourself, I suppose. Nice, isn't it? Don't tell him anything though, will you? He might jump off his ladder."

"I have no intention of speaking to him at all," retorted Olga stiffly. "And, by the way, I have given up nothing."

That evening Olga came home desolate. On her mat she had found Bogat's note: Could he come round to inspect her bureau? At her earliest convenience, of course.

31

"Where is he, then?" asked Sasha at last, pushing back his chair and taking a cigarette from behind his ear.

This was at dinner, a meal which, since Valentina's flit he had taken to sharing with Lizaveta. Tonight she had been unusually expansive after having spent most of the day helping Bogat with preparations for his party. For the host the great draw was to be the reading of his poems, but the old woman knew that if the food and drink were good and plenteous, guests might be better counted on to tolerate art.

After Sasha had regaled himself on the remains of a sturgeon, pickled roes, a tub of red caviare and a loop of lean sausage, Lizaveta helped him to kvass, ice-cold from the fridge. "In there," she said, pointing her jug at the closed door of the Kuznetsovs' quarters, the larger part of which Bogat had commandeered for his show. "And a high old tizz he's in. He was locked in the bathroom so long splashing about with those coloured essences of his that I'm behind with the washing. Aren't you going to rub yourself down, too? Lord knows, you must need it after a day puddling in other people's trash."

"I come home to relax," said Sasha, flicking over the newspaper to the TV programmes. "There's football on tonight and ice-hockey. The Canadians . . ."

"Didn't you know?"

"Know what?"

"You're on the door tonight."

Sasha groaned and pinched out his cigarette. "I might have guessed. Who does he think he is – Bella Akhmadulina? They ought to bribe me not to let them in. Who's he going to spill his poetic innards over this evening?"

"Everyone we know from round here," said Lizaveta dandling a hardly touched chunk of sturgeon flesh in her tea-towel. "That's not locked up, that is."

"Valentina?"

"Hardly," said Lizaveta. "Avid for culture is Pavel Aleksandrovich, and the last person he wants to see is that broomstick *princess* of hers, that foul-mouthed Marina Andreyevna Whatsername, or the fat tirewoman who swells her train." She dropped the salvaged fish into an empty pickle jar and snapped on the lid. "Can't stand that sort, can you?"

"Oh, Valentina's all right . . ."

"No, no – the other one. I don't know how they can face us."

"Us?"

"The People, the People," said Lizaveta irritably.

"Ah," said Sasha combing crumbs to the middle of the oil-cloth. "That *us*."

"After their depredations," mumbled the old woman. "You'd think they'd humble themselves in the dust."

"Brushes off, that," said Sasha, intent on making a little castle from the detritus.

"What?"

"Sackcloth and ashes. Anyway, what's the poor old bag ever done to you?"

Lizaveta wiped her hands and studied the front page of the newspaper. "Nothing, I suppose. Nothing." She gave a chuckle and planted a yellowing nail on the masthead. "Nothing. But it strikes you sometimes – nothing, except, don't you think someone ought to be blamed for letting *this lot* in after them?"

Without looking up Sasha demolished the pile with his thumb and grinned at the tucks of Lizaveta's floral stomacher. "Watch yourself, *babushka*. Any more and they'll be asking for your medal back."

Lizaveta smiled down on him. "No luck, my little son. I sold it."

"Forty years' work and you sold it? What did it fetch?"

"Three roubles," said Lizaveta. "Three roubles. 'No call for them,' said the man. 'No call for them, *matushka*.'"

Bogat was not mean. On the hallstand by the front door was a full bottle of vodka, cap unscrewed, and a tumbler. Propped behind was a card: "Lamp any scruff. I'm depending on you." And I'm depending on you, thought Sasha, addressing the bottle. After dousing his head under the shower, he took the bottle and knocked on the host's door with the glass.

Bogat grimaced. "Shit," he said, wringing his hands and nodding to the partitioned-off bedroom where the Kuznetsovs could be heard moving softly. "I thought I told you – not this door – *that* one."

"I know, I know," said Sasha. "Thought you'd want to brief me first, though. Over a gargle."

At the far end of the room was the great trunk from the lumber room in which Lizaveta stored old boots, broken umbrellas and the feather pillows which Lev had discarded because of Xenia's asthma. Draped over it was the batik coverlet from the Kuznetsovs' marriage bed.

"So that's where you do it, then," said Sasha, motioning to the trunk with his bottle. "Like up in the air, reciting."

Bogat looked nervous. "*Declaiming*, actually."

"Oh, right," said Sasha. "That's the proper thing." He poured himself a drink. "I knew a declaimer once – did I ever tell you about Arkady? He used to do *Graf Nulin* with all the dirty words, but his star turn was one called *Party Piece*. He declaimed the names and titles of all the delegates to the Seventeenth Party Congress, you know, the 1934 one. Brought the house down, every time, the warders were killing themselves. He did their dates, you see. It sort of built up. A bloody scream. Crackers, Arkady, but he could lead an audience."

The doorbell rang.

Bogat slipped across the room to the trunk and shot his cuffs distractedly. "Spare me a moment to compose myself and then you can allow them to enter."

The widow and Marina were standing in the hallway.

"Have you two got invites?"

"What do you think?" said Valentina. "Am I dressed for window-cleaning?"

"Or winding clocks," said Marina. "This is official. We have been expressly requested."

Sasha entered gracefully into the footman's role.

"Is he charging?" whispered Valentina as he took her coat.

"You pay with your body for this one," said Sasha kissing her on the nose.

"Tcha!" said the old woman. "Nothing's free with that lot. They've been handing round the collection plate since 1917."

When they swept in Bogat looked blank: neither woman seemed like a customer for poetry. He advanced towards them, weak from the onslaught of Valentina's corrosive scent, scarlet curls and shocking-pink, full-skirted frock. The weird old woman, tall, scrawny and dressed from head to toe in black, stood to one side staring above and beyond him. Someone had shorn her hair and given the remainder a permanent wave. It clung to her skull like the scallops of a white-petalled bathing cap.

"Introduce me to your friend," he mumbled, turning his eyes on Sasha and extending a hand to Marina.

Before Sasha could open his mouth Marina was gabbling hoarsely in an undertone: "Introductions! What need have you and I of such civilities? All our callings are obligatory. By now, young man, you know us better than our mothers. Our intimacy is deeper than the kissing of hands."

She was so tall that Bogat had to raise himself from his Cuban heels to catch her words.

"Bring me a chair, fellow."

The little man meekly took her arm and steered her towards the only armchair in the room.

"Dear lady," he began. "Pray be seated. You do me honour, honour indeed."

"What the hell do you think you're doing, trundling that old bag of sticks to my *conversazione?*" he hissed at Sasha when Marina was settled and out of earshot. "If I'd wanted a circus, I'd have brought my top hat and whip. Now, she's your responsibility. She keeps *stumm*, right? This is an intellectual enterprise, not artistic soap-boxing."

Valentina overheard. "That's nice," she said, fiddling with the veneered doors of Bogat's stereo cabinet. "Very suave about your guests you are. I'm sticking pins into myself already to make me believe I'm here."

Six champagne bottles stood on a side table by the window in Lizaveta's biggest galvanised pail. The widow sailed across, the layered tulle of her frock drifting up to her knees, assumed her most queenly attitude and waggled an empty wine glass at her host. "Who's this for, then, my man?" she called, taking off Marina's manner. "The dregs or the quality? Whatever way you make the choice, at least one of us gets a drink. Worked it out, you see, her and me, top and bottom of the social scale. We look after one another."

Bogat padded up to the table in his suede crepes and untwisted the wires of one of the bottles. The plastic cork popped out weakly. After a long drink Valentina turned and pinched the lobe of his right ear. Her body heat uprose, rollicking the sheaves of incarnadine tissue as she unloosened from the effects of the wine like a fat rose-bud unpinioning itself to the sun.

"All woman I feel in my dawn-blush frillies – stylish or unstylish, black isn't for me. 'How would I look?' I said to my old lady." She crushed Bogat's ear between her ploughgirl's fingers and her torso swelled out under his nostrils, rank with cold cream. "A blood-pudding in mourning."

Bogat attempted a deprecating grin. "Surely not, nothing so becomes a handsome woman . . ."

"Phoo!" said Valentina. "I'm not taking the veil. Not yet. It's sheer net and shocking pink for me while there's still a dimple in my flesh."

She wandered round the room, overcome at the profusion of Bogat's goods. "Take a look at that! Did you ever see the like? This is the poshest thing out!" Her pleasure in the glassware, prints, limp-leather miniature edition of the poets, a celadon bowl, even the reproduction Imagiste manifesto (because of its anodised frame of white aluminium), was so unfeigned and total that no one cared to interrupt the progress.

Bogat refilled her glass and returned to Sasha who was standing beside Marina's armchair, his arms folded across his chest.

"I did tell Olga Sergeyevna to invite her friends who could perhaps put in a word for me in literary circles . . . With her being at that agency, I mean, hobnobbing with commissioning editors, taking tea with novelists, that kind of thing – but from the sound of her, the only literature your ex warms to is the writing on a fifty-rouble note."

Picking up a tumbler chased with the engraving of a hippopotamus hunt he handed it to Sasha. "Now, you keep an eye on them, there's a treasure, while I circulate. Give the female Don Quixote a few stiffeners before she lets her hair down – what there's left of it."

Sasha laughed. "That's the host's job, isn't it? Lubricating the stiff joints? Here," he said, taking up a bottle of red wine. "You pour and I'll hold while we both charm her into a good opinion of your flash manners."

"How dare you," said Marina when Bogat offered her a glassful.

"But, I assure you, it's French . . ." he said, examining the label.

Marina curved her extravagant nostrils in an equine sniff. "That bouquet is redolent of nothing but an Algerian *pissoir*. Where's the real stuff?"

Bogat turned the bottle in his hands, holding it up to the light. "I took advice," he said. "'Fruity' Petrosian characterised it. 'With the teasy undertaste of elderflowers.' Of course, I'm a tyro at this game, only a budding *cognoscente*, you might say, but Petrosian swore on his mother's . . ."

"An Armenian would bottle his mother's entrails," shouted Marina, "and vend it as elixir. Do they teach you nothing in your job? That would come down on the palate like a whack from a forge-press. Bring me something cellarable, pot-boy."

Bogat, truly willing to learn, reached into the cupboard beneath his Hitachi and tumbled out his small store of wines. One by one he presented the bottles for Marina's evaluation, kneeling by the side of her chair, official notebook and pencil at the ready.

"That's no use," said the old woman as he caressed the venerable labels. "There could be anything in there. Let's get at it, you silly man."

"Actually open them, you mean?" said Bogat.

"How else? Unless you want to poison your superiors with septic colonial whey."

"Oh God," moaned Bogat. "It's the money, you see. I was investing. Can wine go bad? No one ever told me . . ."

"How about this?" interrupted Marina, struggling to keep a magnum of claret upright between her knees. "*Château Haut Brion, 1937, premier cru.*"

"Is that a nice one?" said Bogat, pencil poised.

"How should I know, my little person, without it sullying my lips. You," she ordered Sasha. "Fetch a corkscrew."

There was one on his jackknife. As it was plunged into the darkened cork, Bogat tapped his teeth with his pencil. "Dreadful," he groaned. "It's like a violation, all that glory at the mercy of one twist of an awl. Look at the cellar-stamp – *Oberkommando des Heeres: Hauptquartier, Malo-Yaroslavets.* Handled by the mighty, liquid history . . ."

The cork was crumbling under Sasha's inexpert attack.

"That's right, not too far at first. Blemish its maidenhead with gentleness. Anyway," said Marina, smiling at Bogat, "this is the only way you can be sure your colonel's lady wouldn't be knocking back the seepage of some Armenian drain. Imagine the stains it would make on her porcelain bridgework."

"All right," said Bogat testily. "But it stops here. One bottle only. I'll have to risk the others. Oh dear, why do they have to make them so *big*?"

"A question I have often pleasantly mused on," said Marina lying back and sipping the superb claret. "It has a wide-ranging but a simple answer – that way you can get much more in."

Under an over-coloured reproduction of Monet's *Gare St Lazare* the two men went into a huddle. The wine had scarcely touched Bogat's tongue before he wanted to spit it out. Sasha lifted the damask cloth swaddling Lizaveta's bucket and his companion jetted the crimson stream of his first Bordeaux into the crushed ice round the champagne.

"What a filthy experience," he said, taking a small packet of gum from his top pocket. "Here, have a spearmint. Do you think she really knows anything about wine? Or is it just quantity?"

"Quantity and quality," said Sasha. "She's got herself round some good stuff in her time. They did themselves well, her lot. Know how many bottles Lenin found in the Winter Palace?"

Bogat popped in another spearmint and mashed it vigorously on his wisdom teeth. "Not the kind of thing one's in a position to check, is it? I don't expect he counted them, Lenin." He pondered. "Big family, grandfather was a toper, beer for the kitchen staff, vodka for the ostlers. Oh, I'd say . . . Let's say – five thousand. Give or take a few hundred."

"Two million," said Sasha, gratified to be holding the stage.

Bogat stopped chewing. "Two million! That can't be true. That's . . . that's five thousand four hundred and seventy-nine a day annual intake. Lenin never said that."

"Not Lenin. I never said *Lenin*. He said Lenin *found* them."

"Who said?"

"*He* said . . ." Sasha looked round and put his mouth to Bogat's ear. "*Trotsky* said."

The little man jumped back. "Where?"

"In his *History of the Russian Revolution*. A mate of mine found it in the prison library at Vladimir."

"Two million bottles! A slander!" said Bogat excitedly. "A slander on the Russian people. Scurrilous claptrap." He paused and lowered his voice. "Why didn't they drink it then?"

"You said yourself, five thousand four hundred and seventy-nine bottles a day – how could they?"

"Not them, not *them*," whispered Bogat. "Ours."

"Ours?"

"The Red Guards, stupid," said Bogat, baring his teeth. "Those ours. They must have found it. Lenin didn't have time to count empties, not personally . . ."

"Never touched a drop. Makes you proud, doesn't it? They guarded it, the People's Property."

"Who said that? Trotsky again?" Sasha nodded. "I knew it," said Bogat exultantly. "All bloody lies."

Marina, ecstatically nosing the bouquet of the claret, had begun to sing "Dark Eyes" in a cracked, gypsyish contralto.

"Look, my dear chap, each to his own and all that, but she's getting on a bit, that one. That French lotion won't kill her, will it? I mean, at her age she could do anything. Die, even."

"Don't worry," said Sasha, patting him on the back. "She'll be going nowhere while there's a drop untapped. Just keep the old girl topped up – I've seen her like this before. Anyway," he went on, holding out his own glass. "You don't want us listening to your stuff stone cold sober, do you?"

Cheerful from the vodka Bogat generously dispensed, he started to explain his problem about poetry. Bogat frowned.

"Rhymes, dear? Oh, you don't want to be nervous of rhymes. They went out with nightshirts. Freedom is the watchword now. All right, you can do it the old way, you can corset yourself with spondees and amphibrachs, but theme is all to me, theme and variation. Spread yourself, do a public *turn*. Believe me, people love you for boldness, for the splendour of psychic amplitude. Revelations! Skeletons! The cobwebs of the mind turned in upon itself. What's the best of Yesenin, now? Not the cottage-loaf elegiacs about Mum and Dad miles from the high-road marking time in the rat-infested *izba*, making balalaikas and potsherds until they bark their dear old shins on death. No! It's the little black man that sat on his shoulder in the Astoria and gnawed his ear until he apostrophised him in his own blood! That's the real story, that's what there was in him! Blood, ruin, perversity, and exaltation rain down upon us like stars, and underneath we raise a firmament to burn off the fires, until that moment comes when the flame spumes . . ."

"I never read those," said Sasha. "But I like the one where he got back home – you know, like Pushkin, and sees the old place. I didn't know he went funny . . ."

"Funny?" shouted Bogat.

His stridency appealed to Marina, and she neglected to watch the passage of the '37 claret from the bottle to her jug. For several minutes the wine overflowed at her feet, unnoticed, darkening the white leather uppers of her Hungarian court shoes while the men argued on.

"There's much about poets that puts them off themselves, young man," she interrupted, turning to Sasha when Valentina had at last caught sight of the pool spreading to the chair casters and was gently lifting her mistress's feet in order to mop it up with the champagne cloth. "That's why they require intoxicants. It cannot be pleasant to know yourself or be accountable only to yourself for the utterance of truths. Imagine the temptation to speak irresponsibly! No one would check you, you could take everybody in. Look at their followers, we have them here. What a fate for a man, to be steeped in the plaudits of the vain! Mayakovsky drank himself into self-dispraise. It was a necessity."

Such was her rolling eye that Bogat tried to maintain a prudent attention in case the *détraquée* old woman rose from her seat and began to hurl herself about the room, but his heart was sinking as he watched his valuable wine dog-leg inexorably along the seams of the maple parquet. Unable to bear the strain any longer, he took out his oversize handkerchief and fell on his knees beside Valentina, swabbing back the claret from the fringes of his Kirghiz runner.

Marina tapped his head with her glass. "You, fellow, are you with me?"

Bogat straightened, wiping the sticky lees from his palms on to the houndstooth check of his jacket. "Absolutely," he said. "That's the ticket."

"Hasn't understood a word," said Marina to the Monet. "Not a word. Listen."

She switched sides in her chair so that Bogat's face was on a level with the amber butterfly brooch at her breast. "What happened to this poet, Mayakovsky, the man whose hand was once warm and which once touched this cheek, as I touch you?"

To Bogat's astonishment she cupped his chin in her hand, the black lace flowerets of the half-glove grazing the evening shadow of his shaven skin.

"You knew him? You really knew Mayakovsky?"

"I knew everyone," said Marina in a suddenly tired voice. "A tight little world is mine, locked in this bone ring."

As she spoke she pushed her fingers into the shorn roots of the hair behind her ears.

"Ladies and gentlemen," Bogat began, employing the outmoded phrase in deference to the old woman's past.

"On the 14th of April 1930 Vladimir Vladimirovich Mayakovsky shot himself. But what is most significant for this evening on which we are all assembled to carry forward his glorious Russian lyric torch, is that here . . ." He gestured up and down, making a tall, coffin shape in the thin air at Marina's side. ". . . Here saw I stand – Mayakovsky!

'*Ya vizhu –*
zdes'
stoyal Mayakovskii!'"

After her third glass, the ghostly exaltation died in Marina's face and Sasha realised that she was racing through the bottle, determined to get very drunk. Valentina crouched beside her rolling up a supply of the old woman's cigarettes.

"What a carry-on," she said. "All for a few verses. Better to have left the poor desolate soul behind."

Anna Kuznetsova smiled sadly, drawn by Valentina's solicitude. "Can I help you?" she said, nervously disarranging her hair, lost for occupation now that the food and crockery were set out.

Valentina shook her head. "No harm will come to her. Or him," she said, looking at Bogat.

"I know. If only it would," said Kuznetsova slackly, not far from tears. "My life is suffused by oblique illuminations . . ."

"Then somebody'll catch it sooner or later," said Valentina. "Let's hope we're moving targets." She offered a cigarette but Anna drew back her head with a moue of disgust.

"Not even for the nerves?" she coaxed. "Don't be so edgy, dear. Tonight the keepers are entertaining the inmates. Makes a nice break to the routine."

Kuznetsova seemed inconsolable. Her mouth screwed up into a sob. "If only you knew," she whispered. "The last guest has yet to make an appearance."

Lev was watching closely from his stool by the partition. "Anna!" he shouted. "Xenia says her petticoat won't stay up."

When Kuznetsova whisked back to her husband's side, Sasha lip-read his commands: "Don't interfere. How many more times?"

Bogat had disappeared. Although he was a drag on any idea of festivity, without him the party lost its centre. There was only more drinking to do, but Sasha, mistrusting himself if he took too much on board, initially, with the rest of the evening before him when anything might happen, put his glass by the radiator and wandered over to the table. If he got something solid down, perhaps he could go back to the bottle of Krepkaya, the black-labelled strong vodka which Bogat had laid in for him. In any case, digestion was good for the nerves, or so he had heard on the radio, and he was dreading the arrival of Olga who had been persecuting him with her scorn ever since the day of the dog shooting. A quiet stomach and an unshaking hand – that was it for the fray. Or affray.

He felt cold. That old crane-fly, Marina Andreyevna. Look at her, putting it away like pop. A distillery, her insides must be, exuding the gross fractions through her epidermis and spiralling the pure juice straight into her brains. Bad enough to start with, this intellectual tub-bashing, without Marina's harpy squawks. Kuznetsova, all of a heap, thinking bogey men are going to parachute through the ceiling. Who'd be a woman? It must be like being permanently wired to an electric fence.

Nice cheese, though, smooth cheese with big holes in it, "diplomatic cheese" Bogat called it from the blokes with gold roubles he bartered it off. Should sort out any heartburn from the salt cucumber. Potato dice, dill, pink, tenderised skirt of beef. Lizaveta must have been pleased to have something to work on. And the amber fish. Nice . . .

"Mur-derer!" screamed a voice behind him, a voice as clear and ringing as a young girl's.

His plate was overfull and he was damned if he was going to turn round in a hurry. The meal was too good to waste. Resolutely, he forked anything within reach on to his plate, haphazard, chinking on merrily as the silence became dense. Not murder. Not him. Couldn't kill a cat. None of them could. What was it with intellectuals? Didn't the blood smoke black enough in their fucking poems?

271

The stillness was broken by a deep salutation: "And a very good evening to you."

Sasha put down his plate. God help us. It's him. The cricketer-bastard. That was the digestive process stultified for the next few hours. Not a man to keep your back turned on.

Bogat had his arm round his friend's shoulders, partly in fraternal embrace, but mostly to keep him from falling over. Rocky had been drinking and his knees wavered in that dead-still roll with which Sasha was only too familiar. The glacial, unconciliatory smile swept into the guests like a blast from the tundral scrub. "Now, isn't this just dandy," he said with glottal deliberation. "All the old folks at home for my début."

He bowed from the waist, bringing his arm low with the sweep of an orchestral conductor. Under the other was a shiny black calf briefcase, the handles slotted back into the flap above the open zip. Without moving his feet he leant over to Bogat's trunk and slowly shook out a bottle of Scotch whisky and a loose-leaf folder.

"To the rostrum, my friend," he said, reaching out for Bogat's cheek, missing it and fastening on his tie. "*Ad tribunum plebis*, this is the democratic spectacular, the night-thoughts of the élite. Mount me to the block, dear toilers."

Sasha had been caught once before. He knew by instinct that those argent eyes were glaucous by will, not alcohol. Rocky was the kind who could shake himself to in an instant, if the need arose. The wide shoulders still moved usefully beneath that redskin neck. Sasha's fingers tightened round his chain as he slipped the serrated edges of his keys, points outwards, between his knuckles.

But Rocky seemed to be in no mood for violence. It was literature he was hungry for and Bogat, already demoralised by the unexpected path his carefully-prepared evening had already taken, was frantic to block off this new by-way.

Rocky was performing one of those miracles of drunken balance which Sasha had long admired but which always eluded him: he was sprawling on one spot, shooting out his arms, rubbing up his bristly red hair against Bogat's chin, timing each motion so exactly that his balance was maintained without moving his feet.

"Be a dear," implored Bogat. "This means a lot to me. I've got class coming in a minute. This lot couldn't tell the *Lay of Igor* from Nekrasov. Give yourself a nice douche and I promise I'll bill you second. All right? Ladies present and all that. You know how they take on."

Gradually he got Rocky to the door and pointed out the bathroom. "Just on the right there, by the clothes-horse. Towel on the rack, remember?"

Rocky tottered down the passage.

"Switch is upside down – that's it. Now you have a lovely cool off and then I'll send for you . . ."

"*Assass-in!*" screamed Marina, still frozen in the half-rising position she had taken up at her first sight of Bogat's friend. In profile, with her hooded eyes orbed out under their prominent lids, her veined and crippled hands clawing the air, she looked every inch a crop-headed pythoness hovering above the sacred tripod on a temple plinth: reckless, transfigured, and delirious from strong potations. Valentina disrupted the trance by pushing her gently back into the armchair and fanning her face with the current number of *Literaturnaya gazeta*. The old woman slumped and trembled, her eyes closing, her venom discharged.

"Well," said Bogat, looking at his watch. "Not quite the prelude I myself would have devised but the show must go on." He leapt smartly on to the trunk and held out his arms. "Ladies and gentlemen, although one of the company is still not present, I think the time of waiting is over. We will make a start."

From the inside pocket of his jacket he drew out a thick sheaf of typescript and began to thumb through it as the tenants noisily arranged their chairs.

Four ranks were quickly organised. The front one was left unoccupied. "In case someone else turns up," explained Valentina.

Sasha switched off the centre light and a hush fell.

"This first work," announced Bogat, wiping his forehead with the claret-stained handkerchief, "was composed last year when I was undergoing a certain crisis of soul, the details of which I may leave, until after you have heard the poem, to unscramble for yourselves."

Someone at the back cut short a guffaw but Bogat, his nerves in ribbons by this time, could not risk the probable humiliation which might come from taking on hecklers, and he snow-ploughed through the wintry reserve of his audience.

"*Triste*, downright *triste*, that is how I should describe the mood."

"A question," said Valentina. "May I?"

"If you must, but be quick."

"I'm sure I speak for more than one of us who haven't had your advantages in life, but can you do the foreign words into Russian, like they do in books?"

"A point, a point. *Triste*, you mean? Sad, miserable, forlorn."

"Right," said Valentina. "There's good Russian words for them, there's . . ."

"Oh shut up!" shrieked Bogat. "Call it what you like – fed up, up the creek, pissed off, but let me get to the bloody poem before you start nit-picking."

The bad language took the wind out of Valentina's sails and Bogat felt that at last he was on the verge of mastering his audience. He paused weightily, giving time for further interjection. When none came he swept a hand through his hair and resumed the explication:

"A spiritual crisis . . . a spiritual crisis. Some of the expressions, you will notice, are self-critical. Damaging, even. Let them alert you, those trigger-words: 'out of practice', 'topple'; 'no one has tested me', 'dead' . . ."

With a tall full glass Sasha settled in for a lengthy siege. "Dead." OK. Give him that one. You had to do yourself a fair amount of damage to get yourself dead. He's going to read it in a minute. Then he's going to read them all, every last one of the fistful. Needs a hat to set them off. Not that American film star's. Floppier? Take him an inch or two nearer the stratosphere.

Bogat coughed, then began. "On Watch", he read, holding the typescript a yard from his chest:

> "Where the terraces toppled to the bay,
> We settled in the roads, stilling
> Thick blue water for miles around."

Sasha knew he was in for it now. You could bet your life that there was a string of these in the pipe-line. He began to regret his canvassing of the demerits of rhyme. A bit of assonance might have made the business less balls-aching.

> "Capped guns sweep the somnolent city;
> We're out of practice, capital ship,
> And the artillery makes a dead manoeuvre
> On the citadel, before breakfast.
> No problem in the plump, dark belly,
> An armoured belt encompasses us,
> Cinches out innermost parts. Christ
> Keep us from the spark, no one
> Has tested us."

The delivery had been so slow and the punctuation so emphatic that it was a while before anyone knew Bogat had finished. In the gloom of the back row Xenia snivelled catarrhically.

"Very miserable, ships are," said Valentina with feeling. "Like hospitals. All planks and scrubbing. You need Jesus in a hospital. Especially when you're pregnant."

Marina, drifting in and out of sleep, slapped the widow's hand. "Use your common sense, goose, no women are allowed on warships. You're obsessed . . ."

Valentina was indignant. "He said so – that dark belly-thing."

Over her head, Bogat appealed to Lev Kuznetsov. "The *shape*, Lev Davidovich, the *shape*, is there form there?"

"If we take the content first, I'd say that Valentina Dmitryevna had something there," replied Lev gravely. The widow straightened her back and smiled.

"How do you make that out?" said Bogat. "I can't even stand the sight of a pregnant woman. In any case, nothing was further from my mind – it's nothing to do with babies, it's the world of men, of action . . ."

Lev had long considered his approach. "Ah, that's just it, the poet is the last person to know what lies beneath the surface of the most apparently transparent line . . ."

"He is?" said Bogat uncertainly. "But I wrote it so I must know what it means, mustn't I?"

"Only up to a point."

Bogat smirked. "The demon speaking through the artist?"

"Exactly," said Lev. "The poet as helpless visionary. As seer."

Bogat held forth the typed sheet and silently went through the poem again. "Ye-es," he said. "You might have something there. The trouble is, if I'm unaware of the force working through me, how can I know what it means when I am driven to set down poetic speech? You're saying I'm like a dog which can't wag his tail and bark at the same time."

"Very neat," said Lev. "And why should you try when people can be hired to do the barking for you?"

"Like you?"

"Like me. A mere academic drudge."

Bogat perched above them all on the edge of his seat, elbows on his knees, eager not to miss a word of Lev's delivery. Lizaveta Ivanovna, who up to now had been happy mutely to superintend the food and drink arrangements, spoke up for the first time.

"Be careful of that chair, young man. It's riddled with worm."

"Thank you, Granny," said Bogat patting the cross-tree. "We can take that as a very suitable caution – the canker in the rose. No doubt Lev Davidovich is preparing himself to dig it out."

Bogat's anticipations were fated to remain unfulfilled. From the opening door in the corner of the room, light flooded over the back row of seats, and, for a brief moment Olga Sergeyevna stood at the threshold, the dark image of her body shrunk and intense against the opalescent yellow. As she edged forward along the gap between the wall and line of chairs, something at her neck was caught in the rays from the standard lamp behind Bogat's hunched shoulders, shedding a fire-fly mosaic of prismatic colours at the parting of her modest décolletage.

The host made to rise but she motioned him down and took her place in the front row a yard from his podium. Bogat beamed. He should have waited. But he had to admit she was the more discerning. What more accomplished *démarche* could she have contrived? By this entrance she had asserted their community of spirit; the jokers were put down. All that mattered was this one benign interlocutrix. The rest could go to hell.

"Olga Sergeyevna, we are in your debt for this condescension. Please accept my apologies, but due to untoward events, a hiatus threatened and we thought it better to delay no longer. Lev here was about to lay bare the groundwork of my most recent fancy . . ."

Bogat reached out for the sheaf of manuscript by his chair-leg and swept a glance over the audience. "Now, how shall we go about this? Shall I declaim once more for the benefit of Olga Sergeyevna?"

There was much shuffling of feet.

"Or shall we proceed?"

"Take it as read, Pavel Aleksandrovich, I think, take it as read," said Olga quietly.

"As read," repeated Bogat. He clapped his hands above his head with a ringing smack. "Right. Fine. Now, settle down please. There is work to be done."

"What about that other one?" cried Lizaveta Ivanovna, who, from her position by the door could hear the geyser still rumbling in the bathroom and was worried in case Rocky had passed out and forgotten to turn it off. "He's not responsible. He could drown himself."

"Or gas himself," muttered Sasha.

Variations on this theme passed between the tenants, along the rows, from mouth to mouth. "Or shoot us all." "Or murder us in our beds."

Marina suddenly woke up. "What other one?" she asked Valentina, startled.

"The fucking hiatus," cut in Sasha, too loudly.

"That's it," shouted Bogat. "That's it from you, Biryusov. You're not in the Mechanics' Institute now! Out, out, and take your language with you."

Sasha placed his tumbler upside down over the neck of his Krepkaya and obediently shambled out of the room, overcome with relief at this change in his luck.

At the other side of the door on a high bamboo stool, one classily black-trousered leg stretched full length to the wall, barring further egress, sat Rocky drinking Scotch. Sasha dared not look up but followed the line of the raised satin stripe which ran along the seam. He still had the brown mirror-glass polished boots, the steel quarter plates on the soles flashing at heel and toe like motor-cycle brake discs.

"Have you asked Sir to be excused?" said Rocky, without the least slur in his voice. Evidently Bogat's shouting had not carried through the wall.

"Breath of fresh air," said Sasha, meeting Rocky's gaze. "It's getting a bit tense in there."

Although the hair and moustache were groomed and immaculate, and Rocky's skin glowed from the shower, Sasha saw that the man was very drunk by the way he put down his glass and began to clean out his pipe: slowly poking the inside with a matchstick, loosening the dottle, then turning over the bowl and allowing the ash to fall a good foot away from Anna's wastepaper-bin which he had placed by the stool. He must have been doing this over and over again for there was already a small heap of wet, curly-cut tobacco and white powder on the floor. That and the slightly glazed, blanched veal eyes were the only indications that he was not as sober as a new-born babe.

"I sympathise," he said. "Old comrades can get heated. This is my second party of the night, and there's another one to come. Help yourself to Scotch."

"Thanks, I'll do that," said Sasha, braving a small measure of the spirit he detested because of its caramel tinge.

Rocky filled his pipe from the ingenious silver box which Sasha had noticed at their first meeting. "Have a peep round the door," he said lighting up, and generating blue clouds of smoke. "I should be on soon."

Bogat was shouting. "That can't be right, nothing was further from my mind. So this is what goes on in your university seminars. No wonder discipline has collapsed in this country when anyone is encouraged to say the first thing that comes into his head! Things could get quite out of hand! Back to the . . . I can't say it, I can't repeat such indecency . . ."

"The womb," said Valentina ringingly. "What's indecent about that? Just because you haven't got . . ."

"It's got nothing to do with *having* anything. It's about libel, that's what it's about. I mean, it never occurred to me . . . What sense does it make to tell me I want to go back to somewhere I can't even remember having been?"

"'No problem in the plump, dark belly'," quoted Lev. "And you did invite us to attempt to identify the cause of your crisis."

Bogat took a deep breath. "You do that, Lev Davidovich. You do that. You tell me in simple language what was my root problem."

"As plain as the nose on your face," said Valentina, warmed by her hitherto unrealised literary-critical skill. "Insecurity!"

"*Insecurity,*" began Bogat, on a rising note. "Oh, I see, *insecurity* that's it of course." He hunched his back and stomped around the trunk top pointing at the faces before him, one by one. "What a relief! I've found the answer! Of course, *you* dream sweet, untroubled dreams. *You* are never woken by hammering on the door, no one carts *you* off in the middle of the night." Valentina twitched her skirt as he halted and stretched out a shaking finger in her direction. "Let me tell you, dear, if *I'm* insecure, *you* wouldn't have enough nerve to draw your stockings on of a morning." His voice dropped to a sinister wheedle: "You can't have forgotten already, can you? Or has my generosity dulled you? Convinced you that I'm as open and approachable as the next man, the man on the street, the man you jostle against in the queue? *Insecurity? Security?* Don't talk to me about that! I'm in the business!"

Sasha withdrew his head. Rocky was leaning back, puffing on his pipe, hands clasped below one upraised knee. "Isn't his act over yet?"

"Depends what you mean. They seem to have got on to his job . . ."

"Ah, yes," said Rocky pleasantly. "That's nothing new. The professional always gets the better of the amateur in the end."

Olga bore the tedious altercation between Lev and Bogat, knowing that Lev was making the most of his rare opportunity to engage with an antagonist and she felt glad that, so far, neither man had appealed for her arbitration. But it had been only a matter of time before Lev's interpretation became patently spoof, even to Bogat.

Lev was one of those timid persons whose behaviour was difficult to predict. And while Bogat could be counted on not to overstep a certain limit, so long as she was in attendance, with Lev there was no telling when discretion might be thrown off and horns became well and truly locked. It was a pity, this goading of the little man on the trunk. Although she had not heard Bogat's poem, she instinctively felt that his verse must be execrable and he would make a show of himself simply by speaking it. That ought to have been enough. And would have been, had not Lev drawn him from mere exhibition of his creative club foot into prolonged public contemplation of it, boot and all. Even though he was ineducable, Bogat wanted to learn, and that desire should have been respected by one who taught; or, at least, noted, so that the temptation to strike him down was held over for some unworthier excess. How was Lev with his students? Carefully brutal, she imagined. But the Kuznetsovs had suffered. They had all suffered and Lev was chancing for hits on behalf of the entire company.

Her hand stole to the three-stranded necklet at the base of her throat. The cabochon garnets were smooth and cold to her fingertips, icier than the millefiori spaced between. Too cool and harsh.

"That will do, Lev Davidovich," she said crisply. "We are here to be entertained, not lectured at. Perhaps the next poem — I am sure that we are to enjoy more than one?" Bogat nodded gratefully. "Pavel Aleksandrovich's next poem might benefit from a less technical approach."

"My sentiments exactly, Olga Sergeyevna," said Bogat. "What comes from the heart should be taken up by the heart. This man has the sensibility of a computer."

Bogat retrieved his papers from the floor. After some scrabbling amongst the leaves, he drew out a sheet the size of an ordinary envelope.

"This one should do the trick — a mood piece. 'Partisan'. A cutting from the scrapbook of the Great Patriotic War:

> "He peers greyly at me, the unmannerly one
> Who props his rifle by the biscuit tins
> And smokes, and does everything wrong
> Except promise his children ponies, and
> The sun, and the place where it never
> Rains, when it's all over, when
> The plane comes in."

Rocky, after looking at his watch, had pushed open the door with his foot, and the poem was just audible to both men in the passage. As Bogat stood head bowed, overcome by emotion at the end of his reading, they stumbled along the back row and took the seats at either side of Lizaveta Ivanovna. Each man clung to his bottle.

"Now, show some deference," whispered the old woman to Sasha. "He's upset. Human feelings deserve respect."

"I know this one," said Rocky, just loud enough for the next row to overhear. "It's about his Dad." He poured himself a very large whisky.

Valentina looked back over her shoulder. "Can't be," she said. "He's too young for his Pa to have been with the partisans."

"He wasn't," said Rocky, more quietly. "What do you think the biscuit tins are about? His father was a lad with a weak chest who spent the war at confectionery shop no. 206 in Pushkino. Too young for call-up."

"Be quiet," hissed Lizaveta. "Some of us want to listen. I think it was lovely. What do you want the poor boy to do – produce his passport?"

Without waiting for Bogat to recover from his strange access of piety, she began to applaud. Her ragged, unco-ordinated claps startled the assembly and Bogat looked up, bemused. "Bravo!" screeched the old woman. "A son to be proud of! What's the matter with you all, is it wrong to honour those who begot you?"

Rocky shrugged, put down his glass and joined in. Everyone followed except for Marina who was filing her nails. Sasha whistled and stamped. The applause was so loud and long that eventually Bogat, embarrassed by the unexpected reception, raised his arms for silence. The only good opinion he craved was Olga's. As with restless fingers in her lap she pleated and repleated the folds of her long, ultramarine evening skirt, he looked down at her beseechingly.

Sasha now realised how slow he had been on the uptake: the whole evening had been planned round Olga. They were rubbish, they had been set up. Bogat had no interest in any merit the rest of them might or might not have perceived in his poetry. This was snob calling to snob.

"Olga Sergeyevna, I appeal to you, a published author in your own right, a brilliant translator, a critical biographer of our own Pushkin. Tell me what you really *think*, in all honesty, professionally, as writer to writer."

"I would say you are brave, Pavel Aleksandrovich, rather brave," she said, without raising her head or interrupting the nervous play at her frock. "Braver than I."

Bogat had been prepared for anything but moral praise. "Brave, Olga Sergeyevna?"

"You see," persisted Olga, refusing to meet his eyes. "By this you deliver yourself into the hands of others. At some time in life we all, of course, do that, but privately, as . . . as lovers, withdrawn from the general gaze, not as you have done here. Public avowal of the deepest, most common feelings which we all share, is the bravest of acts and deserves the respect of the good. All art needs feeling, but deep feeling demands great art. Your concerns are not trivial, Pavel Aleksandrovich, but your aesthetic unsureness enables others to trivialise them."

Lizaveta asked Sasha to interpret. "What's she saying?"

He drew his finger across his throat. "No good. Finish. *Kaput*."

"Oh!" cried the old woman. "How cruel you all are. And he never knew his mother . . ."

Disappointment showed in the slump of Bogat's shoulders, but he quickly rallied. "Would you think that there was any chance of publication?"

"Eventually, Pavel Aleksandrovich. The important thing is not to give up. I'll make some soundings for you."

Bowing himself down from the trunk, Bogat fell to one knee and began to cover Olga's hands with kisses. Rocky stood up. "Don't overdo it, Pasha, there's a good lad. She's given you her professional opinion. No need to make love to the woman for a splash in the papers."

"What would you know of an orphan's gratitude?" said Lizaveta. "It's comfort he needs."

Rocky thrust the whisky bottle into her hands and started up the makeshift side aisle, his briefcase under his arm. "Wait till you hear me, Gran – parents aren't the only ones to be missed." His back to Olga, Rocky slipped an arm round his friend before stepping on to the trunk. There were tears in Bogat's eyes when he turned away. "Gifted," he murmured. "But lacks confidence – fated to be an amateur."

Rocky's manner was zestful and direct. "Now listen carefully. I shall say this only once." He might have been a corporal instructing a platoon how to dig latrines. "I am about to give you my best poem. No two ways about it, it's good. Why do I know it's good? I know it's good because I'm in the habit of showing my work to those who know what's good – and since none of them would be seen dead with people like you, I'm telling you what they think so you'll know what to think, too. Have you got that?" No scrape of shoe nor clearing of throat was heard. Marina Andreyevna mooned dumbly, brandishing her nail file at the ceiling.

"This I reserve for special occasions. Tonight is one of those occasions. I have just lost a comrade in the line of duty. A close friend."

Lizaveta put a hand to her mouth.

"Your sympathy is irrelevant. For me, writing is not a form of shop-window self-abuse, and it was only for the sake of that one friend that I started writing poetry at all. You!" he commanded Lev. "What do you think you're here for?"

Lev ventured warily. This one was no poetasting leg-pull. "To listen . . . mmm . . . to appraise?"

"Appraise? Do you seriously imagine anyone above ground gives a fart for the *aperçus* of a Yid harp-twanger like you?"

Anna's face blazed at the insult, but Lev only moved closer to her and kept Rocky in view as his glance swerved to Sasha who was caught in the act of re-filling his glass. "Or this gem of evolution, our orang-utang of the steppes. Understand Russian, do you, my little primate?"

Sasha could barely nod.

"Know what an epitaph is?"

He did but no sound came.

"You know he does," said Olga slowly. "You know we all do."

"Thank you, Milady, for that testimonial. But the ewe must not be suffered to smell out her lambs. Define it!" he called to Sasha, pacing backwards and forwards on the trunk and swinging his arms.

The dustman found his voice. "It's nice words you say about somebody who's dead, and it goes over their grave."

"Wonderful," said Rocky. "And does it matter if it's read?"

Sasha didn't understand the question. "I don't know – if it's written I suppose somebody's meant to read it."

"You?"

Sasha looked around. "Me, her, anyone . . . They might do. Depends on how they're situated at the time."

"Perfect," said Rocky. "Your present situation is perfect. Imagine that I am a stele which reads off its own runes."

Without another word he sank down on the trunk in the posture of a karate *dan*, cross-legged, heels tucked out of sight, arms folded across his chest. An intrigued silence prevailed in the audience as he breathed long and deeply through his nose. As abruptly as it had begun, the meditation ended when Rocky lifted his eyes to the far wall, at the same time releasing the pent-up air from his lungs with an explosive burst which sounded back from the confines of the room. For all the listeners knew of the strangeness of the man, that might have been the poem. No one would have been surprised if he had possessed the skill to expostulate his friend's epitaph as primeval battle-cry or truncated haiku. But they were not to be spared: the queer expletive was evidently some preliminary de-misting of the spirit, for he began to recite in Russian, lingering over each line as if it were a spoke in a prayer-wheel:

> "Who was holding who
> When my friend fell
> Away into the soft sea."

Little Xenia Kuznetsova, her lace-collared party frock of black velvet stained by mayonnaise, had detached herself from her parents during Rocky's silent lead-up to the poem and now stood with her back to him contemplating rows of glasses and bone-china teacups set out on Bogat's walnut chiffonnier.

Above the chiffonnier hung a small, oval mirror in a gilt rococo frame. Xenia took down a balloon brandy glass, blew on it and began to polish the interior with the broad white ribbon unravelling from her hair. Her parents watched, not daring to move.

> "Clutching at spaces the
> Gulls could see, the free.
> My boy died, the one
> Who didn't like me,
> Clouded over by the arc
> Of the sea."

Catching sight of herself in the mirror and entertained by the distortion of her appearance in its convex surface, she placed the glass over her nose, crossed her eyes and grimaced.

Since the antique silvering was so marred by brownstain that only the top half of her face could be observed from the angle at which she stood, Xenia took the rim of the brandy-glass between her lips, thus freeing her hands to grasp both ends of the ogee which formed the back-drop to Bogat's crystal and porcelain along the uppermost ledge of the chiffonnier. As Rocky's invocatory final quatrain swelled forth, the child raised herself on tiptoe and strained her hideously bell-jarred nose up to the overhanging frame.

> "Protect those who follow
> Innocent occupations;
> Tie my horses by silken threads,
> Heap earth, memorialise me."

There was an uncomfortable pause while the audience sought for some indication that the reading was over. No flicker passed across Rocky's impassive face. He could have been in the throes of some further arcane spiritual exercise which temporarily dispensed with the need for breathing. No one could tell. Olga was about to cough when Xenia, enchanted by being able at last to survey the reflection of her head in its entirety, giggled. Escaping bubbles of sound quavered in the hollow of the glass like infant whale-cries. As she rocked delightedly on the points of her ballet-pumps, lost to the world around her, the lines of glassware and crockery began to fluctuate and then touch, giving out a pleasant ripple of variously pitched chinks, reminiscent of a glass harmonica. The nearer the stem of Xenia's glass approached the mirror, the more the tempo of her rocking increased, and as cups began to bounce over saucers, Anna jumped up. She was within an arm's length of her daughter's fluttering ribbon when the brandy glass fell from Xenia's mouth and crashed on to a blue and white Sèvres chocolate pot, the *pièce de résistance* of Bogat's china. In shock, the child leapt back, her hands still grasping the curved ends of the chiffonnier which proceeded to empty itself shelf by shelf over her legs. Anna had just time enough to whisk her away by the hair and thank God that the fall of many of the things had been so deflected by Xenia's body that they remained undamaged, when the whole walnut structure teetered and fell squarely on top of Bogat's eighty-four-piece dinner-service, three suites of champagne, hock and brandy glasses, collection of eighteenth-century pill-boxes, and a pot cock from Erevan.

Valentina pinched the bare arm of the dozing Marina and slid forward on her chair to get a better view as Bogat, hands outstretched, fingers angled upwards to the ceiling, jerked from his seat with the fearful slowness of a blind man fending off an invisible wall. A silent howl crumpled the fine line of his mouth. At last true theatre had broken out, and the audience, so long thwarted by the disconnected progress of the evening's entertainment, was hushed in complacent anticipation of a final act.

For a long moment they sated themselves on the calamitous as Bogat, the sole of one shoe uplifted, pirouetted like a somnambulist, grinding into oblivion under his heel the egg-shell shards of the only intact item of his Kiang-Hshi, a fruit dish once aflame with hand-painted frangipani.

"Fated!" he screamed. "I knew it! All of us – perishable goods! Lay not up for yourself! Lay not up!"

Impervious to the grandeur of stoical gesture but ready for anything after one look at Bogat's ravished eyes, Valentina leapt forward to avert the sacrifice, but the heel was down too quick and the bowl crunched an inch from her hand. She toppled back, reached out, and wrapped a fist round Bogat's ankle. The impact of his back as he shot to the boards gave the final quietus to his *objets d'art*.

While he lay weeping, Valentina heaped fragments of fluted glass stems, gilt teacup handles and masses of frangible Chinese blue and white on to the Kuznetsovs' silver tray. "Here, come and help, Marina Andreyevna," she called. "This is a right fricassée of pots staring me in the face. Can anything be done with it, do you reckon?"

Before Marina could reply, a savage yell floated down the hall from the kitchen where Legless was watching his football match.

"We done it! We done it! What a bunch of lovely boys then, we done it, we done it!"

The rubbers of his Swedish chukka boots squealed on the lino as he dashed along the corridor, tremulous from vodka and news. He grabbed Sasha's jersey, almost pulling him over, and wept out his joy, the big face red and sweaty from pent-up emotion. "In the *bag*," he murmured. "What a sweet little number that striker is – ought to have a statue to him, a fucking great big statue. We was level-pegging at injury time and he banged in a little beauty with a minute to go. In the bag, mate, in the *bloody bag* . . ." His eyes were wide from tenderness. "Come here," he said trying to embrace the resisting Sasha. "You don't want to waste your time with this gang of flop-willies. Have a drink with me, have a little drink and we'll do a replay and see some real poetry. Spartak, I salute thee. Poetry? Fucking epic it was, fucking epic."

"Leave it off," said Sasha, trying to ward off Legless's clammy hands. "This jumper was clean on this morning. We've got enough problems here, mate, without you molesting my laundry. Go and fall under the table with the real poets, they could do with a bit of damp hand-holding."

"Who's that then?" said Legless, squinting across Sasha's shoulder at the pool of light over the trunk on which Rocky still sat cross-legged and unmoved. "Well, bugger me, if it isn't Mr Kiss-my-arse. Hey!" he shouted. "Last you've seen of his doolies, your Lavrenty. Won't come back, you know. Take more than a sonnet to hook him out of the Baltic . . ."

Rocky failed to rise but stared ahead, a blank shop dummy smirk on his lips.

Legless took the hem of an imaginary skirt between forefinger and thumb and made a deep curtsey. "Ah," he simpered. "Have we lost our creamy bum, then? Our darling of the fleet, our little playmate of the heads?"

"What are you talking about?" asked Sasha.

"Didn't you know?" called out Legless. "He was in love with a *Kirov* deckhand. Him and that one down there. Got him on some smuggling charge, then they used to do him at the same time, one at each end. When they got tired of that they passed him round the whole flotilla, from flagship to bumboat. Got so he couldn't stand another pumping from hairy matelots so he dropped himself in front of the icebreaker at Kronstadt."

Anna Kuznetsova gave a whimper and pressed Xenia close to her belly. "Don't worry about her, missis," confided Legless. "Their sort can't stand the sight of any kind of . . ." Legless then used a word which, to all the women in the room, was the ultimate obscenity. Marina screamed.

"You diseased abortion of a man! Get out of here, you lout, before we women herd ourselves together and trample you into the floor."

Thrown off his stroke by this unlooked-for intervention, Legless frowned, sincerely puzzled. "Christ," he muttered. "Christ, I'm doing you a favour, mother, God's truth . . ."

"What a glib, sinister line you spin," said the old woman. "I've sunk pretty low in my declining years and my acquaintanceship has come to embrace dog-shooters and official perverts, but when a creature like you makes pretensions to the truth, then would I prefer to take up habitation with child-molesters. You think that no one can desire anything beyond the instant satisfaction of cravings. Cover your nakedness, you materialistic scum! What can you know of truths?"

Legless was bemused. "Would you care to repeat that?" he asked. "I'm not quite with you."

Marina was staring at his feet. "And just look at those shoes."

Legless lowered his eyes mechanically. "What have my shoes got to do with it?"

"Brown as tea!" crowed Marina.

"And suede," said Valentina joyfully.

Legless raised one foot to the level of his knee-cap and studied his left boot. "I don't get you. My girl got them off a Finnish contrabandist in Leningrad. Cost her a month's wages. He swore they were the last word in masculine *chic*."

Valentina put down the silver tray and assumed an expression of motherly concern. "Perhaps she was trying to tell you something, dear."

Flamingo-like, Legless hopped round in a tight circle.

"Like the language of flowers, only the other way round and what you might call, very appropriately, down to earth," added the widow with a sympathetic smile. "Us women have such roundabout ways of putting things."

"Here," said Legless, caressing the dusty desert-boot nap. "You lay off my girl, she says what she thinks, straight out and no messing . . ."

"She has, too." Valentina concealed a giggle.

Dizzy from his drinking and the one-legged turns but not releasing the grip on his boot, Legless fell back into a chair. "What are you getting at, eh? I know your game, trying to undermine my relationship with the finest girl that ever . . ."

With an uncharacteristic brutality of gesture Marina Andreyevna jerked her thumb in the direction of Bogat, prostrate still, gently sobbing, athwart the hugger-mugger jumble of his irreparable status symbols. "Have a close look at that one," she said. "And tell me – how is the beast shod?"

The boots were identical to those of Legless.

"You know what that means, I take it?" said Marina.

"Can't say as I do," said Legless uncertainly. "It can't mean anything, not a boot. A boot can't sort of actually be more than a boot . . . can it?"

"That's just where you're wrong. Those boots are signifiers."

"No, no," said Legless relieved. "Have a peek at the insides." He hurriedly undid the laces and held up the left shoe for inspection. "There you are, I thought I remembered right. Look at the label: *Husqvarnas.*"

"They *signify*, they *demonstrate*, they *show* something about you."

Legless unlaced his other boot, weighed the empty pair in his huge palms, clumped the soles together and smiled knowingly at Marina. "That I've got big feet you mean?"

The old woman chuckled, tapped a finger against the side of her nose and winked towards Bogat. "That you're one of them, *golubchik*, that you're one of *them*."

Legless went very pale. "But I'm normal," he murmured, gingerly stroking his inner thigh with the boots. "I must be. I'm a policeman."

At this Sasha flung his arms round Lev and the knees of both men buckled; tears streamed down their faces.

"Can you catch it?" ventured Legless, after a pause.

For the first time Rocky made a movement. A smile lit up his face as he turned his gaze on the policeman.

"You will," he said. "Oh, *how* you will."

"Bastard!" roared Legless. "I'll have you put away for this!" He flung the boots at the seated figure. Rocky caught both in the air with a rattlesnake dart of one hand, and held them above his head by the heel-loops. With the facility of a conjuror he produced from his sleeve an unsheathed Japanese short knife of the type which Samurai knights once employed as poignard to the foil of the longsword. One flick and the uppers of the suedes were transfixed and sent whirring across Legless's head, ripped from heel to toe.

"Next time we have words," said Rocky, straightening his arm to allow the weapon to slide back into his sleeve, "we'll be private and that time you'll end up missing more than your footwear."

VI

VALEDICTION

32

At *Feministka* there had been a revolution. Linoleum had given way to carpets of tasteful charcoal grey; the wooden balustrades had been replaced by chromed hand-rails; the walls were emulsioned in pastel tints; and not a single poster had survived from the old order.

Fashion plates hung everywhere in immense silvered frames. The women in them were a new breed, unadapted to the rifle and hay-rake. Their twig-like arms and legs sprouted from puff-ball sleeves and hobbled skirts. The high-heeled slippers were not for walks, the petalled hats were for interior wear, useless except to set off elaborate coiffures. To Sasha, they resembled skeletal cats these sleek, undeveloped and rangy-thighed women, posed with angular bravura in a world of paintbox colours, their undimpled chests graphically exaggerated by the serpentine backs of the curvilinear greyhounds drooping at their mistresses' leashes.

Thin women always used to make Valentina cry. To her they were another race, one which had deprived her of the consolations of haute couture. To him they were no more than counterparts of the equally sexless agitprop commandos who had stared down on him the last time he was here. No woman had ever been like any of them, on this side of the world or on the other. If the wasp-waisted gigolos with brilliantined hair who pursued them with flowers and gin-fizzes along the decks of steamers or alleys of ancient oaks ever caught up, the encounters would be as frosted as the conical glasses. What could such skinny armfuls expect from men whose matador trousers were wallpapered to their backsides?

The old porter was by the lift, his Chaplinesque knees bowing outwards. After a moment's rumination his glassy eyes cleared, and he wheezed, enveloping Sasha in a spirituous haze.

"How's this for a turn-around?" he asked, his croaky voice barely audible above the seething of his effervescent bronchus. "Beg pardon, it always takes me in the tubes before first snowfall."

A prolonged bout of coughing de-congested him satisfactorily.

"Know what this is?" The sound of one foot being firmly planted in the grave would have covered it, in Sasha's opinion, for the want of a more medical term, but the old man meant the décor.

"It's a Ladies', that's what it is now, a Ladies', on three floors."

He came closer, looked round, and banged his fist feebly on Sasha's chest in a sign of male comradeship. "What do you think I feel like, stuck in this bloody boutique all day, suffocating from female deodorants?"

"A quick one?" said Sasha, knowing how the old man habitually proofed himself against life's onslaughts.

"We-ell," said Grigorii. "It puts a strain on a man, being the last bastion."

"A what?"

"A bastion. You know, someone who sticks it out to the end. Never been in the service?"

"Off and on," said Sasha. "I was an officer's bastion once. I spent more time doing his wife's washing than on his kit. I know what you mean."

"There you are then," said Grigorii. "It's humiliating. I'll be shaving legs soon." He squeezed the lift button. "Who do you want?"

"Marya Fyodorovna Osipyenko."

Grigorii winced. "She done it, that one – all this horrible boudoir. Now she's togged up like a feller. Know what frightens me?" he added through the lift gates.

"You tell me," said Sasha selecting the editorial floor on the console.

"I think they're putting something in my food, these women. They're doctoring me . . ."

"No," said Sasha decisively. "It's not them."

"No?" queried Grigorii, leaning forward as the outer doors began to slide.

"No, there's no need. It's the men – they've been putting that kind of stuff in bottles for years."

When he poked his head round the door, Marya Fyodorovna, who was on the phone, motioned him to the seat facing her across Kirilyenko's old desk.

Grigorii the porter had missed the point. She was not so much mannish, in the chalk-striped jacket with outsize lapels from the neck of which a cream jabot splashed exuberantly, as older and more austere. In these clothes and square, heavy spectacles, she was aping some functionary with the likes of whom Sasha could never even have been on nodding terms: a sterling administratrix from the higher echelons.

Her modest partiality for him which he had exploited in order to get this interview seemed unlikely to outlast the first few moments.

Even on the telephone, she acted too grand to be reachable. But Sasha held his ground. He had made an effort over himself, seen to it that his green jumper was clean, likewise his jeans, and he'd washed his hair and left off his cap. Still, now that Valentina was no longer there to give him the final wash and brush-up he couldn't feel entirely at ease. He resisted the impulse to look himself over. If he spotted an undone button he was sure to fluff his errand. Marya Fyodorovna had a way of making you go very small.

Her business-like distraction was a blessing. There was time to piece together his speech. Man to man, that's how it should go. Anyone sprung from the loins of the deceased Fyodor would be case-hardened to the humble plea. In that family the kids probably cut their teeth on petitioners. But how Fyodor had come to sire this little piece was a mystery. Talk about influence, though – to set her up like this really took a long arm from the grave. Was it never curtains for their kind?

Changes there had been. In Kirilyenko's day this desk was bare, except for a ruler, an out-tray and a bag of sweets. Marya Fyodorovna's sloppiness was cocking an expensive, wilful, retrospective snook. In the blue and grey jars, fresh-cut and dried flowers were jumbled higgledy-piggledy encircled by the garbage of yoghurt pots, a bottle of souring milk, squashy note pads, four wicker bowls brimming with hairslides, seashells, bus tickets, gilt buckles, small change, pens without tops, tampons and dried-up cigarettes. It was only later he discovered that every time the inside of her handbag became too chaotic she dumped it out on to the desk for her secretary to sort out.

The carpet, as thick as a palace lawn, he noticed, had also been victimised. Ash spread wide under the overstuffed sofa where the pile had been singed by dog-ends. Only the vertical surfaces had escaped her sluttishness: flashy modernistic canvases screamed from the walls and one abstract in hard-edge layers of scarlet, blue, purple and gold took up a whole expanse from door to window.

"Cor, you've done all right," he said when she put down the telephone and scowled at him, tapping the desk-top with a yellow pencil. Her nails were still the same, ragged to the quick.

"Spare me your reflections," she said brusquely. "I haven't got all day. What's dragged you in from the great outdoors?"

He took a deep breath. "That talk we had once, outside my place, and you mentioned a job . . ."

"A bit late for that now, Tarzan, isn't it?" she said with a sudden grin. "I took the precaution of overbooking. You could have filled a bus with the takers. Not a chance, my little sleuth hound, not a chance."

"That's OK," said Sasha equably. "I told you I was already suited. No, I don't want to volunteer information. I want to request some."

"Do you indeed?" said Marya smoothing her hair and chewing the end of the pencil. "At least your manners have improved. But what makes you think I'm going to give you any?"

He might be mistaken, his resolution could still buckle, but perhaps she still fancied him a bit?

"For old times' sake?" ventured Sasha, giving the old *tendresse* an uncompromising tonk.

She hit the roof. "For *what*?" she squealed in majestic disdain. Sasha quaked. "What time did you ever give me? Just because I shared a fag with you once, you've invested in a bedroom suite on the never-never. The spirit bloweth where it listeth, my lad, and at the moment it listeth nothing that you tuck under your belt."

"Sorry," he said quickly, divesting himself of any artificial notions of pride. "You know me, I say the first thing that comes into my head. It's nerves. You'd be nervous too, my side of the desk in the hard chair. I've been trying to get through to you for three days."

This was true. He told Marya Fyodorovna how, the day before yesterday he had stood in the gaunt Bakery Lane corridor, cursing himself for a half-wit. His line had been blocked by women: from a secretary whose condescension had made him clench his fist so tight that he cracked the bakelite mouthpiece, to a switchboard operator who, when she recognised his voice for the fourth time of calling, cut him off. In despair, he had resorted to falsetto and they'd put him down in the diary as "Aleksandra".

"They wouldn't let me talk to you, otherwise I wouldn't be here, wasting your time."

Marya ran a finger down her list of appointments. "So they did," she said, softened by the energy of Sasha's quest. "'Fri. 5.20, five mins. Biryusova, A.M.' Well, Aleksandra Mikhailovna, you're the worst female impersonator I've met since Mao Tse Tung, and two of your five mins. have gone. What are you going to do with the rest?"

She took off her glasses and quizzed him through a single lens. This time he decided to elude the banana-skin suggestiveness. Why should she help him anyway? His kind were two a penny and he wasn't even cock of his own dung hill. You'd need the Order of Lenin to be allowed an inch above her knees. But she was a cracker all right. Her eyes were as clear grey, her lips as invitingly rouged as the first time he saw her.

"Hey, wake up. Don't play funny buggers, darling. You haven't told me your problem yet. Better make the most of me while you can."

Again he declined to twitch at the ambiguity, and Marya Fyodo-rovna replaced her spectacles.

"All right, all right," she conceded, kicking back her whirligig chair and taking up a stance before the vast abstract so that Sasha was presented to her sideways on. "Perhaps I'd better find kitty's tongue."

Deflected by the failure of his positive line and inhibited by her un-answerable wisecracking, he did not care to move his head to face her. Instead, he swivelled his eyes. In this position, the left penetrated no farther than the blob of his nose as the two-dimensional right butterflied her against the picture plane, the reds of her hair and the black stuff of her trouser suit in lambent macramé to the surface sheen.

"I know what you're here for. I knew all along," she continued, nibbling her finger ends with even teeth. "The trouble is low boredom-threshold. Mine's lower than the Kalahari water table. I wanted you to be diverting. Are you always so dumbstruck when a girl leads you on?"

Sasha nodded, cultivating humility. It obviously made her sport, the lumbering ox bit.

"God," she cried. "Why do I always pick the blokes who want the girl on top? Don't answer that, shrinking flower. It must be something in my upbringing."

Moving astern of Sasha, along the wall, she disappeared from his view, but kept on talking. "Now, the reason you've come to fairy-godmother is because you reckon she can reverse the operation. Right?"

"Right," agreed Sasha, feeling her padding around behind him, and in the dark about her physical intentions.

"You've had visitors and they left you feeling that if they hadn't exactly turned you into a toad, you weren't the man you once thought you were?"

At this implication of cowardice the artery of his neck distended from suffusion of blood and thumped painfully, reminding him of his uncertain temper and the need to disguise it by the semblance of calm. It was a good thing, now, that she was hidden from him.

"Well?" she asked from the back of his head, unseeing but aware of her effect.

"Who've you ever stood up to?" he muttered. "I don't mind a dust-up when I'm in with a chance, but that lot come in armies. Take one on, take on all, down to the regimental bandmaster's lickspittle clerk. They've got resources, that bunch. If one of them can't kick you to death, the rest'll make sure you're trampled under their boots. Life's passed you by in this fairy castle, with sugar-daddies to swat the flies."

"Aa-a-ah," she drawled, her long, narrow palms massaging his clavicle. "Didn't you answer back? I thought you were my peerless champion, hollering for a scrap!" Her cool eyes were suddenly a few inches from his as she twisted his chin round, held him for a moment, slithering round the outline of his lips with her tongue and licking it, burred as an overripe raspberry, up into his nostrils.

"There," she said, having resumed her seat behind the editorial desk and taken up her lipgloss and compact-mirror in order to repair the damage. "There's a gage for you. *Une grande preuve – non d'amour, mais du désir.*"

"What," said Sasha, bowled over by the treatment but lost at the foreign gurglings.

"Nothing for you to worry your thick head over," she said, pursing her mouth to bow the lip-paint, once more the perfect woman of business. "So they bounced you from hand to hand a bit, these upholders of legality?"

"That's one way of putting it. Was it official?"

"Now, come on. You're no mug. Does it ever need to be? Official, I mean? To them a hiding is a hiding whether it's jurisprudential or as the fancy dictates. You may take solace from metaphysics, but their feet are screwed to the ground. They couldn't operate otherwise."

As Sasha pursued his evanescent rights, she smiled indulgently, creasing the barely perceptible lines of her brow and brush-kissing the quicks of her nails. At the end of his recital, she shrieked delightedly.

"Leeches, my dear? Of course they're leeches and like with leeches your only hope is that they drop off sluggish from the ounces they've drawn off! And it is ounces, isn't it, from what you've told me about your set-up? Nothing long-term about investing in you, now, is there? One thing, though. Don't get ideas about putting salt on their tails, if that's the right curling-up mixture for leeches – that'll only make them very lively."

"How do you mean?" said Sasha, disconsolately, unconvinced that Bogat and Co. would just go home when they got fed up with the wallpaper or Lizaveta's primordial fry-ups.

"Don't complain, that's all. I don't mean like this, to me. But to anyone you think is their superior. They're like bison – a protected species."

Without stopping to consider, Sasha found himself making common cause with the Embassy policeman. "That's incredible. It makes me wonder what kind of country we're living in."

"I thought you already had the answer to that. Anyway, the grammar's wrong. It's the country *you're* living in. Mine's got slicker interior decoration. Listen – put your great flat feet up. I'm going to make you a drink."

By the window stood an ingenious drinks cabinet. When Marya Fyodorovna pulled on the handles a shelf slid out between two door-flaps, to the insides of which glasses were attached by their stems. On the shelf stood a bottle of Martini, some lemons and a chubby barrel containing ice. Having neatly sliced a lemon and popped a segment into a tumbler, she dropped in several chunks of the ice, filled the glass to the brim and handed it to Sasha.

"Try that," she said, smiling. "It might sophisticate your image."

As the ice crepitated tantalisingly beneath the alcohol, he stretched out his legs, sat back and drank.

"Any moaning about my house-guests is to be done in strict privacy?"

"That's about it," said Marya Fyodorovna, locking the bottle in her cabinet. "Didn't any of them hint at the possibilities?"

"One did," he said. "Now I come to think of it, yes, the little one, he did, but I didn't believe him."

"Always take that for gospel," said Marya Fyodorovna briskly. "He won't promise what he can't deliver."

"I believe you," grunted Sasha. "And now, I believe him."

Her telephone buzzed and she picked it up, at the same time glancing at her watch. There was no conversation and after a few seconds she replaced the receiver.

"My car's outside," she said. "I've got to be at a fashion house reception in a quarter of an hour. Here, you can help me on with my coat."

Sasha jumped up, took the coat and held it out by the sable facings on the collar. While she was buttoning up the front, he decided to put the question which had been on his mind throughout the inter-view; the question which, until this moment, he had had neither courage nor opportunity to ask.

"Marya." It was the first time he had not used her patronymic. His voice sounded so different that she paused, her fingers on the next-to-last-button. "Marya, somebody did for Lestyeva and that's how I got dragged in. Tell me, was it you?"

She frowned, fastened up her coat and plumped up the fur at her neck. "That's a natural enough guess, I suppose, in the circumstances. Her loss was my gain. But, no, in actual fact, it wasn't me. That's not to say I wouldn't have taken steps in order to get what I wanted but in her case I wouldn't have known where to start. Luckily, it wasn't necessary, the job had already been thoroughly done."

"And you know who by and you're not going to tell me, are you?"

She nodded. "The information would be useless to you now. What could you do with it? In any case, sources are never divulged on principle — surely you see the sense in that?"

"I daresay," said Sasha. "I'd just like to get my hands on the . . ."

"Exactly. And you'd end up in more trouble than you're in already."

He thumped his knees with his fists. "Bastards, bastards . . ."

"I'm already late," she said, looking at her watch again, but propping herself on the corner of the desk. "What the hell, the driver can wait. Help yourself to another drink — you look as if you need it."

The key appeared beside her and he took it and unlocked the cabinet.

"Are you a health freak, too?" he asked, peering at the row of mineral water and kefir bottles tucked in at the back.

She flushed. "I don't like booze much. Never did. There should be a beer somewhere."

Her hair brushed his forehead as she searched for the bottle. "Your hair's going grey," she said, as he snapped off the cap and took up a glass. "Is that what they did to your face?"

The contour of his cheek had been permanently dented and his unstitched wounds had healed into zig-zag scars. Valentina had wanted him to grow a beard. In cold weather there was a numb patch inside his mouth which he had never got used to.

"I fell on a cricketer's knee," he said mirthlessly, downing his beer.

She shivered and continued to stare. She too looked much older than she had in the summer. Faint lines crinkled at the sides of her mouth. That skin, he thought, would never again be perfect.

"I could feel sorry for you," she said.

"Don't bother," replied Sasha. "I'm quite good at that myself." He pulled his cap from his trouser pocket and waved it at her. "Well, I've got to be off, too, or I'll be late for the poetry."

"*Poetry?* You?"

"Yes, yes, one of our leeches has artistic aspirations. There's no charge but you're fined if you're late or don't turn up. Perhaps you know him — dark, very mad, minces like a sausage-maker?"

From her perch on the desk Marya Fyodorovna spread her legs and rocked with laughter. "Know him?" she spluttered. "Everyone knows that one. He's a legend in his own time. Who's playing Ingrid Bergman tonight, then — you or him?"

33

Len was across the road, lobbing snowballs at the over life-size portraits on the Board of Honour which faced the *Feministka* offices.

"Look at this," he shouted as Sasha emerged into the early-evening moonlight. "Vasya's in this lot."

For a few moments they both stood in silence before the line of photographs, mulling over this apotheosis of Vasya, a corpulent foreman three times married and divorced, whom neither of them had ever seen do a hand's turn beyond unscrewing the neck of a bottle.

"Makes you think," said Len.

"What of?"

"I don't know. Hanging yourself — something like that. Anyway, where the hell have you been? I've been stood here for over an hour exposing my parts to the elements."

"I forgot," said Sasha.

"Forgot, forgot?" bawled Len. "That's you all over, that is. You drag me away from a do where I was enjoying myself, dump me in the snow, while you chat up some girl . . ."

This was not wholly true. Earlier that day there had been a bottle party at the main garage in celebration of Len's reinstatement as supervisor. Halfway through someone had brought in a fifteen-litre jerry can of homebrew and a fight broke out over who was in a fit state to ladle it out. Initially, Len, conscious of his restored rank, held aloof. But when Volodya, a six-foot scarecrow of a youth with asthma and no thought on his mind for drink, poured the homebrew into the fluid reservoir of the hydraulic ramp, under the impression that it was some topping-up specific, all hell broke loose. That was the sign for Len to make a tactical exit. His promotion was not effective until next Monday. Until then they could supervise themselves.

In any case he had heard a lot about Marya Fyodorovna from Sasha. So much that he didn't believe a word and wanted to check her out for himself. Though Len loved him like a brother, he also thought Sasha thick — especially over females. Having met an assortment of his girlfriends over the years he could only conclude that all parties to the arrangement looked so miserable that Sasha either paid them to go out with him or he had a medical condition. For a long time they had stayed off the subject of Sasha's conquests. Now he was at it again, boasting, implying, hinting, longing, so Len wanted to confront the latest, eyeball to eyeball.

When he invited himself along, Sasha was not keen. The meeting with Marya was a crucial one. But Len was pushy and when he suggested that they dropped in at his place to freshen up since there was a couple of hours to kill, Sasha reluctantly fell in with the idea. There might be time enough to disinvite him if anything more tempting turned up. Jenny might be home.

Jenny was Len's new girl and although in her dungarees and curlers she was not much of an improvement on Natalya, to Len she was bliss. The flat was empty and the men had a beer. After a while Jenny came back from the site at Khimki where she drove a bulldozer, and fell into Len's arms. Sasha locked himself in the bathroom to wash his hair. When he came out the girl was zipping up her boots. Len had decided: the three of them were going to *Feministka*.

"Well? Where is she then?"

"I don't know, do I?" said Sasha, looking round the empty street. "Don't blame me if your girls keep running away."

"Not Jenny! She shoved off, her boots were letting in snow. No, that little piece you promised me a bit of. I thought I was going to get a peep at the well-upholstered other half. Bloody hell." Len stamped his feet and hunted through his pockets for a cigarette, cheeks raw from the bitter wind. "You want to watch it, tarting yourself up like that. Or have you been taking lessons from Miss Trench Coat 1940? Back-combing is the first step on the slippery slope, Jenny says . . ."

"What Jenny needs is a crash course in intimate hygiene," said Sasha with a laugh. "Was she born in those overalls?" He took Len's arm in his and they strolled off amicably down the road. "I told you," continued Sasha, "there was no point in you tagging along. It could have been five minutes, it could have been ninety. You never know with Marya Fyodorovna's type. I couldn't come away with her because she went straight down to the car pool. There's some fashion show on."

"That sounds nice. Why didn't you wangle us a couple of complimentaries? It might have been bathing suits or scanties."

"Have a heart – in this weather? Any case, I don't have pull like that and we're not exactly in the model-gown bracket, are we? I went to see her strictly on business."

At the mention of the purpose of the visit Len was appeased. He knew about the problem of Sasha's squatters, and was unhappy that he could not help. "Get a result, then?" he asked.

"She knew who they belonged to all right, but she still wouldn't tell me who issued their free passes to my wage-packet."

They stopped on the corner where an elderly woman with the long, still eyes of a Tartar was struggling to raise her wheeled shopping bag on to the kerb. Len released Sasha's arm in order to help.

"Mind your own business!" she snarled. As she trundled into a nearby court, both men wolf-whistled after her.

"That's not all she knows, either." Sasha had gone back to his story of Marya Fyodorovna. "There's somebody responsible for infesting us with that pricklouse Bogat. Somebody who tumbled Lestyeva and gave a ring to the right quarters."

"Could have been anybody, that. That's Granny's work, nine times out of ten. I ought to know — amazing what the rubbish collection vigilantes poison-penned about me. Denounced for uncultured bin-tipping, I was. Moscow's crawling with old-lady guardians of social purity — take that slit-eyed old cat just now. She'd see you hang for a kilo of butter."

Sasha shook his head. "No Granny would have the *nous* for this one. It's beyond scrawls on the back of an envelope. No, whoever did for Lestyeva made a shrewd assessment, took an overview and dug the knife in deep."

"Can't you work on her, this Marya female?" asked Len. "I thought she'd taken a shine . . ."

"Oh, sod it all!" exclaimed Sasha. "I've had enough for one day. Tell you what, let's go to my place. My resident fairy is holding another one of his recitations tonight. The poetry's piss-poor but the drink's free. What do you think?"

Len quite liked the sound of it, but why didn't they club together for a few bottles and have a binge round his? After all, today he had something to celebrate, and Jenny could rustle up a meal. And nobody would be talking poetry.

Sasha squeezed his friend's arm. "I'm broke, mate. That's why. I've been telling you for weeks — don't you ever take things in?"

Len did, very quickly, but tonight his appetite was for Jenny, not poems. "Come on, I'll give you a sub. Work it off when you like."

"Can't be done — I owe half the depot already." On mittened fingers Sasha totted up his obligations: "After the family helped themselves, Valentina was on her uppers. The cracked bird she's set up house with lives off bread and tea, her pension's so small. So I cough up a bit for them, once a fortnight. Then there's forty for

Bogat's skin-cream and eyeliner or whatever he lashes out his pin-money on, as well as another twenty-five for Legless's bottom drawer. That's how I'm situated, so if it's poems and free refreshments I have to take my arse-ache like a man. What else can I do?"

Len spat over his shoulder. "Stop paying. They couldn't do a thing."

"Couldn't they just? You've not had any of it. That screwy little one, he'd frame his Mum for her lottery tickets. They're all in it together – one squawk and they'd have the lot of us inside for wiping our noses."

Len stopped by a row of telephone boxes. "All right, let's go peekaboo at your nasties. Perhaps we can make a fight out of it. Give me a two and I'll ring home. Jenny can wash down the walls or something."

Sasha gave him a clumsy hug.

"Thanks, Len. Next time we'll take her too, and she can flatten them for us."

An ornate black limousine with white coachlines along the side swept up to the major road, halted at the traffic signals and caught Len in its headlights as he stepped out of the box. On the green light the old car hissed towards them like an overladen hearse, the chauffeur sounding a continuous note on the horn. They had plenty of time to see Marya Fyodorovna.

If the rear compartment had been a landau with deep-buttoned cushioning she could not have given herself a more regal spread. She had slipped off her office shoes in the car and was reclining crossways along the whole extent of the back seat. Gone was the mannish trouser suit. Her head nestling in the champagne leather of the arm rest, her pink-stockinged feet playing with the tassels of her feather boa, she smiled indolently at both men over a pair of silvery, open-work high-heels clutched to the sables at her throat. Len sucked in the picture with a ravenous eye: the swing of Marya's odalisque hips under the stuff of the coat above her crossovered thighs, the tapered ankle pressing white through the fine stretch weave of the nylon, the huge eyes spanned wider by goldy-glitter dust trails fading into the matt foundation at her temples, the mane of auburn hair, sprayed with fixative to freeze its rippled, bouncing flow. Marya Fyodorovna was all body, a pampered surface to be creamed, waxed, depilated, smoothed, coated and high-lined, all to someone else's cost and deprivation. Len loved every inch of it. There and then he would have plonked down his wages to perpetuate the unjustifiable expense of so coddling this luxurious creature that her sweet little bottom never touched anything harsher than crêpe-de-chine.

"How close did you say you got to that one?" asked Len in wonderment as the car accelerated into the night.

"Near as I am to you now," said Sasha proudly, taking the big man's arm in his once more. "*And* I've kissed her."

"You? You expect me to believe that your unclean little gob blemished that plutocratic complexion?"

"Only a peck – on the face," said Sasha. If he made more grandiose claims Len would call for evidence. His weak spot was for fancying the unattainable. Once he had an inkling that this piece of sheer impossibility might be walking out with a bin-scourer like Sasha he would turn completely wild. "Sisterly, you could call it. Sisterly."

At this Len was satisfied to be merely glum. They moved off slowly along the icy pavement.

"Where would you take a woman like that?" mused the big man, finding a better foothold in the slushy tyre channels on the road, and striding out towards the Arbat.

"The pictures?" suggested Sasha at a loss for suitable venues.

"That shows everything about you, that. The pictures! You'd take a grand duchess to the flicks. There's something insidious about your small ambitions – everything turns to tat in your flea-pit mentality. Where's your romance?"

Sasha shrugged. Valentina had often asked him that. "Yevgenia Denisovna thinks the pictures is treats." Using her full name and patronymic imparted a pathetic dignity to Jenny.

"Been brought up to it, hasn't she? Topless go-go dancing wasn't on the agenda down her village. Where she comes from the girls put on yokes to cart the water from the well, not ra-ra skirts. Show her a see-through bra and she'd use it for straining cheese."

"Now who's narrow-minded?" said Sasha. "Get some education down her, take her to a disco."

"Have you seen her wardrobe? They'd think she'd come to fix the strobes."

Coming to a gap in the gaunt ranks of nineteenth-century town houses, now largely converted to ambassadorial residences and government offices, the two men turned from the highway into a rutted track, flanked by outgrowths of birch saplings, which gave on to a derelict back lot where in the summer purple scabious poked up amidst the rubble and discarded timber of two-storey tenements in the course of being demolished. A ruined gateway loomed before them, resembling a dwarf triumphal arch. High in the yellow stucco was a Venetian window, its shutters intact.

"Give me a lift up," said Len, taking out his jackknife. "Look at those hinges."

Sasha bowed his back, infantryman-style, allowing the big man to leap up and plant his boots on his shoulders. Len began to prise away the hinges from the rotten wood.

This was a recent craze with him. Nowadays he came out equipped for plunder: bolt-cutters in one leg-pocket, a canvas hold-all under his arm.

Sasha moaned as his friend's soles ground into his flesh. All this for a bloody woman. Len scoured Moscow for Jenny's bits-and-bobs. Simple love-gifts like flowers or chocolates were not her style. She demanded door-knockers, fingerplates, brass keyholes, ceramic tiles, chromed whirler taps – anything to screw on, grout or plumb into the do-it-yourself paradise she was chip-boarding out of Len's slummy bathroom.

"Nice little find, these," he said, slithering down. "Look good on the medicine cabinet."

"You haven't got a medicine cabinet."

"Well, for the china cabinet, then," barked back Len, vexed at Sasha's knowledge of his tumbledown dwelling.

"You haven't got any china." Len and Jenny were normally marooned in an ocean of tin-cans and sawdust, eating off plastic plates. Fat Natalie had carried off every pot in the place.

"Never mind," said the big man, spitting on one of the hinges and buffing it up on his sleeve, his breath smoking. "We're getting there. Rome wasn't built in a day. Once Jenny gets going with her fret-saw . . ."

". . . she'll run up St Basil's in plywood. Come off it, she's too boss-eyed to drive a nail in straight."

Len was used to taking the defects of his women in good part.

"Hamfisted but willing – that's how I like them. Refinements I can teach her."

They sat on a pile of breeze blocks smoking, and blowing on their hands to keep warm while a tom-cat howled languishingly from a distant back-court.

"Ever thought of moving in with us?" asked Len. "A partition wouldn't overtax Jenny's carpentry. A few rumbles in the night would be worth putting up with for the sake of losing your talc-arsed versifier."

Sasha was touched but uncaptivated. Len's private life had a habit of exploding in his face. Besides, he'd had his fill of fat ladies who roped you in for interior design.

"That's a thought. If they start posting me dead cats I'll remember the offer. But, as for now, I might as well stick it out. He might get run over – or the pox – then it'll be home sweet home again. Anyway,

I want to stay close in case one of them gets loose-lipped and drops me on to the nark who's done for us."

"Fair enough. Any time – you know where I live."

I do, thought Sasha. And who with.

The short-cut through the old croft led them out on to a side road half a mile from Sasha's flat. They plodded along slowly, cheerful now because the snow fell thickly on their warm faces and the anticipated drinks came nearer with every step.

"You know," said Sasha, "it's not much fun being in my position. I can't be sure where I am with them – the other folk in the flat, I mean. They all suspect me as well as suspecting each other."

"As this informer you keep going on about?"

"That's right. They've got me at it, too. At first I thought poor old Borya's widow had done the dirty, then it struck me, that tight-trousers has been leading these poetry-reading rambles once a fort-night for weeks now, regular as a sick-parade, and nearly everybody shambled up – even that scrimshanking *dvornik* Baranov and his missus. They'd go anywhere for a meal, but it couldn't just have been the eats, I reckoned. Lately more and more have been crying off, though. Sometimes Bogat makes up the congregation with a pal or two but they're always musclebound headcases, like that Rocky, who put the wind up the old faithfuls so that next time they stay away. Bogat doesn't seem to give a toss. It's Olga Sergeyevna he wants to hear his poems really. We're just the stodge in the trifle. He can't settle till she waltzes in and when he's reading he ogles her like a randy ferret."

"Perhaps they're in love."

"Don't you ever take life seriously?"

"Not that side of it," said Len. "Once a normal man feels persecuted or misunderstood, he looks for the cause of the problem, and more often than not it's one person who's doing the damage."

"That's what I told you," interrupted Sasha. "I want to get the bugger."

"Hold on a minute, can't you? Listen to uncle. Because this is a semi-official affair, you'll never identify him. Meanwhile you'll reckon all your so-called friends are part of the plot."

"Perhaps they are."

"And perhaps they are. The next thing is, you start blaming yourself for forcing them to take sides. They're simple souls, like you, and you know what pressure from above means. That's how your Bogat's fairy wand breaks the back of conscience-stricken twerps. You shut up so as not to cause any more trouble to your pals, and your pals' suspicions deepen. It looks as if you've joined their persecutors. That's what's happened to Olga Sergeyevna and if you don't listen hard, it'll happen to you."

This was too much for Sasha to absorb at once. "I think I get it," he said, as they came round the corner of the lane. "Ideally, they'd like me to suspect you, as well?"

"Marvellous! It's sunk in."

"Why don't I then?"

"Ah, that's the cunning thing," said Len. "They persuade me to lie low in a fly-blown flat, take a dead-end job, eat out of tins and live with fat girls so that I can worm my way into the confidence of wreckers and saboteurs like you. A proletarian mole, I am. Clever, isn't it?"

34

Lopakhina came out of the lift smelling of bleach. She glared at Sasha.

"It's an orgy up there. All that smashing and thumping. I suppose you're here to add to the broken bottles and wantonness?"

Len gave a ghoulish chuckle, and twisted one shoulder into a hump. "Don't be like that, dearie. Come over here," he gibbered. "Come and get frisky with me. I'll make sure you're not a wallflower."

Lopakhina shrank under his leer and hastened to the door, squealing: "One finger on me, you desecrator, and I'll call the militia."

Len's temper was sunny again. "Hope they've not scoffed everything," he said to Sasha. "Bit hoggish with the booze, aren't they, when they let their hair down – poets?"

They took the stairs to the first floor.

At the door Sasha could not find his key. He must have left it in his work trousers back at the depot when he changed into clean ones for Marya Fyodorovna. Len had taken off his fur hat and was slicking back his hair.

"What's up?"

"Bloody key, I've lost it. Hope they're not too far gone to hear me knocking."

"Here," said Len, pressing a new-looking electric push button. "This'll save the knuckles – you've been automated."

Bogat had installed the bell to raise the social tone, Sasha remembered. A touch of the electronic civilisation he was always talking about. By now the little runt would be well into his bombast, strutting on that trunk in his velveteens, and interpreting the breathless hush of the audience as mature appreciation, not catalepsy.

God, did nothing come free in this world?

Len had his mouth to the crack in the door. "Come on," he shouted breezily. "We know you're in there. Where's the girls, then? Bugger the poems, show us a leg."

In his enthusiasm to make the inmates hear, he pressed his lips harder against the wood. Someone must have gone out in a hurry, leaving it on the latch, for the door yielded easily, swung inwards a few inches, then stuck fast.

"Trusting lot, your people – or is it on the chain?" said Len, feeling round the edge. "Ah, no chain. Give it a shove. You ought to know its habits better than me."

Sasha pushed, expecting to hear the crash of Lizaveta's mop-pail overturning in the hall, but the gap would not widen. There must be something weightier than a bucket of water at the foot of the door. For the moment they could think of nothing else causing the obstruction, and stood stupidly inert, gazing at each other.

A noise came from the lower panel as if something were scratching at the wood. The hair rose at the back of Sasha's neck and for no reason he remembered Boris. There was a brief cough followed by someone retching. The noises were evidently human, and Sasha relaxed. "Must be a hell of a party in there – someone's had a skinful already. Here, you try. I can't shift him."

Apart from the one sound, the flat appeared to be totally silent.

Len bunched his upper arms round his chest and shoulder-charged. The hinges scraped back a fraction but there was no perceptible widening. With the high jogging steps of a boxer, he danced backwards across the landing to the opposite flat, gave one deep breath and raced forward, hurling the mass of his thick back, side on.

There was a soft crunch, followed by a loud groan and the door twisted on its mountings making an uneven aperture, twice as wide at the top as at the bottom but allowing enough space for one person to slide in.

Sasha had one leg halfway through the gap when he understood why the door had jammed. With his other foot he had trodden on something pulpy. He looked down and saw a broad, male, and exceptionally well-manicured hand protruding on to the landing tiles. From below the wrist to the beginning of the fingers it was raw red from the contusions inflicted when Len's violent attack had squeezed it out under the bottom edge of the door.

Len explored the outspread fingers with his toecap, assuming that the hand was not real but some kind of gruesome toy. "Is it stuck on to the rest, do you reckon, or is it only a spare?"

"Holy Mother of God," he murmured when the longest two fingers recoiled from the contact.

The hallway was unlit but Sasha, more quick-thinking in practical matters than his friend, was already on his knees attempting to release the pressure of the unplaned edge of the door on the unseen wrist.

Len could not resist the humour of the situation. "Here, let me give you a hand," he grimaced, pushing Sasha out of the way. With a tremendous jerk he raised the door a couple of inches from the floor, shearing off the screwheads in the lower hinge plate.

The noise attracted no one. In the flat all was silent.

Sasha clambered past and pulled the hand free from inside. For one panicky moment, after the outside landing light clicked off, he could not find the hall light switch. Then he remembered that the previous weekend Lev Kuznetsov had re-located it at a more convenient point when he was re-wiring the lobby. "Bloody interfering, useless bloody sod." As he was fumbling and cursing behind the coat-rack a bestial gurgle escaped from the black heap on the floor.

When the light came on, the noise ceased and there was no other sound.

Along the middle of the hall lay a trail of silver coins glinting against something dark and wet spreading over the uneven linoleum. The trail ended at a heavy figure which was heaped face down like an overstuffed kitbag against the skirting board adjacent to the door. A blackening stain matted the short blond hair at the crown of the head.

"My God," whispered Len from the doorway. "That's some wall he's had dropped on him."

With the back of his hand Sasha attempted gently to turn the head into profile. At his touch the dreadful gasping, choking sound began again. From what was left of the face Sasha made an identification. It was Legless.

A doorknob rattled and the two men were suddenly confronted by the spectacle of Olga in a rust-coloured peignoir, her hair disarrayed. The moment she saw Sasha hovering irresolutely over the body she flew at Len, pushed him back against the wall and wrenched the broken front door to.

Her voice was hoarse from suppressed rage. "Where have you been? Where were you? You should have done something. You could have stopped them!"

Her fury was concentrated on Sasha who met her gaze steadily, without replying.

"How was he to know? What do you take us for – mind readers?" Len muttered. Sasha fell to his knees and having rolled up his sleeve as if about to unblock a drain, carefully turned the head again so that the face was directly towards him. The blood accumulated in the well of the ear was disturbed by the movement and began to trickle down the line of one cheek. Although one side had been smashed from chin to brow by something long and smooth, it was recognisably Legless. One eye had disappeared in a welter of blood and bone, but the other was open and seemed to be twinkling at Sasha almost jovially. The half-features twitched spasmodically.

Len raised his voice to Olga. "This poor devil's in a bad way.

What's the matter with you people? Were you going to leave him here to bleed to death? You must have heard noises – he didn't get like this without making one hell of a racket first."

Olga moaned helplessly, corkscrewing strands of her unpinned hair with her index-finger like a picture-book simpleton.

"Get out of it, if you can't stand the sight of blood and brains!" roared Len throwing his hat at the cowering woman and striding down the passage, running his hands down the walls for the switches. "Let's have some lights in this stink-hole. Where's the bugger that did this? Where is he?"

His voice echoed in the dark recesses.

"Out, out, Mr Handyman! I'm going to rub your snout in the job!"

At the end of the corridor he traced the main battery of switches and flicked on all the lights in the communal part of the flat.

Below him, arms and legs stiffly extended like a child's teddy-bear, sat Bogat. Across his forehead, running parallel to his eyebrows was a long, wide cut which bled profusely into his eyes.

"What's this?" called the big man to Sasha. "The annual cull? These characters can't keep themselves to themselves. Here's another one the floor's jumped up to meet."

Bogat's voice was high, and piteously wracked. "I can't see, I'm blind, I've gone blind."

Len tweaked back the little man's head by its film-star quiff. "You'll be OK, sonny boy. You're only going to need a lot of stitches." Inserting a nicotine-stained forefinger into the cut, he pushed up a hanging flap of skin with his thumb, pressing it back into place above Bogat's prominent eyebrows and wiped away the blood from the wound with the back of his hand.

When Bogat recovered his sight, Olga went berserk. She flung herself at Sasha, clawing at his face. "How I hate you!" she shrieked. "Look what you've done to us! This is all your doing, your wicked fault!"

He fended her off as best he could without hurting her, but she was as springy as a terrier and very strong. They grappled indecisively over the recumbent body of Legless, Olga softly screaming, Sasha fighting to avoid her fingernails.

The Kuznetsovs' door was flung open, and Anna came running up behind Len. Conscious of Len's looming towards him, his arm raised to strike Olga, Sasha had just time to burst out with a short: "No!" before the two women collapsed sobbing into each other's arms.

"There, there," said Kuznetsova, her face drained of colour, gazing reproachfully at Sasha over Olga's speckly grey hair. "This isn't like you, Olga Sergeyevna, dear, not like you at all."

Anna tried to lead the older woman away, but only got as far as the door of her room before Olga stopped and seemed to regain her self-control. Beyond the two women was Lev, nervously tapping the side of his spectacles, and holding his daughter by the hand. Xenia still wore her party frock. Sasha suddenly recalled the object of the evening. An hysterical desire to giggle came over him: it must have been some poem to have caused this fracas.

Bubbles of foam winked and popped at the corners of Legless's mouth. Xenia watched, ox-eyed and unmoved.

"Get that child out of my sight," growled Sasha. "This is no place for kids. She shouldn't see this."

Len had seen enough, too. He picked up his hat and wheeled round to the ruined door, but Olga was in no mood to let Sasha's henchman escape.

"Oh no you don't," she screamed, settling her nails into the sleeve of his donkey-jacket. When he tried to shake her off she dug the heels of her mules into the lino. "You're not getting away with it like that, you great thug. Think you can swan in and swan out pretending it's none of your business? You're up to your eyes in this. You two are in it together, I know it, I know!"

Len had a fierce dislike for women who took any kind of physical initiative. The venous birthmark on his face was enlarging rapidly and Sasha knew that he was close to losing his temper completely and felling Olga Sergeyevna to the ground.

But before he could interfere, an inhuman screech emerged from Legless's mouth, his body humped in an arc and his lower limbs twitched violently. Everyone scattered, only to stare back in fascination as the policeman's grossest convulsions expired in shrug-like shudders, and the breath rattled at the back of his throat.

Sasha began counting until he lay still with no apparent quiver of life. After ninety seconds Legless's breathing became audible once again. This time the air was whistling dryly through his clogged windpipe.

"Oh God, *help* him," whispered Anna.

For over an hour Legless and Bogat lay untended while the rest debated what to do. At first there was no sense to be had from Olga, who had to be restrained from taking a comb to the back of Legless's head.

"But we must tidy it up, I must tidy his hair . . ."

Len sat on the hallstand smoking morosely. He had been in action and knew something of wounds. "The skull's crushed and splinters of bone have penetrated his brain. He's a no-hoper, your big boy, a waste of surgical time."

"Perhaps we should call a doctor," said Anna timidly.

"Do you live here, missis?" said Len.

The answer died in her throat. She was frightened of big men.

"You know she does," said Lev. "Surely."

"Pardon me, but you could have walked in from the street for all I know. So this is what you call home, lady, this superb piece of manhood is your caring husband, and those two bleeders making friends with the cockroaches over there are your light-fingered lodgers?"

Anna nodded miserably.

"Now I get the picture," continued Len. "And you want to call a doctor?"

"At least, an ambulance?" said Olga.

"Or an ambulance, says the other lady." He chucked a cigarette over to Sasha. "Now you tell them, Biryusov, why they shouldn't call the doctor, or an ambulance, or the fire-brigade, or police headquarters. Tell them why they'd be safer in Red Square pissing up against the Mausoleum."

Blushing fierily Anna looked down at the floor. Lev polished his spectacles on his tie.

"Because a report will be made out," said Sasha mournfully.

Len slid down from the hallstand and went up to Lev. "A notification of injury in suspicious circumstances. Who did it then? You?"

"Of course I didn't, anyone knows I didn't! We have a child to consider." There was outrage in Lev's voice. Bogat, quiet up till now in his corner, began to blubber.

"He had no right. I wouldn't hurt a fly."

"Now you hearken to that little invertebrate," said Len. "To him it's a question of *rights*. Someone has striped his marble brow, someone with no right at all to do that to *him*. What that someone has rights for, is to do that kind of thing to you, and to me. It takes more than sheer assurance for the weak to go on the attack – we're like him, we need authorisation. So, Kuznetsov couldn't have done it, Biryusov and Bikovsky couldn't have done it. The women hadn't the right *or* the muscle to do it. That leaves meathead and the fairy, the only two fully docketed up for dishing out beltings."

"We know that perfectly well," said Olga sharply. "They fell out among themselves."

"What about?"

"I don't know – plunder, division of spoils – like thieves do."

"*And who will believe one single bloody word you say, you stupid bitch?*" cried Len, gripping Olga by the shoulders and beginning to shake her.

Sasha got between them. "Give her a chance, mate, decent people are always a couple of steps behind."

"*No one*, that's who. *Not a fucking soul.* They're all boxed by the same import/export firm aren't they, with Grade A stamped on their arses. Who's going to let swine-husks like you into the sweet fruit? This little amateur duffing-up will be put down to you – all of you and, believe me, brothers, those two buggers will swear your life away."

Bogat was swiftest to gather the implications of Len's analysis. Wrapping his arms round his chest he began to wail dismally and rocked to and fro like a child with toothache.

"Where has he gone? Why has he abandoned me? Why, oh why? The swine are going to bury us alive."

Len strode down the passage and kicked Bogat's legs. "Bury you, you snivelling little molester? I wouldn't spit on my hands. If I had my way you'd be sawn into joints and flushed down the lavvy in gobbets. Now stick your hanky in your face and cry nice and quiet while I decide the best method of recycling your offals."

Bogat slewed away from his corner, whimpering: "I'll get you, butcher, I'll have you sliced yet."

"What a pretty rattle baby's got then," exclaimed Len, seizing on something hard and warm which Bogat had been sitting on. He threw it over to Sasha and watched as Bogat's eyes dilated with terror. "Look what Daddy's found," he called. "Go on, Biryusov, you had weapons training – identify and display."

"It's a pistol," said Sasha. That much was obvious even to the women, who backed nervously away as Sasha fitted his hand round the butt and waggled a finger through the trigger guard. "Came off the assembly line when they still had horses and carts, though, judging by the look of it." Under the barrel, in front of the trigger, was a rectilinear magazine which looked as if it might drop off any minute and detonate at his feet. He was glad to hand back the gun when Len gave over terrorising Bogat.

Len swopped it confidently from palm to palm. "This thing," he began sententiously, "this thing, although it could be mistaken by the uninformed, like my friend here, for the arm of an antiquated mangle, is a Mauser pistol." He barked at Bogat. "Running out of money, are they, issuing you lot with museum pieces?"

Bogat squirmed. "I don't know anything about it. That's Rocky's. He found it on an old ammunition dump."

"Another scavenger," said Len. Examining the underside of the exposed barrel he found an engraved inscription. "Here," he said to Olga. "You're educated. What does this say?"

"*Gott mit uns*," read Olga. "God is with us."

"Well, He's lost track of them this time," said Len opening up the breech and disassembling the magazine. "It's not loaded. And from the state of the rifling," he said, peering down the sight end of the barrel, "the last gent to fire this must have been the Kaiser."

"That's right," said Bogat eagerly. "Rocky told me, you can't get the bullets any more."

Olga stared. "You mean that foul brigand was threatening us with a water-pistol?"

"What the hell are you talking about?" said Len, mystified.

"His friend," shouted Olga, pointing at Bogat. "His Rocky rubbish. Lizaveta and I saw it all. Rocky hit the other one with a Scotch whisky bottle full of ten-kopek pieces. Broke it over his head."

Sasha tried to piece together the sequence. "What for?"

"The policeman over there," said Olga, nodding at the apparently defunct Legless, "attacked Mr Bogat with a knife."

Unable to make head or tail of what had gone on that afternoon, Len sat down on the floor, grabbed Anna by the ankle and ran his great hand up her leg.

"Cheer us up, sweetie, will you – how about a cup of tea?"

Both Kuznetsovs were only too pleased at this excuse for making themselves scarce for a while, and disappeared behind their door.

Sasha who had greater stamina than his friend, persisted with the cross-examination of Olga, whose nerves seemed to be gradually steadying.

"This is like a dirty postcard," he said. "Now, tell us again – who was doing what to who?"

She started with a résumé. "All of them had been drinking in the kitchen the whole day . . ."

"You know what?" interrupted Len, giving a vigorous rub to his hair. "I've heard that beginning so many times. A truly Russian tale this is going to be."

"Shut up, Bikovsky – the tea won't be long. Now, Olga Sergeyevna, who's 'they'?"

Olga ticked off on her fingers, blinking rapidly. "The big one with the pipe –"

"The cricket fan, Rocky?"

"Yes, that brute. Then that one –" she indicated Legless – "who was revoltingly drunk, became very angry about something, and Rocky drew his pistol and waved it about like a cowboy and shouted some nonsense about how he could shoot the eyes out of potatoes. So the policeman dragged out Lizaveta's sack and started putting her potatoes on the top of the empty bottles. They had some kind of bet

– if the Rocky man hit so many potatoes, he'd get a letter back."

"Len said nobody could have fired a shot."

"Nobody did. Rocky said the other man was a coward, and called him a lot of disgusting names because he refused to put a potato on his head for Rocky to shoot off."

Len laughed aloud. "He should have jumped at the option. Then his headache wouldn't have lasted so long."

"You're forgetting," said Sasha. "A pistol without bullets was as much use as a rubber duck in a drought."

Anna Georgyevna came out of the room where the poetry reading was to have taken place bearing a huge, oval silver tray edged round by a pierced gallery. With the teapot and cups it was almost more than she could lift, and Sasha dashed across to take it from her. She popped behind her door again, only to re-emerge with a tin box marked Red Cross, and a shallow baking dish overflowing with tepid water. In her teeth she held a blue plastic sponge.

Bogat stirred, thankful for her charity. He was going to be cleaned up. As Anna laid out the contents of her box by his flaccid hand he whispered into her ear: "Tell them to be careful with the china, dear – it's my best."

Len scrambled up and took over the tea pouring. Anna had put out five cups. "You take him one," said Len, poking a foot in Bogat's direction. "I might tip it over him. That's the lot. The other poor bastard only needs prayers." He took a hefty swallow of Bogat's best Earl Grey. "And a miracle, and an intravenous drip of holy water."

Sasha handed round biscuits from a straw-lined tin.

"Well, aren't we cosy?" said Olga sardonically, breaking up the comfortable mood induced by food and drink. "We'll even have a ghost at our feast very soon if the poor wretch stops making that nasty noise and dies. Don't you think we had better get a move on?"

"Not until we've got to the bottom of this business," said Sasha, cramming three biscuits into his mouth at once. He turned to Olga spattering the frills of her peignoir with crumbs. "So, Rocky was doing his William Tell with the popgun . . ."

"That was the point, you see. The policeman was not so drunk that he'd risk his life, but he set up six empty bottles each with a potato stuck on the neck, on top of Lizaveta's jars of pickles, right up high on the dresser."

Lizaveta Ivanovna's sister, who lived in the country nearly a hundred miles from Moscow, kept the old woman supplied every harvest time with tomatoes, white and red cabbage, green beans, peas, cucumbers and other varieties of vegetable which she grew on her house-plot. These Lizaveta marinaded, soused, pickled, salted, and otherwise prepared during the whole month of October, when the kitchen was completely given over to the work. This year, because of Bogat's exigencies, the task was beyond her, and most of the vegetables were thrown away, but the previous year's examples of her industry still stood above the highest shelf of her cupboard, glistening colourfully in a magnificent row of vast jars. The sight of the hoard gave her soul a lift at the start of each day. Not for the world would any of the tenants have touched them.

"Well, Rocky stood over by the gas-cookers. I watched him from this end of the passage. He crouched in a funny way, bending his knees, and he held up his gun with both hands to stop it wobbling . . ."

Len was doubled up with laughter. "I've seen the film! And then the Indian pulls out his tomahawk . . ."

"Do you want to listen to this or not?" said Olga, very much on her dignity. "Or have you been drinking?"

Len raised his cup to her. "No, no, I just want to know how Rocky got out of this one. Looks like a pratfall to nothing so far."

Olga smoothed back her hair. "When he pulled the trigger, nothing happened."

Hysterical peals came from Len, but this time Olga was not discomposed.

"Nothing?" said Sasha.

"A click, that was all. A click."

"Not even a little flag with 'BANG' embroidered on it?" screamed Len helplessly.

"Then he swore, stared at the floor, shook the gun very hard and looked down the barrel."

By this time Len was beside himself. His laughter reverberated around the hall.

"All right, all right," shouted Sasha. "We're all a bit hysterical, but there's no need to give in to it. Anyway, where's the joke? Not exactly rib-tickling, is it, our situation?"

"Neither was his," gasped Len. "Look at these." And he stretched out his hand. Nestling in the palm were ten smallish cartridges.

Bogat pretended pain as Kuznetsova gently swabbed the congealed blood from his temples, but he was following Len's every word and action. "Who's been playing tricks on his friend, then? Who stripped out the magazine and hid the bullets in his handbag?" continued the big man, his voice and manner quietly sinister. The chalk-faced Bogat could stand the suspense no longer.

"I was trying to protect you!" he broke out, having long meditated the phrase best suited to explain his action in secreting Rocky's ammunition clip which Len had pulled from his top pocket when he found the pistol. "Rocky's a fool to himself, swaggering about with loaded weapons. He could have done himself an injury. Somebody had to take precautions after last time . . ."

"What time was that?" asked Sasha, already guessing what was to come.

"Last time, he shot a dog."

"Not with this, he didn't," said Len, picking up the Mauser. "This barrel isn't fouled with powder."

"That's the trouble," gabbled the little man, tumbling over his words in the effort to appear responsibly-minded as well as placatory. "He's got a whole arsenal at home. You never know where you are with him, can't tell him anything, he's so wilful."

A wrangle developed about pistol calibres and about whether or not Bogat had any intention of sticking up the rest of the tenants with Rocky's antique weapon, but Sasha had ceased to listen. Bogat was no homicidal maniac – that one had got away and was on the loose.

"Leave him be, the poor wretch," called Olga to Len. "Can't you see, he's not that kind of man, he's a blabbermouth. It's the fantasist you should be exciting yourself about – he puts actions to words, and there's the product dying in his own blood. I saw Rocky kill that man. Not the easy way with a gun, but with a bottle. I saw him. He wouldn't stop, even when he was unconscious on the floor, blood spurting from his mouth – he enjoyed it, battering him like that, he enjoyed it hugely."

"But he was only thinking of me," protested Bogat. "It was like self-defence. Yuri went for me with the carving knife. I might have been . . ."

Len silenced the outcry with a back-hander, square on Bogat's dressing. "When *I* do you," he hissed, "there'll be no might-have-beens."

35

The solution was arrived at by accident.

Weary of Olga's frenzied demands for some action to be taken over Legless's body which, by now, was exuding a sickening, defecatory stench in the confines of the hallway, Sasha and his friend had withdrawn to the landing where they could rid themselves of the smell by deep gulps of less polluted air, cut themselves off from the hideous burbling still coming from the dying policeman's nasal passages, and give themselves time to think.

Calm planning was vital. If the plan were foolproof they could make a clean sweep. Rocky had shot his bolt, they both agreed about that. Bogat was his superior officer. So if Bogat were spared, Rocky could be neutralised.

There were two ways of bringing Bogat to heel: first, they could threaten to kill him – now or later. The drawback there was that once he was off the immediate hook, Bogat could pull them in for the damage to Legless and, with Rocky's co-operation, make the charges stick. The alternative was to spare him now, threaten him with what might later befall (Len was confident that he could instil sufficient fear), and at the same time somehow convince him that if they were driven to desperation, every inmate of the flat would swear blind that they had witnessed Rocky's murder of Legless. For murder it was going to be – that was the *sine qua non* of the set-up. Bogat would do anything, Len reckoned, to keep Rocky out of a murder inquiry. He already had a reputation for eccentric sadism. No one would be amazed if he'd gone over the top. But on Len's analysis, the actual killing fell to them. Although Sasha could not fault it – and the prospect of ridding himself, Olga, the Kuznetsovs, Marina, Valya and Lizaveta Ivanovna of the entire trio of blood-suckers was distinctly life enhancing – who was going to pull the plug on the filth-bag in their vestibule?

Len insisted on complicity in the act: they (the men, that was) must all take a twist at snuffing him. Sasha baulked, not ostensibly on that score but at the disposal: how did they get rid of the body?

"We can't just bag him like peelings and leave him out on the back steps for the collection."

"Well, boy," said Len, triumphantly. "You're not all scar-tissue and trousers. I wouldn't have given you credit, but you've cracked it."

From his pocket he drew out a huge bunch of keys and jangled them under Sasha's nose. "This is what I collected today. As from Monday I'm your new administrator, and that gives me unrestricted access to the lorries. All we need to lay on is a private pick-up, especially for your charming Legless."

Sasha was unhappy. "But he's not croaked yet." If only the policeman would die – if not from natural causes, then at least without any intervention from him.

"He will," said Len remorselessly. "He will."

Lev refused to help when Anna and Olga raised the body. Glazed blood underneath the head fragmented with the tiny crisping noise of fissuring ice-crystals. They dragged Legless round the corner and set him on the bathroom floor; reverently, Olga put his legs in line, crossed his arms over his chest; Anna, averting her eyes from the mutilated face, slid her fingers under the collar of the service tunic and adjusted the set of the lapels. Lev stood over them like a spectator at a street accident.

"This is inappropriate," he said slowly. "I told you, this man is not dead. Until he is, such ceremony does you no honour."

"How can you know?" asked his wife.

"Here, feel," answered her husband pushing up the policeman's sleeve and grasping the wrist. "He is warm. He sweats. He lives."

Anna drew back and began to weep silently. Lev allowed the arm to drop away on to the cork bathmat, destroying the coffin-like symmetry which Olga had devised.

Olga had hated and feared the man on the floor. The pathos of these last, intimate things made her giddy from suppressed feeling. As Lev picked over the corpse – in those moments of fierce despoliation she could not bear to imagine that the body was not lifeless – she envisioned Legless only as a victim. He was forever excluded from a world which this pile of incongruous objects had once made less unbearable and cruel simply by their familiarity. Once their very feel had reassured, but now that talismanic effect was exhausted. Legless had passed beyond touchstones.

One by one Lev threw them into the wash-basin: a cigarette lighter made from a rifle bullet, a torch pen, a Seiko digital watch with videogame still flickering, two tickets for the *Taganka*, and a shiny packet of American contraceptives. Trophies from the far side of the barbed wire where you were seated above the salt in strange company, united only by a taste for gadgetry. Such men are not peculiar to our own breed, she thought, but spring up everywhere when prizes are to be claimed. However paltry the booty, no one is above sacrificing anything or any person to demonstrate entitlement.

"What an adolescent he was," she muttered.

"Will have been," said Lev absently, pulling pockets inside out with the deftness of a man skinning a rabbit. "Your feeling is perverse. Once he was a small boy — what does that justify? What was done to *her*?" He passed Legless's warrant and Party cards to Anna. "Those he fed off will feed him one more time."

"What do you mean?" asked Olga, alarmed at the bitterness in Lev's voice.

Kuznetsov shrugged and turned away. "Go. You have no place here."

Bogat called to her from the Kuznetsovs' room. "Come and have a little sit-down, Olga Sergeyevna, you must be absolutely shattered."

In the absence of Len, his spirits had perked up significantly. With apparently little thought of the changed nature of the relationship between himself and the tenants he had, after dragging himself upright as the front door slammed behind Sasha and his friend, made for the place he had claimed as his own territory, where Anna and Lev had extended to him that same taciturn acceptance which had marked their relations before this afternoon's dire events. Things had been sufficiently transformed, however, for neither they to leave him in sole possession nor he to require them to leave.

In the electric samovar there had been enough water left over from the tea-making to wash off the last traces of blood. The wound throbbed but Bogat took pleasure in the sense of healing promoted by each twinge of the healthful antiseptic which Kuznetsova had so generously applied.

"Absolutely frightful, putting you through such an ordeal." The old sangfroid was returning, she thought. Was it sheer stupidity or was the man a boundless optimist? "I know just how you must feel . . ." Even his clothes, for heaven's sake, had been changed. In place of the Madras shirt he wore a roll-necked green cashmere, and his denims were pristine. Near murder seemed to have given him a curious *élan*, and he pulled on his cigarette like a man who had been dug up alive: gratitude, relief, and the craving for chatter dancing simultaneously on his lips.

"After all, we've come a long way together, you and I. You could say that now, in a way, there is really something between us."

He was calm, he was tidy, he was courteous. He believed every word he said. "Now that we are accessories . . . all topsy-turvy, Olga

Sergeyevna, but we can rise above it. You have so little experience of the real world."

That was all Legless now signified to him – the seal on a relationship which had only existed in his imagination, but which now he had transformed into a pact, a criminal liaison. For the first time she realised how much this little man had wanted to become part of her life and the lives of them all. They hated him, but his presence was now accepted and on that he could build. She had never seen him so relaxed, so curiously established, as if their compliance in his position was unforced. His reign of terror might be over but his cosiness was just beginning. The atmosphere of conspiracy was enjoyable to him.

"Enough," she said, "to know that Tanya and Rocky will never share the same fate."

"But you suffer and are guiltless. Where is the justice? You must forget such matters. Write, think of higher things."

Tanya, Boris, Marina?

"Why, I myself have been writing . . ."

"No!" shrieked Olga. "If you ever mention the word 'poem' to me again I shall go straight to the procurator's office and turn all of us in!"

By the time the plan had been thrashed out, it was ten o'clock. Len went straight to the depot, promising to return with a truck in one hour. Back in the flat, Sasha, hoping that Legless might cause them no further trouble by having already died, made a final check.

Reluctant to touch any exposed part of the policeman's flesh by rooting for a pulse at the wrist or in the bloodied grime of the neck, he put his ear to the great broad chest. When no heartbeat was discernible after several minutes of intense listening, Sasha could have given a cheer – Legless appeared to have settled his own hash – but to make doubly sure he took his own shaving mirror from the glass shelf of the wash-basin and held it before the policeman's mouth. At the touch of his warm fingers in the cold bathroom, the mirror fogged, so he wiped it and tried again. Whether or not the resultant misting was induced by Legless's expirations he could not tell. The technique obviously only worked in stories or on the pictures.

"Don't worry, Aleksandr Mikhailovich," said Bogat softly in his ear, in a voice tremulous with amusement. "For once in his life he's done the decent thing."

Sasha let the mirror fall to the floor. "You creepy little sod. I thought this was your friend."

"A business associate," said Bogat. "And there's no sentiment in business, don't they say?"

Sasha pushed him away. "That's a useful principle – now *we're* in partnership."

"Partnership?"

"Fifty-fifty on this one, right down the middle. You can start by getting that carpet off the wall."

To match his divan and give colour to the Kuznetsovs' drab room Bogat had splashed out on a carpet patterned with dusky crimson roses. Obediently he fetched it in, neatly rolled, the backing side outermost. Bogat knew what it was for and what they had to do. Both men heaved Legless to the side, laid out the carpet woven side up, then lifted the body on to one edge, and in silence and with care proceeded to cocoon it.

At first the arms flopped awkwardly. Bogat unhooked Lizaveta's washing line from over the bath and, making a wide noose of the twine, lashed them to the body. As he did so, the corpse broke wind and Sasha jumped back, releasing his hold, but Bogat carried on as if nothing had happened. When all was secure he crossed the outspread hands over Legless's crotch, patted down the knots at the wrists and sat back on his heels.

"Typical," he said. "The man never had any manners." Strapping down Legless took all the rope. As much again would be needed in order to make fast the roll they were to wrap round the body.

Sasha hunted round the bathroom for more.

"Bit late for etiquette, isn't it?" he grunted. "Now what do we use to keep him nicely tucked in?"

Bogat fingered the shower curtain. "Plastic. Couldn't get enough tension without it ripping. What about those?" He pointed to a bunch of wire coat hangers stacked above the shower pipe. "We could string them together and bale him up like that, but we'd need pliers to untwist them first. Got any?"

Sasha remembered that Valentina had borrowed his toolbag for the repairs at Marina's. "Not worth it," he said. "The old girl's bound to have a hank of twine or something. Start wrapping him and I'll go and find out."

During the struggle in the kitchen many of Lizaveta Ivanovna's jars had been toppled from the dresser, and the floor was slimy with brackish pickling brine. Too devastated by the ruin of her months of work to do more than sweep up the glass into a heap by the window, she had thrown her broom on to the squashy rinds of her preserves, and shambled off, weeping. Since then no one had set eyes on her.

The door opened so quickly to his knock that Sasha almost fell into the old woman's room. She fastened her dry little hands on his wrist.

"Ah, so it's you at last! Have they gone, those villains? Come here, come here, I've got something that will interest you."

"Yes, Gran, but I'm in a bit of a hurry. Have you got . . . ?"

"That can wait, whatever it is. Come here."

Sasha allowed himself to be drawn in, knowing from old that the sooner he yielded the sooner he would be allowed to state his errand.

It was a queer place, this room, another world which each night lay only a couple of inches from his sleeping head. You could hardly move for furniture – most of it junk – and there was a musty smell of odorferous beeswax, incense and heaps of unaired linen permeating the texture of every absorbent surface. When she sat him down facing her, across a round three-legged table on which an extinct candle in a blue and white holder stood next to a photograph of a baby with white-blond hair being cradled by an elderly man in pre-Revolutionary uniform, and a portable ikon of Christ in Judgement, this characteristic scent wafted to him from her clothes and the crocheted antimacassar behind his neck, like some churchy pomade.

The square walnut table and the inlaid wardrobe he knew; they had belonged to his Gran. Like the striped table-cloth with crinkly lace corners, too long for the table.

Beside Lizaveta's bed was a large empty birdcage in which she kept her clean linen, all freshly washed and ironed once a week. From her flat pillow a stuffed hedgehog fixed him with a bead-buttoned taxidermist's glare.

"You didn't think I could do it, did you?" she said, her eyes alive with malign self-gratification. "You thought I was an old fool."

"Nobody thinks you're a fool, Granny. What did you do?"

"The whole thing, I did the whole thing."

She lived among shadows, nourishing herself on the disesteem of others. Who knew what slynesses were being relished in that old noddle? Nothing would surprise him.

"What have you been up to, dearie? Threw in your hand with our lodgers, did you? Anything for a quiet life, eh?"

"There you are," she whispered, craning forward, her scrawny neck aquiver. "Trust you to say that. See how the plague infects – none but the good is unscourged. Say the wrong, do the wrong! I chastised them, you infidel. I, *I* chastised them."

"Gave them a piece of your mind, did you, Granny? Well, good for you. Now, like I said, I'm a bit pushed for time and I was wondering . . ."

"I slew him!" exclaimed Lizaveta, half-rising and grasping the fallen ikon.

If she didn't shut up soon, Len would be round the back with the truck.

"Ah," said Sasha. "That's the way it was, was it? You did for the big lad with the bottle? You won't mind me carrying on the good work then — so if you've a bit of . . ."

"What use was your brawn?" cried the old woman. "I took thought, and acted upon thought. Here, you purblind man, read if you can."

She held out a piece of paper folded into a concertina-like ribbon.

"I never thought such depravity existed in this world."

The folds were so creased and stained that at first Sasha had difficulty in making out what the paper was meant to be. Some sort of letter? But there was no addressee's name and the signature appeared to be cut away. As he struggled with the stilted handwriting he had an obscure sense of something familiar. It *was* a letter, and it was dirty — in both senses of the word. All that impassioned despair tricked out in very rude words, the furtive excitement of the writer leading to a disgusting, an unspeakable climax. That was what it was! The letter from the provincial copper, the filth in the sticks, the one he'd snitched from Tanya's horror-bag over a year ago and lost, dropped from his sleeve when Bobby was still his girl, all that time past.

"Lying about, that was, in the passage for anyone to find, months since. Goodness knows why I picked it up. And I kept it, thank the Lord, I kept it, for it was a sign, a favour from above."

"You haven't read it, though, have you, Granny?" asked Sasha, aghast at what effect such disclosures might have had on an old lady.

Lizaveta clasped her hands piously at her throat. "Not exactly," she said. "Just enough to get the gist."

He shivered and gazed at the inscrutable hedgehog. "You were lucky they never caught you with it. That's pornography, that is."

She snorted. "That big one couldn't have found the end of his nose. But I did *show* it to him."

"You did what?"

"I showed it to him," said Lizaveta imperturbably.

"When?"

"This afternoon. I showed it to Yuri Petrovich when he came in to ask about watching football."

"What for?"

"Well, that was it, you see. May I be forgiven, but I told a lie. I told him that the Rocky creature had dropped it, and it was a letter from his friend, and that there were others, ever so many, and they

324

were *worse*, and did he think it right for policemen to be writing to each other about such frightful things?"

"But you couldn't have cared about that, surely? After the misery they made of your life over the last few months. You were making mischief, weren't you?"

"Of course," said Lizaveta proudly. "And it came to more than that in the end."

"Why, what happened?"

"Outright dissension, that's what. I knew it would, once that Yuri got over his surprise. Very pleased with himself, he was. A very serious matter, that, he said, a disciplinary matter, the sort of thing that would do a man no good in his career. It was an imb . . . *imbroglio*, he said he'd discovered, there might be dozens in it, from the highest to the lowest. I remember every word. 'Lizaveta Ivanovna,' he said, smartening himself up in front of my long mirror. 'My duty is clear: this nest of vipers must be wiped out.'"

"He said that about his mates?"

"He did. However drunk he may have been, he said it, like out of a book, with hardly a slur in his voice."

Then Legless wasn't so thick after all. The chance of some tidy little blackmail had come his way. He could have had Bogat paying out, too, as well as getting his own back for all those snubs and gibes. Crafty. Fancy fluffing it – he could have retired on the earnings. They should teach better man-management at police school. More of that, and he wouldn't have waved that letter under Rocky's nose when they were both as paralytic as ticks in a brew-house.

"You know what happened after?" asked Sasha, breaking into a smile. You had to admit the old crow had style.

Lizaveta nodded. "The flat *shook* with their beastly din. Is he dead?"

"Nearly. You got the wrong one though, Gran. The real bastard hopped it."

"Oh no, I knew my man," said Lizaveta composedly. "It was the big one I wanted. That swine took my son's watch."

Her hard-backed chair creaked as she raised herself. "But he shan't go unhallowed. Hand me that book, and take me to him. But first, what was it you wanted?"

Bogat insisted on washing his hands, then lined up beside Sasha, wiping them dry on his jumper as the makeshift ceremony began in the overcrowded bathroom.

"What a godless pair you make," muttered Lizaveta, picking burrs of carpet thread off the dustman's shirt. "Stand up straight, for

Christ's sake, as the soldiers should have when they diced for His robe. Does either of you know a prayer?"

Bogat stepped forward brightly. "Me, Granny. I know some prayers. Do you want me to say one?"

"Not to me," said Lizaveta. "To yourself, silently, – and to God."

Bogat was the last person she would have thought of as religiously instructed. The notion annoyed her. "Aren't you an atheist, young man?"

"I think so," said Bogat. "But my Gran wheeled me to Novodyev-ichii and got me baptised in my pram, just in case the Communists were wrong. An atheistical Bolshevik Orthodox, that's me – just like Josip Vissarionovich and Leonid Ilyich."

He grinned, but Lizaveta was on her knees by the roll of carpet, her mouth working soundlessly. In her hands she clasped the unopened prayer-book.

Neither man followed suit but Sasha, unlike Bogat, would not join in the devotional mumble. Legless had taken almost everything off him, and he was damned if he was going to have his prayers too. It was grotesque, interceding for that great pillock.

Anyway, they didn't even know if he were dead. Perhaps the prayers would finish him off, and save them all a job. Bastard. Crucifixion would have been too good for him. No TV where he's going. Unless it's closed-circuit so they can monitor his eternal pangs. What will his fiancée do? Cry a bit, God help her, then look for another prick in uniform. Push off, stop hanging about, you lead-swinger. Do us a favour. Croak. Go to hell.

Bogat shut his eyes and crossed himself.

I knew it, thought Sasha. Stark-bollock crazy.

"There, I've done my duty," muttered Lizaveta at last.

"Now I can get on with mine," said Sasha shoving a bundle of rope over Bogat's clasped hands. "By making this little creep finish hobbling his lost shepherd."

"Don't be too down on the chap," said Bogat reproachfully. "'Out of the strong comes forth sweetness and out of the hunter comes forth meat.' Isn't that right, Lizaveta Ivanovna?"

Sasha left Bogat to do the final trussing up and went in search of Lev. The Kuznetsovs had watched the carpet being dismantled from the wall and there was little explaining to do. Lev seemed to have been long prepared for action, and was sitting in Bogat's cane armchair, his black sheepskin already on, hat and fur gloves at his knee.

It took three of them to manoeuvre the bulky parcel out of the

narrow bathroom, down the passage and into the hall. At the front
door they stopped while Bogat slipped into his long suede coat.

"Now, which hat?"

Scanning the selection he kept on the hallstand, he chose a five-
hundred-rouble pastel beige mink. "This is the most seemly, I think,
unostentatious without being totally subdued."

In the glass, he adjusted the front lip of the fur so that it came
down over the sticking plaster on his forehead.

"Tell me," said Sasha. "Doesn't anything bother you for long?"

"Oh no, not now, not since a boy. You see, at the same time as
full-time employment, I took up poetry. Art on regular wages irons
out the bumps of the most recalcitrant experience, don't you think?"

Although the back steps led directly to the courtyard below, there
was always the chance at this time of night, when garbage pails were
being tipped out all over Moscow, that they could bump into some
inquisitive housewife on one of the landings who would demand to
know (if she didn't believe they were burglars) where they had
managed to buy such a fine roll of carpeting, how much they had
paid, and how on earth they could afford it, anyway?

Sasha, more fearful of the lighted street, where people might stare
at their motley group staggering under a load which any one of them
ought to have been able to sling over his shoulder, was for brazening it
out with the Grannies, but Lev took charge and insisted on openness:

"It would be less suspicious via the front."

They compromised and took the lift.

The cabin was small and so low in comparison to the height of the
upright roll that Bogat, having made a guess at the position of
Legless's waist, forced his head against the spot and pulled from
above so that the carpet and contents buckled in the middle. In this
manner they succeeded in stacking their bundle in the far corner, to
which they all then crowded, in order to prevent it sagging over
completely. Once in the main lobby, Sasha was deputed, again at
Lev's instigation, to carry the roll. With the weight distributed across
his wide shoulders and Bogat walking close behind clutching the tight
bands of rope, Sasha stumbled down the steps, stoopbacked, like the
fairy-tale woodcutter under his fardel.

Lev kept look-out through a chink in the main door. When the
Embassy policeman in his *valyenki* stumped over to the ground-floor
flat a few yards from his box, lit a cigarette and began watching the
colour TV through an uncurtained window, Lev tugged at Sasha's
collar and they all managed to round the corner into the archway
without being spotted. Halfway across the empty court, Sasha's legs

were giving way. With a soft thump he deposited Legless across a see-saw in the kiddies' playground before sprawling exhausted into the snow. When he recovered his breath, Lev was by the huge skip at the roadside which Len had fixed on as their point of rendezvous.

Bogat took a folded sheet of newspaper from his pocket, shook it out to the fullest extent, placed it across the other end of the see-saw and hopped over, astride. Taking off his gloves, he cooled his hands by impressing them on the thin dusting of snow along the plank. A slight breeze whined through the telephone wires which spanned the court, and the chained-up swings creaked at their tacklings. Nothing was said as they listened for the heavy churr of Len's truck to come within earshot. Shouts and the clank of car doors floated across with the sub-zero wind from Arbat square, where, in front of the Praga Restaurant, a line of limousines was being marshalled one by one on to the underpass road. All around lights were going out at the curtainless windows of the tenements.

Bogat played with the snow, absorbed as a child succumbing to the necessity of patience, and the oppressive desolation of the playground with its dismal wooden bear lowering over the metal jungle frames and brightly-striped shells of the matchwood pretend-houses. The carpet roll slid down a few inches as he stretched out to reach the snow lying untouched at the fulcrum of the bar, and he hutched back quickly, not wanting to lose the enjoyable springiness at his end of the see-saw which had been maintained by the counter-poised weight of Legless's body.

As he was about to make the final movement to set himself down at the right point, the roll of carpet convulsed. A leg, plainly visible beneath the canvas back, flexed and stiffened. As Bogat came down on his end of the see-saw, the entire bundle writhed, and from its interior was trumpeted a vast, orgasmic roar. Rather than being muffled by the material through which it emerged, the sound seemed to gain in volume from the tubelike form of the roll and streamed out into the frosty air, resonating with a kind of bestial ire. At the same moment, the cylinder of carpet appeared to kick itself off the plank seat, and the sudden release of weight threw Bogat sideways into a drift, while the corpse fell blindly writhing across a heap of overturned dustbins.

Sasha scrambled to his feet, casting about for some weapon to club down the wriggling horror, overcome by feelings of helplessness and the intense desire to still the hidden movement which, as a boy, he had experienced when his mother plucked from their roosts hens which had long since ceased to lay, and had forced them, head down, into a sack. But Bogat was less squeamish, and the dustman stood by incredulous, as the little man flung his entire body over the bundle, wrestling with it like a madman, cursing and striking out in a flurry of snow-dabbled blows.

The bins crashed apart in the struggle, rolling with loud, cheerful clatters on to a paved area around the children's sand-box. Bogat's voice seethed with the filthiest words as in fury and terror he smashed at the hideously twisting and turning bundle. Interspersed throughout the play-area were clumps of birches, their ghostly barks white in the darkness. With a bound Sasha caught at one of the outspread branches, clamped down the end under his boot and wrenched out the bough from its trunk-knot. Wielding the branch like a threshing-flail, he set to, driving inexorably down at the thing in the carpet, pounding at it, detached from all thought that it could be human the moment his body settled to the rhythm of the overhead swing. Bogat clung over the roll, his limbs outflung, gasping, urging him on to bring the nerve paroxysms to a termination by crushing in the head. After many blows, it was done and Sasha flung himself down, branch and all, on the place where the first screams had eddied out, bursting the silence of the night.

Lev had not moved from his post. Now he turned, surveying the few twinkling lights left in the blocks round the court, watching and listening for any sign that the scene had been witnessed or noticed. Only the wind was audible once more, its gentle flow lisping on the wires where the snow-dust teetered, whirled up in an occasional sharp gust, only to be precipitated again in a fine mist which filled out the crevices in the rough timber of the telegraph poles.

Nothing had happened.

The hiss of air-brakes came to them through the stillness as, a quarter of a mile away, Len's truck churned through the winding, uncleared back streets. Lev semaphored its approach by windmilling his arms. This time, neither man wanted to touch the bundle in any way which could revive their sense of its containerised humanity. Grasping the outer lashings of the roll they finally dragged it, bumping and jerking across the potholes, and laid it to rest along the shadowed side of the skip.

The truck had appeared at the intersection to the right, and came trundling slowly towards them, headlights doused. By the time the tail-gate came within reach, they were ready.

Len's original idea had been to take one of the snow-lorries. He would load up slush from the street clearance gangs which worked most of the night in the centre of town, and dump the body in the Moskva at the normal tipping point. But, even at night, something might easily have gone wrong: the gangers were nosey; he would be extra to the night's shift; and, even if they reached the river, there was no guarantee that their cargo would submerge with the snow and not float up in a couple of days' time to attract the attention of scavengers.

On summer jaunts, when he had once or twice taken fat Natalie picnicking to the outskirts of a village some twenty miles north-west of the city, he had been angered by the nearness of a dump for industrial waste. The locals complained that the effluent was polluting their stream and killing the fish. In summer, it was a haven for young misfits and hooligans. In winter it would be desolate. Planted deep down, there was a good chance that Legless would not split his cocoon before the spring rains.

On the way out, there was no trouble. Once off the highway and away from the State Automobile Patrol, they had a free road. It was after midnight when they left the snow-packed trail and hit out, cross-country, for the final two miles to the dump. The moon hung low and pale. Inside the cab the four men were drowsy from the engine's warmth.

"Nobody cops out of this one," said Len. "We're all in it, up to our necks." They knew what he meant. Sasha comforted himself: if Legless, after that beating and this journey, rose again, it would be to perdition on the Day of Judgement, not to glory tonight amidst the tin-cans and bunting discarded from the last village May Day.

From a distance it had looked like the flattened spoil heap of a mine. But when they jumped down from the truck near the crinkle-crankle concrete fencing which enclosed the base of the dump, the vileness of its constituent mishmash sickened them. The great mass of it was tons and tons of oil rag and cotton waste, the outscourings of demolished workshops and factories. Repeated tippings had exerted tremendous pressure on the filthy, soft fabrics and from the interior, wisps of steam escaped through vents in the snow. In the cruel frost at the edges far away from the buried fires, brilliant heaps of metallic refuse, the spirals of huge industrial lathe-turnings, scintillated and winked in the cloudless moonlight. On the concrete slabs of the fencing was the evidence of summertime habitation: swastikas; a crudely incised message in foot high characters: KILL JEWS; slogans for Army Central and aerosolled obscenities about the CPSU. It was plain to Sasha why at this time of year and even in daytime, no one with a care for his life would stray into the neighbourhood.

"Lord God above," whispered Lev. "What better abomination could You have chosen?"

They stood to the roll like pall-bearers, one at each corner. Finding a part where the concrete had been shattered, they passed through the fence at a trot and plunged into the spongy tip. The outlying debris was looser and, at first the going was hard. Eventually, they reached solid footing on the impacted material, unslung the carpet roll and threw it into a deep channel in the melting snow. Len and Bogat had brought spades, but their cutting-edges were blunted by the dense wadding which extended everywhere beneath the snow. Lev produced a switchblade and began to slice, fashioning the outline of a coffin in the putrefying rags. The others squatted on their haunches, watching him and smoking. When he had cut deep enough, they rose as one man and wrenched out the stuff, hollowing a shallow grave. That done, they turned to the body.

It was a moment's work to cut the ropes and unroll the carpet. The face was unrecognisable. Sasha's beating must have broken every bone in Legless's head. Two large front teeth lay at a crazy angle at the corner of what had been his mouth. There was little blood. Only some greyish matter, the consistency of unwashed tripe hung from the smashed nose.

"Right," said Len, pushing the fur hat back from his forehead. "This is it." After kissing his companions twice, once on each cheek, he took the knife and knelt over Legless. The knife, remarkably clean of blood, was then passed to Sasha. When the blade touched, he shut his eyes and did not press it down. Len forced his hand and Sasha felt wetness on the haft. Bogat was swift and business-like. Afterwards he turned to Lev, passing over the switchblade.

"To you, my friend, is reserved the privilege of the *coup de grâce*."

When Lev, with one swift movement, severed the head, Sasha retched.

"OK," said Len taking hold of Legless's feet. "Let's get on with it."

"One moment more," cried Lev, staying the big man's arm. He fumbled in the pocket of his padded jacket. "Here," he shrieked. "Eat! The vomit returns to the dog."

Before anyone could stop him, he had opened the jaws of the bodiless head and rammed down its throat the warrant card of the corpse, and the card which conferred upon it the duties and privileges of a member of the Communist Party of the Soviet Union.

36

"It's absolutely frightful," drawled Marina Andreyevna. "The class of person you find in clubs nowadays."

She had already drained half a tumbler of Sibirskaya, and there was no sign of the cortège.

"Once you had to be someone to get past the doorman. Give me the drink, my dear — it's over there by the window."

Valentina Dmitryevna fetched the bottle and stood by Marina, holding it up by the neck in front of the television. A good third had gone.

"Think you should, lovey? It's still rather early . . ."

"Give it here, woman!" exclaimed Marina, snatching at Valentina's skirt and pointing at the screen. "Too damned late for *some*, isn't it? I may not be far behind, but while I am I shall take great relish in confronting *his* oblivion with a glass in my hand."

Obediently the widow filled up the tumbler, and went back to her rush-bottomed seat in the corner of the *dvornik*'s poky room from where she continued to watch the television in silence.

Between the white half-pillars of the Hall of Columns was a vastly blown-up photograph, almost obscuring the green façade. At each side fluttered scarlet flags. Overcoated figures in trilby hats bobbed around the entrance.

"Look at them," went on Marina. "Our betters. Men in fedoras trying to sell us insurance."

The Baranovs were sitting together on the sofa exchanging glances, and Valentina gave a little cough to remind the old woman that they were in company.

Marina screwed round her head and coughed back, very loudly. "You don't mind an old lady's sourness, dears, do you? The milk has long since curdled in these mortal breasts."

Baranov adjusted his tie, sucking noisily on his empty pipe. His wife squeezed closer to him on the *bergère* which matched Valentina's chair, fanning herself with a paper doily. Every window and door was banged fast shut. Baranova had a terror of fresh air and the heat was stifling.

"No ruderies, please," said Valentina. "You promised to be on your best behaviour."

Marina peered at the seated couple, indifferent to the widow's reproof. The Baranovs fell into whispered conversation and Marina called out into the shadows behind them: "Olga Sergeyevna, what are you doing hiding yourself away, back there? Tell them – It was a club, wasn't it?"

Olga's face was practically invisible. "Yes, Marina Andreyevna, it was a club."

"Ivan Aleksandrovich," barked Marina. "Pay attention when intelligent people speak."

The *dvornik*'s life was lived at the behest of women. How could a janitor survive without rubbing up against them day in day out, at every turn of the stair? He hearkened, dolefully. "What do you read, Ivan Aleksandrovich – newspapers?"

"Of course, Marina Andreyevna. Every day."

"Every day, every day, and every day for more than sixty years we have scanned the newspapers hoping that we are not, by some terrible accident, mentioned in them."

Baranov read the weather forecast, and the television schedules, anything else was too densely glum to do more than flick over.

"Those dear to me once figured in the newspapers, and in that morgue," said the old woman. Her heavy wedding ring made a small clatter as she banged the screen.

"Ah!" shuddered Valentina, her lush bosom goose-pimpling from nostalgia. "Wondrous days of blizzards and roses, caparisoned sleighs at the portico with drivers in pine-marten cloaks."

"Valya, you have a house-serf's soul. I am talking of quite another time, with quite another Social Register." Marina continued to follow her thoughts aloud with no sense, except to herself, of the relevance of what she said while Valentina sat back, prinking the dolman sleeves of her cardigan, content to let her old lady out on her alcoholically-extended lead. Today, was to be a holiday and a celebration for the two women, if for no one else.

"That was where my uncle was arraigned and tried and condemned and led to some noisome place of execution . . ." Marina's voice broke.

"There, there," interrupted Valentina. "Don't take on so, dearie. I told you it would end in tears. Look on the bright side. At least *he* won't be coming back."

Everyone realised that she did not mean Marina's uncle.

"What are you talking about?" shouted Marina who, in this mood, could abandon prostration for rage without observable transit. "Who do you think *he* is, that desiccated policeman with the pig-stuck eyes and Himmler gold rims? That refrigerated mad-doctor, that's *him*. *He* got back!"

After a pause, Marina's face assumed a genteel melancholy to which Vera Grigoryevna instantly reacted by parting her lips in a sympathetic smile and clasping her hands under the point of her chin. "Doesn't it ever strike you," began the old woman, "doesn't it give you that horrible empty feeling inside to see Moscow, our beautiful city of Moscow, thronged on this day with mourners . . ."

Vera elbowed her husband who inserted his pipe between his knees, thus freeing himself to adopt a pose of uncluttered respect.

". . . Drawn from the ranks . . ."

"Drawn from the ranks," murmured the couple, caught up in the solemnity of Marina's prelude.

". . . of the biggest collection brought together under one roof, of larcenists . . ."

"Larcenists" was an ethnic group new to the *dvornik* and his wife, but they let it pass.

". . . pimps, black-marketeers, bawds, time-servers, crooks, racketeers, fiddlers, Nazis and policemen . . ."

A loud male voice put a stop to her attack.

"Marina Andreyevna, you're a seditious old bag. Stop pestering defenceless folk like Baranov. You don't know any better, but neither does he. So let's call truce."

It was Sasha from his chair by the sideboard where Vera Grigoryevna had laid out *zakuski*, iced vodka and sweet Georgian wine. For half an hour everyone, except Valentina, had been trying to freeze him out. Although all threats and harassment had ceased after Len had spelled out to Bogat on the drive back from the dump, that the positions were reversed and now they held him in *their* power, the secret of Legless's death had to be kept from outsiders. While the Baranovs and Marina still retained their suspicions that Sasha was not quite straight, Olga was sure that he was an out-and-out collaborator, especially since Bogat now stuck to him like glue.

"I'm not a deeply political man," said Valentina's taxi-driver friend, who was on his first public outing with the widow and felt obliged to distance them both from Marina's slanders. "But at times like these, when we are in the presence of death, I think that such remarks are quite uncalled-for."

He looked round for support, but nobody spoke. "I mean, it comes to something when we can't pay our respects without Goebbels-like propaganda being . . ."

"Oh dry up, Mikhail Dmitryevich," Sasha called out. "You're no lily-white boy. Where did that turkey come from, the Polish one you had for New Year? Or did you reckon that 'self-service' down that shop meant help yourself and forget about paying?"

The taxi-driver went pink. "That was different, that wasn't stealing, not really. It was more in the way of a protest."

"Protest! What have you got to protest about — that tourists are more fly nowadays and want more than a tenner for a packet of American fags? Rolling in contraband you lot are, everyone knows."

"It was a protest, wasn't it, Valya?" He appealed to the widow. "We wanted to go to Australia."

Valentina retained a soft spot for Sasha and was the only person not to ostracise him. She giggled, and dropped half a biscuit into the mouth of Bootik, the *dvornik*'s dog. "I had to tell him, Aleksandr Mikhailovich, that it would have to be the long way round, via Tel Aviv, so he purloined our dinner out of sheer aggravation."

Even Olga smiled as the taxi-driver swayed in his chair at this betrayal of a confidence. Vera Grigoryevna anxiously handed round plates.

"There'll be no dust-ups here, *if* you please," she said with dignity, regretting that she had invited Sasha to her little television party in the first place. "Not on a day of bereavement." Her eyes filled with tears over the charger of pies. "All those flags and drums. So affecting. It's them left behind I'm sorry for."

"Hah!" blurted Marina. "Aren't we all?"

Sasha meanwhile was leaning back in his comfortable armchair, anaesthetised by Baranova's vodka and the soupy Tchaikovsky. A day off was a day off. It was warm and he was full.

Just as he was falling into a doze, Olga tapped his shoulder. "Someone wants you," she said tersely. "Your baby-faced detective friend."

A figure hovered in the vestibule, its back to the light. Sasha got to his feet slowly, propping his smoky-blue goblet between the side cushions to mark his prior occupancy of the chair. All the others made your behind sore. As he went to the door Olga said something he couldn't catch, and the women burst into peals of laughter.

Bogat stood in the shadows, unusually smart. Under his short wolf jacket was a dark suit, white shirt, and navy-blue tie dotted all over with a dollar-sign motif.

"Thought you'd be at the parade," yawned Sasha.

"Hardly," said Bogat in the subdued tones which were now habitual to him after the Legless débâcle. "It's my job to keep people away from it. A note for you, Aleksandr Mikhailovich." Saluting, he handed

Sasha a thick green envelope. Inside was a buff card: "Come to lunch. M."

Sasha turned over the card and finding no other message, sniffed it. The cream-laid surface smelled of lily-of-the-valley.

"There's a car," added Bogat.

"A what?"

"You know, black, with wheels and everything." Sasha followed him to the main door. A long black car, its motor running, was parked by the kerb.

"Yours?"

"Yours," said Bogat.

Sasha had no coat and the cold was biting. The driver got out, came round to the near side and opened the back door.

"What about you?" Sasha asked.

"Oh, I'm not on the invitation list," said Bogat. "But you'd better accept – otherwise they'll demote me to bicycles."

The driver stood quite still. The interior of the car looked very warm and very plush. The upholstery was scarlet, and there were curtains and polished ashtrays.

"Come on," Bogat insisted. "You'll catch your death out here."

"Only a short drive," said the chauffeur. He wore black leather gloves.

Bogat moved off. "Hey!" shouted Sasha. "Where are you going? This is a set-up, isn't it?"

"Now, do us a favour, Aleksandr Mikhailovich," called Bogat from the entry. "What kind of meat wagon is that? You're on a date, and it doesn't do to keep ladies waiting."

Strains of the *Pathétique* percolated through the grille of the *dvornik*'s ground-floor window. The procession was lining up.

"We shall be late," said the chauffeur politely. "And I have my instructions."

She certainly had a sense of humour, choosing today. "It's not a kidnapping, then?" said Sasha. The chauffeur smiled, running his eyes over Sasha's strong frame. "Not at all," he said. "A perfect match, I would have thought, age-wise."

For a moment Sasha hesitated, then slid across the bench seat to the other side of the car. As they pulled away, Bogat was nowhere to be seen.

On the south-east outskirts, the car was joined by a lone motor-cyclist who led the way down the wide highway. Soon there was nothing but forest on either side. For twenty minutes Sasha lolled in luxurious quietude. The engine could hardly be heard, there was little other traffic and the chauffeur was isolated from him by an electrically-operated panel. Sasha inspected himself in the glass. A good thing he'd bothered to shave that morning.

What did she want? If it were her. Come to think of it, "M" wasn't much to go on. "M" on a scented card. Bogat could have a pile of them. Or Rocky. Rocky was supposed to have been transferred. Where to, even Bogat didn't know. Just up his street, this, to issue a summons in the form of a *billet-doux*.

A wave of self-pity came over Sasha. Nobody would care if he got swallowed up in Rocky's hidey-hole. Valentina was fixed up with her cheapskate taximan, and gormless about old Marina. Len was with Jenny. Olga Sergeyevna still thought he took backhanders. Nobody cared.

Suddenly the motor-cycle swung right into an unmade-up road. Sasha was thrown sideways against the soft upholstery as the car followed. The motor-cyclist pulled over to the ditch and stopped. As Sasha sped past, he saluted. After two or three minutes bouncing over snow-covered ruts they came to a pair of low gates. Beyond the gates several highish buildings showed up beneath the omnipresent pine trees. The driver spoke into a microphone on the dashboard and the gates silently parted.

Some distance away from the high blocks, in a vast forest clearing surrounded by a chain-link stockade, Sasha saw what looked like a single-storey hunting lodge of grandiose proportions with pointed gables and fretted decorative work around the windows. At the tower block farthest from the gateway the car halted by the foot of a flight of steps. The driver came round and opened the door.

"Through there, and straight ahead," he said, pointing up to massive oaken doors. Above the lintel was a monstrous frieze of real elk horns. A couple of dozen beasts must have perished to make up the trophy.

"Do a lot of shooting, do they?" asked Sasha nervously.

"Inside," went on the driver impersonally, without answering, "you'll come to an elevator. You want the top floor."

Sasha gazed at the horns. "Twenty minutes will do it, I should think, so don't shift the car. I'll need you. This place looks off the bus route."

The chauffeur was unsmiling. "I am sorry but I can only take orders from my employers."

The car drove off.

There were no guards, no dogs, no policemen. Sasha had never seen a spot so devoid of the authorities. There was no point getting frostbite on the steps, so he followed the chauffeur's instructions and began slowly to climb the icy stairs. His legs were rather wobbly after the car journey and Vera's drink sloshed round in his empty stomach.

The wooden doors weighed a ton, and there were more inside, then plain glass ones. He stepped on to a chequerboard marble floor surrounded by tall, open storage cupboards stuffed with skis, toboggans, and pairs of enormous boots. The elevator, a wooden-panelled affair with a deep carpet, mirrors and even an armchair, stood open. All around was so uncannily hushed that he expected a robot voice to come out of the wall and ask him what his business was. The moment he stepped inside, the lift doors snake-hissed shut behind him. On the vertical row of buttons which glowed in the brushed aluminium cabin, there was none saying "open". Overhead were more elks: two stuffed heads with enough antlers to hang the hats of a football team were locked in combat on the ceiling. He patted the nose of the less despondent.

The top floor was ten on the control panel. The lift whooshed upwards and stopped almost immediately. The doors opened as quietly as they had closed.

Before him was a plain carpet the colour of moss, stretching under an archway between white walls. Through the archway was a room bigger than the whole of his communal flat, expensively and elaborately furnished. The walls of the room were entirely of plate glass. It was like stepping out on to a high platform without guard rails. The tops of black trees fell away on two sides; at another lay the broad sweep of forest, and a superb view of the city.

He was attracted by another view of Moscow in a florid gilt frame which hung from one of the archway walls. Tiny figures were setting up vegetable stalls under awnings tacked to the Kremlin wall. Things hadn't changed much. The intense light took some getting used to. White leather chairs and smoked glass tables, scattered around the room amongst the antique veneers of clock-cases and briar-dark tables, vibrated with preternatural clarity. At the far end, blocked off by an orangery of dwarf palm trees and rhododendrons, was yet another room out of which music floated down to him. Halfway across the carpet he realised that he had been pursued by the drear schmaltz of Tchaikovsky's sixth symphony. The Andante was still treacling out from the same TV programme he had been watching at Baranova's. He looked at his watch. Someone must have a video-recorder. This was the supporting feature. By now the big picture should be on.

This room was on a more human scale. By the huge colour set were wall-shelves of varying depths for the display of books, two marble busts of Stalin, artists' paintbrushes and palette, a cluster of photographs in hammered silver frames and a big, brass-fitted globe of the world. In one corner stood a set of virginals. The sofa and armchairs matched those outside but in addition there were some tiny ebony chairs with red satin cushions. Quite useless for sitting on, he found out, as soon as he tried.

On the screen the procession was still forming up in replay.

37

"Anyone at home?"

Not a stir. He shouted louder. Somewhere below there was a clangour like that of shoes falling down a fire-escape ladder and Marya Fyodorovna's head appeared through the floor by the book-stacks.

"Good God, man," she said. "I thought you were being raped."

Light filtered through the straw-coloured blinds, picking out the saffron gleams in her tawny hair. Since there were no railings above ground, Sasha had not noticed the spiral staircase.

"I was lonely," he said. "Posh places make me shy. You haven't got any bonecrushers up here by any chance, have you? That chauffeur was a bit stone-faced."

Marya rose fully into view.

"I suppose I should have realised what a touchy little bugger you are. I sent you a message, didn't I? What would you rather have done – walked it?"

"I could have taken a taxi."

"Taxi!" she exclaimed. "No taxi driver could get within miles of this neck of the woods. Strictly out of bounds, you are, my chuck."

Dressed appropriately enough in black, she looked oddly juvenile. The skinny button-through jumper with the tight sleeves which came to a point of stiff gold filigree just above the knuckles, had an air of something from the dressing-up box, and the contrast of stuffs was operatic and swashbuckling. Her skirt was longish and, to Sasha, gorgeously tight: you could just glimpse the stockings below the swish of the flounce which enabled her to move with that swift, energetic step which he always associated with her. The ballet-like pumps stitched with jet round the open-work instep had been chosen pur-posely to show off the slenderness of her feet and ankles. A thin line of beads, the pebble flotsam of a Latvian beach, hung down to her knees.

She picked two cigarettes out of a milky-green glass box, fitted one into a long amber holder and threw the other to Sasha, then flung herself into a leather armchair, her back to the television.

"Sit down, then," she said with an imperious wave.

He perched on the edge of one of the tiny hard chairs, feeling hot and rather foolish, not daring to light his cigarette in case any relaxation caused his weight to snap the legs.

"Well, isn't this nice?" she said, stretching out. "Company at last."

"Do you live here on your own, then?"

She gestured round the room. "A freak bird in a gilded cage, lovey, that's me. One who even changes her own water but pecks only the most exotic seed. I've always been like that: a non-alcoholic loner who makes her own amusements. Not that there's any lack of comedians making me offers."

You bet, he thought, running his eye up her legs. Blokes with their own cars, for a start, and certificated roubles. The type that brought their girlfriends French silk underwear from Romania and showered banknotes on the populace from the upper level of the Slavanskii Bazaar. He knew them. So did Bogat.

Perhaps she was lonely, amongst that shower. It didn't seem too feasible, though.

They'd have a better class of jokes than his.

"Now, why don't you relax?" she said. "I've got some news for you." Sasha stared round the room. "Stop worrying!" she went on testily. "Nothing's going to climb out of the sofa and manacle you. Oh hell, let's get it out of the way otherwise you're going to be too boring."

The leather creaked as she hauled herself up. Pushing aside the big globe she began to revolve a calibrated knob apparently fixed to the wall. He watched her back, and the tigerish stripes made by her hair and the black of the jersey.

"Blasted tumblers," she muttered clicking the disc to left and right. "They've got the temperament of ballerinas." The skirt hugged up as she twisted out the combination.

A few yards from him on a round table was a collection of sea-shells. Attracted by the fossil-shape of one, he abandoned the boudoir chair and went over. It was a nautilus. He recognised the whorl-shape from an old book of engravings his grandmother had shown him when he was small. He pressed his fingers into the uncrusted flutings, trying to recover his childhood sense of some great grey sea through which this creature had pulsed, secreted inside its gay, unturning wheel.

Marya's little bitten nails closed over his hand. "Daddy's," she said. "And very precious."

Under her arm was a big cardboard file fastened with tapes at top and bottom. Pushing the shells gently aside with her elbow, she set the file down.

"All yours," she said. "Take it away and read it."

Sasha put his hand to the tape-bows.

"Not here!" she exclaimed. "This is my *sanitarnii dyen* – cleaning-up time. Business is over for today."

"I'm no reader," said Sasha. "You ought to know that, Marya Fyodorovna."

"Marya, say Marya. I want to hear you say it." She pouted her lips. "M . . . Marya . . ."

She touched his face. "That's so nice. Did you know that men's scars are really s . . . ?"

"Marya, what's in that file?"

"One of the things you wanted. I've been feeling generous since I saw you last." She put up her face and brushed his mouth, not kissing him properly. Her lips were dusted with powder the colour of blanched rose. For the first time it occurred to him that she had prepared herself, because in the flat pumps she stood very little taller than him. His throat went dry as she held his hands to her hips and circled, dabbing kisses at his neck and on the rough underside of his chin. "That's good," she whispered, her mouth moving up to his ear. "That's very good. Who would have thought it? Who will believe you . . . ?"

No woman had ever made up to him in quite this way before. It was relaxing and energising at the same time.

"Aren't you clever?" said Marya. "Look what you can do to me, think what you can do to me, imagine what I'll let you do to me, kiss me all over, put your hand up my skirt, undress me ever so slowly, wet me, lick me, your tongue . . ."

"Marya, Marya," he said quietly. "Is this just one of your afternoon games?"

"Oh God, enjoy yourself," she murmured. "It's more, much more than that."

As he gripped her waist hard a sound of coughing and rustling and the stamping of feet filled the air. For some reason the television had switched itself on.

They were back in Pushkin Street. He shouted: "I don't bloody believe it! Where's the 'off' button? Marya, turn the bloody thing off!"

She whirled round an armchair so that it faced the screen, and leant low over the back, hitching up the elegant skirt to her knees. "Anything, anything while it's on, anything you like," she said, her face almost buried in the cushion. "That's what I want. I want you to do anything you like."

No woman had ever given Sasha *carte blanche* before, and the licence was stimulating.

"As long as I don't switch channels, is that right?" he asked, tugging at his belt.

"Right. Not before the end."

He leant right over, the smooth taffeta cool on his groin, and buried his hands in her coarse, fox-brush hair. It felt more wiry than he had imagined, and so thick that he could scarcely feel the shape of her small head. She made no movement as the little civilian figures, some of them chatting, slouched with bowed heads past the flags and portraits, up from the square and on to the steep carriageway between the Lenin Museum and the Museum of Russian History. He measured her slender neck, slid his hands down the length of her back, then easing out the waist of the skinny jumper brought them up again along the silky skin.

With a deep breath, Marya Fyodorovna snuggled into the warm pit made by her body in the cushioning, and stretching her arms like a swimmer about to dive, took his hands in hers. From her small breasts a fine sweat transpired which prickled between his fingers and salted the nicks and scratches from which Sasha's hands were never free. In her armpits it was profuse, and he lingered there, wetting his fingertips in the stubble, stinging the quicks. He had never felt a girl so small, but with such hard-standing nipples which poppled at his touch, creased and flipped back straight as the winder of a pocket-watch.

He was in no hurry. This time he was in command. He could spin it out, make it last. His nerves had gone. He was completely in control. Marya, quiet and limp beneath him, wanted to be explored.

"Now my little mare," he whispered. "Let's see how you buck."

With a lithe twitch of her waist, Marya raised herself to him. The tight skirt stuck fast at her thighs, and for a moment he stood back, fiddling with the back zip with one hand, calmly stroking himself, underneath, with the palm of the other. Months after he would remember how sharp was that anticipation and how prolonged he made it. For him the domination was uniquely complete. She was offering; he could take or not take. There was no place for niceties. This time he could do as he liked. Teasingly, he slipped in between her legs just above the garter roses in the opaque weave of her stocking tops, pleasuring himself in the slight pain afforded by the dryness of the touch. When she clamped her legs together at the contact, he smiled and dug his nails into the skimpy muslin-like stuff under her skirt, scratching and twisting, pressing downwards with the hollow of his hands on the swell thrust up by the arch of her back. She thrust back at him, squirming, her face twisting from side to side hidden in the mane of clouded orangey hair, one breast leaping free of the

343

crocheted jumper, its broad fluffy aureole violently pink against the ivory leather. He resisted and resisted, held back, dispensing with any thought of satisfaction until he had seen enough of her, had had her in advance with his eyes, slowly stripped her, divested her of the last vestige of coolness and poise. He wanted her drained of fight. Marya was not patient, Marya was wilful, Marya was spoilt. Marya was used to having her own way, and Marya would. But Marya would wait. He could make her. Perhaps she thought she still had power over him when she suddenly ceased, caught up her hair and flung it back, exposing the nettle-rash flush wrought on her profile by the thrashing about of her head. Her tongue curled out, tip-turned and rigid. Over it she searched his face for the effect.

He stared fixedly, close enough to distinguish the tiny roughened buds as she slithered it in and out, all the time gazing at him with dimmed eyes, the line of her lips breaking and reforming wetly. As the band, their instruments correctly aligned against the slope, slow-marched past the spot where in summer the Kremlin tour-guides megaphoned their sales-pitch, Sasha with one outward jerk of his square, powerful hands, tore apart the skirt at the fastening, ripping it down the seam from end to end. The cambric beneath caught in the teeth of the zip and came away simultaneously, leaving long oyster-grey threads strung out against the shiny black taffeta. With a grunt Marya turned her head and relaxed, unclenching herself before him.

At the worst of times Sasha could always reason with himself, but this was so good a moment, the best ever, that his mind spun free from the clutter of past and future and he settled undistractedly on the present task of seeing to it that Marya Fyodorovna was given (in the words of Len) a seeing-to that neither he nor she would forget. After all, this was the one chance in a million; his boat coming home; being handed it on a plate; never drawing the short straw; getting away with murder; without reproach or grudge being descended on out of the blue by an angel who, for once in your life, had chosen your humble portals to mark with a flaming great tick. Undeserved love (or lust – you couldn't really tell with Marya Fyodorovna – and if you could distinguish, did it matter?) had for only the second time in his life homed right in on him, bang on.

Keep your head, save yourself. Not all at once, a bit at a time. Thank God for your proletarian sinews, and make it the longest quarter of an hour since Catherine the Great had her last guardsman.

Marya gave a little gasp and shifted. In the hollow of her back baby down glistened, caught in the declining afternoon sun, as she turned below, lapping in snail-slow orbit around the rigid line of him, her whippy musculature cleaving and keeping fast while he held back halfway there, not wanting to lose sight or sense of the undulating swell in which one moment (but not yet) he was going wholly to sink. Her movements were economical but so efficient when for the first time he felt her, knew what it was going to be like, every inch of the way, knew there was more of it to come, that just holding on to his brains didn't seem to be a simple option after all. All very well, taking it easy, *a bit at a time*, but you needed practice and she'd obviously had plenty at stopping off the calculating part of the male libido. Beating about for some method of cauterising his blind urge to relax, to be taken completely in and up, right to the very end, Sasha, who had had no time properly to undress, gave himself a smart crack on the left ankle with his shoe. The thick heel merely bounded away painlessly. Useless. He should have remembered. They were Valentina's last present and had soles of some Polish composite crap designed not for kicking but keeping your feet dry. Didn't even do that. Bloody Comecon Polack swindle.

Marya whiffled breathily into the eider feathers of the luxurious cushions. "Oh God, oh God . . . it's so *hard* . . . I can feel it . . . More . . . *more* . . . I can see it in me . . . I'm a naughty girl, I'm letting you . . . You're doing it to me . . ."

With this starting up Marya was going to have him away in no time.

Sasha bent his whole mind to a search of the room for some object to fix on. The blank eyes of Stalin bore down on him from the bust over the television. Why hadn't they been painted in? They'd forgotten the colour. It was the same with Hitler, no one could remember. Blue or brown? Except for that, the realism was preposterous, terrific. Look at the miserable bastard. Every hair individually chiselled by hand. With the squint-eyed concentration of an infant nosing out the breast, Sasha started at the left and traversed the walrus moustache, counting each strand.

After each ten, he paused, mentally scored through the tally, tucked the unit away somewhere in the increasingly blank space inside his head and allowed himself to push. When he reached one hundred there was three-quarters of the moustache left. Some business was going on with the coffin at the side of the Mausoleum, and he was left with nowhere further to go – Marya had him complete. If she'd left it at that he would have been all right since there was enough yardage left on Stalin's upper lip to dull the most lively man's sensibility. But Marya intervened, dramatically quickening his steady, arithmetical pulse.

"Hold me down . . . be hard on me . . . it's in my mouth . . . You're doing it to me everywhere . . . Your finger, quick . . . *There*

345

. . . now, now, oh God, it's everywhere . . . I'm going to . . . soon . . . I'm going . . ."

And there was more to it than that even, much more, and totally new, for Marya seemed to have an uncanny charge over the deepest recesses of her body which, with magic impulse she made pucker round him, tweak and compress like the wet wing-beats of a trapped flitter-mouse.

All his resolve forfeit, caught up in the most refined physical pleasure he had ever known, Sasha closed his eyes and lowed like a calf, picturing her blood-flow engorging the tiny muscle-ring as drenched poinsettias wavering in a pitch-black well.

Her words jumped in syncope. "Dear God, don't let it go . . . Hold me under . . . I can't stand it . . . Oh God, let it stay . . . You're doing for me, all of you . . ."

A group of elderly men stood to one side as a woman in furs leant over the open coffin.

"Hard men, all of you . . . everywhere . . . have no mercy . . . a naughty girl . . . teach me a lesson . . . stricter, harder, stricter, harder . . . I'm going to . . ."

Suddenly Sasha felt the minute wrenchings cease and Marya Fyodorovna twisted under him, tore the skimpy jumper up to her neck, scarifying her breasts with her fingers, and stared up at him, her face reddening and wrinkled into a sour, contorted leer. "Let me, let me," she started, her hoarse, unrecognisable voice becoming louder and louder as she clawed at her breasts, crushing the nipples together with her strong hands. "Let me, let me . . . just this once . . . and I'll be good . . . I'm going to be good . . . I'm going to be now . . ."

On the screen the woman brushed the dead forehead with her lips and stepped back.

"I'm going . . . You're killing me . . . I'm going to . . ."

Sasha felt his spine crack as he keeled into her, wanting nothing now except to sweep her over the edge.

"I'm going . . . murder me . . . I'm going to . . . Now, *now, now,* NOW, N-O-W . . ."

The flawless lines of the face of the Marya he thought he knew, the Marya in the office, the Marya on the stairs, the limousine Marya, collected, well-born, cool and smooth as lead, melted under his eyes like a strip of celluloid on which a schoolboy had pinpointed the sun's heat with his magnifying glass. And, as when the image gathered enough liquefying folds to soften it for the first spark of combustion, so her features curled away from him, dissolved into an ecstatic, palsied grimace, and sent out the paralysing scream of an animal being eaten alive.

"Nice?" she whispered in her usual voice, a few seconds after. The rash was already fading from her chest.

"Nice," he said coming out as far as he could without losing touch and lingering on the contrasts of line and curve. Her body had gone heavy, and she trembled involuntarily. Sasha squeezed his hands under her thighs and parted her in front. *"Now don't you dare move,"* he said between gritted teeth. "And I won't keep you more than half a minute."

As he rushed in upon her, Marya took the force of the shock with equanimity, smiling into the cushions. "Take just as long as you like, my sweet. I love playing dead."

Sasha took even less time than he had thought he needed. Afterwards, he collapsed over her and could have slept for an hour but Marya, now busy and composed, slithered from under him and stood with her back to the television set dragging at the tangles of her hair with a silver-handled brush.

"God, I'm a mess," she exclaimed catching sight of her reflection in a great burnished copper dish set on the wall. "I can't breathe, I must get rid of all this."

With her free hand she unhitched the long skirt, bundled it up together with the remnants of her underclothes and threw them all into a tall basket by the rhododendrons. Then, pulling the little jumper over her head, she crooked her legs slightly at the knees and towelled herself thoroughly, all the while smiling and arching back her head to allow the brush bristles free play in her dense locks.

"Heavens, I was sopping," she said, letting the jumper fall at her feet. "Your fault."

Sasha elbowed himself down and came to rest with his feet sticking out over the chair back, his head levelled a few inches above the tops of her stockings. He closed one eye, then the other. "How about that, then?" he said. "Now I can't see further than the end of my nose."

She tapped his head with the back of the brush and made a little jump towards him. The crinkly hair tickled the end of his nose. "Can't?" she said gaily, resuming the long brush strokes. "Or won't?"

Sasha scrambled up and followed her example by removing most of his clothes, but unlike her he tried to make a neat pile of them on the floor, not forgetting first to take the cigarettes and matches from his trouser pocket. He lay at her feet, smoking. "I don't know, I suppose I never really got asked, so if you are curious you come to think you're not meant to be, and it's pushed further and further back in your mind. Perhaps it's something to do with being brought up with only women in the house. A sort of taboo, you know."

Marya moved away to the bright copper bowl and studied her hair carefully before fixing it back with an auburn pin. He stubbed out the cigarette half-smoked and yawned.

"You mean you've never looked, wanted to, but never really *seen*?" Marya was truly astonished. "Good Lord, how unnatural."

She knelt down beside him on one knee, her magnificent hair tickling his face, and stroked the back of his neck. "Come on," she coaxed. "Watch me – watch me. Let me show you what a beastly little exhibitionist I am. Watch me now – not just me when my back's turned."

Sasha let himself slide to the floor. He grinned at her impudent delight in the way he had first taken her, and running his stubby fingers between her haunches, pulled down her head by the loose curls at the nape and kissed her heavily on the lips. For a long time they toyed with one another, Marya joking and chattering, Marya curious and absorbed.

"Let me see, will it? How pretty, my ring hand there. You know, I've searched for nail varnish that colour. A glove puppet . . . let me make it talk. There's a cross Punchinello, working himself up. Let me drown him, cool it, that hardening cherry-stone heart . . ." Every so often she glanced up at him her eyes dancing with naïve pleasure as he unfurled and straightened to her. "This . . . is . . . the way . . . we . . . bob . . . the apple," she chanted, bobbling her lips over him in warm stabs. "This . . . is . . . what . . . the lady does . . ."

He played with her ears, winding around them the longest strands of hair, and pressed her eyelids shut. "Not yet," he whispered. "Not yet. Who was going to show me how natural she was?"

Marya sprang up, squealing as he tickled her behind the knee. He grabbed her by the ankle, and they both fell off the long sofa tangled in the flix of the bearskin.

They lay quiet for a while as she nursed Sasha between her breasts. His body felt nothing but the blur of her hand as she swept the yellow and grey hair on his chest.

"Does this come off?" she murmured. "Or were you born with it?"

Sasha was unwilling to leave her warmth. His voice was muffled. "Does it unzip, you mean – like a gorilla suit?"

"Not that, stupid, this."

His eyes were unfocused as he looked down. "Of course it doesn't. I don't keep it in a glass by the bedside overnight, if that's what you think." He propped himself on his elbows. Their noses touched. "I thought you knew a thing or two about blokes."

"This, you fool, this detainee from the laundry list." Marya dug her fingers into the ribbing of his string vest and nibbled the tip of his nose. "And to think I didn't wear a bra for you. Look what I'm wasting my glories of my maturity on – Granny's knitwear."

"I didn't notice."

"Oh thanks very much," she said in pretended offence.

"No, not that, I couldn't miss that, could I? No, the bloody vest. It's a habit – like a cap. You forget it's on."

She was trying not to laugh. "It does come off, then? You're not sutured to it?"

"Hey, you," said Sasha, blowing hard on her eyelids making the individual lashes bend this way and that. "I take it off to wash. I'm a well-scrubbed lad in spite of my hog-bristles. Been with me through thick and thin, this vest."

She put a finger to his lips. "Shush, I believe you. After that, I believe everything you say. *And then you put it on again . . .*" Marya's breasts joggled under him as she shook from suppressed laughter, *"to go to bed."* For two or three minutes she laughed like a mad thing, tears rolling down her face. There was a break and he spoke, anxious to explain: "I don't have anyone now, you see and, well it gets cold night-times . . ."

This time her screams were so rhapsodic that he joined in, and they lay wrapped in one another, joyously convulsed.

"Oh, you," she said at last. "You're miraculous. I'd never want to change you."

The bearskin seemed to be trapping all the energy of their bodies and re-conducting it as heat over their nakedness.

"God, this place is so airless, lovey," she exclaimed, scrambling to her feet. "I must get a drink."

When she came back carrying a wooden tray on which were two tall glasses and several little bottles, Sasha was sprawled in the armchair stroking himself meditatively. He did not stop as she put down the tray on one of the octagonal chromium and perspex side tables. "There," she said, levering off the caps of two of the bottles. "That's what I like to see."

"I thought girls didn't care much for looking?"

"They don't," she said, handing him a glass of bubbling mineral water. "Except at those."

"And what do they call them, Miss Nature Notes?"

"Oh, there isn't a word you could use – for that, or any part of you and me, or what goes on between us. Only metaphors, locutions."

He remembered Bobby. Bobby's language; and Valentina's odd mixture of prudery and down-to-earth grossness; and Len's hideous candour of speech.

"What are *they*?"

"Ways round it. Names are no good. They're like pieces of money, they may look the same but when they get spent they can mean anything or nothing to the people who use them."

"What's my . . . my . . . metaphor?" said Sasha enjoying this way of seeing the world not as it appeared, but as it was, and as it could be – fresh and novel, depending on who you were with and how they happened to see it too.

"That," said Marya Fyodorovna impishly, standing astride him as nude as a gartered Eve, "that I would call progress."

"Or," she went on, grinning and showing her small, even teeth. "Or a man – a nice man, a man I could be very fond of, who always seems to think he's bought the last ticket on the last train to nowhere – that's a man who's just learned how to extend his repertoire."

From the glass which she was holding at her breast long streams of bubbles twinkled upwards etherising into a chill gas which floresced the blunt nipple.

For the first time he was seeing her entirely naked. My God, she was fragile, so fine-boned she could have snapped when he was over her. Snapped on a plane through the line which dipped in below the last rib, drew taut to her unprotected sides before massing out over the convex swell of her hips. He dwelt upon her, whisking avid eyes across the gentle forward pitch of her belly between the newels of the thigh bone, the fullness of her laid there, pressing earthwards to the open.

Fine-haired and deep-cut; more than nicked, scribed out, poppy-red under white, still broadened from his breaking into her, exfoliating amid the sea-urchin tendrils of pale coloured floss which bunched along the cleft to hatch out her dark separation.

In the washed, ducted air of the room, scents mingled, and the musk of her body lotion was drawn upwards with the sweetish tang of geranium from the trickle of her slackened thighs.

His interest was frank, and obvious.

Marya emptied her glass into a tub of hydrangeas underneath the television console and pounced.

"Again? Againagainagainagain?" she baby-talked, rocking her head from side to side over his, so close that he had gently to pull her back by the hair to look at her eyes. They were sportive, moist and dizzyingly unchaste.

"I think I'm about due," he said, stealing a hand down her back. Marya skipped away at the touch and waved at the television.

"Be a love," she said. "Wind it back for me while I pop away for a minute."

Sasha tried to oblige but was puzzled by the blank screen. "You've missed, it," he called out when only her upper half was visible on the staircase.

"Is that the first one of those you've seen, too?" she called back. "You've no need to have it on to record something. Press the white and red buttons at the same time."

When Sasha did so the coffin was shown being raised from the gun carriage. "O-ooh!" cried Marya Fyodorovna. "My favourite bit." Her cheeks dimpled with childlike joyousness and she crushed her breasts in a hug. "Put it on 'hold' and I'll be with you in a tick."

Sasha was soon bored with the picture and lay back in the wide armchair, pulling idly at his vest. After a while the thought struck him that probably, underneath all that thistly khaki and serge, all those yellow alloy buttons, insignia and nylon medal ribbons, every man in that square was wearing the same regulation string vest. Funny, what people had in common. Like the beetles Len used to go on about. Three hundred thousand different kinds of beetle in the world but they all had exactly the same number of legs. So, in a way, if you knew one beetle, you knew them all. He pulled the vest over his head and, after a quick look round, stuffed it under the cushion-seat. Time to leave it off, like mustard plasters and balsam inhalants, those other preventatives of boyhood. The cleansed, humidified air circulated refreshingly over the previously unexposed areas of his body. Nice. If you lived here, you could forget about clothes. Well, underclothes. Or just go around in underclothes. Bugger everyone. No doors to be knocked on here. No one hiking up the stairs to demand what you thought you were doing sitting in your nothings twiddling on knobs and paralysing State Ceremonial.

On the mezzanine, Marya Fyodorovna was banging drawers and squeaking rapturously, like a baby in a chocolate shop. He was hungry but the place was bare of eatables. Another cigarette, then. Perhaps she had a kitchen down there. Not that cooking seemed much in her line.

Coming up this time, her stockinged feet made no sound on the steps and she could have been standing there for ages had he not turned away from the screen to find an ashtray. It was quite a shock. Her hair was swept up above her ears under two long-toothed ivory combs which matched, as he later discovered, one even longer at the back. Fronting this heaped coiffure which fetched out the breadth and upward slope of her cheekbones, was a purple aigrette made from the tail of some long-feathered bird, its hollow spine stiffened with gold and set with minute brilliants. Formerly she had worn no make-up; now her face was chalked white with some kind of powder, her eyes outlined in harmony with the headdress and her lips blanched over deep fuchsia.

"You do like me, don't you?" she murmured. "You said you liked women's paint and their clothes."

The frock was low-cut for evening, impossible for public wear for at least the last seventy years, probably much longer than that. As she frou-frou-ed towards him, the skirts of black bombazine sweeping along the carpet, he realised what she had done.

This was full-dress mourning.

"You look – *marvellous*," said Sasha. He meant it, literally. By what miracle had such clothes come to be preserved?

Under the extravagant folds of black she dropped to one knee and bowed her head low. "A creation, *Vashe prevoskhoditelstvo*, a creation by *Worth*, your excellency. Have you ever seen the like?"

"Only in picture books. Where's it all from?"

Marya Fyodorovna swung to and fro before him with long, rakish strides, turning like a mannequin on a cat-walk. "Some old dear's trunkful of memorabilia," she said, hand on hip by the indigo rhododendrons. "From a Kiev cellar. A Wehrmacht colonel was carting her entire 'nineties' wardrobe back to Berlin in a half-track when they shot him on the Kreshchatik. Ironic. This little number might have consoled the widowhood of his *gnädige Frau*. Daddy traded it from the partisans for vodka and American cigarettes. Like it?"

Behind the banks of flowering shrubs was a heavy, old-fashioned easy chair with padded wooden arms. Its brass casters squealed as Marya Fyodorovna pushed it in front of the television screen. When she sat down on the edge, gathering her skirts around her, the long seat tightened behind her back.

"Well," she said flicking the remote control switch to start the video. "Didn't you want to see?"

Sasha groaned. "Oh no, not again. Not exactly nail-biting, is it? I must know every cobble in that square by now."

"Come over here," said Marya. "And watch me watching them watch you."

Rifle butts crashed and the wind carried off the high notes of the brass.

With a brisk shake and rustle Marya settled herself at the farthest end of the velvety seat, the antique frock overflowing the straight arms. Sasha knelt before her, glad to compromise his nakedness, but she searched him out with a warm foot.

Fire tenders hooted on the Moskva.

"Going . . ." she said quietly over Sasha's shoulder, and very slowly drew up her skirts to the waist. Underneath she had so disposed her legs that they lay outwards, draped along each arm of the wide chair.

The frock was her only clothing.

"Going . . ." she repeated, beating a handclap in slow time, her eyes brilliant and rapid in the white-masked face. Sasha raised one knee and leant forward without touching as the inappropriately festive screeches from the river rebounded from the Kremlin wall. Second by second before his unmoving head, she flared out, glistening red in the refracted limelight of the television glow, the promise she had made him fulfilled by her laying open of this spearhead mark of her absolute difference.

The rumpus of sirens and water jets ceased. In the square there was silence. The picture flipped brokenly, then the screen went blank.

"Gone," said Marya Fyodorovna over the tape-hiss, and relaxed along the back of the chair. "Take me. Take me for a lady. Don't spare me – you are the master now."

"Why?" asked Sasha, on his back, rubbing himself into the deep pile of the carpet.

"Why what?" yawned Marya.

"Me. You know, why *me*?"

"Is that your basic trouble, then?"

For the past hour or so, Sasha had thought he'd left his troubles behind. He massaged his shoulder blades against the pricking tufts.

"What?"

"Never thinking it's your turn, never thinking you deserve things, always being surprised and disbelieving when something goes right."

Sasha pondered this. "Yes," he said. "Is that a problem, then?"

Marya rolled over and began to rub back the hair on his belly, fluffing it out against the lie of the growth. "Not so much a problem as a condition, a state of mind. You get to live with it, like being a peasant. An easy way of putting it would be to say that you've got an inferiority complex so deep you don't even notice. It's been passed down to you through generation after generation."

"There's nothing complex about it. It's dead simple – I *am*. Well, in most things." He stroked her down between the thighs.

"You're what?" said Marya, rubbing harder, impatient with his contentedness.

"Oh, come on," said Sasha, amused at her irritation. "You know what I do for a living, you've seen where I do the living *in*. There's no fence round my place. Who wants to break into that kind of existence?"

He knew what Marya was going to say. "There must be something people want from you, otherwise those house-trained burglars wouldn't have been padding round your place every hour of the day and night."

"Bogat and Co. you mean? Oh, that lot, you know how those dodgy little articles rank in the real world. Better than most, you know that. They're on my level, aren't they? After scraps, on the fiddle, helping themselves when no one's looking, bending the rules, jumpy as hell in case the boss gets sacked and they get a new one who's less bent and might take their stripes away if they're caught with their fingers in the till."

"But you're not like that," protested Marya. "I offered you a soft job and you turned me down." She clambered back to him on hands and knees and began to trace the outline of his tattoo, making soft, conciliatory noises. "That's one reason why, if you want to know . . ."

"What's the other?"

Marya left the question open. "'MAMA'," she read. "Isn't that sweet? It must have hurt. I don't know any man who would have gone through all that pain just for his mother."

"Get away," he smiled. "Tell me what the other is."

"We-ell," said Marya trying to span his wrist bone with one small hand and pressing his elbow joint with the other. "I'm no chiropractor and it might have been a trick of the light, but there's more to you here than meets the eye."

"Oh, that. That's just a joke." Bobby had never mentioned his tattoo. The fact that she hadn't had been a relief, and also a cause for resentment – as if he'd had false teeth and she'd decided to fancy him in spite of them and pretended not to notice when they clunked. Valentina hated it: sleeping with him with that on, she used to say, was like having her bed invaded by a placard telling her how low she'd sunk.

"Help me, you beast," cried Marya. "I can't get it to . . ."

Sasha bent his arm to the window with a practised twist.

"There. Satisfied?"

"Good God," she murmured, nosing along his arm. "It's more detailed than I thought."

Sasha squinted down. "I suppose it is, now I come to think of it."

She was parting the thick blond hairs to get a better look. "Look, she's even got a . . ."

"Oh hell," he groaned. "She has, too. I never knew what that was until half an hour ago."

"You can bet it wasn't the first one *he'd* seen," giggled Marya, marking the crease with her scrubby nail.

"I could kill him, the bloody, anatomically-minded sod," shouted Sasha. "The bastard never liked me, but I never thought he was out to ruin my love-life."

"Very beautiful," she said, delighted by his indignation. "Nobody'll notice if you keep her legs closed."

"Trust you to find it."

"Be bound to, wouldn't I? After all, I ought to know what I'm looking for."

Sasha wrapped her in his arms and they rolled over and over on the carpet squealing with laughter. They ended up under the sofa.

"Well, are you going to tell me, then?" he said.

"Tell you?"

"Tell me the other reason *why.*"

"Ah," whispered Marya. "Who wants to be told that it's only *his* that works with girls?"

He froze. "It was all right, though, wasn't it? I thought . . ."

"Of course it was, you silly man, it was more, a lot more than all right, but the reason it was, is the other reason *why* and that's got nothing to do with your . . ." She stopped and took his head in her hands, pressing her thumbs over his eyes. "It happens behind those. It's the way it comes out through those. The way you see things, that's what you can't hide and that's what makes a girl swear and shriek and turn herself inside out and want every gap in her stopped and filled by you and be had and had and had."

"God above," said Sasha. "What a fate. Thank God I'm a man."

"And thank God for women to be one with," said Marya feelingly. "That's who you should be grateful to."

In the dark Sasha wrestled with the thought. "You're right, that's what always beats Len. He inspects himself all the time – when he's shaving or in the bath or putting on his clothes. His body has a queer fascination for him. One time he got really obsessed, and he'd stop in the middle of a drink and go up to the mirror and poke at his nose and pull his ears. Then you had to stop him from rolling up his trousers and staring at the hair on his legs. Anywhere he'd do it, once the horror seized him. 'Christ,' he'd say. 'Christ, why are men so horrible to look at?' Then he'd start dragging out parts of himself. 'What the hell women see in *that* I'll never know, God, no wonder they keep their eyes closed.'"

"He sounds nice," said Marya. "I'll bet his girls think he is."

In the void Sasha contemplated Len's virtues. "He's all right. He's straight. He has that way with him. He'd never let you down, well, not yet he hasn't. He wouldn't mess himself about, if you know what I mean, there's some things he's above."

Marya took away her hands. "What a lucky man you are."

Sasha blinked. "Why?"

"You can look people in the face." She straightened her back, stretched and got up, holding a hand down to him. Sasha got to his knees. "How else can you look at them?"

"You're lovely," said Marya. "How do you survive? In my upbringing there were only two ways: through them, or straight over their heads. Now, get off your hideous, hairy behind. I'm sleepy and we're going exploring."

Marya's bedroom was a long way away and hard to reach. There was another staircase hidden behind a vast Dutch tulip-wood press, then a windowless corridor which criss-crossed several little passages branching off to left and right. A buzz-bell sounded continuously. At each junction solid doors opened at their approach and closed behind them, automatically. They were both quite naked and Sasha felt daft. Behind every door he expected to find a Lizaveta Ivanovna with her mop-pail.

"Stop worrying," said Marya Fyodorovna. "Nobody's going to affront your modesty. That's what the bell's for – the staff clear off into the side offices when it comes on and their doors switch shut until we've passed through. You never see anyone here."

Eventually he found himself in a small room like the cabin of a liner. Louvred cupboards extended along one wall. Opposite hung another thick black bearskin. The bed was in between, too large, unmade and with prickly linen sheets.

"Safe," said Marya. "All that glass upstairs gets me down sometimes. I like being cosy."

Sasha looked through a porthole. The light was going, and the sky was blue-black. Gunshots echoed from the forest. "Don't be so jittery," she said, noticing his look of alarm. "That's only my tame Marshal. I think he fancies me." She stroked the bear's hindlegs. "He keeps giving me these."

They slept for a while, uncovered in the warm air. She woke him by ruffling the hair on his chest with a silver fork.

"Come on," she murmured. "You've given me an appetite. I'm starving."

He followed her into a sparkling clean blue-tiled little kitchen where she squatted down in front of a huge refrigerator and began to pull things out on to the floor.

"Steak, potatoes, mushrooms, salad, bread. It's all been done for us. And yes," she added, reaching into the back. "There's wine or beer if you want."

He knelt beside her and wiped the frost specks from her knuckles where she had touched the freezer compartment. "Those little hands are horrible," he said, kissing her neck. "How about you giving up biting your nails and me coming off the bottle?"

She licked up a spoonful of mayonnaise from a jar and bent her head to him. "Mmmm, smooth. Don't martyr yourself for me. I like a man who drinks. Anyway, it doesn't seem to make a wounded soldier out of *him*," she said, flicking the dregs from the spoon between his legs. "Sometimes I think men need drink more than . . . you know . . . in this place. I know I would if I were one. Besides, I quite like biting my nails. I've done it all my life and I promise it won't spread to other bits of me."

Sasha grinned. "All right. I won't give up drinking until you start on your toes."

"I can do that, too," she laughed, pushing him over. "You wouldn't believe the sort of things I can get my mouth to."

She cooked for him, untidily, in a cast-iron pan so wide and heavy that it covered three rings of the stove and was immovable without his help. The utensils fell to the floor around her when she tried, with amateurish slapdash, to slice off the meat and fork it into his mouth. All the carefully-separated items of food had been slung together and the steak, instead of being seared, braised itself in the juices of split-skinned tomatoes and blackening mushrooms. She didn't care a fig, and neither did Sasha. They were ravenous. When he lifted the entire pot on to the pile of bamboo mats at the centre of the scrubbed deal table, they plunged in with Marya's heavy silver cutlery, eating straight from the dish for the want of plates, and spearing the steak on to thick hunks of sour rye bread.

He was amazed to see how much the slender Marya could put away. Long after he was full she was still spooning the rich meat ichor over a fat bagel which she tore apart with greedy cries. It was all good, expensive stuff, the best he had tasted since that time his patrol had looted a charcuterie in Prague.

The afternoon was almost spent, but Sasha had hoped that if he weren't going to stay the night (could he ask or should he leave it to her?) there was still the evening to look forward to. Not now, though, not on your life. Who was this Marshal, anyway? For all he knew half the General Staff might pop in for cocktails at eight thirty and hide behind the curtains for the floorshow. He rubbed the back of his neck and jerked his head upwards.

He tried for an extension by asking to stay the night.

Marya took his arm in a strong grip and smiled, the white make-up creasing round her mouth.

"Look," she said. "I'll be honest. Not tonight. It wouldn't be good any more. I can't stand the place myself at nights and I'd only get on your nerves by not being able to sleep. The only time I ever slept here with anyone something happened and I've never done it since. Tell me about your girls, tell me about one, a nice one, tell me about what you did to her, tell me everything."

Sasha might have forced himself to make an effort of imagination (how could he tell her about Bobby who, in any case, had done it to him?) but he could see that there was some story Marya Fyodorovna would eventually insist on boring him with. Better now than later to ask the routine question: "What happened, then?"

He heard her out, not paying much attention: something had happened to whoever it was in the lift. A heart attack or the elks got to him. Sasha didn't give a damn. He was glad. Maybe it was God slipping through the stockade and clouting him one, Marya's epauletted old bastard.

They made love on the cool floor.

Upstairs, there was no light. Woolly snowflakes plummeted in the windless air at the other side of the glass walls. When Marya pressed the switch the room fluoresced blindingly.

Sasha dived for his clothes: "My God, we can be seen all over Moscow!"

"No," said Marya. "I'm too high up. No one else lives at this level." But, as he dressed, she swathed herself in a plaid rug which lay over the sofa. With the heavy make-up streaking she reminded him of a squaw in brave's warpaint.

"Next time you come we'll take a sauna."

"When is next time?"

"Tomorrow. The next day. Whenever you want."

He would try to believe her.

"Don't forget all this stuff," she said, poking a toe at the file. "And for heaven's sake don't lose it!"

"I don't feel like reading at the best of times, never mind after all this."

"It's a good read." She smiled. "Curl up with it. Anyway, your friends like literature, don't they?"

Sasha was mildly disappointed. "It's OK for them to see it – too?"

"Why not? They might appreciate their own story."

Marya Fyodorovna stood on the bottom step, snow settling thickly around her bare feet. The car's windscreen wipers squealed. She helped Sasha in with the file as the chauffeur stared over the head-lights, imperturbable to their farewells.

"Kiss me – *now*," she said over the whine of the heater.

He did, and clutched at the fringes of the plaid, suddenly desolate. Marya slammed the door. She was still waving when the wall of flakes cut him off from the night.

38

Olga was translating aloud from a thick book:

"'This brave group knew little about women's movements in other parts of the world.'"

"What group?" interrupted Marina Andreyevna from the opposite armchair.

"That lot," said Sasha from the floor where he was crouched at Olga's feet. On the dust jacket was a collage of women's faces which formed up into a group portrait. "Or didn't you smile at the dicky bird?"

Marina leant forward and narrowed her eyes. The faces, drawn from disparate epochs, regions and classes made a pleasant graphic hodge-podge.

"Cut-outs from old newspapers, pasted together. Wouldn't be seen dead with any of them."

"I think she means us, dear," said Olga quietly.

"Never belonged to anything in my life," snapped the old woman. "Except a circulating library, until Mama stopped that because the books were risqué. I knew there was something funny about that girl. Never asked me about women's movements. All of a piece, aren't they? Chiefly from the supine position – on your back and . . ."

"Now, dear, you're forgetting yourself," said Valentina. "It's mixed company we're in at present."

"Him, you mean? Don't tell me that one hasn't been privy to a few female squirms, strapping fellow like . . ."

Olga raised her voice: "'Never before had these women been asked how they felt about sex.'"

"What did I tell you?" shouted Marina Andreyevna. "Never said a word to me . . ."

"'Never before . . .'" repeated Olga.

"Never *before*? What does she mean, never before? Listen," said the old woman, fully awakened now and sitting bolt upright, flourishing her cigarette. "By the time men had finished with *me* there were *no* questions unanswered, not a square inch of lusts left unexplored: Like this? Like that? How often? Again? Hard enough? Tight enough?

Long enough? Did you, didn't you? What's it like for you to be a woman, to feel it there? Fast? Slowly? Do you scream? Do you moan? Can I do it there, or there? Will you take it, stroke it, put it in your . . . ?"

"Marina Andreyevna, that's enough!" shrieked Valentina. "It's quite obvious why she didn't ask a phenomenon of profligacy like you. Some women," she went on, pulling her skirt over her knees. "Some women haven't abused their bodies with such licentious industry."

"Then they're fools," grumbled the old woman. "We are, all of us, born to be stripped bare, and subject to hard usage."

"Isn't that rather what she implies, in a wider context?" asked Olga again finding her place in the book.

"'Most of the women I interviewed answered frankly and tried, for the first time in their lives, to express how it was they experienced the idea of love in relation to the shortcomings of the reality they had to confront every day.'"

"'That's a nice way of putting it," said Valentina, tousling Sasha's hair. "I could have felt more objective about you if I'd been fetched up in sociology."

Sasha tried to move out of range but she clutched at his ear and tweaked it affectionately. "Where's my little 'shortcoming of reality' then? Covers everything, that, when you come to think of it. Next time this pint-sized Lothario is paralytic he can ask himself what he's not confronting – reality or the gutter!"

"Love in the biggest garret in the world," muttered Marina, eyes closed. "Roofless to the stars. And she asks for bread. What did she want, that joined-at-the-ankles girl – a panderess, and a supermarket at every street corner?"

Sasha settled himself at Olga's knees, beyond Valentina's reach. "That would take in just about everything, wouldn't it, in the way of human needs?" he said, knowing better than any of them what the needs of Bobby Weston had been.

"For some people here, I mean," he added, when Marina showed no response. "Some can remember when the goodies were on tap, some long for that day again, but Bobby never knew anything else. How will they be, those drabs on the cover, if the lights start flashing for them? Like *her*? Is that what they've got to look forward to – homes of their own, and not only full bellies but full everything else?"

"Not you, too!" cried Valentina. "As if I hadn't got enough on my hands already with this one." Politeness had kept her seated but she patted and smoothed the divan cover avid for some occupation which would conceal her impatience. It was like being back at school, all this being read to, and she had expected no more of it after that dreadful pervert's verse-evenings had come to an end. In any case, what could any American fly-by-night tell her about how she felt in her bones? Most of the time, if she were truthful, she would admit to being miserable. So was almost everyone she knew. She also knew that a programme of re-jigging the male sex wouldn't raise her spirits. You were stuck with men, like you were stuck with the government. Changing them was a job for native heroes, martyrs, saints; nothing changed – not fast enough for her benefit, anyway. If things became better, they became better for men first because they'd always pushed to the head of the queue. Women could only be had; never have. Marina was right: the ageless problem with men is not that they're on your back – but that you're on yours.

"Is there much more of this, Olga Sergeyevna? Marina can't stay up like she used to and this awful American's dressed-up espionage is not her kind of bed-time story."

Olga was in no mood to make exceptions. She had been reading ahead. Bobby had used them all. They all had to know how.

"Valentina Dmitryevna, I beg you, indulge me. You will see the point of it all quite soon."

Marina raised her eyebrows. Olga resumed before the old woman could interrupt:

"'Whenever I met one of my friends, the response was always the same: a desperate, clinging affection, but, simultaneously, a reticence which could quickly develop into suspicion towards new ideas. This suspicion, even, at times, hostility, is noticeable amongst the working-class; even with the poorer, but better-educated women of the intelligentsia, male supremacy, although it has been officially diluted by war and revolution, is still preserved.'"

"Well, there you are," burst out Valentina. "That's the real bitch yelping. The working classes indeed! It's the same old story, the world over. 'Hostility to new ideas' she calls it! I remember the look on the face of that little glass-arsed concubine when I whipped her away from Russian meat. Very gamey he was then, our Aleksandr Mikhailovich, high enough to set before a queen, and she was all a-slaver to snap him up. The origin of those feelings isn't class, Olga Sergeyevna – it's a fount between your legs. Couldn't admit to her own gush, that lady, after it stickied her up to no good purpose."

Marina Andreyevna chuckled as Valentina's face grew redder and redder.

"I know you laugh at me behind my back," the widow went on. "Because of him, isn't it? That pipsqueak hiding under Olga Sergeyevna's skirts. How could I have? Fancy fighting over him!

Fancy ever thinking that deformed Nebuchadnezzar was the bacon you once wanted to bring home! Well, let me tell you what I thought then and what I think now – that ribald apology for the male sex" – Sasha covered his head – "who everyone thinks is so common, so vulgar, so uncultured, that spavined beast of burden is living witness to what that brass-hearted street walker calls 'male supremacy'. Why? Because he's the only person I've known who's valued a woman higher than she values herself . . ."

"And how does woman esteem herself?" interposed Marina serenely.

Valentina turned to her, and hesitated. But only for a moment. "As a walking parcel of tripes, my dear."

"Oh dear," said Olga. "This is not quite . . ."

Sasha peered through his fingers. "You'd better be carrying on Olga, before they start enjoying themselves."

As Olga ploughed further through the unleavened paragraphs of Bobby Weston's tract, he took comfort in the widow's belated recommendation of his powers. He was gratified that she had once liked him more than he had thought. Everyone needed as much of that as they could get. Niceness. Marya had been nice to him, Valentina had tried. Marya was sure of herself; Marya could hand herself over, please herself – literally. Deep in the whale was Marya. That was security.

A quarrel had broken out over the reading. All the women were talking at once.

"What are we, an African tribe . . . ?"

"Just because folks can't buy . . ."

"A man is the pole of the bell-tent . . . Even in Rostov and that's almost as big a dump as this place you're . . ."

"Please hear me out," shouted Olga. "I agree with Aleksandr Mikhailovich when he said that you should take this through to the bitter end . . ."

The widow glared at Sasha. The same old Valya, he thought: suspicious, even of her own credits. "Did he write it with her, then?" she said. "Is that what's being kept from us? Ah, the ingratitude! I can imagine how she wheedled it from him, snug in the crook of his Judas arm, seething with the excess of his loins, close-cropping the strength of him with her cut-purse Babylonian exhortations . . . All our hidden places descried! Our night-cries uncoiling for the delectation of the Philistine . . ."

Olga shouted again. "Have you no patience, woman? Control yourself. Twenty minutes ago you must have heard me, raving at Sasha, just like you. Now the world has changed. Your condemnations are futile." She appealed to the older woman. "Marina, Marina, I can't . . ."

"Valentina Dmitryevna!" barked Marina. "Not another word! The good parts are coming."

As Olga resumed the narrative, Valentina sulked and bit her handkerchief. Olga's soft voice diminished as Sasha cut himself off. She doesn't know the half of it. Not a change but a revolution. Marya had known the world in all its aspects before he knew he was born.

"You can't trust anyone. Not round here – or round *there* – for that matter," she had said, helping him to steady the awkward packages on the springy back seat. No sooner had she waved him off than he was untying the ribbons of the stiff, red folders and leafing through sheet after photocopied sheet, each with its quota of rubber-stamps, pencil squiggles and stick-on warning labels. It didn't take him long to discover what she meant by *there*. One folder was almost entirely composed of departmental correspondence extensively min-uted down the margins, where someone had very carefully collated a series of requests which had obviously been made by the other party to the correspondence but copies of whose letters had since been removed. The requests had been complied with; you could see that from the log of letters dispatched to various academic and professional organs. The buggers were on to someone. He remembered his own pity.

"'Life appears to be a battle of the sexes, which on the whole, the women will lose. The application of male power is controlled, occasionally, I found, by subtle, pervasive displays of retaliation.'"

"That sounds like a queer sort of physics," said Marina. "Each action having its own equivalent reaction."

Olga marked her place in the book with a knitting needle. "Yes. But there action can't lose to reaction. Parity is always preserved."

"Then it's the language of physics she wanted to take off. As if what she describes is as foreordained as the pulling away of the stars."

"Or a love affair."

"Or marriage."

Valentina jumped up at the word "marriage". "The damnable cheek of it! You don't need to travel to faraway places to write about that. What did she know, anyway? She never got a wedding-ring on. Not even once. Where are the people in all this? Or is it just rules and laws and principles, and no sight of flesh and blood?"

"How about this, then?" said Olga flicking to a later part of the book. "'Personalities'. The raw stuff of it. That ought to fill your bill, Valentina Dmitryevna." She had evidently read this section beforehand, for the corners of several leaves were folded over. "Here we have character anatomised, in concrete detail."

There was something grim in her manner which caused the widow to subside.

Sasha burrowed his head into his arms. They'd asked for it, all of them, taking her in, thinking the silent leap could be made privately, individually, with friendship, hospitality, open arms, operation on the human level. Misunderstandings cleared up by threefold kisses and the exchange of gifts. By romance, a few mildly daring jokes, and gossip about prices, bargains and peace. A book had attracted someone's attention. Not here, that came later. Abroad. The title was uncatchy: but our drudges are conscientious. It was bought; paid for in dollars. Expensive, but worth it. Vigilance costs. He had only heard of this kind of thing being done back home. Clever young people, better-paid than him, spent their days raking over the dust heaps of foreign reports, and analyses and commentaries and studies on the look-out for slanders and pornography committed to the post by the well-meaning or crackbrained for the benefit of their Soviet friends. But this one was a beauty. No wonder some attaché had snapped it up. The author had done their work for them, footnoted every source. Here were names, here were photographs. In Moscow the demands rolled in: "Under the auspices of which academic body?"; "How did this person gain access?"; "In what guise was the application presented?" That was only somebody's outrage at having to save his bureaucratic skin, but there were soon other, quite un-cultural queries: "Why has the personnel file of this woman not been forwarded?"; "What is the extent of her involvement?"; "Has an investigation been initiated into this whole circle?"

When he got home he found the book in Marya's box together with a bundle of articles from learned journals. He couldn't read a line of any of them except for the name. He remembered the shape of it from the credit cards.

"'... they take their roles as Soviet mothers very seriously. "If I am not a mother, what am I?" was a remark I often encountered. Nevertheless the burden of motherhood combined with the strains of marriage create a rapidly ageing female population . . .'"

"There we are again," said Valentina. "She sounds so sure of herself, saying that some woman said this and that, but how do we know she hasn't made it all up? I've never heard such an ignorant remark – 'What am I?' I've no kids but I know what I am."

"Yes, yes, you've already told us, in striking imagery," said Olga. "Don't go on so."

"Well, it's enough to make the saints spit, putting us in this goldfish bowl. I ask you: who can have said such an absurd thing?"

"I did," murmured Marina. "And I remember when I did."

Poor cow, thought Sasha. Quicker on the uptake than Valya. She's got it now. She'll know what's coming.

Valentina became frightened and lashed out at Olga. "Now look what you've done. She's all confused, doesn't know whether she's coming or going. There, there, don't you upset yourself, Marina Andreyevna, my dear. Wouldn't it just take a foreign slut to pen all this venom?"

Marina tapped the side of her nose appreciatively. "A scrupulous girl. A girl with a notebook, a girl with drive and a career to make. Tell me, Aleksandr Mikhailovich, who took the precautions – you or her?"

Sasha blushed and cleared his throat. "Bobby was one step ahead, in most things."

Valentina pounded her great knees. "The suppurating Jezebel! Americans! Liberty! Everyone making free with everyone else! They'd lie with their aged fathers for the dirty thrill of telling about it afterwards, in those rich, clinical words. There's no silence in them. Gobbling down their own bodies in talk! And casting about for others to feast on . . . !"

"When, Marina?" said Olga, frowning at the book.

"That evening when Andrey broke the nose of my sweet, my gawky girl, the girl I once had. Then. When else would I have spoken so?"

"'A remark I often encountered'?"

"Olga Sergeyevna, think of the temptation! To generalise is to give authority. Isn't that what we suffer from here? At least, though, we offer figures, statistics. She was less scientifically literate. For her the phrase does the work, the work gets the job, the job means promotion. Who are we to judge?"

"But it's lies!"

"And seen for what it is. Should we love one another less for our frailties?"

"Listen," said Olga. "We come to the naming of names. 'I had a long talk with my closest friend in the Soviet Union, a journalist on the women's magazine *Feministka*, Tatyana Borisovna Lestyeva.'"

"God have mercy upon her," said Valentina.

"'Tatyana's distressing vulnerability in both a male-orientated household and a male-dominated profession, is a reflection of Soviet society generally. At *Feministka* the male editor is in a superior position to that of the women staff, thirty-five in all, only half of whom were married. Few had children or could afford to have any.

Tatyana herself is childless, and her situation, although senior, is far from enviable.'"

Olga's extempore translation grew more practised as she became accustomed to reading the clumsy terms of art.

"'Even educated women like Tatyana Lestyeva regard the husband as head of the household. The continual drunkenness and brutality of Andrey Lestyev horrified me. Frequently he would be absent all night, returning home violent just as his wife was about to depart for a day's work. Perhaps as a consequence of this Tatyana ran her home with startling inefficiency. Poor meals of bread, cheese and fatty cutlets and overcooked cabbage were all she had the energy or resources to provide. Inevitably the vodka bottle always appeared on the table. Tatyana herself drinks and her elderly mother is rarely sober. At forty-six Tatyana looks almost sixty. Her hair is white . . .'"

"No good saying that mine was at thirty or that we fed her as best we could. This will go beyond personal memorabilia, Olga Sergeyevna, will it not?" said Marina.

Sasha reached for the correspondence file by Olga's feet. "This'll take all night. Never mind this women's stuff. Let's have the real story. Read us . . . Oh, hell, I'll do it myself . . . It's all been done into Russian."

He pulled out a sheaf of papers, stapled together. "Here's something more like it: the copy of an official report made seven or eight months ago. 'Subject of Report': A series of magazine articles published in the United States of America. 'Abstract begins'; The Formation of an Illegal Organisation within the territory of the RSFSR: Item one: *Leningradskaya oblast* . . . That was Tanya and Masha dishing out pamphlets on birth control to girls in a restaurant along the Griboye-dev Canal." He made a try at the lumpy, official prose, then stopped. "Oh God, what's the point? We all know Tanya's in prison but this isn't *why*. Some friendly American academic translated one article – would you believe? – and passed it to one of our people in New York for onward transmission. Do we pay such creatures? Or is it just prestige of some kind they're after? Anyway, he wasn't alone – there must be at least three translations of the very same article there, all from pro-Soviet hands." He threw page after page into the old woman's lap. "It's all there for you to read, Marina Andreyevna. Dossiers, files and particulars, scheduled to the day, like astrological charts: dates, places of birth, education, residence and work. Here am I, here are you, laid between the box for social origins and the box for decorations and awards."

"And here," said Olga, turning to the end pages of the book. "Here are the illustrations. A snapshot of Tanya, enlarged. Pictures of the outside of your house and our block here. In the snow, in the sun, every season recorded. Nothing escaped her."

"Stop it, stop it!" screamed Valentina trying to snatch the papers from Marina's hands. "Leave her in peace, you tormentors! Do you want her to die?"

"Hush your noise, girl," said Marina. "Fetch my spectacles and be silent. Let me see how carefully my daughter's life was spilled."

She put on her wire-framed glasses and held the book close to inspect the photograph of Tanya.

"Tanichka, Tanichka, my love, where have they taken you?"

"I only worked it out myself half an hour ago," said Sasha over Marina's shoulder. "No one else could fit the frame but they'd what Marya Fyodorovna called 'de-personalised' the file by inking out most of the names before she got her hands on it. It took the book to give us final proof. Thought it was me, didn't you?"

"I never," said Valentina. "Not really. Not most of the time."

"Never crossed your mind, I suppose, that it might be a cover-up?"

"What? Disguising themselves as tramps, now, are they?"

Marina continued to stare at the picture of her daughter. The enlargement of Tanya's passport snap brought her into pleasing soft-focus. "Looks like a film-actress with those silly, moony eyes," said the old woman tartly. "And what has happened to *her*, Olga Sergeyevna? Do we know?"

"Only from the biography on the jacket. She landed a prestigious job in some institute and is seen as an authority in her field. Appears on television occasionally when the going gets rough over here. That sort of thing. Another book is . . . what's the cant phrase? – yes, another book is 'eagerly awaited'."

"Eagerly awaited," repeated Marina without taking her eyes from Tanya's face. "As she was here, at some time or other, by us all. Now why should that have been?"

"Because she held out promises?"

"That was it, Olga Sergeyevna. You felt better for her optimism. She was the climber who had crested the hill and waved back to encourage you on."

"And how do you feel now she's stoning us with rocks?" said Sasha.

"Now?" said the old woman. "I would put her to death."

She turned the pages: an Arbat of back streets, of grey lopsided houses, garbage, boarded-up windows, graffiti, fat old women with shopping bags, Uzbek recruits in Army fatigues, tattered newspaper boards, illicit advertisements flapping from telegraph poles, litter from lottery booths, bruised apples on packing-case stalls and everywhere, everyone rushing and bumping along, slithering on the phlegm of countless Russian expectorations.

"So that's how she saw us. A mêlée of roughnecks, gobbing and hawking, foundering in our own squalor. The alternative tourist brochure."

One look had been enough for Sasha. She had even included his own decrepit beer-shop. For the queue. What else? He had never seen her with a camera. Neither had Marina. Otherwise her shack kitchen and scrofulous front door wouldn't have been featured.

Bobby was on the frontispiece. The swish photographer had signed his name on the print. Bobby had done herself up. Hair short now, brushed back, no spectacles, shoulders bare beneath diaphanous blouse. A camera-conscious face tilted archly to the left, fixed on an unseen audience. Very cool, very professional in the book-lined room, a miniature samovar on her desk, Mother and Child ikon at her elbow. Eyes limpid with mendacity.

"Reptile," hissed Valentina. "I loathed her on sight. Trust you, Aleksandr Mikhailovich Biryusov, to open your front door to all and sundry."

Olga, who had so long mistrusted him, seized the opportunity of making amends. "Sasha has suffered enough false accusations already. It was I who invited Bobby Weston into this flat. If he hadn't discovered the truth, we would have gone on believing a lie."

Valentina started to cry: "Oh, Lord, Lord, I can't understand you educated people. What is all this about truth? What good does it do?"

She embraced the unresisting Marina. "Look at this old woman," she said, covering the wrinkled forehead with kisses. "How can it help her? You folk think life is better for righteousness, but tonight and tomorrow and for all the days left she will suffer torments because now she knows more than is good for anyone to know. Isn't it enough that her girl is taken? Isn't it worse to know why? You rob us of our goodness with your truth – are we never to trust ourselves to one another again for fear of deceit? How can we live in the world forearmed against it? Better believe the lie than perish from the real."

She went on in a soft, howling whine and kissed Marina's hair. "As the darkness closes over her light you blanken her eyes with the pennyweights of truth. Because you know you have nothing to offer, you clever weaklings. No battle, no justice, no vengeance."

Marina gently rocked herself in the widow's arms, tears streaming down her face.

When the two women had stumbled off into the night, Sasha took Olga by the arm and stared hard into her eyes. "Was she right? Have we nothing?"

"Nothing," said Olga. "Except knowing we have nothing. Truth saves."

Sasha was quiet for a time. "Letters," he said suddenly. "You mentioned letters. What letters?"

Olga studied the pages of acknowledgments. "It says here that her articles began appearing more than a year ago. She must have written some while she was still here, and posted them home through her Embassy. I seem to remember that last evening . . ." She looked round the room as if the way the furniture was disposed held the key to memory. "Roberta stood here and I . . . She'd been round there, making xeroxes . . . It must have been a regular arrangement." She picked out an off-print. "Yes, that's right. This first article must have gone to the press while she was still here."

At the bottom of most of the pages were transliterations from the original Cyrillic. "Interesting," said Olga, tracing the unwieldy romanised words with her fingernail. "Look at these."

Sasha followed her direction to the abbreviated words followed by numbers which cropped up at the end of many of the romanisations: fol 23v. And so on.

"What are they?"

"Archival numerations. Has *Feministka* an archive?"

"What do you mean – archive?"

"A sort of library where they keep all their old papers, back numbers, files . . ."

"Correspondence?"

"Yes. Everything like that. Do they?"

Sasha hedged. "How should I know?"

"Well, from that girl, for instance. Your crazy Marya."

"They used to burn a lot of papers, I know that."

"I'm not surprised, looking at these. Oh my God, what horrible things! These were never meant to see the light of day . . . Quite obscene . . ."

With a laugh she let the off-print flutter to the ground. "Don't ask me to translate for mercy's sake, Aleksandr Mikhailovich."

Sasha stiffened. Out with it, Biryusov, get it over. "I won't," he said. "I've read them in Russian."

"Impossible! That kind of thing's unprintable here."

"The originals. I pinched them."

"What on earth for?"

"For fun, I suppose. I thought they might be fun to read."

"Well, someone else has had all the fun. She stole them from you?"

"Borrowed, really. I got them back, Olga Sergeyevna."

"Young man, you are technologically sub-normal. So did she. Back to the USA."

"The xerox?" asked Sasha miserably.

"The xerox, Aleksandr Mikhailovich."

"Then it's all down to me. It's my fault. I started the whole thing."

"Fault? Fault?" Olga had tipped all the articles out of the box on to the floor and was on her knees, scanning the small print of the footnotes. "Aleksandr Mikhailovich, you never stood a chance. This is a very determined little lady indeed. You know what she's done? She's invented an archive, given exact references to papers that don't exist in the place she says she studied them. It must have taken weeks to work out this system of numbering so that it looked plausible."

"Is that bad?"

"Bad? In her line of business, it's criminal!"

"Well, won't some other bright American come over here, one day, to work on the same stuff? And find it's not where it's supposed to be?"

"Don't you see, you silly boy? That's just what can't happen. On your application form you must first specify what papers you want to see, give their location, and exact references to them. Then the Ministry or the Academy check. It'd be half an hour's work to find there's no such collection and the application would be rejected out of hand. It's foolproof."

"But that'd look fishy . . ."

"Not at all. They'd blame it on us – *typical Soviet bureaucracy.*"

Olga shuffled through the papers. "Now, as if that weren't bad enough, there's a long piece here, written by Tanya herself. Ten months ago this came out. Part political, part personal. Tanichka at her maddest and most possessed. Her style all right." She held it up to the light. "Now this is no letter, so how did the girl get her hands on it? The fact of its existence alone would have been a danger to . . ."

Sasha wiped the sweat from his face. He had not expected this. He had been prepared to tell Olga the whole truth about the letters, but Bobby had drawn him in deeper. He was to blame for Tanya's betrayal. With Tanya's own writings he should have taken no risks.

But would that have made much difference? Tanya had been monumentally indiscreet in her talk with Bobby. That was obvious from all those reported conversations. All the same, he had inadvertently supplied the proofs, the documents. Since when, though, was hard evidence required for our lot? Talk was enough. Enough for Bobby, too. No such thing as disinterested chat on either side. No one was innocent.

He went back to the book and flipped through the photographs again. She'd snapped a lot of blokes. On the quiet, too, because none of these characters' wives could have fancied them in full colour in the family album after she'd roughed them up with her Leica. Not one had shaved for three or four days, and a good half of them were caught in some un-social posture which spoke as much of the photographer as about the subject. If this girl had worked for an undertaker she'd have tripped over a corpse outside her hotel and then pictured Moscow's gutters as choked with dead. All right, they were around, this crowd and he'd seen them and knew what she meant when she caught them blowing their noses through their fingers, tottering from beer stalls, scratching their behinds, bellicose and red-eyed. They'd taken a lot of tracking down.

"Olga Sergeyevna, I thought this book was about women?"

She smiled up from the floor. "And so it is – mostly."

"You mean men get a look in sometimes?"

"Well, let's say they get looked *at* from time to time. It's about women's problems, and you can't write about them without taking men into account. You must have got the flavour when I was reading about Andrey."

"I'm in it, aren't I?"

Olga's smile widened. "I haven't had a chance to read it properly, Aleksandr Mikhailovich. But yes, I think I detected some passing references to someone you might be said to resemble."

Sasha hunted through the pages. "Just show me where," he said. "I want to know where, show me my name, how many times she mentions . . ."

Olga took the book and ran her finger down the contents page. "No need to worry, Aleksandr Mikhailovich. I seem to remember that you'd been anonymised. Which is only to be expected in a section of that nature. Now, where were we – 'The Plight of the Single Mother' . . . 'Child-Care at the Workplace' . . . Ah, here you are, 'A. M. B.' I told you, no names. Simply initials. No one could tell."

"Tell what?"

"That it was you."

"That *who* was me, for Christ's sake?"

"The person with the problem, of course."

Sasha sat down beside her and pointed to the chapter heading. "Olga Sergeyevna, what does that say?"

Olga put her hand up to her mouth and tittered. "Let's say it's a specialised chapter, a chapter about Russian men. A certain side of Russian men."

With relief he remembered the rogues' gallery of photographs. "Oh, the *drink*. She was always going on about that." Olga didn't need to translate. He could guess what was in the chapter. Such a shrewdly choosy memory as Miss Weston's would have sopped up every beer stain. But what had driven him to it wouldn't merit a footnote. "I bet she really went to town there. You'd think a drop had never passed her lips. Come on, Olga Sergeyevna, had me for a hopeless alcoholic, didn't she?"

Olga was trying to be tactful, but she would read it herself, he didn't doubt.

"Not quite, Aleksandr Mikhailovich. Not quite."

Bobby went up in his estimation. "I wasn't a total write-off, then? Not like poor old Andrey?"

"I don't think comparisons come into this – at least, I hope not," said Olga skimming rapidly through whole pages, looking for initials other than Sasha's. "No, no, one might accuse her of rather narrow sampling in her fieldwork, that's all. Her A. M. B. takes such a lot on his shoulders. Oh, I can't really accept this. Very far from what I'd consider plausible in the circumstances."

Sasha looked so bewildered that it was hard for her to keep a straight face, but after his reprehensible prurience in the matter of Tanya's letters, he deserved to wriggle for a while.

"Good gracious! I would never have thought it possible!" she went on, stretching out on the floor and propping the open book against a table-leg in order to have a more luxurious read. "Well, this is a side of you I never imagined."

Sasha snatched away the book and glared at the chapter heading as if the rabbit of the roman script would yield to his concentration and turn into a Cyrillic duck. "Worse than drink?" he asked tentatively.

"Something to do with it, apparently."

"Have a heart, Olga. We can't play quizzes all night. What's that bitch said about me? I must know. Somebody might read it and ask. Just the title – the title!"

Olga read off the words like an unlettered child, giving equal expressionless weight to each: "'Sexual Mores of the Urban Working-Class: Case Study 1: A Pathology of Male Unresponse.'"

The language was impenetrable to him. He thought for a moment. "Is that all?"

"In the title."

"Yes, but what I mean is, is the rest like that, in that kind of words?"

"Mostly, yes."

"Thank God for that," he said. "Len won't be larking round the depot shoving it under my nose, then. None of my friends could make head or tail of it, either. That's a relief. What does it mean?"

"It means that you, like us, were duped and that Miss Weston was not only unscrupulous and lying but also very spiteful." Olga decided that he had been teased enough. "Unless you, my funny boy, have some very outlandish tastes . . ."

At last Sasha understood. "Ah, *that*," he shouted. "*That's* what she's been swinging me round by!" Scrambling to his feet, he stood over her and pointed a finger at his own chest. "And she's written it all down so that strangers can imagine how they would have filled her in more satisfactorily, if they'd been there instead of me; how co-operative they'd have been with a girl who begged to be violated, raped, tied down and ravaged. There's a lip-smacking scene for you! A quaking virgin spreadeagled, bound to the wheel. And what does he do, this wolf from the tundra, with his pillaging Cossack eyes? What does he do? I'll tell you what he . . ."

"Aleksandr Mikhailovich!" shrieked Olga from the floor. "Please, that's quite enough local colour! Not another word!"

But Sasha had not yet done with injustice. He took a step forward and thumped his chest sturdily in the fashion of statuesque oratory. "He pulls on his trousers – and runs!"

Olga dissolved into breath-catching screams of laughter, and Sasha was slightly miffed at the collapse of his rhetorical flight.

"Well, that's what I did," he grumbled. "What's so funny, Olga Sergeyevna?"

"I'm sorry, I'm sorry, Aleksandr Mikhailovich. Awful for you, I'm sure. But it's just the picture of that wolf . . ."

"I don't know – wolf – it's what she had at the back of her mind – animals – wolf, bear, elk . . ."

"An elk, now," spluttered Olga, giving in to another sally of hysterics. "Fancy an elk trying to put on his trousers!"

Olga had boiled the samovar and they sat round it at the table, stirring dribbles of plum compôte and harsh Soviet cognac into their tea. After the excitement of the last two hours, her spirits relapsed and her mind flew to thoughts of her brother.

"Aleksandr Mikhailovich, what can I do? Once I laughed at Boris's fears. Now I can't even beg his forgiveness."

Had they been closer, or he cleverer, Sasha might have worried

about her, wondered how much reality she could stand. Her brother's
memory was not a helpful resource. At the first shock of illness he
had crumbled and taken himself off into dream. They were too social,
these creatures of books. Art had made them companionable beings,
the iron in them corroded by feeling and taste. They mourned too
readily at the depletion of their own circle and forgot both present
plight and common fate.

He simply knew that he didn't want to talk about Boris, but that
she did and she would, right over the dead man he had helped to put
down and whose memory called up nothing except a snowswept tip
lit clean by the moon.

"Forgiveness for what?" he said, tapping the samovar with his
spoon to see if there was water left for a couple more cups.

"For doubting the sureness of instinct. He told me you could have
been a good friend to me, but I allowed myself to be swayed by fools.
Now it's rather late for real friendship, Aleksandr Mikhailovich . . .
but I shall always be in your debt and I shall always feel desperately
ashamed."

Her face was close to him, smooth now in the shaded light.

Oh Lord, not another gracious gentlewoman clean out of luck.
This was Valentina's department. He couldn't tell her that she was
only upset because Boris, for once in his life, hadn't made a bosh
shot. How wrong could a man be, about almost everything, and still
get out of bed in the morning? Boris had been the kind of man who
metaphorically (thank you, Marya) stopped to light a fag and bits of
an aeroplane fell on him.

Sasha rose from the table and walked over to the window. He drew
back the curtains. Chandeliers blazed in the Embassy. As he glanced
across, the figure of a man, bronze-dark and mother-naked, sprang on
to the inner window-ledge opposite, sporting the biggest and blackest
erection Sasha had ever seen in his life. When he blew him a kiss, the
man's teeth flashed, and he jiggled ecstatically on the sill. Very carefully
Sasha wrote a mirror-message in the condensation of the glass: HOW
WOULD – At these words the man gave token of understanding by eager
shakes of both head and body – YOU LIKE – The grin became brilliant
as he pressed himself flat against the window – FIVE – By now abandon
was almost total, and lumps of snow fell from the outside ledge into
the street as the window-frame rattled – YEARS?

Sasha watched second thoughts percolate from brain to physique
as the man slowly made sense of the whole from the parts, his
cinnamon-hued splendour curling under like a soft toffee flagpole.

"What is it, Aleksandr Mikhailovich?" said Olga. "What are you
doing?"

"Nothing. Nothing, really." He sighed. "Just improving my out-look on the Third World."

"Him! Don't tell me he's started on men." She rushed over. The Embassy was now in darkness but by the light of the street lamps they both seemed to detect a glint of bared white teeth.

"Was he . . . ?"

"As a Georgian aubergine," said Sasha laughing. "And nearly as thick. Does he always while away the evenings sticking up his posters?"

"You shouldn't be so coarse, Aleksandr Mikhailovich," said Olga when they resumed their places at the table. "He's really rather sad."

Not about that thing, thought Sasha. You could go a long way with that.

"Your deprived friend was bumping at the wrong window. Where's Bogat tonight? Still hangs around here, doesn't he?"

She smiled wanly. "He's in the kitchen giving a cooking lesson to Lizaveta. He's teaching her to shirr eggs."

To his surprise she fiddled with her hair in the old nervous way and avoided his eyes.

"Leave him alone, Aleksandr Mikhailovich. For my sake. He's quite friendly these days. He does us no harm and you got your money back, you and Lizaveta. She calls him *synochka*, now, little son, and he calls her *rodnaya*, my own."

"That's disgusting!"

"Pure *folie à deux*, my dear, but it's useful." She leant behind him and took something from the long drawer of her bureau. "I suppose you may as well know . . . I had . . . have, a friend – you remember? Someone abroad." She blushed and dealt out a wedge of air-mail envelopes on to the pink tablecloth. Each was addressed to her in foreign-looking, curly Russian script and all were smudgily rubber-stamped in French: *ADRESSE INEXACTE, ADRESSE INCONNUE, REF-USÉ*.

"Yes?" he said, baffled.

"They're from him, all of them. They were supposed to have been returned: 'Not known at this address', and so on – a way of discouraging him from writing to me, don't you see?"

"Well, why weren't they?"

"Because he intercepts them, Bogat, he gets them for me, from the postroom. Before, they were always confiscated or returned. But James kept on writing. I couldn't bear to be cut off again. You do understand now why I tolerate . . ."

He looked at the floor. Marvellous, these people, the way they oblige you to spare them the pain of confronting your own embarrassment at their ruthless self-interest.

It was late. He yawned. She was talking for herself, without an auditor, the way she had talked with Boris. "They're out of date, of course, but he may still mean what he says."

The dead walked in her midst. As if there'd not been enough transformations. Sunrise to sunset. Gold-sheathed Bobby with iris *imperator* eyes, sloughing off her skin to nest for a space with blindworms; Olga ushering the burglar towards the family silver, converting him to seedy retainership for the cause of a man who could never have known her, and would never return. Lizaveta spooned with the blackmailer, while the blackmailer, true to his nature, continued to fribble and pry.

"I'm sure he does, Olga Sergeyevna, I'm sure he does. Otherwise, how could we live?"

She gave a cry of delight, and tears came into her eyes. "He'll come to me, won't he? He'll come soon! Oh Sasha, what joyous hopes I have!" She kissed him on the brow and on the lips. "How kind, how noble to comfort me so. After all my unworthy doubts of you."

Doubts? Another time, but in the same place, those little reservations could have got him shot. It was hopeless. Soon she would want him to leave so that she could drown in her James. Sasha knew only his name. Was he married? And did he sleep with his wife? For Olga the ache of routine torments would be marred by distance, and if memory were insufficient, absence gave ground to glamour. So handsome! There must have been others before. Sasha had seen them, their counterparts, pressing up to the barrier at the Berliner Ost-Bahnhof, leggy blondes garlanding hoar brevet-majors with stephanotis, whilst he lugged string-bagged *delicatessen* alongside the curving troop train to the officers' van, and joined in the thump and whistle and cat-calls as hundreds of conscripts clawed out their arms in embrace and farewell from mounting-step and window. To him, to them, to the place and the past. *Tam*, there, our sandspit jetty into the Mark of Brandenburg. As far as Olga had ever gone. Beyond them were the illustrated papers out of which ladies condescended to roll their liquefacient eyes eastwards, across the North German plain. There was her competition. He was luckier in the dip: Marya Fyodorovna was homegrown.

But tonight he didn't want to be alone to think of Marya, he wanted distraction from wanting her, not to have to think that she was on the spot and might no longer want him. Still, he was in with a chance. No one intercepted her communications.

"I'd better leave you all this stuff," he said, huskily, kicking the heap of papers on the floor. "I've no use for it and no room, either. You make your own peace with Bogat. As long as he knows me and Len are still around he shouldn't give much trouble. You're a fortunate lady, Olga Sergeyevna, to have so many bodyguards."

She wasn't listening. The letters were out of their envelopes all over the table and she had begun to re-read them in sequence.

"Are you going to tell poor Lev? That it wasn't Anna's fault, I mean, and they were just casualties in someone else's scrap?"

"They've gone to his sister's," said Olga. She was miles away. No interest in the Kuznetsovs, or anyone else this side of the Oder. If Mr Sunshine could get a visa for another jaunt she'd ditch the lot of us. A. M. B. would be the one traipsing to Chistopol, or wherever, to visit Tanya.

He left silently, without farewell. His room was bleaker than ever. Everything except the mattress had been given to Valentina, but somewhere, he knew, there was the sweet lingonberry liqueur which Olga had given to Lizaveta and which she had passed on to him. There should be enough to put him out for the night.

In the corner of the window-ledge where he kept the bottle was a note in Lizaveta's crippled hand:

"Pavel Aleksandrovich says it's just right for his soufflé. Knew you wouldn't mind."

39

The following day Olga Sergeyevna did not go to the office but lay on her bed all morning, reading. At noon voices sounded in the hall:

"Clear off! Can't you see I'm busy? This is urgent."

There was a smart rat-a-tat on her door. Carefully marking the place in her book she placed it on the cover of her sewing-machine.

Bogat gave her a shining smile and held out a bottle and a letter.

"Post. Your mailman. I thought you might like a drink as well."

"How considerate," said Olga absently. The sight of Bogat's perky face made her feel very tired. Down the hall Sasha was hunched over the telephone, shouting: "On the south side, on the south side! It's big enough, for God's sake — you can see it for miles. What do you mean, it can't exist if it's not in your book? Of course I'm sure, of course it bloody exists, I've been there, haven't I?"

The dead may green in the earth but with him, my God, things don't change. He's back to where he was: pursuing females. No peace now, he'll be on there for hours. Poor girl.

"What's got into him?" whispered Bogat. "Is he in some kind of trouble?"

Olga shrugged. "No more than usual, I'd imagine. But I thought you knew everything about everyone?"

Bogat was rueful. "Well, you know how it is, Olga Sergeyevna, put a foot wrong once and they never let up on you. I'm on probation now, at work, and they've severed my connections. No access now to inside stories."

"I'm glad you take it so philosophically, Pavel Aleksandrovich."

"Oh yes. I do that," said Bogat. "Where else would I get two forty a month?" He sighed and examined the label on the wine bottle. "Graves," he said. "Is that a good place?"

"The quality depends more on vintage than region, I believe."

"The cork has a funny smell. I never get anything right."

"You have your poems," Olga reminded him. "They keep rather better than wine."

"Not if they're like this — rubbish to start with. I've had my fling

with the muse, Olga Sergeyevna. I'm getting on. Time to settle down
with a hobby."

"A fickle mistress, Calliope," said Olga turning the letter over to
see the sender's address.

"Oh no," said Bogat. "I couldn't stand that. I've turned my face
against that side of life, too. Not that it was *mistresses* with me. I
suppose you've gathered, I'm . . ."

Sasha's fury was gaining momentum. "You stupid little bitch, they
must have a phone, they must have hundreds of phones. In that sort
of place the bloody dog-kennel's got a through line to the meat
market. Put me on to your supervisor."

Bogat watched Sasha's ears turn red. "I've got something here for
him, too, but he's in such a mood," he said, taking a small rolled
package from his inside pocket. "Would you mind awfully if I asked
you to give it to him, Olga Sergeyevna? I haven't got the stamina for
a set-to before lunch."

He buttoned up his coat, looked sideways at the wine bottle with
his slanting eyes and tittered. "I expect the French have a certain flair
even with rubbish so get that down you, my dear. It'll do you good."

Sasha's voice had become very quiet. "Ah, the lines are down, I
see. Out of order. You can't say when . . . I know, I know, and we
won the war, and we're still a teeny-weeny bit behind the bastards
that lost."

He threw the receiver at the wall and turned in Olga's direction.

"Aleksandr Mikhailovich, special delivery for you."

Sasha turned over the parcel several times, squeezing it gently.
There was no name or address. "I've never had a parcel before, Olga
Sergeyevna, not once, not even on my birthday."

"Things change," said Olga. "Perhaps somebody loves you, Aleks."

At this unprecedented show of affection, he looked up sharply, but
she had already stepped back and the door closed on him. Oh God,
thought Sasha with a pang – remorse, she must have embroidered
me a kaftan. He began to pick holes in the wrapping paper.

Olga had guessed immediately who the parcel was from. She was
glad. The situation was almost romantic. In the end something had
been given him to keep: a secret known only to him and the girl. Two
parties to a correspondence, safeguarded by the very people who
feasted off the indiscretions of others.

She laid James's letter unopened on the lid of her sewing-box and
traced around it with her ring-finger, gently pressing back the ash
and greenheart veneers which lifted every winter in the arid heat of
the room, hazing the eyes of the marquetry heliotropes. Aunt Lily's

motif: any flower which set its face at the sun was deserving of light. What was the point of reading what had already been read, sieved for the implications of its punctuation, tested for magic inks, photographed and stapled by a girl with a university degree and mascara smeared on her fingers (the airmail paper so readily took prints), who boxed it with all its predecessors under a spring clip and made the appropriate entry on her worksheet before slipping out to the shops in her lunch hour? A very ordinary person. And no doubt they all had to be very ordinary persons, these people who usurped the attributes of God so unthinkingly.

At the window, a line from Bobby's book came to her: "An unmarried woman of forty-five, Olga Sergeyevna considers herself to be an inferior member of society." The light in this room used to make me look younger; the dank winter light of Moscow under an upturned dish of sky the colour of zinc, fuzzing the sheen of the hooded crows. When will the snow come? Boris used to say that they were trying to take even that away from us by seeding the clouds with crystals and precipitating the falls in the forest, out of reach. Yet more secrets.

Inferior? That wasn't it. And whoever thought of himself as a member of any society? That was other people being considered by outsiders in books. Not up to much as a woman perhaps. An unmarried mother of forty-five might have had something to console herself with, but if the father had fled what was it they gave you for the child – four roubles, five roubles? Tanya had told her once: enough for two bars of chocolate a week.

How can I trust James, now, after Bobby? How can I see myself as I am seen when I myself have never learned to read foreign faces?

The lights were still on across the road. When he saw her standing quietly, the dusky man twitched back his curtain. Today he was in a suit, a gold watch-chain across his waistcoat. Listlessly she raised a hand and watched him smile and wave again. On his bed was a suitcase. Going home with his story, no doubt: of how he made love to a beautiful Russian girl who offered herself to him across the street. Over there, under the palm trees, clustered round the oasis with his camels he would make her his for ever. That was the way to possess – inside the head, no need to share a narrow bed.

Ever since she had overheard two old women on Kropotkinskaya Street looking at the statue near the Metro, she had done that with the city.

"Who's that?"

"Him? Engels."

"Oh God, can't you ever get away from the bastards?"

After that, for her, the Gogol Boulevard became again the boulevard of the Immaculate Conception and now she never crossed a street without murmuring its old name. And, in winter, a few inches of snow obliterated all changes and titles so that you were left with only the ancient contour of streets and faces. It was all there, underneath: the general with the scarlet facings to his greatcoat had only changed places with the cab-driver muffled up on his box outside the Bolshoi. Both had the sullen glare of the *muzhik* who had heaved himself up to unship a leery eye at the metropolis. Only? James had said. *Only*, she had replied.

He had wanted to be part of her life, but how could he have fitted himself for a people which had no way of accommodating his name? James, *Dzhems* stigmatising himself, consonantally.

In spite of his Vladimir Osipovich, Sherwood had reverted to west European origins with that sinister, miniature house which might have been an *Hôtel d'Angleterre* at Biarritz or a Baden-Baden *Hof*; anything, in fact, except a *barskii dom*, the house of a Russian gentleman. *Almaz almazom rezhetsya*, only diamond cuts diamond. *Dzhems*. There was no future with him here, or her there. Better to turn away.

Olga looked at her watch. There was time to drink tea before the shops became too crowded. When she went through to the kitchen, Sasha was on the telephone again. On the hall table lay a man's string vest.

"*Milashka*," he was saying, in the words of a peasant caressing the muzzle of his horse. "*Milenka*, sweetie. Yes, about half an hour ago. He left it for me. You should be more careful though. I nearly threw the card away with it . . ."

Author's Notes

Readers who are not familiar with contemporary Moscow may find the following notes helpful:

Vodka and beer: Although there are many flavoured and coloured vodkas, Sasha prefers the clear, unadulterated sort, which ranges from the stark Vodka, marketed at Soviet beer-shops in bottles with tin-foil caps, through the posher Moskovskaya, Stolichnaya, Russkaya, Sibirskaya, Kubanskaya and Golden Ring to Krepkaya (very strong), most of which are for export. Both Brezhnev and Andropov reduced the price, hence the names Brezhnevas and Andropovkas for bottles of the cheapest vodka. Russian bottled beer (Kolos, Moskovskoye, etc.) is sold in half-litres and, at thirteen per cent alcohol by volume, can be stronger than most wines.

Working clothes (page 16): Soviet liquor stores are forbidden to sell alcohol to customers in working clothes – a rule widely evaded, especially in the case of uniformed policemen.

Ryazan (page 20): A town about one hundred miles south-east of Moscow. "I'd know your Ryazan mug anywhere" is an insult – characterising someone as a half-wit from the back of beyond.

Kasha (page 24): Staple Russian cereal dish of buckwheat groats which, cooked properly, leaves the grains as fluffy, separate, and moist as rice. In raw state contains unthreshed black specks, *grits*.

Beriozka (page 43): Russian – "birch tree". Name of chain of luxury food, gift and book shops in large Soviet cities, generally accessible only to foreigners or those with hard currency.

Okhotnii Ryad (page 44): "Hunter's Row". Game market formerly in the centre of Moscow, demolished to make way for the Gosplan building and Karl Marx Prospekt.

Manège (page 44): French – "Riding school". Large building in central Moscow, formerly used by Tsarist cavalry officers. After the Revolution it became the Kremlin garage and is now an exhibition hall.

Valyenki (page 59): Thick felt snow-boots for winter work in the country; vital for survival in labour camps; and most seen in Moscow on the feet of policemen on point-duty.

Shchi (page 61): Rich soup of meat, vegetables and pickled cabbage.

Pelmeni (page 61): Siberian dish of pastry envelopes containing minced meat, similar in size to Italian ravioli, served in clear soup.

Room-cards (page 81): Issued to residents in Soviet hotels and presented at the reception desk in exchange for the room key. Without a card one can have problems getting past the hall porter.

Dezhurnaya (page 85): Woman who, day and night, is posted on each floor of a Russian hotel to issue room keys and supervise the movements of guests.

Sobor (page 129): Russian – "Cathedral".

Marina Vlady (page 156): Film actress, once married to the popular, mildly subversive singer Visotskii, notorious for his hard drinking and bitter humour.

Potyomkin (page 159): Lover of Catherine the Great, noted, among other things, for his girth and stamina.

Kolomenskoye (page 161): District a few kilometres south of Moscow; site of a former palace of Peter the Great, now famous for its churches. Popular with Muscovites for summertime bathing in the Moskva. The village has a pump, a pub and a duckpond.

Samogon (page 190): Very potent illicit alcohol distilled in the country and widely consumed there as well as in towns.

Marina Tsvetayeva (page 209): Russian poet who wrote much anti-Soviet verse before emigrating in 1922. Eventually returned to Russia where she killed herself in 1941. Her work is currently very fashionable but under Brezhnev it was hard to obtain, except by foreigners and the privileged.

Baba Yaga (page 216): Witch in Russian fairy tales who lived in a house on hens' legs and ate unwary Russian travellers unless they were distinguished or well-born.

Bella Akhmadulina (page 262): Contemporary Soviet poet, noted for temperament.

Nekrasov (page 272): Mediocre nineteenth-century poet whose verse finds favour with Soviet educationalists because of its progressive social commitment.

Board of Honour (page 299): Large notice boards prominently sited in busy city districts displaying over life-sized photographs of Soviet citizens who have distinguished themselves in Party and Union activities.

Zakuski (page 334): Salty, sharp titbits of fish, meat, and vegetables eaten as accompaniment (and antidote) to intake of neat vodka *apéritifs*.

Certificated roubles (page 341): Since the authorities recognise that the official rate of exchange grossly inflates the value of the rouble against hard currencies such as dollars and sterling, some privileged Soviet citizens who earn money abroad are allowed a far better rate but the proceeds are issued as certificates which must be spent in Government shops, restaurants, etc.

Slavanskii Bazaar (page 341): Well-known Moscow restaurant specialising in Russian dishes.

Sherwood, V. O. (page 382): Nineteenth-century architect, sculptor and artist of British origins. Designed Russian Historical Museum on Red Square.